MISTAKEN IDENTITY

LISA SCOTTOLINE

MISTAKEN IDENTITY

**A ROSATO &
ASSOCIATES
NOVEL**

HARPER

NEW YORK • LONDON • TORONTO • SYDNEY

HARPER

HarperCollins books may be purchased for educational, business, or sales promotional use. For information, please email the Special Markets Department at SPsales@harpercollins.com.

FIRST HARPER PAPERBACK PUBLISHED 2012; REISSUED JULY 2019.

FIRST HARPERTORCH EDITION PUBLISHED MARCH 1999.

FIRST HARPER HARDCOVER EDITION PUBLISHED MARCH 1999.

Library of Congress Cataloging-in-Publication Data has been applied for.

ISBN 978-0-06-210457-1 (pbk.)

19 20 21 22 23   LSC   10 9

*For J., new-found,
and for Peter and Kiki, as always*

MISTAKEN IDENTITY

BOOK ONE

Doctor of Medicine: What is truth?
Doctor of Law: Whatever can be proved by two witnesses.

—August Strindberg, *A Dream Play*

1

Bennie Rosato shuddered when she caught sight of the place. The building stretched three blocks long and stood eight stories tall. It lacked conventional windows; instead, slits of bulletproof glass scored its brick façade. Spiked guard towers anchored its corners and a double row of cyclone fencing topped with razor wire encircled its perimeter, attesting to its maximum security status. Exiled to the industrial outskirts of the city, Philadelphia's Central Corrections housed murderers, sociopaths, and rapists. At least when they weren't on parole.

Bennie pulled into a parking space in the half-empty visitors' lot, climbed out of her Ford Expedition, and walked down the sidewalk in June's humidity, wrestling with her reluctance. She'd stopped practicing criminal law and had promised herself she'd never see the prison again until the telephone call from a woman inmate who was awaiting trial. The woman had been charged with the shooting murder of her boyfriend, a detective with the Philadelphia police, but claimed a group of uniforms had framed her. Bennie specialized in prosecuting police misconduct, so she'd slid a fresh legal pad into her briefcase and had driven up to interview the inmate.

THE OPPORTUNITY TO CHANGE read a metal plaque over the door, and Bennie managed not to laugh. The prison had been designed with the belief that vocational training would convert heroin dealers to keypunch operators and since nobody had any better ideas, still operated on the assumption. Bennie opened the heavy gray door, an inexplicably large dent buckling its middle, and went inside. She was immediately assaulted by stifling air, thick with sweat, disinfectant, and a cacophony of rapid-fire Spanish, street English, and languages Bennie didn't recognize. Whenever she entered the prison, Bennie felt as if she were walking into another world, and the sight evoked in her a familiar dismay.

The waiting room, packed with inmates' families, looked more like day care than prison. Infants in arms rattled plastic keys in primary colors, babies crawled from lap to lap, and a toddler practiced his first steps in the aisle, grabbing a plastic sandal for support as he staggered past. Bennie knew the statistics: nationwide, seventy-five percent of women inmates are mothers. The average prison term for a woman lasts a childhood. No matter whether Bennie's clients had been brought here by circumstance or corruption, she could never forget that their children were the ultimate victims, ignored at our peril. She couldn't fix it no matter how hard she'd tried and she couldn't stop trying, so she had finally turned away.

Bennie suppressed the thought and threaded her way to the front desk while the crowd socialized. Two older women, one white and one black, exchanged recipes written on index cards. Hispanic and white teenagers huddled together, a bouquet of backward baseball caps laughing over photos of a trip to Hershey Park. Two Vietnamese boys shared the sports section with a white kid across the aisle. Unless prison procedures had changed, these families would be the Monday group, visiting inmates with last names A through F, and over time they'd become friends. Bennie used to think their friendliness a form of denial until she realized it was profoundly human, like the camaraderie she'd experienced in hospital waiting rooms, in the worst circumstances.

The guards at the front desk, a woman and a man, were on the telephone. Female and male guards worked at the prison because both sexes were incarcerated here, in separate wings. Behind the desk was a panel of smoked glass that looked opaque but concealed the prison's large, modern control center. Security monitors glowed faintly through the glass, their chalky gray screens ever-changing. A profile moved in front of a lighted screen like a storm cloud in front of the moon.

Bennie waited patiently for a guard, which cut against her grain. She questioned authority for a living, but she had learned not to challenge prison guards. They performed daily under conditions at least as threatening as those facing cops, but were acutely aware they earned less and weren't the subject of any cool TV shows. No kid grew up wanting to be a prison guard.

While Bennie waited, a little boy with bells on his shoelaces toddled over and stared up at her. She was used to the reaction even though she wasn't conventionally pretty; Bennie stood six feet tall, strong and sturdy. Her broad shoulders were emphasized by the padding of her yellow linen suit, and wavy hair the color of pale honey spilled loose to her back. Her features were more honest than beautiful, but big blondes caught the eye, approving or no. Bennie smiled at the child to show she wasn't a banana.

"You an attorney?" asked the female guard, hanging up the phone. She was an African-American woman in a jet-black uniform and pinned to her heavy breast had been a badge of gold electroplate. The guard's hair had been combed back into a tiny bun from which stiff hairs sprung like a pinwheel, and her short sleeves were rolled up, macho style.

"Yeah, I'm a lawyer," Bennie answered. "I used to have an ID card but I'll be damned if I can find it."

"I'll look it up. Gimme your driver's license. Fill out the request slip. Sign the OV book for official visitors," the guard said on autopilot, and pushed a yellow clip ID across the counter.

Bennie produced her license, scribbled a request slip, and signed the log book. "I'm here to see Alice Connolly. Unit D, Cell 53."

"What's in the briefcase?"

"Legal papers."

"Put your purse in the lockers. No cell phones, cameras, or recording devices. Take a seat. We'll call you when they bring her down to the interview room."

"Thanks." Bennie hunted for a chair and spotted one in front of the closed window for the cashier and clothing exchange. The families had left the seat vacant because it was the equivalent of a table by the front door in a busy restaurant; when it opened, the exchange would be mobbed with families dropping off personal items, such as plastic rosaries the inmates liked to wear and do-rags necessary for gang identification. And the inmates always welcomed extra cash; for what, Bennie didn't want to speculate. She wedged into the seat next to a stocky grandmother, who smiled when she spotted Bennie's briefcase. A prison waiting room is the only place where a lawyer is a welcome sight.

"You're up, Rosato," called the guard.

Bennie rose and went through the metal detector to the other side of the front desk. She set her briefcase down on the gritty tile floor and raised her arms while the female guard ran a professionally intrusive hand down her arms and sides. "Tell me I'm the only one," Bennie said, and the guard half smiled.

"Go on up, girl."

"Fine, but next time I expect dinner." Bennie picked up her briefcase as a male guard unlocked another gray metal door, double-thick. Attorneys signed a "no-hostage waiver" to get an initial ID; a misnomer, it meant that their release would not be negotiated if they were taken hostage. Once she passed through the door, Bennie would be locked in with a general population of violent inmates packing knives, straight-edge razors, garrotes, shanks, forks twisted into spikes, and possibly a blowtorch or two. Bennie's only weapons were a canvas briefcase and a Bic ballpoint. Anybody who believes the pen is mightier than the sword hasn't been inside a maximum security prison.

Bennie crossed the threshold with a nonchalance that fooled no one and walked down a narrow gray corridor, as stifling as the waiting room but mercifully quiet. The only sounds were echoes of faraway shouting and the clatter of her pumps down the hall. She hit a battered button and rode the empty cab to the third floor. On the landing was a smoked glass window that obscured the guard sitting behind, who accepted the request slip Bennie passed through a slot. "Room 34," said the guard's muffled voice, and the door to Bennie's right unlocked with a mechanical *ca-thunk* and opened a crack.

She walked through the door to another gray corridor, this one with a set of doors on the left, each leading to a gray cubicle. Inmates entered the cubicles from doors off a secured hallway on the other side, and all the doors locked automatically when they closed. Each cubicle, about four feet by six, contained two chairs facing each other and a beige wall phone for calling the guard. Only a

Formica counter divided felon from lawyer. Though it had never bothered Bennie before, it felt oddly inadequate today. She walked to the end of the corridor, opened the door to Room 34, and did a double take when she saw the inmate.

"Are you Alice Connolly?" Bennie asked.

"Yes," the inmate answered with a cocky smile. "Surprised?"

Bennie eyed the prisoner up and down, her gaze ending its bewildered journey at Connolly's face. The inmate looked like a prettier, albeit streetwise, version of Bennie herself, though her hair was a brassy, fraudulent red and had been scissored into crude layers. She had Bennie's broad cheekbones and full lips, but wore enough makeup to enhance those features. She looked as tall as Bennie, but was model-thin, so her orange jumpsuit seemed almost fashionably baggy. Her eyes—round, blue, and wide-set—matched Bennie's exactly, rendering the lawyer momentarily speechless.

Connolly extended a hand over the counter. "Pleased to meet you. I'm your twin," she said.

2

Bennie stared at the inmate in disbelief. Her *twin*? "My *twin*? Is this a joke?"

"No, not at all," Connolly said. She let her hand fall unshaken to her side and spread her palms. "Look at me. We're identical twins."

Bennie shook her head slowly. It wasn't possible. Despite the similarity in their features, there was a chill to the inmate's affect that Bennie had never seen in a mirror. It made the comparison between them that of a cadaver to a living person. "We may look alike, but we're not twins."

"You're just surprised. I know, I was, too. But it's true."

"It can't be." Bennie couldn't wrap her mind around it. She kept shaking her head. Her own eyes looked back at her from the prisoner's face. "You didn't say anything about this when you called, Connolly. You said you needed a new lawyer."

"I didn't want to tell you over the phone, you wouldn't have come. You'd have thought I was nuts."

"You are."

"You didn't know about me, huh? I didn't know about you either, until the other day." Connolly sat down on the other side of the counter and gestured to the chair opposite her. "Better sit, you look kind of pale. It's strange, finding out you have a twin. I know, I just went through it."

"This is crazy. I don't have a twin." Bennie sank into the plastic seat on her side of the counter, slowly regaining her emotional footing. At almost forty, Benedetta "Bennie" Rosato was the only child of an ailing mother and a father she'd never met. She didn't have a twin, she had a law firm. Plus a young boyfriend and a golden retriever. "I don't have a twin," Bennie repeated, with confidence.

"Yes, you do. Give it time. It'll sink in. Look, we're built the same. I'm six feet tall, and I can see you are, too. I weigh a hundred and forty-five pounds. You're heavier, but not by that much, right?"

"I'm heavier. Leave it alone."

"You're kind of muscular. Do you work out?"

"I row."

"Row boats?" Connolly appraised Bennie with a critical eye. "It's built up your shoulders too much. You know, you should lose some weight, do something with yourself. You have a pretty face but you don't wear enough make-up. Your hair needs a cut and some color. I got a friend on the outside could shape it up for you. Make you look hot. You want my color?"

"No, thanks," Bennie said, taken aback.

"Look, it's weird for me, too, seeing you. Trippy. Somebody who looks like me, without makeup. You're another me."

"I'm not another you," Bennie shot back reflexively. The very thought. An inmate, maybe a murderer. "We're not twins just because we look a little alike. Lots of people look alike. People tell me all the time, 'I know someone who looks exactly like you.'"

"This isn't that. Look at my face. Don't you believe your own eyes?"

"Not necessarily. I'm a trial lawyer, the last thing I believe in is appearances. Besides, I know who I am."

"You only know half the story. I'm the other half. Listen. I even sound like you. My voice." Connolly spoke quickly and her tone was direct, a vague echo of the lawyer's tone and cadence.

"You could be doing that on purpose."

"You mean, fake it? Why would I do that?"

"To get me to take your case."

"You think I'm *lying* to you?" Pain creased Connolly's brow, and because it looked so much like Bennie's own, it made the lawyer regret her words, if not her thoughts.

"What else can I think?" Bennie said, defensive. "I mean, something's wrong here. I don't have a twin. There's just me, there always has been, my whole life. That's it."

Connolly cocked her head. "My birthday is July 7, 1962, same as yours. How could I fake that?"

"My birthday? You could find that out anywhere. It's listed in my alumni directory, *Martindale-Hubbell*, *Who's Who of American Lawyers*, a hundred places."

"We were born in Pennsylvania Hospital."

"Most of Philadelphia was born at Pennsylvania Hospital."

Connolly's blue eyes narrowed. "You were born first, at nine in the morning. I was born fifteen minutes later. You weighed ten pounds at birth. How would I know that, huh?"

Bennie paused. It was true. She was born at 9:00 A.M. She used to think, just in time for work. Had she mentioned that ever, in an interview? "You could find that out. I'm sure birth records are public."

"Not the time of your birth, what you weighed. That's not public."

"It's the information age, everything's public. Or maybe it was a lucky guess. Christ, you can look at me and guess I weighed ten pounds at birth. I'm an Amazon."

"Okay, how about this?" Connolly leaned forward on slim but sturdy arms. "Our mother is Carmella Rosato and our father is William Winslow."

Bennie's mouth went dry. It was her mother and father. Her father's name hadn't been published anywhere. "How did you know that?"

"It's the truth. Our father took off before we were born. Carmella gave up her second-born twin. Me." Bitterness puckered Connolly's lovely cheeks, but Bennie noted she was avoiding the question.

"I asked you, how do you know my father's name?"

"Bill and I are friends. Good friends."

"*Bill?* You're good friends with my father?"

"Yes. He's a very nice man. A caretaker. You didn't know that, did you? Bill told me he never met you and that Carmella was too sick to visit. What's the matter with her, with our mother? Bill won't talk about it, like it's a secret."

Our mother? Bennie shook her head in confusion. She couldn't understand how Connolly knew about her father. Her mother had hated the man who hadn't stayed long enough to marry her, and as Bennie had grown to adulthood, her father had simply become irrelevant, a footnote to a busy life. "None of this makes sense."

"Hear me out," Connolly said, holding up a hand. "You need some background. I was the sick twin, you know, from before we were born. We had something called 'twin transfusion syndrome.' That means the twins share one placenta and the blood meant for one twin goes to nourish the other. When we were on the inside, my blood went to nourish you. I weighed four pounds at birth. Most of those babies died, especially in those days. Bill said they can't even find my birth certificate."

"Oh, come on," Bennie said, suddenly annoyed. "I took your blood? What a bunch of crap."

"It's the truth, all of it, every word. Bill told me when he visited."

"Are you saying that my father visits *you*? In prison?"

"Sure. Comes in his flannel shirt, no matter how hot it is, and his little tweed coat. Said he was looking out for me. That was when he told me you were my twin. He told me to call you. He said you're the only lawyer who could win my case, that nobody knows more about the Philly cops than you."

"Gotcha there, Connolly. My father has no idea what I do. He doesn't know me at all."

"Oh no? He follows your career. He has your clippings."

Bennie paused. "Clippings, you mean from the newspaper?"

"You know, I couldn't wait to meet you when I found out about us. I have so many questions. Do you remember anything, like, from the inside?" Connolly edged forward on the counter, but Bennie leaned away.

"Inside?"

"I do. I have memories of you, like a ghost. A phantom, but close to me. They have to be from the inside, it's the only time we were together. When I was little, I always felt lonely. Like a piece of me was missing. I always hated being alone. Still do. Then Bill told me about you and it all made sense. Now, tell me about our mother. What's the matter with her? Why doesn't anybody want to talk about her?"

"I have to go," Bennie said, rising finally. The inmate was a con artist or delusional. The police conspiracy was paranoia. Some clients weren't worth the trouble, no matter how intriguing the case. She reached for her briefcase. "I'm sorry, I wish you the best."

"No, wait, I need your help." Connolly scrambled to her feet like a shadow left behind. "You're my last chance. I didn't kill Anthony, I swear. The cops killed him. They're covering for each other, they set me up. There's a group of them."

"You already have a lawyer, let him handle it." Bennie snatched the wall phone off its hook. It would ring automatically at the security desk.

"But my lawyer doesn't do anything. He's court-appointed. He's seen me maybe twice all year. The most he's done is keep me here. He's part of the conspiracy, too."

"I'm sorry, I can't help you." Bennie hung up the phone and edged to the window in the door. Where was the guard? The cinderblock corridor was empty. There were three locked doors between her and the outside. A panic Bennie couldn't explain flickered in her chest.

"I was hoping you'd believe me, but I guess not. Read this before you decide. Our mother hasn't told you everything. It'll prove what I'm saying is true." Connolly pushed a manila envelope across the counter, but Bennie left it there.

"I don't have time to read it. I have to go, I'm running late. Guard!"

"Take it." Connolly thrust the envelope over the counter. "If you don't, I'll mail it to you."

"No, thanks. I have to get back to work." Bennie jiggled the doorknob and pressed against the window in the door. A heavyset guard hustled down the hall, her pant legs flapping, her expression more annoyed than alarmed.

"Take the envelope," Connolly called, but Bennie ignored her and twisted the doorknob futilely. *Come on.* The guard finally reached the cell, jammed a key into the lock, and swung the door open so wide Bennie almost stumbled into the hall.

"Guard!" Connolly shouted. "My lawyer forgot her file." She stretched over the counter with the envelope in her hand, but in a swift movement, the prison guard drew a black baton from her belt and brandished it.

"That's far enough, you!" she shouted. "Sit down! You want a write-up?"

"Okay, okay, relax!" Connolly said, folding instantly into the chair and raising her arms protectively. "She forgot her file. I'm trying to help. It's her file!"

Bennie backed against the door, her feelings in tumult. She didn't want to take Connolly's file, but she didn't want to see her clubbed. The inmate who looked so much like her cowered in the chair, and Bennie felt frightened for her and of her at the same time. "She wasn't going to hurt me," she heard herself saying.

The guard turned under the raised club. "That your file or not, lawyer?"

"Uh, yes." She didn't want Connolly beaten, for God's sake.

"Then take it!" the guard ordered.

Bennie lunged for the file and stuck it under her arm. Her mouth felt surprisingly dry, her chest tight. She had to get out of the prison. She hurried out the door and for the exit, clutching the unwanted envelope to her breast.

3

Four patrolmen crammed into a booth at Little Pete's, taking the table farthest from the door by habit. Blue cotton epaulets buckled as they squeezed onto vinyl benches and radios rested silently at their thick leather belts. In the middle of the table, black nightsticks rolled together like an urban logjam. Corded blue caps, each with a heavy chrome badge affixed above a bill of black patent, sat in a row on a nearby ledge. It was early for lunch, as the night tour called every meal they ate, but James "Surf" Lenihan had another bug up his ass.

Surf got his nickname because he looked the part: sun-bleached white-blond hair and a tan, muscular build from summers spent lifeguarding in South Jersey. Surf had the antsy metabolism of a natural athlete and was always worked up about something—the new contract, the reassignments, the court time. He leaned over the table to talk, even though Little Pete's was practically empty. "It's for real," Surf whispered, but Sean McShea laughed so hard he almost choked on his cheesesteak, and Art Reston called Surf a horse's ass.

"Why you swallow stuff like that?" Reston asked, shaking his head. He was tall and strong, with a well-groomed dark mustache that hid a too-thin upper lip and brown eyes that glinted with occupational skepticism. Reston's fifteen years on the force had taught him never to believe anything unless ballistics, forensics, or the union president swore to it.

"It's true, okay?" Surf raked a hand through a thatch of bangs. "Rosato is Connolly's twin. I heard it from Katie's girlfriend, the one who works at the house. She told Katie that Rosato visited today."

"The girlfriend's puttin' you on." Reston dropped his pepper ham hoagie into a red plastic basket shaped unaccountably like a boat. Next to him, Sean McShea, still laughing, wrested a napkin from the steel dispenser. A chubby, cheerful man with a bulbous nose and ruddy cheeks, McShea was a natural for the Santa Claus gig at Children's Hospital. His large face reddened with mirth as he wiped his mouth, leaving a blot of ketchup on the pebbled napkin.

"She's not puttin' me on," Surf said. "Why would she?"

"How would I know? Maybe she's got the hots. Wants you to throw her a bone—yours." Reston laughed, but Surf's face remained a mask of alarm.

"You don't believe me, we can check the logs. I'm tellin' you. Rosato was there. Katie said they look alike, too."

"Bull." McShea finally stopped laughing and wiped his eyes with the other end of the stained napkin. "If they looked that much alike, somebody woulda noticed it."

"No." Surf shook his head. "Connolly's hair is dyed red. Rosato's a blonde. Also, Rosato's heavier, remember?"

"No, I never even saw Rosato. I could give a flying—." Reston snorted. "It's a con, kid. A hustle. Connolly is the master of shit like that. Look how she scammed us."

"So what if it's a scam? It doesn't matter. If Connolly gets Rosato on her case, we're screwed."

Next to Surf, Joe Citrone listened in his typical stony silence. Joe was near retirement age, tall, with a bony nose that was bracketed by elongated wrinkles around a small mouth and a sharp chin. Joe didn't talk much and always looked sad to Surf because he had those dark circles under his eyes that Italians get. Still, Joe was the smartest cop Surf knew.

"Joe," Surf said, turning to him. "What do you think? Katie's girlfriend says they're look-alikes. Why would she mess with us?"

"Don't know."

"Do you know Katie's girlfriend? You know everybody."

"Scotty's daughter."

"That's her. So, would she lie to Katie about something like this?"

"Don't know."

"You think they're twins?"

"Don't know."

McShea started laughing again. "Joe on the witness stand: 'No.' 'No.' 'No.' 'No.' 'Don't know.'"

"The Joe Game! The Joe Game! The Joe Game!" they shouted, banging on the table, except for Surf. It was the Joe Game and they played it all the time to get a rise out of Citrone. "Here's Joe at home," Reston said, starting. "The wife says, 'Honey, you want spaghetti?' 'Don't know.' 'Honey, you havin' fun at Disney World?' 'Don't know.' 'Honey, you love me?' 'No.'"

McShea slapped the table with a heavy hand. "I got one! Joe in bed." His animated features fell into deadpan. "'No.' 'No.' 'No.' 'Oh.'"

Citrone ignored their laughter and finished his cheesesteak, which only made McShea and Reston laugh harder. Surf couldn't stand it. What was the matter with these losers? Maybe Joe wasn't smart at all. Maybe he just never said enough to sound stupid. "I shoulda never got involved," Surf said. "I knew it. Dammit, I knew it."

"Shut up with that, you're embarrassing yourself." Reston made a face. "Ooh, I'm ascared of Rosato."

Surf kept shaking his head. "She's smarter than that turd who's on the case now. And she ain't ours."

"Big deal," Reston said. "She got an all-girl law firm. Hey, you think they get their periods at the same time?" He nudged McShea. "What a nightmare. Lawyers on their periods."

McShea stopped laughing when he caught the concern on Surf's face, then reached over and chucked the junior cop on the chin. "Don't worry, girlfriend. If Rosato takes the case, which I tell you she won't, she won't have time to get ready. What is it, a week away, and half that time she'll be givin' interviews. Newspapers, TV, cable. You know how she is. When she's not at the bank, she's in front of the camera."

"*Cha-ching!*" Reston said, but Surf only glowered.

"I'll do something about this, if you won't."

Citrone rubbed his fingertips together, brushing off invisible crumbs. "Don't, kid," he said quietly.

"Don't what? Deal with it?"

Citrone's expression didn't change. "Just, don't."

"I can deal with it. I know what to do. I can't sit around with my thumb up my ass."

"I'll take care of it," Citrone said, and everybody accepted it as the last word.

Everybody, that is, except Surf.

4

Alice Connolly lay on the thin bed in her cell. No inmate stayed in her cell during unrestricted time unless she was doing something she didn't want the guards to see or was doing something with the guards she didn't want anyone else to see, but Alice spent all her time alone in her cell. She had laid down the law with her white-trash cellie, Diane. *Stay the hell out.* Diane had gone along. She was only twenty-three, but looked fifty because of the crack. Pipers looked like they were born at fifty.

Alice squirmed to get comfortable in the bed. The cell, of gray cinderblock, contained a stainless steel sink and over it a plastic mirror the size of a tabloid. A skinny Formica ledge built into the wall was supposed to be a desk, with a beat-up stool bolted to the floor next to the stainless toilet bowl. The bowl had no lid and the cell stank all the time. Alice didn't turn away from the toilet; it wouldn't do any good. She lay in the uncomfortable bed and stared at the blank wall opposite her.

Alice kept no personal articles in her cell, unlike most inmates. No pictures of boyfriends with beer cans in their hands or school photos of kids in front of a fake blue sky. The latest fad in the house was magazine pages folded into an accordion fan. The women set them in pencil holders like flowers, trying to make the dump a home. Christ.

Alice didn't see the point. Ever since the day they handed her her blues and showed her the cell, she had spent every minute of every day thinking of a way out. She'd be convicted for sure. She wasn't about to go to trial and let Pennsylvania plug her full of joy juice.

So from day one, Alice became the model inmate. Scrubbed the kitchen floor, scraped scum off the shower stalls, taught computer. Tried to find anywhere she could slip out, any way. Connected with the gang leaders, the do-rags and the spics, trying to learn what she could. Even tapped her little wetback mule, Valencia, for information. But in a year Alice had gotten nowhere. Her trial was around the corner.

And then it had fallen into her lap. The only bit of luck in her life. It happened the day the guard knocked on her cell door and told her somebody named William Winslow had come for a visit.

I don't know any Winslow, Alice had said, but she was curious. She'd changed into the ugly orange jumpsuit after the pat-down, gotten the plastic bracelet with the bar code on it, and gone down to the visiting room. It was a large room, with steel chairs facing each other in groups of four, and the seats were full. Families yapped and boyfriends copped feels under the NO KISSING sign. Sitting by himself was an old man who looked like a scarecrow. He was tall and thin and his head dipped forward like his neck was stuffed with hay. He wore a tweed sportjacket with a flannel shirt and a brown felt hat that he tugged off when he spotted Alice.

This old coot was her visitor? Alice had almost laughed out loud. She went over and sat down opposite him. The man kept clearing his throat, but he couldn't seem to get a word out. Up close his face was thick with tan and wrinkles. Alice asked him who he was and why was he here. Then he'd told her she was his little girl. He said he'd given her up for adoption.

What are you talking about? she'd said. She wasn't adopted, not that she knew, but her parents were too dead to ask. Not that they'd been the greatest parents anyway, even when they were alive.

This is you, as a baby, the scarecrow had said. Holding a black-and-white photo in a shaking hand.

Fine. Whatever. He was a geezer, maybe he was senile. She took the photo, of a fat baby with round eyes. It looked like every baby in the world. Alice handed him back his picture and told him to get lost. He'd been in the cornfield way too long. But from then on, Bill kept coming back to visit, once a month for about six months. The guards kidded her that she had a groupie, it happened all the time. Crazy johns who liked bad girls, bringing them stuff. Some of the stuff they made, like the young Jamaican who brought Diane little boxes with pictures pasted on them. Others brought money.

Winslow never offered Alice money, but she took his visit most months, figuring he could be used down the line. Everybody could be used somehow, even a wacko. He always asked about her defense, frowning every time Alice said her lawyer sucked. She noticed his reaction and worked it, playing him to get her a new lawyer. Then, the other day, the old man dropped the bombshell: *You're a twin, Alice. Your twin sister is the best lawyer in the city. She knows all about the police. It's time for you to call her. Show her this.*

He'd held out an envelope. Alice took one look at the stuff inside and felt like she won the lottery. She didn't care if it was true or if the coot was just plain crazy. Alice could spin this straw into gold. It was her ticket out. Only one thing she didn't understand: *Why didn't you tell me before? I been rotting in the hole for a year. I coulda called Rosato a long time ago!*

The scarecrow was startled at her sudden anger, clenching and unclenching the brim of the hat hanging in his hands. *I thought you'd be okay, Alice. I thought you had a good lawyer. Now I know you need Bennie.*

Alice shifted her weight in the sagging bed. What a joke. Bennie Rosato, famed hotshot lawyer, was her twin? So what? She didn't know if Rosato was her twin and she didn't really care, just so she got off. But Alice had to convince Rosato they were twins, so she got busy. Read the newspapers and memorized the articles about Rosato and her cases. Cruised the Internet to see if Rosato's firm had a website, and when she found it, saw how the lawyer looked and dressed. Started eating to pack on the pounds and decided to grow her hair in like Rosato's. Even watched the TV news and COURT-TV, so she could imitate Rosato's voice.

Alice became a twin expert, too. Crammed like her life depended on it, since it did. Logged onto the Net, researching books and webpages about twins, so she could pick up a few details to sell Rosato the story. Studied the medical angle and picked up the memories from the womb. Alice hadn't had much time and learned what she could in a few days. She almost became convinced of it herself. Maybe she was adopted. Maybe she really was a twin. It would explain some things, like how she didn't like being alone. And how she never thought she looked like her parents. They were so different from her. Boring. Stupid. Losers.

Alice got herself psyched to meet Rosato. She knew she was ready the night the lawyer came on the news. Just one quick shot of Rosato and a do-rag watching TV had called out, *She look like you, Alice.*

She sure do, Alice had thought to herself. She'd called Rosato the next morning and the lawyer had come running. Their meeting hadn't gone that well, but Rosato would come back. The lawyer was confused, but she'd get past that. She'd be curious about Alice. About herself.

Alice's thoughts were interrupted by a chubby figure in blues scuffling down the hall. Valencia Mendoza arrived at the door and stuck her head inside the cell. Long, thick curls framed features smoothed by excess fat and thick makeup. Alice sat up in bed with a loud sigh. "What do you want?" she asked, as Valencia's cheap perfume filled the cell. It overpowered the stench of the toilet, but Alice wasn't sure she preferred it.

"I don't want nothin'," Valencia answered, in her baby voice.

"Then why are you here?"

"I worryin'."

"I don't have time for your worrying." What a pain in the ass this spic was. They made good workers, used to taking orders, but they could be such a damn pain. "You have nothing to worry about."

"I no hear my Santo for a week," Valencia said, anxious. "My mother, she call every week says how he is. She put him on the phone. She no call this week. Somethin's wrong."

"Santo is fine. Your mother got her money yesterday." Alice paused, double-checking in her mind. It was hard to keep track of the payments without the laptop, but nobody was giving out Powerbooks to prison inmates. It was cruel and unusual. "Santo is fine."

"She got de money yesterday? Why she didn't call?"

"I don't know, Valencia. I don't know your mother. Maybe she met somebody."

Valencia's black-lined eyelids fluttered briefly. "Santo, he had 'nother ear 'fection, las' time I talk to her. Doctor say he get one more ear 'fection, he need tubes. Tha's 'spensive."

"You shakin' me down, Valencia?" Alice's eyes narrowed, and Valencia's crimson nails flew to the blue plastic rosary she wore around her neck.

"No, no, Alice. No. Not me."

"It's not like you. I thought you were a good girl," Alice said, eyeing her employee. Valencia was the girlfriend of one of the bantamweights, and Alice had recruited her right away. Valencia was smarter than most of them, timely on the pickups, and always did what she was told. Then she got pregnant and it ruined her. She'd stuck powder in Santo's diaper and got busted. Oldest trick in the book.

"I am good," Valencia said. "I no shake you down. Never. Not me."

"Your mother gets her money every week, if you stay quiet. That's the deal. You know the deal, even though you're not so good with de English?"

"Right."

"Right, what?"

"Jes, I know the deal." Valencia nodded. "I swear."

"Ain't nothing else in the deal. No tubes, nothin'." Alice stood up, put a hand on Valencia's soft shoulder, and squeezed. "As soon as you stop being a good girl, I stop the money. What happens to Santo then? Huh, Valencia?"

"I don' say nothin'." Valencia's eyebrows sloped downward. They were so heavily penciled it looked like a kid scribbled outside of the lines. Same with her lipstick, the color of cherry Jell-O, crayoned on puffy lips.

"You love Santo, don't you?" Alice dug strong fingers into Valencia's shoulder.

"O' course I love my Santo. He my baby. I don' say nothin'."

"Miguel's not gonna take care of Santo, is he? Not on the fights he gets. Hell, he won't even marry you. Now will he?" Valencia's brown eyes welled up, and Alice felt disgusted. "Will he, Valencia?"

"No," she answered, almost a whisper.

"Who takes care of Santo, Valencia?"

"You do."

"That's right. I do. Remember that." Alice released her grip. "Quit crying. If the baby needs tubes, he'll get tubes. From me. You hear?"

"Jes." Valencia's lower lip trembled and a tear rolled down her cheek.

"What you gotta do, Valencia? Do you know?"

"I know."

"You gotta shut up. You gotta shut the hell up."

"I shut the hell up," Valencia repeated, bursting into tears, and Alice smiled grimly. Valencia was definitely a loose end. And Alice couldn't afford a loose end anymore.

5

"Please hold my calls," Bennie said, and hurried by the startled receptionist with a stride that warded off associates and secretaries. She hustled down the corridor of her firm, past pine console tables and a print by Thomas Eakins of a rower sculling on the Schuylkill River. An elite rower herself, Bennie sculled daily on the same river, gliding under the stone arches the artist so faithfully detailed. She usually glanced at the prints as she walked by, but not this afternoon. A twin? Could it be? No way.

Bennie hadn't opened the envelope in the truck. It had ridden beside her on the passenger seat, intrusive as a hitchhiker. *It'll prove everything I say is true,* Connolly had said. Her voice sounded a lot like Bennie's and her laugh was almost an echo. But it was a trick, it had to be. Prison was packed with hustlers, all wanting free legal help. Bennie got letters from inmates almost every day, and the mail spiked every time she was on TV. Connolly just had a more original approach.

Bennie reached her office, shut the door, then yanked the envelope out of her briefcase and opened the wrinkled yellow flap. Inside were three photographs, one eight-by-ten and two smaller ones, snapshot size. The large photo drew her eye. It was in black-and-white, of twelve pilots in front of a grainy airplane. The shadow of a propeller fell on its riveted skin and the airmen faced the camera in two rows, like a jury. The back row was a lineup of men in bomber jackets, grayish ties, and caps with badges on the front. In the bottom row of the photo knelt another line of pilots, in envelope caps of grainy wool. The pilot on the far right, poised uncertainly on one knee, had light eyes that Bennie recognized. Her own.

She swallowed hard. The soldier's eyes were round and large as hers, though he was squinting against the sun. His nose was longer than Bennie's and his lips less full, but his hair was a sandy blond, like hers. Bennie felt a jarring in her chest and turned the photo over. "Formal crew photo," it said on the back, in a neat, careful pencil. "Lt. Boyd's Crew, 235th Bomb Squadron, 106th Bomb Group, 2nd Division, 8th Air Force." The names of the airmen on the top row were written in the same handwriting and they were all lieutenants. Bennie's eyes raced to the end of the second line. A list of sergeants, then the last sergeant's name. S. Sgt. William S. Winslow. Bill Winslow.

Dad.

Dad? Bennie checked her watch. There was still a chance she could find out today. She grabbed the group photo and snatched up the little photos with only a glance. She'd look at them on the way. She had to get there before visiting hours were over.

The last rays of the sun streamed dark gold through the Palladian windows, burning long, glowing arches into the Oriental rug. The sitting room was spacious, with worn antique chairs and couches grouped around mahogany coffee tables. Oil landscapes hung on the plaster walls, and a portrait of a somber physician in three-piece suit and watchchain was illuminated by a dim brass fixture. The setting was a model of old-money elegance. Nobody would have guessed it was a mental hospital.

Her mother's wheelchair had been positioned against one of the windows, apparently to view the front lawn, newly shorn. The wheelchair cast a distorted shadow, its handles elongated and its wheels elliptical. Her mother's head made a rumpled silhouette above the plastic sling of the wheelchair. Bennie felt a pang as she crossed the empty room toward the chair. Her mother's condition was expected to remain stable with medication. It was both the good and bad news.

Bennie pulled up an ottoman needlepointed with fox-hunters. "Hey, good lookin'," she said, sitting down. Her mother's head didn't turn from the window. "Ma. How are you?"

The sunlight streamed onto her mother's face, but she didn't blink. A tiny woman, her chin and cheekbones were delicate, framed by dense, wavy, gray hair. Pale, papery skin covered her soft jowls, and deep frown lines furrowed her forehead. Her eyes drooped a listless brown, her lids hooded with age. Her only strong feature was a hawkish nose that had always seemed feisty to Bennie until recently.

"Ma, you gonna say hi to me?"

Nothing, not even the blink of an eye. Her mother had been this way for two weeks now. The doctors were tinkering with her dosages, but she wasn't coming around.

"Ma, the sun bothering you? You want me to move you?"

Her mother suddenly slipped down in the wheelchair. A blue cotton blanket rode up her legs, exposing knobby ankles under the hem of a chenille bathrobe. Her spongy slippers fit poorly, curling up at the toe. Dark, spidery veins looked sketched in india ink against the translucent whiteness of her shin.

"Ma, here. Let me help you." Bennie tilted the chair out of the sunlight, then grasped her mother by her thin shoulders and hoisted her higher. The old woman offered neither resistance nor help; her body was light as an old paper lantern. A scent clung to her, not the Tea Rose perfume she favored, but a bitter and medicinal smell. Bennie pulled the blanket down over her mother's feet. "Better?"

No response, but her mother slipped down again, her knees flopping wide open. If she had been sentient she would have been mortified, and Bennie shuddered for her as she pressed her knees together and tucked the blanket tight around them.

"Ma, sit up straight. You gotta sit up. Can you sit up?" Bennie leaned over, eased her up again, and held her there a minute. "Isn't that better? Do you feel that? I'm gonna let go now. When I let go, see if you can stay up. Ready? One, two, three." Bennie released her grip, but her mother slid down into a deep sea of blue cotton, her chin barely above water. Bennie permitted herself a sigh and rearranged the blanket over her mother's legs and ankles. "You're not at dinner tonight, Ma. Did you eat in your room?"

Her mother's expression remained unchanged.

"Was Hattie here to visit today? She told me she was. She said you had lunch together. You had some soup, right? Chicken noodle." Bennie grasped the green-padded armrests of the wheelchair and pulled her mother closer. "You're not gonna talk? What, do I have to take your deposition?"

But even that didn't get a reaction. Her mother's eyes rested on Bennie without seeing her. If Bennie hadn't lived it, she wouldn't have believed it was physically possible. As long as she could remember, Carmella Rosato had been ill, and the daughter had grown up taking care of the mother instead of the more conventional arrangement. They'd made a breakthrough with electroconvulsive therapy, but the old woman's heart had grown weaker. Bennie called a halt to the procedures because she'd rather have her mother depressed than dead. At times like this, she doubted her decision. "Ma?" she said. "Mom?"

Her mother blinked, then blinked again, and Bennie realized she was falling asleep. Then Bennie remembered. The envelope. The photos in her briefcase. She wasn't sure what to do. As much as she wanted to know, Bennie felt torn about raising the subject. Her mother was already so fragile. What if the questions sent her into a deeper catatonia? Gave her a heart attack?

Still, Bennie had asked nothing of her mother all her life and all she wanted now was an answer. Of course she didn't have a twin and she was entitled to have it confirmed. Anger glowed in her chest, but Bennie ignored it, ashamed. It wasn't that her mother wouldn't help, it was that she couldn't. Still Bennie didn't reach for her briefcase. She froze on the ottoman, as motionless as her mother in the wheelchair.

The sunlight faded to the shade of tarnished brass and the room grew cold. Bennie watched her mother's eyes close and her head nod slowly forward. Her skin looked waxy and pale. Her breathing was shallow. Soon the old woman would be dead. *What?* Bennie caught herself, in surprise. Not dead, *asleep*. Soon her mother would be *asleep*. Bennie ignored the lump in her throat, fished out the envelope, and set it on her lap. "Ma, I have something I want to talk about. It's important. Wake up. Wake up,

Ma." She patted her mother's knee, but it had no effect. "Ma, I'm sorry, but there's something I have to ask you. It's crazy, but I want to hear you say that. Ma?"

Her mother stirred, lifting her head with an effort that sent a guilty ripple through Bennie.

"Great, Ma. That's great. Now can you see me? Do you see me?"

Her mother's eyes were open but unfocused. As far as Bennie could determine, her mother was seeing nothing.

"Ma, I met a woman today who says she's my twin sister. She says that I was a twin, that I am a twin. That's crap, isn't it? Of course it is."

Her mother blinked so deliberately it was almost slow motion.

"I know it's strange. Shocking, kind of." Bennie smiled, because her mother didn't look shocked. Her mother had no expression whatsoever. "Don't look so surprised," she said, with a laugh that faded fast. "Ma. Did you hear me? I know you heard me. Will you answer me?"

But she didn't.

"If you don't answer, I'm hauling out the heavy artillery. Don't make me go there. I got pictures. Of my father, she says. You want to see?"

No reaction.

"You want *not* to see?"

Still no reaction.

"Okay, since you asked." Bennie slid the group picture from the folder, the one with the airmen and the airplane. "Take a look at this." Bennie held it up in front of her mother's face and noticed fibers of black construction stuck to the four corners of the photo's back, as if from a photo album. Then she peeked over the photo and scrutinized her mother. The old woman's eyes didn't move toward the picture or even appear to see the pilot, so Bennie moved the picture into what she figured was her mother's line of vision. Still her mother's eyes didn't focus on the photo at all.

"Ma, they're tellin' me this is Exhibit A. Is this my old man?" Bennie hooked a finger around the side of the photo. "This one, with the eyes that look like someone you know?" Her mother's eyelids were sinking again, and Bennie's hopes with them. "Ma? Are you signaling or sleeping?"

Her mother's head dropped onto her chest and she slid under the blue blanket, which engulfed her like a riptide. Bennie's breath lodged in her throat, then she let her hand and the photo fall to her lap. Why wake her mother up or show her the other photos? There was no point.

Bennie returned the photo to the envelope and slipped it back into her briefcase, but didn't move to go. She stayed still, keeping her mother company, watching her slack chest moving up and down, her breathing too shallow to lend any reassurance. Bennie had no answers and she barely had her mother, but she remained. It felt good just to be around her, in her flesh-and-blood presence. Bennie didn't dwell on how many such times they would have left. In that moment it was the same as it had always been: Bennie and her mother, the two of them, still breathing against all odds.

And now was there another? A third? Bennie couldn't imagine it. The Rosatos weren't the ideal nuclear family, but it was *her* family and she took its structure for granted, like stars fixed in the firmament. A constellation couldn't be changed; there was a Big Dipper and a Little Dipper, and that was it. There couldn't be another Little Dipper, could there?

Bennie's gaze strayed through the arched windows to the sky, where the earliest stars were peeking through a transparent canopy of dusk. She remembered that stars weren't forever, but died from instability within, spewing glowing heat, light, and color into deep space. She'd seen the photos in the newspaper: stellar deaths like pinwheels, cat's eyes, and whorls of light. From their showy deaths came life and new stars were formed, yet to be discovered, named, and recorded. To be sure, they existed before Bennie knew of their existence. Maybe Connolly was like that, an unnamed star.

Bennie reflected on it, her eyes bright. She had to concede it was at least theoretically possible. Her mother, dozing in her wheelchair so soundly, could have borne twins. She was tough as a young woman, defiant of convention, and tight-lipped enough to keep a secret of that magnitude. Maybe the secret had contributed to her illness. Maybe it had even caused it. If new stars could be formed and old ones die, didn't it follow that constellations could be reconfigured? A Big Dipper and *two* Little Dippers? The thought made Bennie shiver with an admixture of doubt and wonderment, and she sat by the window until night shone with an almost unbearable brilliance.

On the other side of town, a white police cruiser idled at a gum-spattered curb. Its headlights were on but its radio crackled to an empty car. Joe Citrone was on the pay phone at the intersection. It was dark and this was a rugged section of the city, but he had nothing to fear here. He had grown up only a block over, in the house near the corner. There used to be a luncheonette on the corner, Ray's and Johnny's, and Angelo's Market, the grocery store right across the street. Joe used to like Ray's, it made the whole corner smell like the steak sandwiches that sizzled on the flat grill. Now the corner stank like garbage.

"He in?" Joe said into the phone. The receiver was all black and greasy. He hated that. Everything dirty, from the crackheads. He couldn't use his home phone. He didn't want it in his phone records, in case some mamaluke got ahold of it.

Joe never took chances. It wasn't his way. He didn't have to do anything extreme, just prevent Rosato from taking Connolly's case. He knew people who could make that happen. "You there?" he said into the receiver. "Now listen up."

6

Starling "Star" Harald yanked open his locker to get a towel for his shower. He felt so low. His sparring match had gone bad two days in row. Inside the locker door was a yellowed picture from the newspaper. Star at fifteen years old, with his arm looped around Anthony. *The future heavyweight and his manager, Officer Anthony Della Porta of the Philadelphia police,* read the caption. It was only four years ago, but seemed like ages.

Star had felt heavy during the sparring match. His arms went sore early and stayed that way. He couldn't land his right cross. It was pitiful. Star caught sight of himself in the mirror stuck on the locker door. His hair was a soaked, shaved fade, and his eyes, bloodshot slits of brown. His nose was wide, still not broken, and a trace of mustache covered his upper lip. He was too fat; he was about two-fifteen and he liked to be around two hundred. Damn. He used to be so pretty, like Ali. He didn't look so pretty now. Harris fight was comin' up, but the way he was boxing, Star would get killed. Was he ready for the top of the card, a twelve-rounder? His first professional fight?

Star grabbed the washcloth that Anthony used to replace every day with a clean one. He felt empty inside. It was a year since Anthony got killed, and every time Star opened his locker he felt like hell. Anthony was dead and

Star had nothing left. No manager, no sparring partner, no friend. He'd been managing himself all this time. Couldn't bring himself to pick a new manager. Kept the same trainers and worked hard, taking the crappy fights promoters threw you when they wanted you to hire a manager they could play ball with. Star had beaten them all; his record was thirty-two wins, thirty by knockout, and only two losses.

Star wiped his forehead with his hand, his handwraps flapping. He couldn't keep on the way he was. So much business he had to take care of, it was takin' him away from his training. Star didn't know what to do. Anthony would know, he was like a father to him. Didn't matter Star was black and Anthony was Italian. Anthony discovered him in a PAL program, taught him to box, got him all the way through Golden Gloves. Took him to amateur fights in Philly, Jersey, and New York. Even Tennessee and Kentucky. Put him up against class boxers and punchers, plus down-and-dirty brawlers who stuffed their gloves, so Star would know how to fight all kinds when he turned pro. Star fought his way through all of 'em, knocked out Irish and Dominicans and even a black guy with a British accent.

Anthony found the backers, white stiffs in suits, and picked a name for the syndicate, Starshine Enterprises. It would pay Star a decent salary for a change, plus fifty percent of his purses. Anthony only wanted ten percent to manage Star. He didn't care about the money, he cared about Star. Anthony was the first man to make Star feel like he was worth anything, like his name wasn't a joke. Then Anthony got killed, shot dead. Star had known that Connolly bitch was trouble from the jump. He just didn't know how much.

"Hey, Star," said a deep voice to his left, and Star looked over. It was Leo Browning, who managed one of the older heavyweights. Browning was fat, fifty years old, and white, but he talked like a brother and wore double knuckle rings. "It's comin' up on Harris, man," Browning said in his gravelly voice. Anthony always used to say that Browning sounded just like Barry White, but Star didn't know who Barry White was. "I watched you box that boy, just now. You're bigger, you got a longer reach, and you're quicker. Only you got your ass whipped, man."

"Shut up," Star said, though he knew it was true.

"Look, I know Anthony managed your career real good. Took real good care of you. You don't want to blow it now. You a heavyweight, man. You need a manager. You a boxer, you got to box."

"Don't be tellin' me what I gotta do."

"I know you thinkin' that nobody can do as good by you, but that ain't right. I can. I know your talent. I know where you want to go. I know how to get you there. The promoters, they know me. You don't let me manage you, the promoters gonna pull you out of Harris."

"Bull. Contract says I'm top of the card."

"They find a way out of that. You got to stay strong, like nothin' changed. It's like when the president dies, you know, like when JFK got assassinated. You know JFK?"

Star wanted to hit him. He hated it when whites talked down to him. Anthony never did that. Anthony knew he was smart. Anthony showed him respect.

"When JFK, the president, got shot, they had to swear in the vice president right that day. Same day. You know why? They had to show the world that just 'cause a great man died, the line of power was okay. The country was in good hands." Browning shifted closer in his fake alligator shoes.

"You know, man, you're all screwed up over Anthony. You got to get clear, man. You been in a funk for a year, mopin' like a little baby."

Star's neat head snapped around. He didn't like to be talked to that way.

"You heard me. You need somebody to tell you the truth, man, not like those yes-men you got. You upset about Anthony gettin' whacked, you do somethin' about it. You hear me, stop cryin' and do somethin'. But don't let it mess up Harris, man. Lotta money to be made on Harris. A *career* to be made on Harris."

"Screw you!" Star shoved Browning in the chest, and the man flew off his feet and crashed backward into the lockers.

Star stood in the hot shower. Water pounded on his shoulders and coursed down the muscles of his naked body. His skin was sleek as a Thoroughbred's, a rich, dark chestnut. Thick veins ran close to its surface and snaked down his forearms. Star stood under the water, his head thrown back, trying to keep his mind blank. Trying not to think about Anthony or the bitch who capped him. Or Browning, with the alligator shoes.

You upset about Anthony gettin' whacked, you do somethin' about it.

Star twisted the knob on the wall, turning up the water temperature. He let the hot water hit his shoulders. His muscles tingled. His veins opened wide as tunnels. Star imagined blood gushing through them like a red tide, rushing to the muscles. He felt bigger, stronger. Pumped.

You upset about Anthony gettin' whacked, you do somethin' about it.

Star squeezed his eyes shut tight and twisted the knob

'til the shower was hot as he could stand it. Then, hotter. Water scorched his biceps and blistered his chest. He opened his mouth and steaming water rushed in. His tongue was on fire. Star could take punishment, everybody said so. Blows that buckled the knees of other men, sending them to the canvas like they were prayin' to God. But this was a blow that Star never took in the ring. This was a hurt like nothin' he ever felt. He couldn't make it stop and he couldn't take it neither.

You upset about Anthony gettin' whacked, you do somethin' about it.

Hot water rained like flames from heaven, and suddenly Star roared. He never made no noise in his life, not in all his fights, but he kept roaring, not knowing where in him the sound came from. He heard it echo off the tile walls, turning the dingy shower into his den. He roared louder and louder until his skin burned like the sun. It made him feel strong and clear like never before. Star got tougher in the fire, like steel.

And then he knew what he had to do.

7

At home, Bennie set the envelope to the side of a makeshift plywood table and arranged the photos while Grady Wells watched. A tall, skinny North Carolinian with light, curly hair, Grady had been Bennie's associate and was now her live-in lover. They were renovating an old rowhouse together, rebuilding the shell floor by floor, even though Grady was a business lawyer who had as little spare time as Bennie. They talked about getting married in the house if it didn't collapse first.

"Okay, that's everything," Bennie said, whisking sawdust off the plywood with her hand. "You ready to examine Exhibits A, B, and C?"

"Ready," Grady said. He leaned against the two-by-fours that would reinforce the dining room walls. His gray eyes scanned the photos from behind gold wire-rimmed glasses, and he had already changed into the white DUKE T-shirt and jeans he wore to work on the house. "You say her name's Alice Connolly?"

"Yes. Now. The first photo, Exhibit A, you saw already. It's the one with the airmen in front of the plane, the one I showed my mother. Exhibit B, the second photo, is of the same pilot, Bill Winslow, my father. Holding two babies about the same age."

"The same age?" Grady leaned over the black-and-white picture and compared it with the pilots' group photo; a young, fair-haired man in a white T-shirt and rolled-up blue jeans was sitting on a brick step, grinning. It did appear to be the same pilot and in his arms were two infants swaddled in white blankets. "I can't tell if they're the same age. The photo's so grainy and the babies so tiny, I can't see their features."

"Me neither. They could be twins, but who knows? It's Winslow, though."

"How do you know for sure? You never met your father, did you?"

"No, but I think it is. Maybe he came back for this photo, I don't know. That's his name and his eyes are like mine. Now, this is Exhibit C." Bennie picked up the last photo, suppressing the emotion it evoked. It was a picture of her mother and two other young girls, seated on a round stool at the type of luncheonette counter that didn't exist anymore. Her mother's eyes were fully made-up and her dark hair pin-curled around her ears. She had a rich mouth, vivid with lipstick, and her body curved amply in a sweater set and a slim skirt with a slit up the back. "Check this out, Grady. The hot number is my mother."

He grinned. "She looks so pretty. How old you think she was?"

"Sixteen, seventeen. A lot younger than I am now. Isn't that weird?" Bennie gazed at the photo. She was far too old for it to be a revelation that her mother had a life before she came along. The revelation was that she was ever healthy.

"I don't think I've ever seen a photo of your mother that you haven't taken. Let me see that." Grady slid the photo from Bennie's hand and flipped it over. There were tufts of torn black paper in its four corners and on the back, in a feminine script, was written, FOR BILL. "Interesting," he said.

"That's my mother's handwriting. I'm supposed to believe she gave the photo to Winslow, who gave it to Connolly. Who says she's my twin."

"Do you believe her?" He raised a faint eyebrow.

"No, of course not. Although it's strange that she had these pictures, especially the one of my mother."

"Wait a minute." Grady handed Bennie the photo with a frown. "This is a photo of your mother with two young women. The photo could have come from anywhere. Connolly could be the child of one of the other women."

"But it says 'For Bill' on the back, in my mother's writing."

"Maybe Connolly forged it."

"Yeah, but how?" Bennie turned. "And what about the tufts of paper on the back of the photos? It looks like they were all taken from the same photo album."

"I don't know, but I don't like you being manipulated by some con." Grady folded his arms and his T-shirt edged up over slim, ropy biceps. Golden hair covered his forearms, and his wrists were narrow, so his Swiss Army watch seemed crudely oversized. "Does Connolly look like you?"

"There is a resemblance, a definite resemblance."

"A resemblance doesn't cut it for identical twins." Grady pursed his lips. "Identical twins look identical. They come from a single egg, fertilized by a single sperm that splits. The DNA in identical twins is the same, and I'm sure you can test for it. Why don't you ask Connolly for a blood sample and we'll find a lab?"

"That's bizarre, don't you think?"

"No. Not if you're even considering representing this woman, which I hope you're not, by the way."

"You don't think I should represent her?"

Grady laughed softly. "Under no circumstances should you represent her."

"Why not?" Bennie didn't necessarily want to represent Connolly, but she didn't like being told she shouldn't. "Because she could be my twin?"

"Not exactly." Grady shook his head. "Whether she's your twin or not, you shouldn't represent her. You don't know who she is."

"How well do I have to know someone before I take their case? My God, Grady, I've represented people I barely knew, even barely liked."

"But this one may be your twin, and that makes you emotionally involved. You'll get all bollixed up. How can you prepare a defense and maintain your objectivity?"

Bennie laughed abruptly. "You represented me once, remember? You were in love with me and you represented me."

"That was different," Grady said, maintaining an even tone. If they were going to fight, he wasn't going to let fly with the first round. A Civil War buff, Grady was never as quick into battle as Bennie. His study of war had only reinforced its futility. "We weren't that involved then, it was the beginning. Besides, it's not your field anymore. Connolly's case is at bottom a murder case, not a police brutality case."

"It's still cops. Who better to investigate cops than me?" Bennie plucked the photo from the table and held it protectively to her chest. "Not everybody can handle a case like this, and Connolly has a lousy lawyer."

"If you're concerned, get her a good lawyer. The lawyer you'd hire for me."

Bennie considered, then rejected, the suggestion. "If there's even a remote chance that we're related, I wouldn't want another lawyer to represent her."

"Why not? It doesn't follow that because Connolly may be your twin, you have to be her lawyer. On the contrary."

Bennie felt momentarily stumped. Grady, a former Supreme Court clerk, was making complete sense as usual. He forced her to think; it was one of the things she loved best about him. But this issue was about feeling, not thinking, and she couldn't help the way she felt inside, even as she knew her feelings wouldn't stand to reason. At her core, Bennie believed that blood was everything. Blood *mattered*. If Connolly were her blood, then Connolly mattered. And if Bennie walked away now, she'd never know the truth.

Grady sighed. "You're gonna represent her, aren't you?"

"Yes," Bennie said, and the answer surprised even her.

"You comin' to bed?" Grady asked. He stood in the door to Bennie's home office, the hall light silhouetting the leanness of his form. Grady was a full six feet, the only man Bennie had met who wasn't threatened by her height, and his limbs were long and sleek. He was naked except for a pair of boxers. Bennie knew from his not-so-subtle display that he was inviting her to make love, but she couldn't accept tonight.

"Can I get a rain check?" she asked, sitting at the computer keyboard. She was researching articles about the Della Porta murder, which she needed before she met with Connolly again. Resting at her feet was an overweight golden retriever, Bear. The dog was the exact color of pumpkin pie and his feathered tail started beating against the floor as soon as Grady crossed the threshold and walked over.

"You can't get a rain check, babe." Grady put warm hands on Bennie's shoulders and gave them a gentle massage. He smelled of Ivory soap and mint toothpaste. "It's not like a lunch date. It's spontaneous."

"Spontaneity is overrated. Have your girl call my girl."

"As long as we're negotiating, I'll settle for the morning."

"But I hate the morning."

"Don't whine. You have to pretend you like it."

"So what else is new?"

Grady laughed and read the monitor over Bennie's shoulder. "You on NEXIS? That's a good idea. What's your search request?"

"I plugged in 'Alice Connolly' and limited it to a two-year period." She punched the ENTER key to retrieve the articles.

"Use 'w/15 Della Porta.' That'll get you only the articles about the murder."

Bennie took the suggestion. "You're helping, even though you think I shouldn't take the case?"

"I support all the stupid things you do."

"What a guy."

"So you do appreciate me." Grady leaned over and kissed her cheek. "Good night. You're off the hook, for now. I made you a pot of coffee. Don't work too hard." He scratched Bear's head. "Take care of her, boy," he said, and left the room, padding out in bare feet.

Bennie bade him good night, then hit the keys to learn what she could about Alice Connolly.

8

Star glanced at the squirrelly dude in the passenger seat. Dude all but disappeared in the bucket seat, he was so short. Flabby even for a white guy and he had those hair plugs. Brown hairs sprouting out of his head like rows of tomato plants. To look at him, Star couldn't believe the dude had juice, but T-Boy said he did. "T-Boy think your friend can help me out," Star said.

"T-Boy's right. My friend knows everybody." The dude nodded. "Everybody. He'll help you out, no problem."

"Your friend know somebody in the house, is what I'm axin'."

"He knows everybody in the house. Everybody who matters anyways."

"Gotta be somebody who can do the job." Star steered the Caddy up the street, past boarded-up crackhouses. Nobody was on the street, but Star still flipped up the collar of his Starter jacket. He couldn't afford to be recognized and he was too big a man to hide. He used to be too good a man to be doing this. "Nothin' can go wrong, you hear?"

"Nothin's gonna go wrong."

Star hesitated. Not because he was scared, the deal wasn't even illegal. The Champ used to say it all the time, *Frazier in ten*. No, the problem was that Star felt like such a bitch, payin' somebody to do it for him. Man should do his own killing, but Star had his future to think about. "You know the bitch, right? Connolly, Alice Connolly."

"I know her name."

"He gotta do her by the weekend. That's it, a week. You only got 'til the trial."

"My friend will get it done. You make sure *you* get it done."

Star shouted, twisting toward him in the seat. "Don't be usin' that tone with me. I don't need nobody tellin' me. I got the deal. I carry Harris 'til the seventh, then he goes down. It'll be the farthes' he get with me. Tell your friend to put his money down. Harris gets knocked out in the seventh."

"Can't be a decision, got to be a knockout."

"I know that! I said that!"

Dude looked out the window in the dark. "My friend hearin' about you. Heard you lost your touch. He don't think you can deliver."

"I don't give a damn what your friend say, bitch! I deliver!" Star slammed the steering wheel. He hated this little rat. He hated that Anthony was gone. He hated himself. "The seventh, Harris will be knocked *out*! Man won't know his own *mother*!"

"Chill. My friend has a lot of money on you. A lot of money. He ain't the kind of friend you mess with."

"*I* ain't the kind of friend you mess with!" Star rumbled like a volcano inside. Didn't mean nothin' to the dude Star fought Golden Gloves, was the next Tyson. He could never get over. Star twisted the Caddy to the curb and jerked open the passenger door. "Get out, freak!"

"What? In this neighborhood?" the dude said, his voice panicky.

"I said, get out!" Star shoved him onto the sidewalk and slammed the door closed. "Better run, bitch! It's gettin' dark out."

9

"I'll represent you, on two conditions." Bennie set her briefcase on the Formica counter, yanked out a metal chair, and faced Connolly. The inmate was smiling, though her eyes remained icy, and Bennie tried to ignore the resemblance between them. "Number one, you have to tell me the truth. I have to know more about you than anyone else in that courtroom."

"That should be easy," Connolly said, standing on her side of the counter. "You already do. We're twins."

"Which brings me to condition number two. The only way I can represent you is if we keep the case, and only the case, in focus." Bennie unzipped her briefcase and retrieved a legal pad. "Table the twin issue. I have to prepare your defense. That has to be paramount."

"Does this mean the photos convinced you?"

"It means it doesn't matter to the court case. Now, sit down and let's get the facts." Bennie gestured to Connolly, who sank slowly into the chair opposite her, her brow knit in disappointment.

"It matters to me," she said. "I still want to meet my mother. My real mother."

"Look, if we take time talking about personal issues, you won't be alive to meet anybody. You answer my questions and we'll do fine. It's Tuesday already. We have less than a week until trial unless I can get a continuance. I have a hundred things to do on this case, in addition to my other cases."

"Just tell me one thing. What is our—my—our—mother like?"

Bennie glared her into silence. "I have some background questions for you. Ever been addicted to drugs or alcohol?"

"No."

"Any prior convictions, or been arrested or questioned for any reason?"

"No."

"You were raised where?"

"New Jersey. Vineland."

Bennie made a note. "Went to Vineland public schools?"

"Yes."

"Quick rundown of your childhood."

Connolly nodded. "Okay. Strictly business, I get it. I was an okay student, not great, a B, C student. I lived with my parents, at least I thought they were my parents. They never told me I was adopted. They were weird, no friends or anything, real quiet. I don't remember a lot about my childhood except that we had a great dog. I love dogs, crazy about them."

Bennie thought of her golden retriever. "Go on."

"That's it, basically. I wasn't that close to my parents, and my mother, not my real mother, was sick a lot. She had multiple sclerosis. They both died in a car crash when I was nineteen. I was about to start college, at Rutgers, on full scholarship."

Bennie couldn't help but notice that Connolly's youth echoed hers. "How'd you get a full scholarship? They're hard to come by."

"Basketball."

"Athletic?" Bennie hid her surprise. Her own scholarship to Penn had been academic, but if they'd been giving them out for women's rowing she would have gotten one. "How'd you do?"

"Lousy. I blew out my knee. Never lived up to potential, that was what the coach said. I dropped out when the scholarship wasn't renewed. I was an English major."

So had Bennie been, but she wasn't about to mention that. "Ever been married or divorced?"

"No."

"Ever lived with anybody?"

"Not before Anthony."

Bennie made a note. "Okay. Tell me how you met Della Porta."

"In a laundromat in town, when I first came to Philly. He was washing towels, tons of towels, and drinking coffee. I'm a coffee freak, so we started talking."

Bennie didn't say anything. She was a coffee fanatic. The similarities were impossible to ignore, or was she looking for them? "When did you and Anthony start living together?"

"We dated for about a half year before I moved in. I had been living with him for about a year when he was killed."

Bennie didn't have to make a note. It was a year ago that she and Grady bought the money pit. "How did you and Anthony get along?"

"Great. We were happy. He was a great guy."

"No fights?"

"No more than normal. We were happy. Really."

"Ever talk marriage?"

"A little, but nothing definite," Connolly answered,

and Bennie thought of herself and Grady. If Connolly and Della Porta were renovating a house, Bennie would kill herself.

"Okay, what happened the night Anthony was killed?"

"I came home from the library and he was lying there, dead. There was so much blood." Connolly's voice trembled. "It was horrible."

"What time did you come in?"

"About eight at night. I'd been at the Free Library all day. I always used to leave at six-thirty and it takes an hour or so to walk home."

"Did you work at the library?"

"No. I wrote there, on the computer, because it was quieter than the apartment, with the construction going on across the street. And the room in the library was real pretty, with ironwork all around."

"What were you writing?"

"A novel. I was almost finished with the first draft. It was sort of literary fiction, I guess you'd call it."

"Where's the book now? Do the police have it?"

"I think they took the disk, but the book was protected with a password. If they insert the disk and use the wrong password, it'll erase."

"Your whole book will erase? All your work, wasted? You don't have a hard copy?"

"It wasn't much good anyway, and I have bigger worries right now, like proving I'm innocent."

It seemed strange. Bennie jotted a note to check the property receipts when she got the D.A.'s file. She wanted to know everything the police had seized. "All right, back to the night Anthony was killed. You found him. What did you see?"

"He was lying on his back, facing up, and there was the most awful expression on his face." Connolly looked away, her attention apparently focused on the memory. "There was so much blood on the rug, on the couch, on the wall. At first I just stood there in shock, then I went over to him. I knelt beside him and I saw he was dead."

"How did you know that?"

"You could tell. God. There was a hole right in his forehead, like someone had . . . drilled it." Connolly bit her lip, which was a light, glossy pink. "I didn't know what to do. I just knelt over him. I guess I was in shock. Then I ran out."

Bennie scrutinized Connolly's expression, limned with grief. She couldn't determine whether Connolly was telling the truth. Bennie was usually able to pick up lying in her clients, but the resemblance between her and this client was throwing her off balance. She worried that Connolly wasn't the woman she appeared to be, even though the woman she appeared to be was Bennie. "You ran out? You didn't call the police?"

"Not a smart move, I know." Connolly brushed her hair back with nails that had been filed into neat half-moons. "I was in a panic. I was worried whoever did it was still in the apartment. I wanted to get out of there."

"What did you do when you ran out?"

"I ran down the street. Then I saw a cop car coming around the corner and I freaked out. I ran into the alley at the end of the street and out the other side."

"You ran from the cops? Why?"

"I was afraid of them. I didn't know what had happened to Anthony. I knew it would look like I killed him and I had no good alibi."

A human reaction, but the wrong one. If it was true. "What was the patrol car doing there, if you didn't call for it?"

"Maybe somebody else did, I don't know. Going down to set me up, probably."

Bennie checked her notes. "You and Anthony lived on Trose Street, about twenty blocks from the Roundhouse. Were they on patrol?"

"I don't know. We were sorta close to the Roundhouse, that's why Anthony kept the apartment. He used to stop home to get his stuff before he went to the gym."

Bennie wrote it down, but it didn't make sense. Had a neighbor heard the gunshot and called it in? What was the time of death? She didn't know the most critical facts, which was why she hated taking a case this late in the game. All trial lawyers did. They even had a saying for it: stepping into someone's else underwear. "Okay. You ran out and the cops saw you. Then what?"

"It was McShea and Reston. They threw me down onto the ground, cuffed me behind my back, then took me in the patrol car down to the Roundhouse."

"Who're McShea and Reston? You know them?"

"I met them once or twice, and they testified at the preliminary hearing. Anthony used to be friendly with them, at least Reston. The two of them were both in the Eleventh until Anthony got promoted to detective. They had some kind of falling out but Anthony never wanted to talk about it. It was in the past, I thought. Until they framed me."

Bennie held up her hand. "Wait on that. Keep it chronological. What happened to you after your arrest? They took you in?"

"They took me down for questioning. I was the only suspect, right off. They didn't look for the real killer. I was charged and put in jail that day. I've been rotting here, since there's no bail for murder in Philly."

"Did you answer their questions?"

"No. I asked for a lawyer and they set me up with this kid who got court-appointed."

"The same night?" Bennie's hand remained poised above her legal pad. She didn't know how Connolly had gotten representation and hadn't had time to check the docket for counsel of record. "I never heard of somebody getting a court-appointed lawyer that fast. I'm surprised you didn't get a public defender."

"My lawyer's worse than a public defender. His name is Warren Miller, in town. He's an insurance lawyer, real corporate."

"Can't be. Not in a homicide case."

"I'm telling you, it's all part of the setup." Connolly leaned over the counter. "They framed me, they planted the evidence, then they set me up with a lousy lawyer. I wouldn't be surprised if the judge is in on it, too."

"Judge Harrison Guthrie? Not likely," Bennie scoffed. Guthrie's reputation was sterling and he was one of the most scholarly, respected judges on the Common Pleas Court bench. "You didn't sign a statement, did you?"

"No."

"Figures." The cops could question somebody for hours but unless the suspect made a full confession there would be no statement. It was only the first step in ignoring evidence that pointed away from a suspect's guilt, all in a process intended to do justice. Bennie came back to the crux of her problem with Connolly's story. "What I don't get is why the cops would set you up."

"I don't know either. I wish I did. Whatever happened in the past, they killed Anthony for it and framed me. You see what I mean?"

"No." Bennie skimmed her notes. "Let's go back to the

apartment, the living room. Were there signs of a struggle? Furniture turned over, things broken or messed up?"

"No."

"Was the door locked?"

"Yes. I used my key to get in, even downstairs."

Bennie made a note. Della Porta had known the killer. He had let him in. It jibed with what she read about the crime in the online newspapers. "Was Anthony supposed to be meeting anyone at home?"

"Not that I knew of."

"Was there music on, anything like that? Drinks around?"

"I don't know. I didn't notice. I just saw the body. I don't remember anything but that."

Bennie checked her notes from the newspaper. "The D.A.'s case is that you shot Della Porta, got his blood on your sweatshirt, then changed and threw the bloody sweatshirt in the Dumpster in the alley. They found a Gap sweatshirt, size large. Was it yours?"

"It was my sweatshirt, but I wasn't wearing it that day. I had on a workshirt. That's what they picked me up in and it was clean. If I was going to kill Anthony, you think I'd put bloody clothes in a Dumpster next to the apartment? How dumb do you think I am?"

"Did anybody see you at the library wearing a workshirt that day?"

"I don't know. Maybe."

Bennie's eyes narrowed. "You think Reston and McShea set you up. How well do you know these guys?"

"I met them at a cop thing, a barbecue, but I didn't really know them. Like I said, they were old friends of Anthony's from when he was a uniform. He used to hang with them, used to go out at nights. They called them board meetings because they were all bored at home."

Bennie considered how to phrase the next question tactfully, then gave up. "Was Anthony involved in anything dirty?"

"Of course not." Connolly sat back in her chair, her eyebrows bent in offense. "Anthony was as straight as they come. You don't know what he did, for Star. He lost money on Star, to help him."

"Star's the boxer Anthony managed, right? I'd like to talk to him."

Connolly paused. "Don't bother. He won't help us. He hates my guts."

"Why?"

"I'd hang at the gym with the boxer's wives. I got to know them, became friends. Star didn't like me around the gym. Thought I distracted Anthony."

"Did you discuss this with Anthony?"

"No. Anthony had his work and his boxer. He did his business, I did my book. We understood each other." Connolly cocked her head. "Do you have a boyfriend? I know you're not married, you don't wear a ring."

"I have a boyfriend, but we're not discussing me."

"Ever been married?"

"None of your business."

"Me neither, like I said. I didn't get along with my father, my adopted father. They give us workshops here, on relationships. They're mostly bull, but they say you can't have good relationships with men if you don't have a good relationship with your father."

"That what they say?" Bennie flipped the page, surprised to find herself tensing up. "Where does he live, by the way?"

"Who?"

"My father. Bill."

Connolly paused. "He never said."

"No? Did he ever say how he got here, to visit?"

Connolly smiled. "I thought we weren't supposed to talk about family stuff."

Bennie's thoughts clicked away. The prison wasn't easily accessible by public transportation, so he had to be close by, within driving distance. Odd. She had always imagined her father living far away—California, for some reason. If you're going to abandon your family, at least change area codes. Bennie slapped her legal pad closed. "Okay, that's enough for now. I've got to file for a continuance. I'll be in touch."

"Okay, sure. I'll see you when?"

"Soon as I need you. Stay tuned." Bennie left the interview room, preoccupied. Where did her father live? She hadn't wondered about it in years. Did she care now? She went through the prison's exit procedures—a perfunctory pat-down, trip through the metal detector, and signing out—which gave her an idea. It shouldn't be difficult to find out where her father lived; if he had visited Connolly he'd have to give an address. Bennie should check the prison records, if only to verify Connolly's story.

"Could I see the visitors' log book?" Bennie asked, and her hand shook slightly as the black-uniformed guard slid it across the desk.

10

Alice entered the prison law library, a large gray room carpeted with a thin gray rug, and handed her pass to the guard at the door. She would have only fifteen minutes of unrestricted time here. It would be enough. She spotted Valencia's mass of oiled curls bent over a law book at the bank of gray metal carrels in the center of the room. The girl was always trying to get her conviction reversed, complaining in letters to Congress, the President, and for some reason, Katie Couric. Valencia's argument was that mandatory sentencing for coke possession was unfair, mainly because she'd been convicted for it.

Alice laughed to herself. Valencia had known what she was getting into when she took the job. She carried the powder for money and used it to buy Santo the frilliest baby clothes ever made for a boy. Plus a stroller with a plastic cover like an oxygen tent. Not real useful, in Alice's view, but neither was Valencia, any longer. Alice crossed the room, lined with secondhand case reporters and maroon statute books, and slid into the neighboring carrel. "Hey," she said, and when Valencia looked up from the law book, her cherry-red mouth broke into a sticky smile.

"I talk to *mi madre*!" she blurted out, then looked around and lowered her voice. Two other inmates looked up briefly.

"Shhhh!" Valencia giggled, holding a matching cherry fingernail to her lips. "Sh! Ees a library."

"Shhh! Ees a library." Connolly mimicked her voice almost exactly, and Valencia laughed.

"My mother, she say she got de extra money dees morning! For de tubes! Thank you, thank you!"

"How is Santo doing?"

"She say he has the 'fection, but he so much better. She say he take the medicine every day, ees pink medicine, like bubble gum. He no fight!"

"I told you he'd be okay. Now, you keep the money, tell your mother not to spend it. If he needs the tubes, he'll have the tubes. You don't have to worry." Alice peered at the open law book. "How's your appeal?"

"Look what I find!" Valencia said, excited. "Look at dees." She turned the book eagerly toward Alice. It was the report of a legal case, an onionskin page of fine print in two columns.

Alice scoffed. "You're no lawyer. You can't understand this stuff."

"Sure I do." Valencia nodded, and her scented hair bounced like in the commercials. "De judge say de sentencing unfair. He objec' to it. He say he no take drug cases anymore. The judge, he *quit*!"

"Really? A judge quit?"

"*Sí*. In New York."

"New York? That doesn't help you in Pennsylvania, dummy."

"*Cómo?*"

"New York law is different from Pennsylvania law, and you're looking in a federal reporter anyway, which is only about federal law. You don't know what you're doin'."

Valencia's sticky lip puckered with disappointment. "I can write it in my letter. I have *de cite*."

"So what? They don't have to listen to it. It doesn't mean anything in Philly. God, are you dumb." Alice reached over and closed Valencia's book. "I have a better way to help with your appeal." She leaned closer so the others couldn't hear and almost choked on the smell of imposter Giorgio. "I have a new lawyer, a great lawyer, and I told her all about you. She has an idea for a new appeal. A new argument. She thinks she can get you out of here."

"*Díos!*" Valencia blurted out, covering her mouth like a Miss Venezuela contestant. "*Díos mío!*"

"I know. Isn't it great? Just don't get too excited yet. I'm meeting with her about you. I gave her your court papers, the ones you gave me from before, and she promised she'd read them and get back to me. Then she wants to meet with you and tell you all about your new appeal." Alice held up a finger. "You have to keep this quiet. If anybody finds out what I'm doing for you, they'll want me to do it for them. The lawyer will drop your case in a minute."

"I no say nothin'." Valencia glanced quickly around. "You see."

"Not even to your mother or Miguel. Nobody."

"Nobody, *sí*."

"You're good at keeping secrets, I know. You've proved that to me." Alice patted her hand, because that usually got a big reaction. "You don't have to worry about any-thing. I'm taking care of you and I'm taking care of Santo, too."

"Than' God," Valencia said softly, squeezing Alice's hand. "Than' God for you, my friend."

11

Bennie hustled across the gray marble lobby of her office building running, pushing thoughts of her father to the back of her mind. It was almost noon. Her pumps clattered across the glistening floor to the elevator bank, where she punched the UP button. She had an emergency hearing to stage and the rest of her caseload to either squeeze in, farm out, or get done. She grabbed the first elevator, swimming upstream against the lunchtime crowd, and hurried off the cab into a scene that no longer struck her as remarkable.

Rosato & Associates was staffed entirely by women. The receptionist, sitting at a long paneled desk after the glass-walled conference rooms, was a woman, as were all five secretaries and lawyers, their offices arranged around a horseshoe adjoining the reception area. Bennie hadn't hired only women intentionally, but she thought of the firm as an experiment in what would happen if women ran the world. She wasn't surprised when it turned out to be less warlike and more color-coordinated, even if the coffee stank, a point that defied both explanation and stereotype.

"Hey, Bennie," said the receptionist, Marshall. With her hair woven into a long French braid, Marshall looked fragile in a pale-blue dress with a matching ribbed sweater. No appearance was more deceiving; she had run Bennie's old law firm with a manicured fist and remained the office administrator at Rosato & Associates. "We got incoming," Marshall said, handing Bennie a thick packet of yellow message slips.

"Any word from Judge Guthrie's chambers about the emergency hearing?" Bennie set her briefcase by her feet and thumbed through the messages.

"Not yet. I have your entry of appearance ready in *Connolly*. You want to sign it?" Marshall fished a form from a neat stack on her desk and pushed it across the blotter to Bennie, who stuffed the messages under her arm, plucked a ballpoint from a jar, and scribbled her name.

"Way to go. Don't file it, I have to talk to her old lawyer first, Warren Miller. I called him from the car and left a message. Did he call back?"

"Yep. He's at Jemison, Crabbe. His message is in there somewhere."

Bennie frowned. "Miller is at Jemison? Jemison is Judge Guthrie's old law firm, from before he ascended the bench."

"That's not unusual, is it, for a judge to send his old firm a case?"

"It is when it's a homicide case, going to a white-shoe firm. You can't make any money on those cases and you have to qualify to be court-appointed. I never heard of Miller."

"He did sound young." Marshall gathered a stack of correspondence, creased in thirds. "You've got mail. You won a motion to dismiss in *Sharpless*. You didn't get an extension on the brief in *Isley*. Also, the bar association says you're behind on your ethic credits. You need to take two continuing-education courses."

"What a waste of time." Bennie hugged the mail to her suit, a plain cut of tan gabardine. "I'm too busy being a lawyer to learn how to be a lawyer. Anything else happening?"

"I'm not letting you go that easy." Marshall produced a brochure paper-clipped to correspondence. "This is from the bar. If you don't fulfill your credits, they can put you on inactive status."

"They say that every year. I'll pay the late fee."

"You did that already. You're Group Four and you're out of the extension zone."

"Out of the extension zone? That sounds scary. I don't want to be out of the extension zone. I live in the extension zone." Bennie picked up her briefcase and hurried to her office, nodding to the secretaries and one of the young lawyers, Mary DiNunzio, who glanced up from a casebook when Bennie charged past. "I'll need you in fifteen minutes," she said to DiNunzio.

"Sure thing," Mary called back, swallowing visibly, and Bennie pretended not to notice. She had to keep a professional distance from her employees, even her colleagues, since she was solely responsible for their performance evaluation, hiring, and firing. Bennie hated firing people. It was why she dreaded her first phone call of the day.

"Warren Miller, please," she said, after she'd set down her briefcase, slipped into her chair, and called one of the city's most prestigious law firms, Jemison, Crabbe & Wolcott. She guessed Miller was an associate there, a caste she knew well from her days as a serf at the equally medieval Grun & Chase. Knowing the significance the big firms placed on pro bono work, Bennie figured the kid would love to off-load the Connolly case. God knew what screwup had sent it to him in the first place.

"Miller here," said a young man's tenor. Bennie visualized him in corporate peasant garb, three pieces and pinstripes.

"Warren, this is Bennie Rosato. How are you?" Bennie stalled.

"*The* Bennie Rosato? I know all about you. I admire the work you've done in civil rights. I saw you speak last year at the Public Interest Law Center. You were amazing. In fact, I help out at the moot court program at Penn and we were hoping you'd judge it this year. The committee is sending you the invitation."

"I'd be honored," Bennie said, then took a deep breath. "That's not what I'm calling about, Warren. A client of yours, Alice Connolly, has contacted me and asked me to represent her."

"We know that. We're objecting."

"What? You can't object."

"We're opposing, then."

"You can't do that either."

"Well, we . . . intend to continue our representation."

"Who's 'we'? And why?" Confounded, Bennie reached for her coffee, but there wasn't any. "And how do you know she contacted me?"

"Jemison has represented Ms. Connolly for a year. She's our client."

"Warren, I don't get it. You want to keep this case? Are you even a criminal lawyer?"

"I attended Yale Law School, where I was a member of the Law Review. My comment, a review of current search and seizure law, was the most requested reprint last year."

"Last year? Are you a *first-year* associate?"

"I've already taken several depositions and I've had an arbitration. Ms. Connolly is a client of Jemison, Crabbe, and we're retaining the representation."

"We're talking about someone's life here, Warren."

Bennie's bewilderment turned to anger. "You've had two consultations with the client in one year on a capital murder case. That's ineffectiveness *per se*. Have you notified the malpractice carrier? You're an insurance lawyer, aren't you?"

"That's just my specialty, one of the services offered by Jemison, Crabbe," Miller said, but Bennie could hear his tone stiffen. She imagined him sitting as straight as anybody without a backbone could.

"How did you get on the homicide list anyway, child?"

"There's no need for that. The captain of our trial team is a former district attorney, Henry Burden. He receives many court appointments. I'll be trying the case with his guidance."

"Aha, so Burden is the one on the homicide list and he's delegated this case to you, is that it?" Still, Bennie couldn't understand it. Henry Burden was going to prop the kid up in a major trial, but she couldn't see why. "Look, Warren, I don't know what your problem is and I don't care. I've already asked Judge Guthrie for an emergency hearing on the continuance. We'll slug it out in court. You up?"

"I . . . guess so."

"Lock and load. I'm looking forward to it." Bennie hung up the phone and didn't wait a beat before getting up. Now she had one more battle on her hands and no time for any of it. She left her office, strode to Mary Di-Nunzio's, and slipped into the cloth chair across from the associate's pristine desk. Bennie needed a bright, resourceful lawyer, and it didn't hurt that Mary had an identical twin, whom Bennie had met last year.

"Bennie!" DiNunzio said, startled, sitting at her computer keyboard. She was on the short side, well built, with dirty blond hair. Her makeup was simple, and her navy-blue suit modest and smart. Despite her professional appearance, DiNunzio always looked vaguely nervous to Bennie, who tried to put her at ease.

"I thought I'd visit you, instead of having you in my office." Bennie scanned the small office. The desk was clean, devoid of pictures or stand-up calendars. Leather-bound hornbooks stood in a straight-edged row on the bookshelves. Red accordion files were arranged alphabetically on the top of the credenza. An antique quilt hung on the wall, its patchwork colors the only disorder in the room. "Nice quilt," Bennie said.

"Thanks."

"Enough small talk?"

DiNunzio smiled. "Yes."

"Good. How busy are you?"

"I'm in the middle of a Third Circuit brief in *Samels*. It's due on Friday, and I have another motion due to Judge Dalzell in *Marvell*."

"They're writing assignments. You got any trials?"

"No."

"Arbitrations or hearings? Any stand-up time at all?"

"Not recently."

"You're starting to sound like a big-firm lawyer. You want trial experience, don't you? I thought that was the reason you and Carrier came here."

"It was. I just haven't felt . . . ready." DiNunzio colored slightly, and Bennie felt a guilty pang. The associate had been lying low after the Steere case. Not that Bennie blamed her, but it was time to get back on the horse.

"You're ready, Mary. I wouldn't ask you to do more than you could. You want to be a trial lawyer, don't you?"

"Yes," DiNunzio answered quickly, though she had

spent most of the morning thinking of new careers. She could be a cat-sitter, a pastry chef, a teacher. Daydreaming about other jobs had become her full-time job. Somebody had to do it. "Sure, I want to be a trial lawyer."

"Then you can't keep doing clerk work, can you?"

"No," Mary answered, though clerk work sounded fine to her. Law clerks never left the library, which cut down significantly on the opportunities for them to sleuth around or get shot at. Clerk work sounded great, even without dental. "I'd love a new case."

So Bennie began to explain the case, and Mary tried not to panic.

12

The computer lab at the prison was a shoebox of thick cinderblock, windowless and painted the standard washed-out gray. Inmates sat at the counter of computers and bent over the smudgy keyboards. Alice stood behind them as they powered up the ancient machines, since her gig was to teach computer technology. To Alice, anybody who would give up dealing smoke for word processing needed a course in economics, not computer tech.

A guard stood at the door, his arms linked behind his back, but for the first time it didn't bother Alice. In the upper corners of the room hung large curved mirrors that hid the surveillance cameras, but even they didn't bug her anymore. Rosato had called and said to expect an emergency hearing today. Things were starting to happen on her case and happen fast. She was on her way out of this hellhole. Good-bye.

Alice folded her arms in satisfaction over the V-neck of her blue cotton top. Navy-blue pants hung loosely on her thin frame, ending in white Keds she'd bought at the shop. Keds had the lowest street-status in the joint, but Alice didn't give a crap about the things the inmates cared about. One of them had been caught after a family visit trying to smuggle a pair of Air Jordans in her bra. *Shouldn'ta pumped it up*, Alice had cracked.

"This computer ain't workin'!" an inmate called out from the seat nearest the door.

Alice ignored the outburst. She had a rule against calling out but the inmates called out all the time. They couldn't follow basic rules, yet they were supposed to master Microsoft Word.

"Hey, *I said*, my computer ain't workin'," repeated the inmate. It was Shetrell Harting, the leader of the Crips, in a blue do-rag.

Alice pretended not to hear her. She didn't like Shetrell. Shetrell made her own rules.

"Piece a crap!" Shetrell shouted, and suddenly slapped her monitor with a loud *thwap!* The monitor wobbled on its base, and the other blue do-rags laughed. The red do-rags frowned, and the Muslims, their heads covered in short white keemar, suffered in holier-than-thou silence. They were all dummies to Alice, who walked over to save Shetrell's skinny ass.

"You gotta problem?" Alice asked, and Shetrell's bandanna pivoted angrily around. Her face was long and angular, junkie-bony, and her skin was the color of light coffee, bringing out the jarring green of her eyes. Shetrell was in for dealing rock and had kept the business going on the inside, making a bundle because there was less competition. Alice could have taken Shetrell, with her better-organized operation, but she didn't want to do business with a murder rap over her head.

"*I* don't got no problem, this *piece a crap* got the problem," Shetrell said. "Bang, bang!" She shot the monitor with a finger gun turned sideways. The other do-rags laughed on cue. Leonia Page, the gangbanger who sat to her right, always laughed the hardest. It was her job.

"Chill, home," Alice said in a passable black accent. She was in too good a mood not to play. She peered at Shetrell's monitor. "Whatchoo tryin' to do?"

"I ain't your home," Shetrell said with open contempt, and Alice grinned crookedly.

"Don't you want to be my girlfrien', girlfrien'?"

"Screw that," Shetrell said with a snort.

"That a no?"

"Yes. No." The blue do-rags fell quiet at Shetrell's confusion, and the red do-rags chuckled under their breath. The Muslims continued to suffer, and Alice dropped the accent.

"What's the problem?"

"I said, I saved my document and now it won't give it back."

"The document is a file, so you have to open the file folder. Did the file open when you clicked open?"

"No."

"Give it another chance," Alice said, knowing Shetrell hadn't tried it the first time. "Move the mouse to the yellow folder and click it."

Shetrell grabbed the mouse and slid it left. The computer arrow hovered uncertainly over the folder icon on the toolbar. She clicked the mouse and her list of documents appeared.

"Guess the slap helped."

"Always does," Shetrell said, and glanced at Leonia, who was sizing up Connolly.

Shetrell knew Leonia could do Connolly, no problem. Leonia spent all of her free time in the weight room and lifted every day. She had her weight up to two-twenty-five now and she could put a serious hurt on a man, even. Leonia had to cap Connolly by the weekend. It meant a lot of money to Shetrell, though Leonia didn't know how much. If Shetrell wanted it done, Leonia would do it. She'd *love* doin' it, now that Connolly had dissed her.

Shetrell made a little nod to Leonia, who cut her eyes sideways, understanding.

13

Mary DiNunzio perched on the edge of her chair at counsel table, looking as jittery as she felt. Mary wasn't the only lawyer nervous about making court appearances, but she was one of the few who would admit it. The modern courtroom had muted slate rugs, sleek black pews, and no windows to leap from, undoubtedly designed to prevent prisoners from committing suicide. Nobody cared if the lawyers committed suicide.

The emergency hearing was about to start. Bennie was conferring with the deputy at the dais, flanked by the royal-blue flag of the Commonwealth of Pennsylvania and an American flag with a gaudy yellow fringe. Courtroom personnel with plastic ID badges were pulling over a separate defense counsel table. The assistant district attorney, Dorsey Hilliard, drummed dark fingers on the prosecutor's table, his head shaved to a bumpy polish and glistening brown, wrinkling into a bullish neck. Aluminum crutches rested on the floor at his feet, their elbow cups stacked like spoons, but it was almost as if they belonged to someone else, since Hilliard looked muscular and strong in a suit of custom pinstripes. The prosecutor had a reputation as one of the toughest in the city, and Mary fidgeted in her seat. ANYWHERE BUT HERE, LORD, she wrote on her legal pad. NOT INCLUDING THE OFFICE. OR

LAW SCHOOL. She stopped writing when Bennie strode toward her and sat down at counsel table.

"This ought to be exciting," Bennie whispered.

"Can't wait," Mary said, forcing a smile. *I'd rather set my hair on fire.*

"All rise for the Honorable Harrison J. Guthrie, presiding," called the deputy. The lawyers stood as Judge Guthrie entered from a small door, ascended the dais with some effort, and settled his wizened frame into a high-backed leather chair. His head was a wispy white cap and his face bore the refined yet craggy lines of a patrician and an accomplished sailor. His blue eyes shone bright behind tortoise-shell reading glasses and his trademark red tartan bow tie perched like a plaid butterfly at the neck of his black robes.

"Ms. Rosato," Judge Guthrie said, his voice firm despite his age, "you have requested an emergency hearing, and the Court has granted your request. As I recall, you don't usually make such requests frivolously."

"Thank you, Your Honor," Bennie said, pleased. She rose to her feet, recalling the last time she had been before Guthrie. The Robinson case, in which a cop had beaten a small-time drug dealer, apparently for thrills. The judge's healthy damage award had drawn substantial criticism, though it was the right result. "I would like to enter my appearance in this matter, Your Honor."

"A rather perfunctory chore, Ms. Rosato."

"Usually, Your Honor. However, former defense counsel has refused to accede, even though the defendant wishes to retain me. I therefore find myself forced to seek resolution of this matter by the Court."

Warren Miller, the young associate from Jemison, Crabbe, rose halfway to his feet. A slight, dark-haired lawyer, Miller wore rimless glasses, a three-piece suit, and the pallor of a hothouse orchid. "For the record, uh, we take issue with . . . that recounting of the facts, Your Honor."

"The Court will hear from you in due course, Mr. Miller," Judge Guthrie said, and Miller withered into his seat. "Now, Ms. Rosato, you have also requested that we bring down the defendant, Ms. Alice Connolly, and I granted that request, though the notice was short. You must know it was a great deal of trouble for the Court and the sheriffs."

"I'm sorry the Court was inconvenienced, Your Honor. I didn't have much notice myself and since this is a capital murder case, I was sure the Court would want the defendant to be heard."

"Yes, yes, of course," Judge Guthrie said. He slid his reading glasses from his nose and waved at the deputy with them. "Perhaps we should have the defendant brought in. Will you, Mr. Deputy?" A courtroom deputy in a navy blazer disappeared behind a side door in the paneled wall and emerged a second later, followed by a Philadelphia police officer with a black windbreaker over his uniform and an earphone plugged into his left ear. Behind the cop walked Alice Connolly in her orange prison jumpsuit.

Bennie stood when Connolly entered, but Mary sat as if fixed to her chair, her eyes widening. Alice Connolly looked so much like Bennie she could be her twin. The defendant had a cynical smile, her hair was bright red and raggedy, and she was thinner, but her features looked the same. What was going on? Mary didn't think Bennie had a twin, much less one accused of murdering a cop. This case was looking worse and worse. She grabbed her pen. *Anybody got a match? I'll bring the hair spray. It'll only take a minute.*

"You can seat the defendant with us, Officer," Bennie said. "Right here." She got up and pulled out the chair at counsel table next to Mary, who flipped a page in her legal pad quickly.

"Excuse me," Miller interrupted, pulling out the chair next to him. "Ms. Connolly should be seated here, as I'm counsel of record."

The cop glanced from one lawyer to the other, powerless to choose, but Mary couldn't focus on the seating dispute, she was too distracted by Connolly's looks. Didn't anybody notice the similarity between the defendant and her new lawyer? The D.A. barely looked at Connolly. The lawyer from Jemison, Crabbe didn't react. Maybe nobody noticed because the context was so different: Bennie was a prominent lawyer and Connolly a criminal defendant.

Bennie was standing before the dais. "Your Honor, I'm not going to fight over the physical location of the defendant. Mr. Miller seems to think that possession of Ms. Connolly makes him her lawyer, which of course it doesn't. He's welcome to sit with my client, with my permission."

"So ordered," Judge Guthrie said. "Mr. Deputy, you heard her." The judge cleared his throat as the cop in the windbreaker escorted Connolly to Miller's table, where she sat down. "Now that the defendant is safely ensconced, please explain your position, Ms. Rosato."

"Your Honor, Ms. Connolly contacted me by telephone yesterday and requested that I represent her effective immediately. She has an unfettered right to counsel of her own choosing and I am happy to undertake the matter, on a pro bono basis, but I seek a continuance. The trial is set for next week. I am requesting a month postponement, Your Honor, so that I may prepare my defense."

"Thank you, Ms. Rosato." Judge Guthrie tilted his chair to face the Jemison lawyer. "Mr. Miller, may I have your comments now?"

The associate stood up, clutching an index card like a security blanket. "Your Honor, I, my supervising counsel Henry Burden, who unfortunately was called out of the country this morning, and the law firm of Jemison, Crabbe, were appointed by this Court to represent this defendant and have done so for almost a year now. There is no reason to remove us as counsel and no reason to delay this matter. We hereby oppose the request for removal and the request for a continuance."

"Your Honor," Bennie argued, "Jemison has no standing to object to defendant's choice of counsel. Until now they haven't shown even a modicum of interest in this defendant."

"Settle down, Ms. Rosato. I have your argument." Judge Guthrie eased his reading glasses on and peered at the case file, turning the pages with care. "Does the Commonwealth wish to enter into this fray?" he asked, without looking up.

Dorsey Hilliard rose heavily, slipped his aluminum crutches under his elbows, and walked to the podium. His suit shifted at the sleeves, unnaturally bunched around the crutches, but Hilliard's handicap was otherwise not an issue. "The Commonwealth takes no position on Ms. Rosato's entry of appearance. However, the Commonwealth strenuously opposes granting a continuance in this case at this late date. This matter has been the subject of six successive postponements, most by the defense. The People would not be served by a seventh. The Commonwealth is fully prepared for the upcoming trial and is ready to go."

Judge Guthrie frowned. "How about it, Ms. Rosato?"

Bennie took the podium as Hilliard shifted to the right. "Your Honor, none of the delays have been at defendant's behest and none were chargeable to her for purposes of the speedy trial rule. The defendant's right to counsel of her choice and to a fair trial should not be jeopardized because of circumstances beyond her—"

"Wait a minute, please," Judge Guthrie hushed her, holding a nimble finger over the papers on the dais. "The Court would like to consult the record on this. Perhaps it would save us some time."

"Yes, Your Honor." Bennie gripped the podium and struggled to remain still while the judge read. The restraint almost killed her. She considered silence an unnatural state for a lawyer.

"Let's see," Judge Guthrie said finally, still reading. "There are far too many continuances for a case of this gravity, Ms. Rosato."

"I agree, Your Honor, but they appear to be the fault of current defense counsel, who have barely worked this case. The defendant shouldn't be punished for her lawyer's lassitude."

Warren Miller shot between the two lawyers like a chaperone. "That's not true, Your Honor. We have consulted, as needed, with the defendant. The continuances in the record were due to an illness of mine, then of Mr. Burden's. One was because he was on trial on another matter. There's no justification for removing us as counsel, Your Honor."

"My, my. Please, all of you, take your seats," Judge Guthrie said. The lawyers sat down as the judge focused his stern gaze on the defendant. "Ms. Connolly, it would appear that two skilled criminal lawyers wish to represent you. It's an enviable position for someone accused of such a grave crime, and certainly rare, in my experience. Kindly take the stand and lend us some aid."

"Yes, sir." Connolly stood up, walked to the witness stand, and was sworn in. Bennie watched every move to try to determine what kind of witness she'd be, if she had to testify.

"Ms. Connolly," Judge Guthrie said. "The Court would like to ask you a few questions to determine your wishes in this matter. As you know, this Court appointed one of the most respected criminal experts in this city, Mr. Burden, working with his associate, Mr. Miller, to represent you. Now Ms. Rosato tells us you wish her to act as your counsel. Is that truly your wish, Ms. Connolly?"

"Yes, sir."

"Ms. Connolly, please state for the record why you wish Ms. Rosato to represent you."

Bennie held her breath as Connolly answered. "I think Ms. Rosato cares more about my case than anyone and she's a great lawyer. I trust her. We have a very close . . . trust."

"Well. My, my." Judge Guthrie paused. "There remains one question, Ms. Connolly. Why didn't you raise this issue earlier? You've been incarcerated for quite some time."

"I didn't know Ms. Rosato would represent me before, Your Honor."

"I see." Judge Guthrie made a quick note with a thick black fountain pen. "Please step down, Ms. Connolly."

"Thank you, Your Honor," Connolly said, and as she walked back to counsel table flashed Bennie a quick smile. Bennie smiled back, but it was only for show. Connolly smoothly hadn't revealed her belief that Bennie was her twin, which was at least a material omission. Connolly was a completely believable liar, and it worried Bennie.

Judge Guthrie skimmed the record. "Well. Having considered this matter and taken all of the relevant factors into account, the Court grants Ms. Rosato leave to file an entry of appearance on behalf of defendant Alice Connolly."

Bennie half rose. "Thank you, Your Honor."

Judge Guthrie held up a wrinkled hand. "In addition, after due consideration, your request for a continuance is hereby denied. This matter has already been characterized by a number of continuances and delays, and this Court must not add to it. It is the Court's responsibility to use judicial resources efficiently and effectively. Trial remains as scheduled. Jury selection begins Monday."

Bennie gulped loud enough for Mary to hear. "Your Honor, Ms. Connolly is on trial for her life. It's almost impossible to prepare a homicide defense in a week, in a death penalty case."

"The Court understands your task is a difficult one, Ms. Rosato." Judge Guthrie closed the case file. "However, Ms. Connolly is switching lawyers at the last minute for no reason that is apparent to me or anyone else. Jemison, Crabbe is one of the best law firms in this city, and my alma mater, I might add. While the Constitution mandates my decision on your entry of appearance, our forefathers, mercifully, chose not to tell me how to run my courtroom. The Jemison firm is to turn over its file to you forthwith and I'm sure that file is complete. So ordered." Judge Guthrie banged his gavel, and Bennie took the file from Miller's reluctant hand.

• • •

After the hearing adjourned, Bennie pushed through the revolving door of the Criminal Justice Center with Mary DiNunzio struggling to keep up. They charged past the curious stares of uniformed cops waiting in front of the courthouse and kept ahead of a pair of news stringers with notebooks. "Bennie, why are you appearing in Connolly?" they shouted. "What's the story, Ms. Rosato?" "Please, Ms. Rosato, gimme a break here!"

Bennie hustled down the narrow sidewalk on Filbert Street into the sunlight. The stringers were rookies compared with the full-court press that would come later. Bennie expected the attention, but noticed that Mary had gone an unhealthy shade of white. She grabbed the associate's arm while she hailed a cab and opened the door when it slowed to a stop. "Come on, DiNunzio," Bennie said, pushing the associate in ahead of her.

She gave the driver her office address as her thoughts clicked away. She'd have to prepare the main defense and the death penalty defense at the same time, because if she lost the case she'd be on an hour later to save Connolly's life. She'd have to find psychological witnesses, experts, school records. She'd need another associate and maybe an investigator, too.

Bennie was so busy making a mental list of things to do that she didn't notice the gaunt old man lingering behind the crowd, dressed in a tweed coat despite the warm weather. He stood in the large shadow cast by City Hall, a felt hat pulled low over his eyes. Bennie wouldn't have known him anyway, unless she remembered the photo of the airmen.

It was Bill Winslow, and he was watching her with a tight smile.

14

Back at her office, Bennie tore through the Connolly file in disbelief. Jemison, Crabbe hadn't prepared any defense at all—no witness interviews, no investigation, no neighborhood surveys, not even lawyers' notes. What were Burden and Miller thinking? She reached for the only full folder, bearing a label that read D.A. FILE—DISCLOSED AT PRELIMINARY HEARING. It contained a skinny transcript of the preliminary hearing and a bare-bones collection of incident reports, list of seized items, autopsy and toxicology reports, and mobile crime reports. There were no activity reports, the detailed logs of the police investigation.

"Bear with me, kids," Bennie said as she flipped through the manila folder. The two associates, Mary DiNunzio and Judy Carrier, sat across the desk like Mutt and Jeff with J.D. degrees. DiNunzio was short and dressed like Lawyer Barbie in her blue Brooks Brothers suit; Carrier was almost as tall as Bennie and dressed like an artist in a loose denim smock, blue tights, and suede Dansko clogs. Bennie finished skimming the file and looked up. "I want you to drop everything, Carrier. You have to subpoena the police dispatch records. I want to know who called in this murder."

"No problem," the associate said, making a note on the pad on her lap. Her hair, shorn around her chin in a blunt, lemony bowl, fell forward like a bloodhound's ears. "They keep that on tape, don't they? The 911 records?"

"Yes, but by now the tapes have been erased. You'll have to apply for the transcripts, the computer-assisted records. Now go get the office camera, will you? Marshall knows where it is, ask her. DiNunzio?" Bennie said, turning to the associate as Carrier left the office. "You know anybody at Jemison, Crabbe?"

"Sure, it's huge. Two of my classmates went there, I think."

"If they survived, give them a call. I want to find out how Henry Burden got this case and if he has any connection to Judge Guthrie. Be discreet, though."

"How do I do that?"

"Take 'em to lunch or something. Get the dirt. You heard what Miller said in court, that Burden was called out of the country. What's up with that? Run it down. Now grab your bag and the file. You're ready to rock and roll, aren't you?"

"I mean, sure. Right. Absolutely." Mary was too intimidated to say anything else. Secretly she wanted to go to home, climb into bed, and read the classifieds. Were there jobs in America where you could tell your boss the truth? Nah.

Drizzle tinged the sky gray and dotted the windshield of Bennie's Ford. She pulled over and parked on Trose Street, across from the rowhouse where Della Porta had lived with Connolly. The house was squat, only two stories tall, with a wooden sign that read APT FOR RENT creaking on rusted hooks. It had black shutters that peeled unnoticed and its brick was a low-rent rust color, unlike the muted orange hues of Colonial brick. It sat next to a storefront day-care center and a rowhouse, also two stories, with a shutter missing on the second floor. Next to the rowhouse stood a defunct bistro and a tattered pink zoning notice glued to its boarded-up glass announced someone's mistaken optimism.

"Let's go, kids," Bennie said, cutting the ignition. "DiNunzio, bring the file. Carrier, get the camera. I want you to take pictures of the street and the area outside."

"Got it." Judy climbed out of the Ford and flipped up the hood of a yellow Patagonia slicker. She looped the camera around her neck and began snapping pictures, shielding the lens from the weather.

Next to her, Bennie took a legal pad from her bag and made a fast sketch of the street, holding the pad close to avoid the raindrops. She drew the houses and the alley where the bloody clothes were found, which lay on the far side of the day-care center, going west. Beyond it were two more rowhouses to the corner, Tenth Street. Bennie walked to the alley as she sketched in the dented blue Dumpster. It still sat rusting against the brick wall of the alley, on the right. The alley went through to the next street and so could have been entered from behind. Cleaned up and spray-mounted on foamcore, Bennie's sketch would become Exhibit D-1.

Her eyes swept the block when she finished, thinking about possible witnesses to the comings and goings at the rowhouse. The south side of Trose Street, where Della Porta's house was, contained several rowhouses between it and the alley. They would be the houses from which most of the witnesses would come and, as such, they'd be the primary focus of the defense in the next few days.

Bennie pivoted on her heel. Across the street, directly

facing the Della Porta rowhouse, was a newly constructed apartment building. All but four rowhouses had been demolished to make room for the building, eliminating the possibility of witnesses who would have had the best view of the Della Porta house. A plastic banner on the building read NOW LEASING FOR SEPTEMBER, and Bennie remembered the construction that Connolly had mentioned in their interview.

With the Nikkormat in front of her face, Judy snapped photos of both ends of Trose Street, until she realized Mary hadn't gotten out of the truck. She sidestepped to the half-open window. "Mare," she whispered. "Mare, come on out."

"No." Mary sat in the backseat. "I'm not coming."

"What? What do you mean you're not coming?"

"I'm not coming. Which word don't you understand?"

"Are you kidding?"

It was a good question, and Mary wasn't exactly sure. "I've never been to a crime scene before. I don't want to go to a crime scene now. Why do you think they put up all that yellow tape? Because crime scenes are not good places to go."

"Mary, it's your job."

"No kidding." The associate's head popped from the window and she blinked against the rain. "I know it's my job, why do you think I hate it? If my job was making chocolate eclairs, I wouldn't hate it."

"Are you crazy? Get out of the car."

"If my job was buying clothes, I wouldn't hate it. Or reading books. Also I like to eat. Maybe I could get a job eating. Are there jobs like that, Jude?"

"What's the matter with you? You want to get fired?"

Mary brightened immediately. "Why didn't I think of

that? Then I could collect unemployment, like the rest of America."

"Carrier! DiNunzio! Let's go!" Bennie shouted, the impatience in her tone impossible to miss. She was already climbing the front stoop of the rowhouse.

"Come on, she'll fire me, too." Judy opened the Ford's door and grabbed the sleeve of Mary's suit. "You'll be fine, you'll see," she said, yanking out her friend and slamming the door behind her. They walked together to the front door, outdistanced by Bennie, who had slipped inside the entrance and already had her finger on the buzzer under a dented aluminum mailbox.

"We caught a break," Bennie told them. "The super lives on the first floor."

"How do you know?" Judy asked.

"It says so." Bennie pointed to a nameplate: J. BOSTON, SUPER.

"Ace detective work," Judy said, but Mary wasn't laughing.

The super was short and wore a dirty T-shirt, baggy pants, and a grizzled, apathetic expression. When he spoke, a scotch-scented wind wafted toward Bennie. "No, I didn't hear nuthin' the night Ant'ny got killed," he rasped in a voice sandpapered by cigarettes.

"But you live downstairs," Bennie said. "You heard the gunshot, didn't you?"

"The cops already axed me that. I told 'em, I don't hear nothin' at night."

"Even a gunshot?"

"I didn't hear nothin'. So I'd had a few. That agains' the law?"

"Did you ever hear Connolly and Della Porta? Talking, arguing, anything?"

The old man's watery eyes lit up. "Anything? You mean *anything*?"

"Fine. Anything."

"No." He burst into laughter that ended in a hacking fit. Judy and Mary exchanged glances, standing in the hallway in front of his apartment. The television, specifically Oprah Winfrey's theme song, blared from behind a white door grimy with fingerprints. "I hardly ever saw 'em. They was never around. Him bein' a cop and all, I figgered he was busy."

"Did they have a lot of visitors?"

"Hell if I know. I stay in my place. My brother-in-law, he owns this dump, he likes it that way. Any way he likes it is fine with me." The super squinted. "You say you're a lawyer? All a youse are gal lawyers? Do they have that?"

Bennie let it go. "Does that sign out front mean that Della Porta's apartment is vacant?"

"Hell, yes. That apartment's nothin' but trouble. I could show it all day, ain't nobody gonna rent it. Nobody want a place with a man got shot, even furnished and all. Plus he's askin' too much."

"The apartment's been vacant since the murder? With the original furniture?"

"Sure. Got everything 'cept the rug. I throwed that out when the cops was done with it."

Bennie sighed. Trace evidence would be long gone. "Is the furniture the same as it was? You didn't rearrange it, did you?"

"I don't get paid enough to move nothin'."

"I need to see that apartment. Can I borrow the key?"

"What the hell." The super fumbled for his pocket and

dug around inside. "Who you think cleaned that mess upstairs? Yours truly. Who you think took up the rug, had blood all over it? Yours truly. Who sanded the floors? Repainted the bloody wall? Packed all their junk up and put it in the basement?"

"Yours truly?" Judy said, and the super grinned in toothless appreciation.

After they got the key, Bennie charged up the stairway with the associates to the second floor. The stair was long and skinny, covered by a dirty red runner, and on the second floor was a door without a sign or number.

Bennie unlocked the door. "Keep your eyes open," she said, stepping inside the apartment. "Take note of the layout of the place. Look at the orientation of the rooms, the furniture. Check views from the windows, lighting. Try to remember what you see, no matter how insignificant it seems now. Got it?"

"Yep," Judy answered. She snapped a photo, but Mary lingered at the threshold, unnoticed.

Bennie scanned the apartment. The large room had two windows that faced the street, a northern exposure, and contained a table with four chairs to the right, making up a dining area on the east side. On the left side of the room a couch sat flush against the wall and in front of it was an oak blanket chest. A Sony Trinitron sat on a TV cart between the windows and an oval mirror hung on the wall. Bennie made a note of the brighter squares in the textured wallpaper where pictures had been hung, and there was a light square in the center of the floor where a rug had been. "Take a picture from this spot, Carrier," Bennie said. "Take a bunch."

"Gotcha." Judy clicked away as Bennie crossed the room to the couch.

"Here we go. Here's the bloodstain." Bennie strode directly to a discolored patch in the hardwood, which was glossy in uneven patches, the refinishing sloppy. Della Porta's blood must have seeped through the rug. She remembered from the police file that the bullet had been a .22 caliber. It had made a small hole in Della Porta's forehead and blasted through the back of his skull. The loss of blood had been significant.

"Jeez." Judy walked over and took a picture. "No wonder the super hasn't rented the place. Nobody sweeps blood under the rug."

"Which way did the body fall? Where's DiNunzio?" Bennie asked, and both heads snapped to the doorway where Mary stood rooted. "DiNunzio, what are you doing? Come over here."

"Coming." Mary walked over as purposefully as she could and looked down. On the floor was a dark brown stain shaped like France. Her stomach flipped over. "Is that what I think it is?"

"Della Porta was found face-up," Bennie said. "Was his head tilted east or west?"

"East? West?" Mary couldn't think clearly. A man had died here, shot in the head. She visualized a slug of hot lead tearing apart the soft wetness of his brain. Destroying what should have been inviolate.

"West is to your left, east to your right."

Mary couldn't take her eyes from the bloodstain. She'd seen the autopsy photos and the mobile crime unit photos. So much blood in a line of work that was supposed to be bloodless.

"Which is it? East or west?"

"Can I . . . check the file?" Mary slid the accordion from under her arm.

"No. You read it, didn't you?" Bennie snapped, and Judy touched her sleeve.

"What's the point, Bennie? It's hard for her—"

"Quiet, please. Mary doesn't need a lawyer, she is a lawyer." Bennie was doing this for a reason, but she didn't need to broadcast it, and she even knew the answer, which didn't matter anyway. "DiNunzio, this is a murder case, so blood is a prerequisite. Don't think of the body, think of the file. Think of the paper. It's just another case. Now, was he facing east or west?"

"West," Mary said, the answer materializing from a police photo she didn't know she remembered.

"Good girl. What did the coroner have as the time of death?"

"The coroner said between seven-thirty and eight-thirty. It was in his report."

"There you go. Now, Connolly told me she was at the Free Library on Logan Circle. She left at six-thirty and walked home. The shooter was somebody Della Porta buzzed in, and the murder took place almost immediately after. Della Porta was standing at the time and was shot point-blank. He crumpled and fell backward, face-up. It's all consistent with the M.E.'s report, that's what they're going to say. You think I'm right, DiNunzio?"

"That's what they'll say."

Judy looked puzzled. "You know what I don't get? It's a long walk here from the library, an hour or more. Why did she walk? There's buses, cabs, everything."

"I don't know, maybe she likes to walk."

"Then she has no alibi. If she left at six-thirty, she could still be walking home at the time of the murder."

"I'm aware of that."

Judy swallowed hard, then risked job termination. "Did she do it?"

"She's our client, Carrier. Whether she did it or not is beside the point." Bennie checked her growing annoyance. "Legal Ethics 101. It's not prosecutors on one side and defense lawyers on the other, with equal and opposite functions. That's sloppy thinking. The roles are different in kind. The prosecution is supposed to seek justice, and the defense is supposed to get the defendant acquitted."

"You don't think Connolly's guilt is relevant? What about justice?"

"Connolly is my client, so I have to save her life. My job is about loyalty. Is that noble enough for you?"

Judy cocked her head. "So it's a conflict between justice and loyalty."

"Welcome to the profession."

Mary heard the edge to Bennie's voice and recognized it as anxiety. If Bennie and Connolly were the twins they appeared to be at the emergency hearing, Mary could imagine the strain Bennie was feeling. Judy, who hadn't been at the hearing, was missing the point.

"Then I'm confused," Judy said. "If we're not solving a murder, why are we here?"

Bennie looked at Judy directly. "We need to understand the D.A.'s case and develop a credible theory of what happened that night. When we get into that courtroom, the jurors have to look to us as the font of all knowledge, so they take that confidence in us into the jury room. Shall I go on?"

"No, but—" Judy started to say, and Bennie waved her off.

"We don't have time to discuss this any longer. Connolly has a right to effective counsel, so get effective. Take pictures." Bennie glanced around the living room, bothered. Carrier's question had been nagging at her from the beginning. Did Connolly do it? Bennie didn't think so, but why? She suppressed the thought. "This place is too fucking clean. Let's start with the kitchen, DiNunzio, and check through in an orderly way."

"Okay," Mary said, though Bennie was already at the threshold to the kitchen, hands on her hips.

It was a small galley kitchen with cherrywood cabinets, new appliances, and a fancy Sub-Zero refrigerator. Bennie opened the cabinets, which were empty except for one stocked with heavy white dishes. She double-checked the others, which were bare, then went to the window. "Who called 911 about the gunshot, DiNunzio?"

"Mrs. Lambertsen, from next door. She testified at the prelim. She also saw Connolly run by, and so did other neighbors. Three or four, I remember reading."

Bennie nodded. "Assume 911 dispatch gets the call and radios it out right away. Who was the first patrol car to respond?"

"I have to check that."

Mary slid out the accordion, pulled out a folder, and thumbed through it with Bennie at her shoulder. Yellow highlighting striped every page, evidence of DiNunzio's careful work, and Bennie thought the associate would make a fine lawyer if she'd just get out of her own way. "Here it is," Mary said. "Patrol Officers Pichetti and Luz."

"Not McShea and Reston?" Bennie thought a minute. "Where were Pichetti and Luz when they got the call?"

Mary ran her finger down the page. "A couple blocks away, at Seventh and Pine."

"What we need to know is where Reston and McShea

were and why they were so close to Della Porta's apartment."

"The file doesn't have a report from them."

"I'm not surprised, but there must be one. That's the report we want. We have to find it. It should have been in the police file or the file from Jemison, Crabbe. Check that when we get back to the office."

"Okay." Mary was starting to feel useful and she couldn't see the stain anymore.

"Good. Let's look at the other rooms." Bennie left the kitchen, walked through the living room, and entered the bedroom, which was as nondescript as the kitchen. A queen-size bed frame and box spring sat against the wall between two windows, and a walnut veneer dresser against the far wall, with three drawers. Bennie crossed the room and opened the drawers. Nothing.

"Here's the bathroom." Mary waved a finger behind her, and Bennie nodded.

"Have a look. I'll take the other bedroom. I wonder what they used it for."

Bennie walked to the spare room and stood dumbstruck at the threshold. It was a home office and it looked like a replica of Bennie's—even the furniture in it was arranged like Bennie's. Around the walls was a lineup of file cabinet, bookshelves, in the far corner a computer table, then another bookshelf. The table matched Bennie's; a tall, white workstation from IKEA, with two shelves above the table and pullout trays on each side. Bennie used her trays all the time. Did Connolly?

Bennie walked over to the computer table and pulled the right-hand tray, which slid out with a familiar, gritty sound. Centered on the tray was a brown circle. Bennie knew what it was because hers had one, too: a ring left by a coffee mug. Her gut tensed. Did it mean anything? Logically, no. Most people drink coffee while they work and arrange their home offices the same way. And the lines at IKEA are endless.

"Nothing in the bathroom," DiNunzio said from the door.

Bennie shook her head. Without knowing why, she crossed the short distance to the door. "There's a peg here," she said, and closed the door, revealing a peg stuck from the top panel.

"How did you know that?" Mary asked.

Bennie had a peg in the same place, but she didn't want to explain that to DiNunzio yet. She needed to know more about Connolly before she gave any credence to this twin business. "Everybody has a peg on the door, don't they?" she said casually.

"I'm just surprised Connolly did. She never used it. This office was a sty."

Bennie pivoted in surprise. "How do you know that?"

"The photos, in the file. They were in an envelope from the mobile crime unit."

Of course. She had forgotten. "Let's see them."

"I don't have them with me." Mary's attack of usefulness vanished. "We're not allowed to take originals out of the office, remember?"

Bennie gritted her teeth. It wasn't the kid's fault, so she couldn't strangle her. "What do the photos show?"

"The apartment with all their stuff in it. You can see how they decorated it. It's pretty much the same, except for this room. The apartment was neat, but Connolly's office was a mess."

"I want to see the photos tonight. Remind me when we get back."

"Okay, sorry. I didn't understand."

"Forget it." Bennie raked a hand through her hair. Connolly's home office was a revelation, raising more questions than it answered. It was time to find the answers. "Get Carrier," she said suddenly. "Let's go."

"Where?"

"Downstairs to see the super. I'm renting this apartment."

"You want to *rent* this place?" Mary was appalled. "But this is a crime scene."

"Understood."

"A man was killed here."

"There are worse ideas than renting a crime scene," Bennie said, but Mary couldn't think of a single one.

15

Judy sat across from Mary in the conference room, typing a pretrial motion on her laptop while Mary organized the Connolly file. They had worked this way forever, holed up in a war room until late at night, readying for trial on a conference table dotted with open law books and take-out lo mein. "You're nuts," Judy said as she hit the ENTER key.

"You weren't in court today, I was." Mary pressed an orange label onto the coroner's report and marked it Exhibit D-11. "I saw it. Her. Them. I'm telling you, Connolly is Bennie's twin."

"I don't believe it." Judy stopped typing. "Bennie never mentioned she had a twin. She's private, but not that private."

"All I can tell you is, Bennie and Connolly are twins. Same basic face, same height, same eyes. Not just sisters, either. They're twins, I can feel it."

"How?"

"Because I'm a twin. Twins know these things."

"You're starting to sound like me." Judy cocked her head and her Dutch-boy haircut fell to the side. "You're getting a twin vibe, is what you're saying."

"Catholics don't believe in vibes. Just take it from me, they're twins."

"If they look that much alike, how come nobody else in the courtroom saw it?"

"Nobody was really looking at them, they were following the proceeding. And Connolly and Bennie look different. Connolly is thin and her hair's red. She wears makeup, she's pretty. Foxy. Bennie's hair is such a light blond, messy, and she always looks like she put on whatever she grabbed first, like a jock." Mary finished choosing and labeling the defense exhibits. "And the cues weren't there. My God, Bennie's a big-time lawyer and Connolly's a state prisoner. One's a winner and one's a loser. Nobody made the connection."

"What do you mean? Either Bennie and Connolly look like twins or they don't."

"Not necessarily. It's like with me and Angie. There was a time, I don't know if you remember, really early at Stalling? I was a second-year associate. I lost twenty pounds. My face was sunken in, I broke out constantly, and I looked terrible. The worst I've looked in my life."

"Worse than now?"

"As I was saying, I remember Angie was entering the convent. We were allowed to go to the ceremony and watch from behind a carved screen. Wasn't that big of them?"

Judy smiled. "Without your religion you'd have nothing to whine about."

"Yes, I would—what about my job? Anyway, I took pictures of me and Angie that day, and you could never tell we were identical twins from them. There's Angie, looking all happy and serene. Relaxed, fulfilled. On a first-name basis with the Holy Spirit."

"The Holy Spirit has a first name?"

"Al, of course. You can call him Al. Now will you shut up and let me tell the story? In the picture, I looked the worst I ever looked and Angie looked the best. She was becoming a nun and I was becoming a burnt-out associate. She was serving God, I was serving Satan."

"I get it," Judy said, though Mary remained undaunted.

"You know those ads with the 'before' and 'after' pictures? I looked like the 'before' picture and Angie looked like the 'after' picture. Especially with me in the suit and her in the nun costume." Mary sipped cold coffee from a Styrofoam cup. "It doesn't help when you dress differently, like Connolly and Bennie were, in court. It's not only in the way you look, anyway."

"How so?"

"I can tell in other ways that people are twins. I knew fraternal twins in school. They sat closer together than other people. When they talked to each other, they stood nearer. They were just used to being physically close. They gravitated to each other, like meatballs in a bowl. Angie and I used to be that way."

"That's so cool." Judy straightened in her swivel chair, and Mary felt suddenly special. It was good to feel special about something, even if it was an accident of birth.

"There are things about twins no one would mistake. No one knows how to look for it like a twin. When I look at Angie, I see me. It's not only how she looks, it's how she acts."

"How?" Judy asked, though she had a rough idea. She didn't know Angie that well, but she'd noticed it, too. It was as if Mary's twin were an echo of Mary. The same person, but not the same. A physical clone, but emotionally a different person.

"You know Angie's body language? She sits like me. She always tucks her right leg under her butt, like me. Plus she talks too fast, like me. My mother has to ask her to repeat herself. I'm the only one who can understand her."

Judy scoffed. "That doesn't count. You both have South Philly accents. Nobody can understand either of you."

"I'll ignore that. It's the tone of voice. And the gestures, the way she talks with her hands."

"You're both Italian."

"Guilty as charged." Mary thought a minute. "We like the same clothes. When we go shopping, we fight over the same dress. It used to happen all the time."

"That doesn't count. You were raised together. You've developed the same taste in clothes. Didn't your parents even dress you alike when you were little?"

"True, all the time. Same birthday party, same toys. Until we were three we called each other by whatever name was handy. Angie, Mary, it didn't matter to us." Mary thought harder. "But there's other things. Nature, not nurture. Stuff that you couldn't learn. I finish her sentences."

"We finish each other's sentences."

"That's because you're always talking about food. It's not the same thing."

Judy pitched a paper clip at her. "Like what, then?"

"Well, sometimes, I know what Angie is thinking. I knew when she was unhappy in the convent. I knew when she was worried about me, or about my father. I know when she's thinking about calling me. Lots of times, I'll pick up the phone to call her and it's busy because she's calling me."

"Maybe you call each other at the same time, as a habit."

"We don't. It happens at all times." Mary's voice softened. "When she got into paralegal school, after she left the convent, I knew she got in. I could just feel how happy she was. I knew it the very minute she did. I was in the library, working on a brief. All of a sudden I felt something inside, like a rush of great feeling. Like I accomplished something. The minute I felt it, a voice inside me said, 'I got in.' Not 'Angie got in.' '*I* got in.' It was like I was having her thoughts."

"Whoa." Judy's eyes widened, Delft-blue. "Like telepathy."

"Not exactly. Don't get carried away." Mary flushed with sudden regret. She hadn't talked about this to anyone but Angie. Even she thought it sounded wacky. She wanted to change the subject, but Judy was already leaning over the conference table toward her.

"You're telepathic, Mare! You and your twin. That's what it means."

"No, I'm not."

"Yes, you are. You had *her* thoughts. Can you tune her in, right now?"

Mary rolled her eyes. "No, you idiot. It's not like a radio."

"Tune her in. Call her up. Do whatever."

"No. Stop. Forget it. You make it sound like the movie *Carrie*. It's not like I can move things with my eyes." Mary pulled over the police file and opened it. "We should get back to work."

"Can Angie read your thoughts, too?"

"I don't know. Get to work."

"Yes, you do. Tell me."

"We have work to do. Write your brief. And don't tell anybody what I told you, okay? Or I'll set you on fire with my finger."

"Okay. Fine." Judy fell silent. If the subject was too personal for Mary, she'd let it go. She didn't want to upset her. But what Mary said had implications for the Connolly case. Judy felt suddenly uneasy. "Mare, if Bennie is Connolly's twin, she shouldn't be representing her in a murder case. She can't see the facts objectively. She'll be swayed by her emotions. I think she already is, the way she snapped out in Della Porta's apartment."

Mary looked up from the file. "Sure she is, but she has to take the case. No question. It's an emotional decision. If Angie's in trouble, I'm there. If Connolly is Bennie's twin, Bennie has to defend her. Period. Whether she should or not. It's a no-win situation."

Judy thought about that. "You show unusual insight, grasshopper."

"Just one of my superpowers," Mary said, and got busy.

16

Bennie barreled down I-95 South as the rain evaporated, supersaturating the dusky sky. She didn't turn on the air-conditioning in the Expedition; she liked the humid air on her cheek. So did Bear, who leaned out the back window with a doggie smile. His ragged ears took flight and ropes of saliva dripped from the corners of his mouth. Bennie had stopped home to let the dog out and had succumbed to his whimpering to come along. She didn't bother to examine whether taking the golden was a good idea; if she were the type of person to examine what she did before she did it, she'd never have taken Connolly's case. Or, for that matter, this little trip.

To 708 Lakeside Drive, Montchanin, Delaware.

The address had been in the prison logs and Montchanin was right outside of Wilmington. Bennie was going to see Bill Winslow. Maybe he was her father, maybe he wasn't. In half an hour she'd know. Her fingers tightened on the wheel. And if Winslow were her father, could Connolly be her twin? She switched to the fast lane and pushed a button for the CD player. It was all Bruce Springsteen, all the time, and a clear road to Delaware. She brushed the hair from her eyes and accelerated smoothly.

In time the four-lane highway narrowed to a two-lane road that wound past towns and long strip malls with new stucco refacing and neon signs. By the time Bennie was on the second CD of the boxed set, the streetlights had been replaced by split-rail fences and lush green pastures. Trees a century old formed a verdant backdrop; the sun had set and the sky was the color of blueberries. The humidity had lifted as she drove south and the air wafted sweet and earthy. Horses grazed silently, their long tails switching at the bites of unseen flies, and raised their heads to watch Bennie cruise past. The Expedition negotiated skinny country roads that led to estates so vast she couldn't see the houses.

Lakeside Drive. Bennie slowed and looked around for number 708. She read the numbers on dented mailboxes and burglar alarm logos until she reached a sturdy aluminum mailbox for 708. Her mouth felt dry, but she ignored it. She had found a man who had been a question mark her whole life; now a man who had an answer she needed.

Bennie pressed the gas pedal, twisted the truck onto the asphalt road on the property, and traveled the road until it forked. The right fork continued in black asphalt, tree-lined in a grand manner; the left fork was gravel and stone. If one belonged to the caretaker, it would be the left. Bennie steered onto it, and the woods grew denser with each foot, so she turned on the high beams. Crickets chirped loudly in the woods and in the distance a horse whinnied to her colt. Bennie slowed the truck, its heavy tires making popping noises on the gravel, and in a clearing she came upon a cottage of white stucco.

Could this be Winslow's house? It stood two short stories high and was encircled like an embrace by a flower garden, dense and mature. Bennie could see white and yellow daisies, a thatch of pink and red rosebushes, and maroon bleeding hearts with other perennials. A raised wooden box contained rows of green vegetables, and pink and lavender cosmos, all leggy stems and feathery foliage, swayed in the cool evening breeze. Bennie felt a prick of resentment. Her father lived in a charming cottage; her mother lived in a mental hospital. How long had Winslow enjoyed these comforts while her mother was renting a series of spare efficiencies on crowded, dirty city blocks, in Philly's lousiest neighborhoods? With a baby in tow, yet. Maybe two babies.

Bennie cut the ignition, climbed out of the truck, and stretched her legs. Her back window was streaked with doggie saliva at a 60-mph-slant, and Bear swiped at the door with his paw. Bennie let him out, and he bounded to the gravel, sniffed excitedly, then loped ahead. Her heartbeat quickened as she walked to the cottage's front door, painted a fresh hunter green. Wind chimes tinkled from a small pitched roof protecting the entrance. Bennie willed herself to be calm, then knocked. Nothing happened. She knocked again. No answer. There was a square, bevel-cut window in the door, and she peered inside. It was dark in the house and nothing stirred.

Bennie turned and looked behind her. There was no car in the driveway or anywhere else. Maybe Winslow wasn't home. She knocked harder. She hadn't come this far for nothing, had she? She tried the knob and the door twisted open. She hesitated, startled, but Bear scampered through the open doorway. "Damn you!" Bennie cursed, always a sensible response to a golden. "Come, dammit!" She gritted her teeth and leaned in the shadowy doorway. What she saw amazed her.

The cottage was filled with books. They lined the entrance hall, papered the walls of a tiny living room, and traveled up the steps out of sight. Hardbacks were piled on end tables and overflowed into stacks sitting on the thin hook rug. Suddenly Bear charged from a room on the right. "Hey!" Bennie shouted. "Bad dog!" Bear plopped on his feathery hindquarters, thumped his tail, and smiled up at his mistress. "Act sorry," she said, pointing a finger, but Bear only sniffed her fingertip. Goldens never understand when you point.

Bennie gripped the dog's red collar and looked where he had been: a tiny kitchen with a white linoleum floor and immaculate white-painted wood cabinets. On top of the cabinets sat a lineup of books and a box of Saltine crackers. The kitchen was as still as the cottage. "Winslow?" she called from the hallway. "Anbody home?" There was no reply, no sound. Bennie waited, listening, then an idea presented itself. Winslow wasn't home, but maybe his cottage contained the answers she needed. She squared her shoulders. Until now a guardian of individual liberties, Bennie proceeded to search the house and seize if at all possible.

She walked into the living room. It was spare, furnished with a flowered sofa and chintz chair. She turned on a ceramic lamp on the end table, which cast a gentle yellow light on the volumes on the shelves, and she was able to read the authors' names. Milton. Spenser. Sandburg. Chaucer. Frost. Bennie slipped a slim paperback off the shelf. Ferlinghetti's *A Coney Island of the Mind*. She skimmed through pages bumpy with water damage. The pages had been thumbed and the book's skinny spine had been cracked. So Ferlinghetti had been read, at least once. By Winslow? It didn't fit the way Bennie had imagined him, in the few times she allowed herself to think about him. She flipped to the front of the book, looking for an inscription or maybe the stamp from a library sale. It was clean. She snapped it closed and moved on to the next shelf.

Fiction, mostly classics. *An American Tragedy. Ulysses. Robinson Crusoe. The Divine Comedy. The Possessed.* The authors were among the best: John Steinbeck, P. G. Wodehouse, Aldous Huxley, S. J. Perelman. But it was too disparate a group. Could a man clever enough to appreciate S. J. Perelman endure *Finnegans Wake*? Did Winslow really read all these books? Bennie turned and glanced around the sitting room. There was no television or stereo, just an old black rotary telephone. She didn't see a radio, and nothing hung on the walls. A wall of newer books sat behind the sofa, and she crossed the room to read the titles. *Raising Roses. Every Gardener's Guide to Perennials. Gardening for Small Spaces.* Bennie ran a finger along the books and no dust trail appeared.

She jumped to conclusions, a specialty of hers. Winslow was a neat man, who collected and apparently read a wide variety of books, almost without discrimination. He kept a flourishing garden, so he appreciated nature and beautiful things. His home was in excellent repair despite its age, so he was disciplined and hardworking. He cared for a large estate, so he was responsible enough to hold the job a long time, judging from the maturity of his garden. By all accounts, Winslow was a gentle, nurturing fellow. If not for the fact that he may have abandoned a mother and an infant. Maybe two.

Suddenly Bennie had to know. She went through the shelves, peeked between the volumes, felt behind the books. There had to be something here, something that would tell her more about Winslow. She went to the kitchen and searched through the cabinets, also neat and clean, and even opened the refrigerator, empty except for a bottle of French Merlot. She hurried upstairs, with Bear's toenails clicking up the stairwell at her heels. At the top of the stair, she found herself on a small landing with a bathroom to her left, a study next to it, then a bedroom. She hurried into the study and found a switch for an overhead light that barely illuminated the room.

Filled with books, the study was no different from the rest of the house except for an undersized wooden desk with an old green blotter on top. Bennie hesitated, then opened the desk drawers, expecting to find bills, papers, or receipts. But there was nothing that would tell her anything about Winslow. Odd. The second drawer contained pencils and pens, Scotch tape in a plastic dispenser, glue, scissors, paper clips. She closed it and opened another drawer. Inside sat a stack of heavyweight black paper. Very odd. Only black paper? Bennie picked up a piece and fingered it. It reminded her of the black paper that was left stuck to the back of the photos. It had the same soft texture and weight, like paper used in a photo album or scrapbook. Then Bennie remembered something Connolly had said at the prison.

He told me he has all your clippings.

Clippings! Where? Was Connolly lying to her? Was Winslow lying to Connolly? Bennie thought a minute. The clippings could be in a scrapbook of some kind, on a shelf like the other books. Bennie replaced the paper, closed the third drawer, and searched through the bookshelves for a scrapbook. There were books about World War II, Roman civilization, the Civil War, and the British monarchy. She reached behind biographies of Gustave Flaubert and Benjamin Franklin. Still no clippings.

She left the study and hustled to the bedroom, dismayed to find Bear lying on the floor, chewing a roll of toilet paper into bite-size bits. "That's helpful, Lassie," Bennie said, and yanked the soggy roll from the dog's mouth. She bent over and picked up the clumps of toilet paper, which was when she spotted something in the shadows under the bed. A large plastic bin.

Bennie set the toilet paper down and peeked underneath. Bear peeked, too, his hindquarters in the air and tail awag. She muscled the dog out of the way, reached under the bed, and pulled out a storage bin. It was about three feet square, with a blue plastic top that said RUBBER-MAID. She pulled off the lid. Inside was a stack of small, homemade books, lying side by side, six across and several books deep. Bennie picked up the top book and saw that its pages were black, like the paper from the drawer in the study. From the back of the photos.

She stared at the closed book in her hands. It was only ten pages thick and its cover was of thin cardboard, punched through with a three-hole puncher and fashioned together with common twine. Did she have the right to look inside it? Did she want to? Bennie opened the first page. It was a black-and-white photo of a little boy on a pinto pony that stood incongruously on a suburban street. The boy was outfitted in a neckerchief and cowboy hat. Winslow? Bennie wanted to see the back of the photo, but it was glued in the book. If she pulled it off, he'd know someone had tampered with it. She flipped the page. The next photo took her breath away.

A snapshot of Winslow with her mother. There was no mistaking it. He had the same masculine grin and wore a T-shirt like the one in the photo Connolly had given her. In fact, the picture looked like it might have been the next shot on the roll, and Bennie wondered who had taken it. She looked at the photo again, breathing it in. Her mother looked young and had curled her arm through Winslow's. Her lipsticked mouth smiled gaily and her eyes shone with happiness.

Her mother? Her father? Bennie tried to dislodge the photo but didn't force it. What year was it taken? And what about Connolly?

Bennie turned the page. It was blank, with the top layer of paper torn away where a photo had been ripped out. She ran a finger over the ragged patch. The threads of paper matched the tufts on the back of the photo Connolly had given her. Had it been taken from this book? Bennie turned the next page. Another wartime photo. Airmen in groups. She found Winslow quickly in the photo, but it didn't answer any questions about Connolly. She flipped another page. A bomber with a pinup painted on its riveted nose. Winslow and two other pilots posed in front of it. Were there photos of Connolly and Bennie, together?

The last page of the album was blank, its picture torn out, too. Was this the page that held the photo of Winslow with the two babies? Bennie scratched at the heavyweight paper and its fibers came off under her nail. She squinted at the tangled threads, and Bear leaned over to sniff. She closed the book and reached for the next. Not a homemade photo album, a homemade scrapbook of newspaper articles.

The clippings.

Bennie read the first page, a newspaper listing of law students who had passed the bar. She found her name easily, even in the tiny letters, because it was circled in pencil. Her heart thudded hard within her chest. Winslow had cut out the article and pasted it here, decades ago. She turned the page. A clipping from the *Inquirer* five years later, a brief mention that Bennie had successfully defended one Guillermo Diaz on a murder case. Again her name had been circled in pencil. The page after that was a report of another murder case she had defended, with her quote, "This is a case only a fool would bring. Need I say more?"

Bennie winced, but she didn't know if it was the cockiness of the quote or the fact that it was circled in the same careful hand. The rest of the book was full of clippings, as was the book after that and the one after that. The homemade scrapbooks—fifteen in all—constituted a chronological account of her career and life. The revelation left her shaking. Winslow had to be her father, and at some level, he had to care. About her.

Right?

Bennie stared at the scrapbook, her emotions turbulent: a combustible brew of anger, exhilaration, and confusion. That the feelings couldn't be parsed didn't gainsay their potency. She had always known Winslow's name, now she knew his face, and his way of life. He lived simply. He loved books and tended perennials. As a young man he served on a bomber and loved her mother. For one night.

Then Bennie reprimanded herself. *Think like a lawyer, not a daughter.* The scrapbooks proved only that Winslow knew her mother and that he had kept track of Bennie. It was slender evidence on which to assume that Winslow was her father or that he loved her. And the clippings contained nothing of Connolly, neither proving or disproving their relationship.

Right.

Bennie closed the book and placed it on the top of the stack. She sat motionless for a minute, then replaced the books in the plastic bin in the order in which she had taken them out. The last one to return was the one with the missing photographs. She ran her fingerpads over its dark, pebbled cover. It was all she had of a secret history and she wanted to hold it in her hands another second. Her fingers encircled the back of the book, where she felt something cool, papery, unpebbled.

She turned the book over. There was a small pink envelope taped to its back. Bennie hadn't seen it the first time around. She turned the book sideways so she could read the envelope. The ballpoint ink was faint and clotted in spots. "To Bill," it said, in a woman's hand. Her mother's hand. There could be no mistaking it. Bennie had seen her mother's writing a thousand times, on powers of attorney, medical releases, and informed consent forms. What Bennie held in her hands now was a letter from her mother to her father. Maybe.

Bennie felt her throat thicken. She hadn't heard them utter a word to each other, but she could read their most intimate thoughts. She freed the envelope from the scrapbook.

17

"Five minutes to lights out!" shouted the guard, and inmates began shuffling to their cells for the night.

Alice was already washing up in her cell. She dried her face and spotted Shetrell's girl, Leonia, glancing at her as she lumbered by. Weird. Leonia's cell was on the lower tier of the unit, underneath the ground floor. What was she doing on the upper deck so close to lights out? Goin' up to Shetrell's for a quickie? Disgusting. Alice didn't get it. She liked her men with dicks. Anthony had been the exception, and Alice used to call him the only dick without a dick. She wasn't sorry he was gone. She was only sorry she'd ended up in jail for it.

Alice stepped close to her cell door and watched Leonia amble down the hall. The big girl's arms hung apart from her sides, the steroid shuffle. Alice flicked out the light and edged away from the door, watching. Leonia looked back over her shoulder in the direction of Alice's cell.

Alice stood motionless in the darkness at her door.

Leonia turned back and walked past Shetrell's cell without going in, then continued down the hall and took the stairs down to her tier, where Alice lost sight of her.

"What're you doin'?" Alice's cellie whined from her bunk. "I was readin'."

"Shut up," Alice said. Wondering.

18

Bennie slipped a finger in the small pink envelope. Inside was a slip of rose-colored paper and she tugged it out. It came only reluctantly, apparently unopened for years, and she unfolded it.

August 4

Dear Bill,

Please try to understand. I have to go. Someday I will explain it all. Until then, please know how much I love you.

Yours always,
me

Bennie stared at the letter, reading it again and again. What? I'm leaving *you*? She had been told that Winslow had left her mother, not the other way around.

She shook her head, astounded. The date on the letter was roughly a month after Bennie was born. Had her mother left her father with a newborn? Maybe newborn twins? It didn't make sense. It seemed incredible.

But there it was, on paper. The letter wasn't signed, but it had to be from her mother, it was her handwriting. Still, Bennie wished it had been signed with at least a "C," just to be sure. The photos, the handwriting, the way it was faithfully kept and even hidden, all of it taken together indicated the note was from her mother, but it struck Bennie as a circumstantial case. Or maybe she was thinking like a lawyer, not a daughter.

She refolded the note. She felt shaken, her body hollow. She returned the note to the envelope, then held the letter in her palm, feeling the old-fashioned heaviness of the stationery. Smelling the vaguely perfumed scent to the paper. Tea Roses, her mother's perfume, or did she imagine that? Still, she couldn't bring herself to put the note back right away.

Then Bennie paused. Whose note was it anyway? Whose secret to keep? It was truth, after all, and to keep it secret was to treat it as if it were property, fencing out others like trespassers. But truth wasn't property, to be owned and held exclusively by anyone. Truth was to be shared, commonly and collectively owned. Bennie had a right to know the truth, certainly of her own birth, and no one else had an equal right to keep it from her. No, the note belonged to her. She placed it in her jacket pocket, put the scrapbook back in the bin, replaced the lid, and shoved the box under the bed.

Bennie rose unsteadily. Her history had changed, or at least her view of it. She questioned everything she'd been told and much that she hadn't. Would her mother leave a man with a newborn, or twins, with no means of support? You'd have to be crazy.

But her mother was crazy. Stone-cold crazy.

Bennie felt vaguely sick inside. She needed to know the truth about Connolly. She had a piece of the puzzle, but not the whole picture. "Let's roll, Bear," she said, and left Winslow's cottage with the golden lumbering sleepily after her.

From the front step of the cottage, she could see the gabled roof of the main house against the darkened sky. Maybe Winslow was there, or at least they would know where he was. Bennie hustled to the Expedition and tricked Bear into jumping in without her.

She hurried through a pasture with grass barely long enough to tickle her ankles. A green, fresh scent filled the air and fireflies glowed on and off, oblivious to mounds of horse dung that Bennie avoided like land mines. She reached the main house, a stately mansion covered with the same white stucco as Winslow's cottage, glowing alabaster in the dark. Huge white pillars supported its slate roof and front porch, which soared to four airy stories. Green-painted shutters framed rows upon rows of bubbly mullioned windows. Bennie paused at the imposing front door and rang the brass bell under a working gaslight.

The door opened almost immediately, and the sweet, aged face of a uniformed maid appeared. "Can I help you?" the woman asked.

"I'm an attorney, Bennie Rosato. I need to speak to the owner of the estate."

"At this hour?" The maid's gray eyebrows made a snow-dusted roof over her eyes. "Why, they've all gone to bed. Is something the matter?"

"Uh, no. I'm trying to find the caretaker, Bill Winslow. I went to his cottage but he wasn't there. Do you know where he is?"

"Mr. Winslow is on vacation this week and the next two. He takes three weeks every year."

Bennie wondered if it was a coincidence. "Do you know where he went on vacation?"

"No. Shall I tell him you called?"

"I was wondering, how long has Mr. Winslow worked here?"

"Let me see. Mr. Winslow and I came to the family about the same time, almost thirty-nine years ago."

Bennie hid her reaction. All her life, he had been here. "So you must know him well."

"Well, no."

"In almost forty years?"

The maid's eyelids fluttered. "I have my duties in the house, and Mr. Winslow works the grounds. He does like his privacy."

"Does he have any family?"

"No, not that I know of."

"Any children?"

"No. I must say, I know nothing about that, and I'm terribly uncomfortable discussing Mr. Winslow's personal business any further. Please call again when Mr. Winslow returns." The maid closed the heavy door with a solid brass click, leaving Bennie on the outside with her questions.

It was a feeling she was getting used to.

By the time Bennie got home, her bedroom was dark and Grady was sound asleep. It was just as well. She didn't want to explain about her trip to Delaware or her lease of a crime scene. She had never done anything like that and didn't know a criminal lawyer who had. Bennie sensed she was crossing a line, but decided to go with it. Coming so late to Connolly's defense called for pulling out all the stops.

She undressed quickly in the darkness, piling her skirt on top of the exercise bike and stepping out of her pumps. She felt exhausted and there was still so much work to do.

She padded to the bathroom, followed by Bear, and stopped halfway in the dark hallway. Her home office was on the right, still unpainted.

Bennie stood at the doorway and looked in. Moonlight streamed through the window, casting a cool white square on the messy files and law books. She scanned the configuration of the room: file cabinet, with the top drawer left open, overstuffed bookshelves, computer table with right-hand tray slid out, then another bookshelf, as unkempt as the first. Last night's coffee mug still sat on the table tray; it would have a thick, sticky ring on its bottom. Her office was the lived-in, under-construction equivalent of Connolly's.

Bennie picked her way through the clutter on the floor, unpacked files and wallpaper books, down the narrow path to her computer table. Bear followed and nestled into his customary circle under the table as she sat down, accidentally nudging the cord for the computer mouse. The monitor came to life with a prickly electrical sound and drenched the room in vivid cobalt. Bennie moved the mouse to the Microsoft Word icon and clicked a white page onto the screen. She faced the blank page and wondered what it would be like to be a writer like Connolly. Bennie had always wanted to be a writer, but had never admitted it to anyone.

Bennie clicked off the blank page and dialed up the Internet, then plugged "twins" into the search engine. She came up with a list of webpages and surfed the sites, most of them made by twins for other twins. She clicked on a photo of little girls with identical grins and matching orthodonture, feeling a surprising stab of envy.

She went back to the search engine, typed in "adoption," and got lists of websites about the subject. She skimmed the first few stories about how adoptees had found their birth parents and researched companies that located birth parents and siblings, with endorsements from satisfied adoptees. None of the endorsements were from the newfound parents or siblings. Why?

She eased back in the chair. Being found was at best an ambivalent experience, not the stuff of short, poignant testimonials. Bennie knew from experience.

She had never felt so lost until Connolly found her.

19

The first thing Wednesday morning, Bennie hurried along Twentieth Street to the Free Library of Philadelphia, swimming upstream against the businesspeople striding to work in lightweight suits and dresses, smelling of mousse and determination. Noisy rush-hour traffic flooded the Benjamin Franklin Parkway for the start of the business day and swirled around Logan Circle, clogging the four lanes into the city. The sun burned hot; it felt muggy even at nine o'clock in the morning, setting horns honking.

Bennie reached the arched façade of the Free Library, a massive, columned edifice of marble, sitting majestic as a lion at the foot of the Parkway. She climbed the steps and pushed open the brass door as soon as the blue-shirted security guard unlocked it for business. Bennie needed to find a defense witness, someone who remembered the clothes Connolly was wearing the day Della Porta was murdered.

She hustled into the entrance hall with its grand staircase, a chamber as hushed and elegant as she remembered from her childhood. Glistening glass display cases lined the huge room, the high ceiling was vaulted, and the marble floor was fawn-colored, inlaid with malachite. Bennie dug in her briefcase, retrieved her legal pad, and skimmed her notes. Connolly had said something about the pretty wrought iron in the library. One pretty room with iron-work, coming right up.

Bennie ducked into a large room on the right under a sign for Lending Library. Two desks flanked the front door and the main area contained shelves of new releases. A wrought iron balcony ringed the room, but the room wasn't pretty, and she guessed it would be the busiest room in the library. Not the best place to become an author. Bennie left and went back to the entrance hall. On its other side was another large room, its entrance under a sign for Music Department. The room was dim, owing to the odd green tint of its windows, and the requisite wrought iron was scarce.

Bennie crossed to the grand staircase, also of tan marble, running her fingers along a sleek banister of polished brass. She hustled past a bronze cast of the library's founder and a bizarre Victorian candelabra of carved marble set on lion's claws, which looked like a lamp with toes. She chugged to the top of the staircase and entered the first room. The Social Sciences room contained a bank of computers, but it was dark because the curtains were closed. She left the room, betting it failed the pretty test, and walked out to the staircase landing again, where she spotted a pebbled sign that read LITERATURE.

Sounded pretentious enough.

Bennie strode down the marble corridor and slipped inside the room. It was a city block long, three stories high, and ringed by curly wrought iron balconies. The plaster ceiling was carved with elaborate Victorian curlicues, swirls, and figures. Indirect sunlight shone from the windows, falling softly on the vacant tables, and a row of computers sat off to one side. Standing by the book-shelves, Bennie ran a finger along the plastic-covered volumes. Milton. Pope. Tennyson. Thomas. She experienced a vague déjà vu of her father's cottage in Delaware. Had Connolly written in this room? Could she be drawn to books for the same reasons Bennie's father had been? Was it in their genes, and hers?

Bennie heard the sound of a chair being pulled out, and looked around. A librarian was returning to her desk. "Excuse me," Bennie said, walking over. "I'd like to ask you a few questions."

"Certainly." The librarian was a slim, middle-aged woman with brushy silver hair, punctuated on either side by onyx dot earrings. She wore a loose, light-blue dress and red sailcloth espadrilles, and her smile was pleasant.

"Do you know a woman, a library patron, named Alice Connolly? She used to come here to write, every day until about a year ago."

"I don't recall that name." The librarian turned and faced an old gray computer monitor, then hit a few keys. "There are twenty Alice Connollys listed here as members."

"Her address would be on Trose Street."

"Sorry. She's not here. She didn't have a card, not in the Philadelphia library system."

Bennie frowned. "Maybe she didn't take books on loan, but I believe she used this room to write in. She mentioned that she wrote on the computer. Do you know the people who use these computers, at least by sight?"

"Yes. I recognize the regular patrons. Most are students, because our collection is scholarly. We tend to be responsive to academic needs, and I see the same faces. What does Ms. Connolly look like?"

"Like me, only better." Saying it out loud validated the connection. "Her hair is different. Red and short, styled in layers, and she's thin."

The woman looked Bennie up and down. Librarians were nothing if not forthright. "No. I'm sorry."

Bennie thanked the librarian, confused. She'd have to double-check the other rooms. She left the room and was hurrying down the marble corridor when she felt something brush her shoulder.

"Alice," said a soft voice from behind. "Is that you?"

Bennie turned. It was a slight young man wearing a black T-shirt, black jeans, and Doc Martens. He carried a black knapsack on a bony shoulder. "You mean Alice Connolly?" Bennie asked, stepping forward.

"Wait, wait a minute." The young man's eyes were dark behind his tiny matte-framed glasses, and they searched Bennie's face. He had to be twenty-five, but bewilderment reduced him to a small boy. And there was another emotion, one Bennie couldn't quite place.

"You know Alice Connolly, don't you? You thought I was her, didn't you?"

"Yes, but—"

"Have you seen Alice here, writing on the computers?"

"Who *are* you?" The young man edged backward, toward the staircase.

"Who are *you*? If you're a friend of Alice's, talk to me. I'm her lawyer."

"I can't. I have to go. I have to get going." He backed down toward the grand staircase and hurried down the stairs. Bennie hustled after him, her pace quicker. She could outrun an art student, for Christ's sake. His Doc Martens clomped down the stairs, with Bennie at his crepe heels. Three feet away, then two.

"Stop," Bennie called out, almost nabbing him in the middle of the staircase. "Just stop and we'll talk."

"I don't know anything. Leave me alone!" The young man reached the landing and whirled around the corner to the next set of stairs, almost slipping on the marble. Bennie swung for him and missed, and he hit the lobby and raced across the floor toward the exit door. In front of it was the security desk, with a guard and a turnstile that gave Bennie an idea.

"Stop that kid!" she shouted to the guard. "He took my purse!"

"No! That's not true!" the young man called, too late. The turnstile caught him in his slim waist and he doubled over.

"Wait right there, sir," barked the guard, a heavyset black man in a blue shirt. A baseball bat with duct tape around its handle rested in the corner next to his perch. "Lady says you stole her bag."

"I didn't!"

Bennie feigned surprise. "My goodness, how silly of me. I just remembered. I didn't bring my purse today. I'm so sorry."

The guard scowled, looking from Bennie to the young man. "Sorry about that, sir. If you have no library materials to declare, you're free to go."

"Thanks," he said, though Bennie clamped a hand on his shoulder.

"I have no library materials," she told the disapproving guard and pressed through the exit into the sunlight. The streets were alive with businesspeople, summer tourists, and heavy traffic. Bennie tightened her grip on the kid and pressed him out of the foot traffic and toward Logan Circle. "I have to talk to you about Alice Connolly. I'm trying to help her. If you don't talk to me now, I'll subpoena you. Either way, we're gonna have a chat."

"You won't hurt me, will you?"

"I'm a lawyer, not a thug."

"Is there a difference?" the kid called back, and Bennie gave him points for humor. She led him by the elbow across the street and walked him to the benches under the shade trees around Swann Fountain.

"Now," Bennie said, "how do you know Alice Connolly?" She plopped him onto a bench and stood over him, close as a lover.

"I don't know Alice Connolly."

"You want me to call the cops? Right now?"

"You gonna say I took your purse again?" He pouted up at Bennie in the hazy sun.

"I'm gonna say you're obstructing justice in a capital murder case. How do you know Alice Connolly?"

The kid slumped into the bench, his back spiny in the thin T-shirt. His forehead looked damp to his George Clooney hairline. "Okay, I know Alice. Knew her."

"Did she come to the library to write?"

"Yes, for a while."

"What were you doing there?"

"Papers, for school. I'm at the Academy. PAFA."

"Did you meet her in the library?"

"Yes."

"When?"

"Fall semester, the year before last. She was new in town. So was I."

"What was your relationship?"

"We were friends. We talked about things. Not much though. She was kind of hard to get to know. She would work on the computer, I would do research or sketch. We'd break for lunch. You know, friends." His prominent

Adam's apple bobbed up and down, and Bennie didn't have to be a detective to come up with the next question.

"You didn't date?"

"No."

"But you wish you did."

"Does it show?" He squinted at Bennie, and she sat beside him on the bench. It was too hot to be shaking down the heartbroken.

"Don't run away now. I'll chase you and make you wear plaid."

"I believe it."

"What's your name?"

"Sebastian Blair."

"Bennie Rosato." She shook his hand and it buckled in her grasp. "You talk to the cops about Alice?"

"I never talked to the police about anything. I've never been in trouble in my life. I don't want to get in trouble now."

"Relax. Just talk to me and you can go on your way. You thought I was Alice."

"Yeah. Are you related?"

Bennie wiped her brow. "So let's talk. I want to help Alice and I need to know what you know about her. What was the story between you and Alice?"

"I was in love. She wasn't. We stayed friends. I never even told her."

"This was when?"

"September."

"Alice was living with someone at the time, a cop. Did you know that?"

He nodded regretfully. "They weren't solid."

"No?"

"Her boyfriend was at the gym all the time, I think he worked out, or boxed or something. She used to go with him to the gym, when she wasn't working on the computer at the library."

"She told you this?"

"Yeah. Then, in October she met someone else, another guy. Then she stopped coming to the library."

"Where'd she meet this other guy?"

"I don't know. He didn't hang at the library. He looked like a lawyer."

Bennie frowned. "A lawyer? What was his name?"

"I don't know. She never said."

"You didn't press it?"

"No."

Bennie sighed. "Sebastian. You lose the woman to another man and you don't bother to find out who he is?"

The artist smiled weakly. "I tried, but she didn't want to talk about him. She didn't want to talk much after she met the lawyer. After a while, she stopped coming to the library. She kind of ditched me."

"Her boyfriend was murdered in May of last year. I need to know her whereabouts that day. When she came and left the library, even what she was wearing."

"Can't help you there. She stopped coming to the library a long time before that." He looked away, at the Swann Fountain, and Bennie followed his gaze. For the first time she noticed three kids playing in the fountain, drenched to their shorts and T-shirts, oblivious to the workday crowd. They kicked and splashed in the circular pool, and Bennie was distracted by the slick nudes at the fountain's center.

"You think she was sleeping with this lawyer?" Bennie asked.

"Duh."

"So who was he?"

"Some rich guy. He drove a Mercedes. He came by once or twice to pick her up."

"What kind of Mercedes?"

"Sedan. New."

"What color?"

"Dirt brown."

Bennie tried to puzzle it out. Connolly hadn't told her any of this. "What did the lawyer look like?"

"Rich. Preppy." The young man's chin sunk onto his hand, like a lovesick version of *The Thinker*, which sat in front of the Rodin Museum down the Parkway. "Mainly he looked richer and preppier than me."

"Was he white or black? Light hair, dark hair? Sebastian, you're an artist, with an alleged eye for detail. Give me a description."

"I can't. The subject depresses me, and I'm no good with words."

"Can you draw him, then?"

Sebastian raised his chin from his hand. "You gotta pencil?"

20

Alice stood behind the inmates at the computers. Their blue shirts bent over the keyboards and they poked at the keys. Her cellie hunted-and-pecked in the middle, and two seats from her was Valencia, reeking like a funeral home. Leonia anchored the end of the row, a mountain of muscle next to Shetrell and the rest of her crew.

Alice kept her eye on them, wondering about last night. There had to be a contract out on her. It would have come to Shetrell, who was connected inside and out. But why? And from who? It didn't make sense, but Alice wasn't taking any chances, not with freedom this close. She knew how to deal with it. Leonia, not Shetrell, would do the dirty work. Alice strolled down the row of do-rags and Muslims and stopped when she got to Leonia's chair. "How's it going, girl?"

"S'all right," Leonia said, without turning around.

"You should save that document. You typed a page already. You don't want to lose it."

"I did save it."

"No, you didn't. If you did, it wouldn't say Document One at the top, right here." Alice reached over and pointed at the monitor screen. "It would have a name."

"Uh-huh," Leonia said after a moment.

"So save it."

Leonia sat still in front of the keyboard. Her short hair

made a spiky silhouette in front of the bright white monitor. Alice knew Leonia had no idea how to save the thing. She could smell her brain overheat.

"Leonia, you know how to save it, don't you? Move the cursor to FILE and click. Then click SAVE."

Leonia moved the mouse, then clicked SAVE with deliberation. A blue-bordered window popped onto the screen, and she sat still again, stumped. Alice smiled. This bitch was going to take her out? She didn't have the gray matter to double-click.

"You have to name the document before you can save it, Leonia. Type the name in the blank window." Alice glanced at Leonia's document. "Is it your resume?"

"Yuh."

"So what would you name the file? Remember what I taught you about file names? Name it what it is. So name it 'resume.'"

Leonia typed, "R E S U M A Y."

"Perfect." Alice held a critic's finger to her chin. "The resume looks very good. What kind of job are you looking for when your bit's done, Leonia? Doctor? Lawyer? Contract killer?"

Leonia kept staring at her monitor.

"I see." Alice folded her arms and bounced on the tips of her feet. "Keeping your options open. Smart move. Very smart. Don't want to be mired in a life of crime, stuck in that vicious cycle of the repeat offender. The possibilities are endless for a woman of your skills and abilities."

Leonia glanced over her shoulder coldly. Shetrell's slitted gaze slid to the side. The black-uniformed guard standing at the door cracked a smile, but none of the do-rags or Muslims did.

"Class, everybody look up a minute." Alice clapped to

get their attention. "Everybody, eyes up! Everybody, give me your attention!"

Heads popped up from the keyboards, ten of them. Diane looked dull-normal and Valencia was attentive, tossing glossy curls back onto her shoulders.

"We can all take a lesson from this lady," Alice said, slapping a hearty hand on Leonia's shoulder. "If you're working on your resume, keep it good and general. Don't limit yourself. You can do anything you set your mind to, like Leonia!"

Valencia grinned, completely missing the irony. Diane blinked stupidly. Leonia glared at the monitor. Shetrell went rigid with anger.

"You can make your dreams come true!" Alice called out, managing to keep a straight face. "One person can make a difference! All you have to do is work out every day! And save your documents at the end of the page!"

Valencia burst into spontaneous applause. "Ees the truth!" she shouted, and Alice curtsied deeply.

21

Bennie hiked the ten blocks back to the office, sweating by the time she turned the corner onto Locust Street, where she halted in surprise. The front door to her building was blocked by news vans, their brightly colored logos an alphabet that spelled disaster. Could something have happened at her office? She didn't get halfway up the block before the reporters rushed toward her.

"Ms. Rosato, is Alice Connolly your long-lost twin?" "How does it feel to have your twin sister in jail, Bennie?" "What's it like to represent your own flesh and blood?"

"No comment," Bennie shot back, shocked. She knew the twin story would break sooner or later, but this was sooner than she'd thought.

Cameramen pushed videocams into her face. Reporters coagulated around her, jabbing the air with microphones. "Ms. Rosato, Ms. Rosato, have you seen the district attorney's statement?" "Do you have any reaction?"

"No comment!" Bennie answered, thinking furiously ahead. The D.A. knew and was making statements. That meant the whole city knew. How? She plowed ahead, parting reporters with her briefcase like a prow does icebergs. "I have no comment on the matter."

"Come on, Rosato, cut us a break!" "No comment at all?" "Is Connolly guilty or innocent?" "What do you say to the criticism by the bar association? Reports have it that you failed to take courses in legal ethics. They're revoking your license to practice law. Any comment?"

"None at all!" Bennie spat out, so infuriated she didn't care that the camera recorded her reaction. What was going on? Every lawyer was behind on the ethics requirement, they were going to yank *her* license? She ducked into her building, ran up the stairs, and by the time she reached the third floor, was beside herself. "Did you see them? They're all out front," she said to Marshall, who sat worriedly at her desk in the waiting area.

"I know." Marshall's French braid had loosened and stray wisps of hair had slipped out. "I tried to reach you at home this morning, but you were already gone. I tried your cell phone, too, but it was off. They've been calling all day. The story was on the news by midmorning."

"They're screwing with my license. Without a license, I can't represent Connolly. Without a license, I can't represent anybody. They can't put me on inactive. Do I look inactive?"

"I warned you."

"I know, but this stinks to high heaven."

"I got on the phone with them as soon as I heard about it. A man named Hutchins. His phone number is in the file."

"Where's the file? I'll call that jackass." Hearing herself, Bennie realized she was losing it. Her practice was in danger. Her livelihood. Her firm. She grabbed the file over the desk. "Now, get word to Connolly. Say you're calling for me. Tell her not to talk to the press. No interviews. Nothing."

"Will she listen?" Marshall asked. "I mean, the leak had to come from somewhere."

"You think Connolly leaked it?" Bennie's eyes widened slightly. She hadn't even considered it. She hadn't had time to consider anything, only to react.

"I'm not accusing her or anything. I mean, you know her, don't you? She's your—" A quizzical look crossed the receptionist's face, and Bennie read it instantly.

"You want to know if Connolly's my twin, right? Well, so do I." She raised her arms and turned to face the office. "Everybody, I have an announcement! Everybody please, can I have your attention?"

Secretaries looked up from their computer keyboards. Lawyers popped from their offices like seedlings through topsoil. Mary and Judy, in the glass conference room, appeared relieved there was a wall between them and their boss. Everybody was looking at Bennie like she was crazy. Nobody said a word.

"You have a right to know the truth, so here it is!" Bennie said. "I don't know if Alice Connolly is my twin. I have no earthly idea. She's news to me, too. As soon as I know, I'll let you know. Meanwhile, don't talk to the press! Thank you!"

The secretaries returned hastily to their typing. Lawyers' heads shot back inside their offices. Mary and Judy got busy with the file. Marshall's lips curved into a tense smile. "If your tantrum is over, take your mail," she said.

"Thanks." One look at the packet told Bennie it was correspondence, phone messages, and court papers. She wanted to throw it all in the air. The sketch of Connolly's lawyer/boyfriend was burning a hole in her pocket, but she had to get her license back. She tucked the mail under her arm, strode to the conference room, and opened the glass door with a free finger. "Hey, gang," she said, and the two associates looked up.

"You need help with that stuff?" Judy asked.

"No thanks. You heard the news about Connolly and me."

"Yes," Judy answered matter-of-factly. She held a pleadings index pressed against her jeans smock, worn with a ribbed yellow T-shirt and matching yellow clogs. Bennie was supposed to be a civil libertarian, so she had to pretend she didn't mind when her associates dressed like clowns.

"Nice outfit. You heard, too, DiNunzio?"

Mary reddened. "Yes."

"I was going to discuss it with you, later. So we may have something in common."

"I guess so."

"The press is all over this. I'm sure we'll be the big story on Action News tonight, evil twin and all. So don't talk to the press, you both know that. There'll be a gag order on this case for sure. Understood?"

"Understood," they both said.

Bennie nodded, calming slightly. "Now, Carrier, did you apply to the court for the activity reports?"

"Yes, but Judge Guthrie's clerk hasn't gotten back to me on the argument. I'll keep after him."

Bennie turned to Mary. "DiNunzio, did you find the report from the cops, Reston and McShea, in the file?"

"I looked but it's not there."

"Call that weasel at Jemison about it."

"Miller? I did already. He says he never saw one, and Hilliard isn't returning my calls. Stall city."

Bennie frowned, wondering if the report had been "lost" by Jemison or by the D.A. She wasn't a conspiracy theorist, but some very peculiar things were happening. The yanking of her license couldn't be an accident; the timing was too good. Who was messing with her, and why? "Did you get in touch with either of your classmates at Jemison about Guthrie and Burden?"

"Neither stayed at Jemison. One went to Cravath in New York, but one is still in town. I don't know where she works. I have two calls in to her house."

"Good. Follow up. What are you doing now?"

"Everything," Judy said. "Preparing a trial checklist, lining up experts, drafting jury instructions—"

"No, you're not. I have a new assignment for you. Come into my office. DiNunzio, you, too."

"Sure," Mary said, and scrambled out from behind the file, finding her pumps under the table with her stocking feet. She stood up when she found them and smoothed down a lightweight blue suit. She'd been right about Bennie and Connolly. The twin thing would be all over the papers. Bennie's decision to represent Connolly would be fodder for the editorial page and second-guessed by most of the bar.

The associates hurried out the conference room door and walked to Bennie's office, where she dumped her mail onto an already cluttered desk, pulled the sketch from her pocket, and showed it to the associates. "Do either of you recognize this man?" Bennie asked. "I think he's a lawyer in town."

"Nope," Judy answered, studying the drawing. It was of an attractive middle-aged man with longish hair, round, close-set eyes, and a chin like granite. "Looks like Superman."

"He drives a brown Mercedes, if that helps."

"A lawyer with a Mercedes? How unusual."

"DiNunzio? You know him?"

Mary shook her head. "No."

"Why? Who is he?" Judy asked, and Bennie waved them into the chairs across from her desk and told them everything she'd learned at the library. She began to get a handle on the situation as she spoke and its implications crystallized. If Connolly had a lover, then she'd not only lied about the happiness of her relationship with Della Porta, she may have lied about where she was the day of the murder. Worse, she'd given herself a motive to kill Della Porta. If the D.A. knew about it, he'd have a field day. Bennie felt unsettled, her confidence in Connolly shaken.

"I don't like surprises, not this close to trial," Judy said. Her worried features were as readable as a Girl Scout's. "If Connolly didn't tell you about this, she's lying to us."

"I've never had an inmate not lie about something," Bennie said defensively. "The only question is whether they lie about something important."

"This is important."

"Maybe not. Maybe the lawyer is married and she wanted to keep the affair a secret. Or maybe it was irrelevant, so she didn't mention it." Bennie heard herself making excuses for Connolly, but she didn't want to start in with Judy again, not today. "In any event, don't tell me how bad the news is. We're advocates, remember? Tell me how we can deal with it if it comes up at trial. Turn it to our client's advantage."

Mary fought the impulse to raise her hand. "Maybe we can offer this lawyer as a suspect. You know, suggest to the jury that he's the killer."

Bennie brightened. She should have thought of that herself, but she'd been too preoccupied with Connolly's betrayal, her license to practice, and the evening news. "Sure. If Connolly has a boyfriend, she has a motive to kill Della Porta—but so does he. He's a jealous lover."

"That's lame," Judy scoffed. "Connolly and Della Porta weren't even married."

Bennie checked her impatience. "We have to develop it, find out a little more. We don't have to convince the jury that this lawyer did it. We just have to make it colorable, give it some weight. Make it plausible enough for reasonable doubt."

"That's what I meant." Mary nodded. She could always take credit, couldn't she? This was America, and it was her right as an employee. "So, do you want us to try and identify this lawyer?"

Bennie shook her head. "No, I have something important I want you two to do. What do you know about boxing?"

"Boxing is cool," Judy said. "I watch it on TV sometimes. *Tuesday Night Fights*."

"Good." Bennie relaxed. Carrier could be a tiger if she was working on something that interested her. "How about you, DiNunzio? You a fight fan?"

"Boxing?" Mary wrinkled her nose. "I think it's disgusting. People trying to give each other concussions. I've never watched a fight past the first round."

"You're about to become an expert. I want you to go to the gym where Anthony's fighter trains. I want you to see if he's talking to the D.A. Find out if he's testifying." Bennie scribbled an address on a yellow Post-it and handed it across her desk to Mary, who took it reluctantly.

"But I'm supposed to be interviewing Della Porta's neighbors. There's so much work—"

"Carrier can't go alone, not to this neighborhood. You're going with her, for protection."

"Protection? Me?"

Judy grinned. "Kapow!" she shouted, throwing an imaginary punch.

22

The gym was in North Philadelphia, far from the glistening business district. Going north on Broad Street, the white marble of City Hall was replaced by the red plastic of Kentucky Fried Chicken, the dark glass of vacant storefronts, and the fake wood paneling of check-cashing agencies with lines around the corner, like opening day of a first-run movie. Unemployment was higher in this area and the evidence was on every street corner, where the homeless shook McDonald's cups of change. And if the City Hall area was spotless, the result of hard work by a privately funded team of uniformed cleaners, the north end of town was littered with newspapers, coffee cups, and cigarettes. This was why they used to call the city "Filthydelphia," but nobody was hiring green-uniformed elves to clean this part of the city, and never would.

Judy surveyed the scene from the window of the cab. They sped by a used-car dealership, whose banner of yellow glitter caught the sunlight like fool's gold. REVIVAL TIME read a sign on one of the many churches that dotted the street. Judy wondered what the church was like inside. "You know, Mare, we should get up here more often."

"Why?" Mary asked. Her head was buried in the Connolly exhibits, which she read as the cab lurched from one stoplight to the next. "We don't have enough to do?"

"Work isn't everything. We should get out a little. See things that are different. A different way of life."

"Catholics aren't interested in different, okay?"

"Come on—"

"In fact, we hate different. Different threatens us."

Judy smiled as the cab pulled up in front of a concrete building about ten stories tall. The upper floors looked dark and vacant, but the first floor was a block-long expanse of glass. A wire cage covered the glass and had trapped every passing handbill and hamburger wrapper. The cabbie, a young man with a shaggy red beard, snapped down the meter's red flag. "That's ten bucks, even," he said over his shoulder.

Mary cracked the window. "This is it?"

"Sure. It's one of the best gyms in Philly."

"There's no sign."

"Don't need no sign. It's almost as famous as Smoke's."

"Smoke's?"

"Smokin' Joe Frazier's." The cabbie glanced at Mary in the rearview. "Philly's a great boxing town, you'll see. How long you girls here for?"

Mary bristled. "Take that back. I'm a native Phila-delphian."

Judy handed the driver the fare. "We're tourists, up here."

"Thanks," he said. "You want I should come back, pick you up? It's a bitch to get a cab this far up."

"I knew that," Mary said.

"I'll get her out now," Judy told the cabbie, who laughed.

Two muscular black men were sparring in a ring that was the heart of the gym. Red leather headgear obscured their features and sweat glistened on their shoulders as they hustled around the blue canvas, behind ropes covered with red and blue velveteen. Centered over the ring hung four strips of fluorescent lights, illuminating the dark faces of the men who stood around. They cheered or winced at each punch, alive with the thrill of the match. The harder the punch, the more animated they got, but Mary flinched as she watched. To her, boxing was assault and battery with tickets.

She looked away, around the gym. Glossy mirrors covered the walls and wrinkled boxing posters blanketed any leftover space. Speedbags hung like teardrops of leather from plywood stands and a brown heavy bag spun slowly on a chain in the far corner. Boxing gloves of gold and silver hung on the far wall; the air smelled of perspiration, stale cigarettes, and filth. Mary hovered behind Judy's broad shoulder. "We don't belong here," she muttered. "We're lawyers. We should be making commercials."

"Stop complaining. We're on a secret mission."

"We're the only whites and the only women. How secret can it be?"

"Follow me." Judy pushed her way to the middle of the crowd to get a better view of the fight. She felt instantly intrigued by the skill of the contest, the movement of the fighters, the whistle of gloves through the air. She couldn't tear her eyes from the ring.

Huddling behind her, Mary squinted at the ring, where one boxer slugged the other so hard his head snapped back like a bullwhip. She gave up being adult, much less professional, and covered her eyes. "Did he kill him?"

"Not yet."

"I hate this. Let's run away."

"No."

"I'll meet you outside. In the suburbs."

"You will not." Judy grabbed Mary's hand and scanned the crowd for Star. She picked him out quickly, recognizing him from the posters around the gym. Starling "Star" Harald was larger in person than his photo, if that were possible. "There he is."

"Where?"

"The hulk in the back row," Judy said, and Mary looked. Star was huge, almost superhuman, even at a distance. He wore a black silk shirt with a black sportjacket that was big in the shoulders even without shoulder pads. He stood apart from the crowd and there was an aloof air about him—the aura of a star, but a dark one. Mary thought he'd be handsome if he weren't so remote, but emotional distance was probably a job requirement for a man who could kill with his fists. "Now can we go?"

"No," Judy said over her shoulder, and felt Mary's hand clutch her dress as she made her way around the ring through the crowd, ignoring stares both curious and lecherous. It was less noisy in the back row, and Judy wedged boldly next to Star. "Are you Star Harald?" she asked. "My name's Judy Carrier."

Star's expression remained unchanged, his concentration riveted on the sparring match in the ring.

"My friend and I are lawyers in the murder case involving your manager, Anthony Della Porta. We represent Alice Connolly."

Star didn't even like the sound of the bitch's name. He kept his eyes on the fight.

"Anthony Della Porta was your manager, wasn't he?"

Star didn't answer. The kid in the red shorts was throwing his jab but he couldn't connect. Kid didn't train hard enough. Kid had no discipline. No respect for himself.

"Did you know the woman Della Porta lived with? Her name was Alice Connolly."

Star didn't say anything. The kid's trainer should tell him to move his freakin' feet, but he didn't know jack. Even Browning, the fat slob Star just signed with, knew more than him. Star folded his arms and his biceps bulged under the custom jacket.

"I see you have muscles. Do you have manners?"

Star snapped his head around and his eyes bored into Judy. He wasn't Tyson, so he didn't tag her, but he thought about it. "I talk if I want to talk."

Mary tugged at Judy's dress for a warning. Antagonizing a prizefighter didn't seem like a good idea, but Judy was from California, where they did self-destructive things all the time.

"Fine," Judy said. "I'll ask a question, and you answer if you want to answer. Did you know Alice Connolly?"

"I know she killed Anthony, tha's all I have to know," Star said matter-of-factly, and Judy hid her alarm at his response.

"How do you know that?"

"I jus' know."

"Did Della Porta tell you anything that would make you think that?"

Star shook his head. He didn't like the chick calling Anthony by his last name.

"What makes you say Connolly did it?"

Star didn't say anything. Bitch was givin' him attitude. He watched the kid in the ring stagger back to his corner.

"Did you tell the cops what you think?"

Star shook his head, no.

"Why not?"

"Didn't ax."

Judy thought for sure the cops would have interviewed Star. His manager had been killed and the police didn't question him about it? "The D.A. didn't ask you to testify? Will you testify?"

Star shook his head again. Testify, go to court. He had the situation under control. He hadn't got the word it got done yet, but he knew it would be. Without another word, Star turned his back on the lawyer and walked away, into the throng.

Judy moved to follow him, but Mary held her in place with a fistful of shirt. "This is me, saving your life."

"But he's getting away."

"That's because he's bigger and faster than you."

Judy watched Star disappear into the locker room. "He can run but he can't hide."

"He can do what he wants. That's why they call him a heavyweight. Now let's go," Mary said, and pushed Judy safely toward the exit.

23

Bennie had squandered an hour wrangling on the telephone with functionaries from the bar's licensing authority before she reached the aforementioned Mr. Hutchins. "Look, Mr. Hutchins," she said, "you require twelve credit hours a year, is that right? Ten hours of substantive courses and two of ethics."

"Yes, that's correct," said Mr. Hutchins, a nice man if you liked those just-following-orders types.

"And I'm in Group Four, so I should have had my credits completed by August."

"Last August."

"Okay, last August." Whatever. Nit-picker. "I paid the hundred dollars for the extension. So what's the problem?"

"The problem, Ms. Rosato, is that the extension brought you only to October of last year. We have received no notice since that time that you have fulfilled your remaining two ethics requirements. Therefore you were placed on inactive status."

"I didn't receive notice of this action. You can't take my license without notice."

An official *click-click-clicking* of computer keys came over the line, and Mr. Hutchins said, "Our records show you were sent notices of your delinquency in November, March, and June."

Bennie took a slug of coffee, but it didn't work. Life was tough when you were totally in the wrong. "So what do I have to do to get my license back?"

"You have to take the required courses immediately, then apply for reinstatement."

"I can't do that. I'm kind of busy right now." Bennie rubbed her forehead. "Why me, that's what I want to know. I can't be the only lawyer behind in her ethics credits. Can you check that?"

"Yes, I suppose I could. If I wished to."

"Don't you wish to? Procedures are important, Mr. Hutchins. Rules are important." Bennie almost gagged. "Don't you want to make sure your agency is following its own rules? It's a question of administrative integrity." There was silence on the other end of the line except for *clicking.* "I bet I'm not even the only one as far behind as a year, am I?"

"Well, no, you're not."

"That's a shocker."

"My, this is terrible. There are quite a number of attorneys in Philadelphia County who are at least a year behind in their ethics credits."

Bennie's sense of humor vanished. Connolly's conspiracy theory gained a notch of credibility. "Why was I singled out, Mr. Hutchins? Does the computer show how that came about?"

"No, it's irregular. The computer usually runs down the alphabet and kicks out the delinquencies in alphabetical order."

"Did I go before the A's or not?"

"Yes, you did. That isn't the way the program is supposed to work, I'm afraid."

"I'm afraid, too. Why was this information about my

license released to the media? Is that standard procedure as well?"

"I wasn't responsible for that."

"Who was?"

"I'm not sure."

"Get sure. It had to be someone from your organization who released that information to the public. No one else knew it."

Click, click, click, went the keys.

"I used to teach libel law, Mr. Hutchins, on one of your dumb panels. You want some free legal advice? The statements your organization made are damaging to my reputation as an attorney and you've exceeded any privilege if you made them to the press."

"What did you say?"

"I said I could sue you blind."

"No. About teaching."

"I said, I've taught libel law, on one of your . . . panels." Bennie omitted the "dumb" as a goodwill gesture.

"Did you apply for your credits from the panel, for teaching?"

"I get credits for teaching? I didn't know that."

"It's often overlooked."

Bennie's heart leapt up. "I overlooked it!"

"If you can let me have the course name and number, I can determine how many credits are due you and apply them to your delinquency."

"Hang on." She was already tearing backward through her Week-At-A-Glance and stopped in February. "On February eleventh, at two o'clock. The course title was Prior Restraints: Harness or Handcuffs? Who names these courses anyway?"

Click, click, click. "I'm showing that that seminar was

substantive and also encompassed an ethics session. You were entitled to two credits as a result of teaching that course. If you can prove you taught it, you will be entitled to the credits, bringing your licensing requirements current."

"I taught it, I swear, Mr. Hutchins. I'll fax you an affidavit right away. In the meantime, you'll reinstate my license, right? I need that license."

"Reinstatement should take some time."

"Not in this case it shouldn't. Somebody screwed up, big-time, and it stinks. Unless you want me to make a very high-profile inquiry, you'll reinstate me effective immediately."

"Did you retain your course materials?"

"My course materials?" Bennie scanned her office bookshelves for the characteristic yellow binders. She didn't see them anywhere, but they had to be there. "Yes, I have them right in front of me."

"Does it show your name as a speaker?"

She rustled some papers on her desk. "Yes, absolutely."

"Then Xerox the title page and fax it to this office, to my attention." *Click, click, click.* "I'll temporarily reinstate you pending receipt of those materials."

"Bless you," Bennie said, and hung up the phone with relief. Now all she had to do was find the course book. She hit the white intercom button on her phone for salvation, and Marshall picked up.

"Back in business?"

"Only if I find some course materials. They're in my office somewhere. Rescue me, would you?"

Ten minutes later, Marshall was still rooting through the bookshelves for the course materials, tossing onto the dhurrie rug everything she thought should be thrown away. The shelves were empty and the rug was full. "We should have all of these materials centralized," she grumbled.

"Yes, we should."

"In the library, not the lawyers' offices."

"I quite agree." At her desk, Bennie was ransacking the lawyers' listings in the Yellow Pages to identify the lawyer in the art student's sketch. She flipped through grainy photographs of lawyers perched on desks and holding fancy pens. Thank God lawyers had started advertising. How else could you find the murderers?

"You can't find anything in here. This is disgusting."

"I know." Bennie closed the Yellow Pages, shoved the thick book aside, and reached for her marbleized legal directory.

"Why don't you clean up or at least let me do it?"

"I'm a maverick, a renegade. The kind of gal who colors outside the lines." Bennie cracked the legal directory. "My clients expect a messy office."

"Nobody likes a pig."

"Don't sugarcoat it, Marshall." She skimmed the legal directory. None of the faces in the photos matched the pencil sketch. The phone rang on Bennie's desk and she picked it up. "Rosato."

"What's up, doc?" said a man's voice on the other end, and Bennie grinned.

"Sammy!" It was Sam Freminet, the tax lawyer who was her oldest friend. He had started with her at Grun & Chase and had remained, becoming a partner. "You get my fax?"

"Yes. He's hot. Is he single?"

"Stop fooling around. Do you know him? He's a lawyer

somewhere in town. I need to ID him for a murder case."

"You're back doing murder cases? Why didn't I know that? Sufferin' succotash. You don't write, you don't call."

"I'll fill you in when the dust settles. Listen, I sent the fax to everyone I know and I'm striking out all over. Do you recognize him?"

"He looks like Elmer Fudd, with that chin."

"You're no help. I gotta go. Call you later," Bennie said, and hung up. She glanced at her watch. 11:45. Damn. She couldn't spend much more time on this, not with the other things she had to do.

"Here it is!" Marshall said. "I found it!" She held out a yellow paper-covered book, and Bennie scrambled out from behind her desk to look.

"You sure? Does it show my name?"

"Yes." Their heads bent over the book and they found Bennie's name at the same time. Marshall gestured to the papers covering the rug. "I'll fax this to Hutchins if you let me throw that mess out."

"No, I need that mess."

"It's trash."

"It's essential."

"Then forget it." Marshall stuck the course materials under her arm and a brochure sailed to the floor. She bent over to pick it up and her smooth brow furrowed. "Who gives these legal education courses? Professors?"

"No. Practitioners, other lawyers."

"Isn't this the lawyer you're looking for?"

"What?" Bennie took the slick brochure from Marshall's outstretched hand. *Accounting for Attorneys* was its title and under the course description was a thumbnail photo of the instructor. The eyes, the face, and the cleft chin were the same as the pencil sketch. *Lyman J. Bullock, Esq.*, read the caption, and next to it, *Bullock & Sabard, Attorneys-At-Law*.

Bennie reached for the telephone.

24

Alice was waiting in line to use the telephone. In the house she waited in line for breakfast, lunch, and dinner. She waited in line to drop off her dirty uniform; she waited in line to pick it up clean. She waited in line to leave the unit and to enter it again. It made her want to kill somebody. Like the bitch in line in front of her, using the phone. Alice didn't recognize her. She must be from Unit B.

"I have to talk to him," the inmate said, her voice high with anxiety. She picked at her scalp with long fingernails; her limp, brown hair had grown thin from the habit. "I need to discuss something important with him. I'm his wife."

Alice felt a drumming in her head. She ignored it and checked the clock on the wall. Only five minutes left before she had to get back to the unit. She'd have thrown the wacko off the phone but the guard was watching, his eyes shifting back and forth.

"Just tell him, tell him it's me. Janine. Neenie. No, no, I have the right number. I know this is his number."

The phone was on the wall in the hallway, next to the line for the commissary window. The inmates put in special orders and once a week the commissary packed transparent trash bags full of Doritos, potato chips, and Fritos. The dummies gobbled the junk like it was manna from heaven.

"No, no, no. She's not his wife. *I'm* his wife. I'm telling you, I made him what he is today. He owes it all to me. He still loves me. Put him on right now."

There was a line on the right, too, at the drug window. Inmates were lined up to pick up the legal drugs that got them off the illegal drugs, and suburban candy like Prozac and Ativan. The other inmates used the rock that traded freely in the house; the talk about instituting random drug testing never came to anything. Alice had had her stint with powder, then turned her experience into money. She was almost out of here, back in business on her own, the way she always wanted. But right now all she wanted was the goddamn phone. "Say good-bye, Neenie," she said, reaching over and hanging up the phone as soon as the guard looked away.

The inmate turned. "How dare you? Don't you know who I am?"

"Shut up or I'll punch your face in," Alice muttered. She picked up the phone and pounded in the number, checking her watch while the phone rang on the other end. Only two minutes left. The drug and commissary lines were almost finished. "Let me speak to him now," she said when Bullock's secretary picked up.

"Yes," he said, on the line after a split second.

Alice fake-coughed into the receiver. "I think I caught a cold," she said. She didn't say more in case Bullock's lines were tapped. She didn't need to, Bullock would understand. They'd worked out a code for the business and for times like this. Alice had given Bullock a name to call if she got into trouble on the inside. They'd try to stop the contract from the outside. It wasn't exactly Bullock's element of society, but he'd do it for her because he had no choice.

"A cough?" Bullock said. "Sorry to hear that."

"Gotta go." Alice hung up, satisfied for the time being. Bullock was reliable, if nothing else. It was good to have an accountant and lawyer in one shot. Bullock was one of the suits from the Chamber of Commerce who'd wanted to invest in Star. Then Alice found a surer way for him to make a buck, only tax-free.

Alice's eyes swept the last of the lines and Leonia wasn't anywhere in sight. Bullock would get to work on the outside, but on the inside she'd have to watch her back. She slipped into the housing unit and headed for her cell.

25

Bennie reached the ground floor of her building with a problem. The press thronged in front of the building and she had to get to Lyman Bullock's office. She lurked at the elevator bank, unsure how to leave. She couldn't lead the press to Bullock. If he were Connolly's lover, she'd be giving away a part of her defense; if he wasn't, they'd plague him without cause. The lobby, paneled in glossy gray marble, was empty except for an older guard at the security desk. It was Lou Jacobs, a recently retired cop who liked Bennie as much as most cops. Not at all.

"Lou," Bennie called from the elevator bank. "We got trouble."

"I ain't blind," he said. "I been putting up with those jerks since lunch. Already they're finding who else is in the building and makin' up fake appointments." He scowled at the reporters, his crow's-feet wrinkling deeply in skin thickened with tan, from weekends on his motorboat. He wore his silvery hair slicked back, and his nose was strong as a seagull's beak. A compact man, Lou wore his navy-blue uniform with a certain pride, which Bennie liked.

"I have to get out of here, Lou. Can I take the freight elevator?"

"No way. You don't have freight."

"Pretend I'm holding a fax machine."

"Forget it."

"Come on, Lou. You gonna throw me to the dogs?"

"If I can watch."

Bennie gritted her teeth. "Either I take the freight or I stand in the lobby and hold a press conference. Your lobby fills up with reporters and your tenants can't get in or out. You like that better?"

Lou shook his head. "You can't use the freight. It's against the rules."

"Christ, Lou, don't give me the rules. You want rules or you want reporters? Your choice, bucko."

Lyman Bullock leapt to his wingtips behind his mahogany desk, his light eyes wide and his small mouth partly open, emphasizing his cleft chin. His pale skin reddened and his neck bulged over a stiff white collar, fastened by a collar pin that threatened asphyxiation. The lawyer's demeanor told the truth, though he never would. "I don't know anyone named Alice Connolly," Bullock said firmly.

"You obviously do, you're not even a good liar. Didn't you go to law school?"

"I thought you said you wanted to see me about a case."

"I do, Alice Connolly's case." Bennie hadn't told Bullock the purpose of her visit when she'd telephoned. She'd just said she was a lawyer in need of ethics advice, with a possible case referral. "We need to talk, Lyman. By the way, is anything short for Lyman?"

"No."

"Listen, Lyman. I'm not here to disrupt your life or to pry. May I sit down?"

"Absolutely not."

"Thank you." Bennie slipped into the Windsor chair across from Bullock's desk. His office was large and sunny, with English antiques arranged conventionally on a blue patterned Sirook. The ethics business had evidently been good to Lyman Bullock. Lucky for him, lawyers were getting less ethical every day. "We need to talk about Alice Connolly. The man she lived with was murdered and she was charged with the crime. Her trial is next week. I'm her lawyer."

"I don't know what you're talking about." Bullock remained standing, his back stiff as a Chippendale chair. Behind his desk, twin diplomas hung on the wall, evidencing law and accounting degrees, and framed photographs of his family rested on a cherrywood credenza. His wife, with frosted hair and graduated pearls, smiled untroubled from a photo in an engraved silver frame. "I told you," he repeated, "I don't know anyone named Alice Connolly."

"I have reason to believe you do. You were seen picking her up at the Free Library. You drive a late-model brown Mercedes."

"I don't know what you're talking about." He bent from the waist, only far enough to pick up the phone. "Martha, call security. There's an intruder in my office."

"It's in your best interest to talk to me. If you'll talk here, we won't have to chat in court, where there's an almost criminal lack of good taste."

"Think twice before you consider serving me with a subpoena. I wouldn't make a very good witness at all." Bullock let the telephone receiver clatter to its cradle. "I have a terrible memory. I couldn't answer any of your questions. It would make you look foolish in front of the jury."

"You and Alice were having an affair."

"I don't know any Alice and I'm offended by such an accusation. I'm a married man."

"What were you doing then, picking her up at the library?"

"I never did any such a thing."

"I have an eyewitness."

"Your witness must have seen someone else."

"Christ, who are you kidding?" Bennie rose, her anger sparked, as a security guard burst through the door, a blur of black uniform with a revolver drawn.

"Mr. Bullock?" the guard said, looking around for the terrorist he'd been told to expect and finding only a pissed-off blonde.

Bullock waved a soft hand in Bennie's direction. "Get this woman out of my office immediately. She's creating a disturbance."

Bennie knew when she was licked, if only temporarily. "You were Connolly's lover for a year. She could get the death penalty."

"I don't know what you're talking about."

"Don't you care about her at all?" she asked, hating the emotion in her voice, but her question was mooted by the security guard, who propelled her from the office.

Back in her building, Bennie stepped off the freight elevator and ran into Lou Jacobs, the security guard. She put up her hands. "Don't shoot. I won't do it again, Officer."

"I don't give a damn what you do," Lou said grimly. He carried a cardboard box that held pictures of his grandchildren and the blue squeeze ball he palmed most of the day. "My days of baby-sittin' you are over."

"You going somewhere?"

"Looks that way. I'm retired again."

"You hate being retired. Why did you quit?"

"I didn't. I got fired."

"Fired? Why?"

"Breach of company policy. Step aside, please. I got freight."

Bennie felt stricken. "They fired you because of me?"

"Forget about it. Move over." Lou edged past her and walked into the elevator cab, draped in blue quilting. He hit the DOWN button, but Bennie held the elevator door.

"But what are you gonna do?"

"I told you. Retire. Take the boat out. Go diving. Ride my bike. Fish."

"Fish?"

"You know, those things that swim in water."

"You won't get another job?"

"It'll take time. Not many jobs for men my age, even as good-lookin' as I am. Now step aside," Lou said, but Bennie didn't see it that way.

"Lou, I need an investigator. You want the job?"

"You're kidding." He smiled dryly.

"No. Not at all." Bennie nodded toward the entrance where reporters thronged. "You see what I'm dealing with. I need you."

"On Della Porta? Forget it, he was a cop. Besides, it ain't like you and me get along." Lou hit the DOWN button, but Bennie kept a strong hand on the elevator door.

"It ain't like you and me are getting married."

"I don't need your charity."

"I'll work your ass off."

The elevator beeped loudly, and Lou winced. "I'll think about it. Don't take it personal."

"You want it, it's there. Tomorrow morning, nine o'clock in my office. I'll match your salary."

Beep. Lou frowned. "It's all women up there, isn't it?"

"Only if you're all man," Bennie told him, as the elevator doors closed.

26

Mary remembered Joy Newcomb as aloof and re-served at law school, which was the last time Mary had seen her. At school, Joy had always worn her dark brown hair back in the same low ponytail and dressed in pressed jeans with white turtlenecks and Fair Isle sweaters, authentically threadbare in the elbows. Joy had gone to Harvard undergrad and was therefore, in Mary's thinking, automatically smart. Mary felt that almost everyone else in her law school class was automatically smart, and never doubted that Joy Newcomb would make partner, again automatically, in any top-tier firm in the country. So Mary was doubly surprised when she tracked Joy to here.

"So, you just *quit*?" Mary asked, astonished as she strode beside Joy, who led a white pony named Frosty. Atop the pony perched a little boy who was about four years old, with densely black bangs. His thick glasses were slightly crooked under a black riding helmet and he clutched a spray of coarse white mane with a small fist as he bumped along. The four of them—pony, boy, and two lawyers—walked around in circles in a riding ring in an unassuming cinderblock arena. "*You* quit law?" Mary repeated.

"Yes, *I* quit. I'm allowed, aren't I?" Joy smiled. Her hair swung free and her expression was more relaxed than

Mary remembered, though her clothes remained the same. White turtleneck and jeans, but no crease ironed down the middle.

"Why did you quit? You were so . . . good at it."

"You know how being a lawyer is. It was too many hours, too much stress, and too little fun. Clients want everything yesterday, the world hates you, and you can't please anyone. So I just quit."

Quitting. The thought made Mary dizzy, but it could have been the walking in circles. She thought about quitting every day, but had never met anyone who had actually done it. "How did you do it?"

"I wrote a memo and said, 'I resign. Take my federal rules and shove it.' Now I do this, which I love." Joy led the pony to the left by a pink nylon halter. Sunlight streamed through the open window, catching her hair and setting it aglow. The air was fresh and clean and swallows chirped from a tall oak outside the window. They were in the horse country of Chester County and the only other sound was the steady *clump clump clump* of the pony's hooves on the soft footing. "It's not that hard to quit. You just have to take a risk."

"Did you have this job before you quit?"

"No, but I'd been riding since I was little. I knew I could teach it. To teach these kids, you have to learn all over again, though. It's not the same." Joy coaxed the pony to a cartoon-red mailbox set improbably beside the ring and patted the little boy's leg. "Go for it, Bobby!" she said, and the boy bent over, opened the mailbox, and extracted a beanbag. He giggled and held it up in triumph, though he said nothing. "Good for you!" Joy told him. "Now put it back, just like yesterday, remember?"

The child bit his lip while he held the pony's mane,

squeezed his legs into the sheepskin saddle pad for balance, and thrust the bag back into the mailbox. Then he flipped the lid closed. Joy gave him a hug, which went unreturned. "You're the best, you know that?" she said, though the boy didn't answer. When Joy turned around, her face was flushed with happiness. "Yesterday he couldn't do that. Today he can."

"Congratulations."

"Bobby did it, not me." Joy clucked to the pony and they began walking again. "Why don't you congratulate him?" she asked, so pointedly that Mary realized she'd been avoiding the child altogether. Why, she didn't know, but whatever the reason, she felt instantly guilty about it. On many days, Mary woke up guilty.

"Congratulations, Bobby," Mary told him, but she couldn't determine if he'd heard. "Does he understand?"

"He understands more than you and me," Joy answered tersely, then looked over. "When you called, you said you needed to talk to me about Jemison, for a case. You didn't drive all the way out here to talk about quitting."

"No? I mean, no." Mary stopped daydreaming and remembered the Connolly case. "You were at Jemison when Judge Guthrie was there, weren't you?"

"Sure. He was one of the gray hairs, in litigation. He was there from forever. He took care of all the old-line house clients. His billings were huge, all of it inherited from the gray hair before him."

"Did you work for him?"

"Only a little, and I wasn't even on the briefs. He was a nice man."

"Then he became a judge."

"Yes." Joy nodded, keeping a hand on Bobby as the pony walked.

"Were you at Jemison when Henry Burden was there? He was a former D.A."

"Sure. He'd been there a year or two when I got there. I never worked for him. He was *muy macho*. I didn't need it."

"Did Burden work for Guthrie at all?"

"Sure. He was Guthrie's boy, totally."

"So they were friends?"

"Not really. Guthrie was a loner in the firm, not political. He was into his family and was always the legal scholar. He wanted to be a judge for a long time. He even published while he practiced and wrote all the articles himself. How incredible is that?"

Mary put her head down, mulling it over. Dust covered her pumps as they marched next to the pony's hooves. The *clump clump clump* was helping her think. "So at some point, Burden comes over from the D.A.'s office. Burden is very connected in city politics, but has no client base. Guthrie has a client base, but isn't connected in city politics. Guthrie wants to be a judge, but you can't be a judge without connections. Not in Philadelphia."

Joy smiled at Bobby. "Sit up, buddy. Try to sit straight as a board."

"So they formed an alliance," Mary said, thinking aloud. "Burden got Guthrie a judgeship, and Guthrie turned over his clients. As a result, they owe each other, and they also owe a lot of powerful people in the city. Isn't that interesting?"

"No, not at all. This is interesting. Ho, Frosty." The pony halted next to a toy hoop mounted low on the cinderblock wall. Joy handed a lightweight basketball to Bobby, who squinted over his glasses and pitched the ball at the hoop. It veered wildly off course, arced into a wall, and rolled into the center of the ring. Joy ran to fetch it. "Put your hand on Bobby's leg, Mary!" she called back.

"Huh? Why?"

"So he doesn't fall off!"

"*What?*" Mary clamped a panicky hand on the boy's leg. "Stay on, okay, Bobby? If you fall off, the guilt will kill me."

Joy came back with the ball, panting. "You know, Mary, you could quit, too. If you don't like your job, just quit. Just do it."

"I can't. I'll fall off the edge of the earth. Now take this child. Put a hand on him. Save him from me."

Joy handed Bobby the basketball and placed a confident grip on his leg. "You'll find another job, you'll see. In this economy, there's tons of jobs. We have two openings. You want to work here?"

"Here?" Mary's throat caught, and Bobby looked down at her, basketball between his hands, as if waiting for an answer. His eyes were brown, magnified by his dense lenses, and his gaze didn't waver. Though his expression remained remote, Mary could see that he accorded her the same trust he did Joy, merely because she was an adult. She felt distinctly unworthy. "I don't think I can," she answered simply, and the boy turned away.

27

It was a business day at the prison and the interview rooms were full. Three-piece suits sat on the left side of the counter and orange jumpsuits on the right. Public defenders huddled with their clients next to tall stacks of accordion files. For their visits, the prison guards became air-traffic controllers, lining up the inmates like jets waiting to land.

"This is a surprise," Connolly said. She stood up when Bennie banged into the interview room and let the door slam locked behind her. "I didn't expect you today."

"Expect me every day." Bennie tossed her briefcase onto the Formica counter, where it landed with a loud *thud,* and she dropped into the chair behind it. "We got trouble. How did the press find out you might be my twin?"

"I don't know. Maybe the way we look?"

"You didn't tell them?"

"No, of course not." Connolly sat down. "They've been calling here, but your secretary got me a message that said not to talk to the press. Not that they'd let me take those calls anyway."

Bennie thought about it. It was true, calls in and out of the facility were limited. "Did you tell any friends in here who could have blabbed it?"

"I don't have any friends."

"How about on the outside?"

"Like I said."

Bennie scrutinized Connolly to see if she was telling the truth. Her eyes, another set of Bennie's eyes, were alert with what looked like genuine surprise, and she sat tense on the edge of the chair, her hands clasped on the counter. A tiny crease in her brow betrayed her anxiety; it looked like the kink that Grady always kidded Bennie about in her own brow. "You have no idea how the press found out?"

"No, not unless somebody in your firm told them."

"No." Bennie laced her fingers into a fist over the counter. "Let me ask you another question. Why didn't you tell me about Lyman Bullock?"

Connolly's mouth twitched and anger flickered across her features. She leaned back as if absorbing a blow, then seemed to compose herself. "Bullock," she said with a sigh. "So you know about him."

"Why didn't you tell me?"

"You didn't ask."

"I shouldn't have to. You're supposed to tell me everything, and I decide what's important for the case. You don't make that decision, I do. I'm your lawyer."

Connolly's temper flared. "That doesn't mean you're my boss, lording it over me."

"It's not about who's the boss."

"The hell it isn't."

Bennie bristled. The similarity between her and Connolly's reaction to authority no longer struck her as a complete surprise. Still, she had a defense to stage. "Look, you called me to represent you, I'm trying to represent you. Knocking myself out to represent you, in fact, and so are my two best associates. Cooperate or die, okay? That incentive enough for you?"

Connolly sulked. "What do you want to know?"

"Everything."

"Except who you really are."

Bennie straightened in her chair. "I know who I am."

"No, you don't, because you don't know who I am. I change who you are, and you don't like that one bit."

"About the case." If Connolly was playing a mind game with Bennie, she wouldn't win. "We're talking about the case."

"You don't like your cage rattled, huh? Well, deal with it." Connolly stood up, and her chair squeaked noisily on the gritty floor. "That you're on that side of the table, with your suit and your briefcase, so full of yourself. You think you can come up here and tear me a new one, then get back in your car and go home. You don't want to believe that you're my twin, huh? That you could have had the lousy luck. That you could have been here. You could have been *me*."

"Lyman Bullock," Bennie said evenly. "Sit down and discuss Lyman Bullock or I leave. When did you start seeing him?"

Connolly's lip twisted. "October, that year," she answered after a minute, and fell defiantly into her chair.

"Where did you meet him?"

"On the street. A hot dog stand."

"A preppie lawyer, at a hot dog stand? Try again. The truth."

Connolly didn't bat an eye. "We met at the hot dog stand in front of the library. He pulled up in the car, to grab a dog. We got to talking."

"Then what?"

"We had an affair, okay? Surprised I got a man like that?"

Bennie retrieved a legal pad and ballpoint from her briefcase. "Where did you go with him during the day?"

"An apartment he kept on the side. I wasn't the first."

"You have a key?"

"No, I met him there."

"How many times a week?"

"In the beginning, once or twice a week. When he could."

Bennie made a note. "You had sex."

"No, we played Nintendo." Connolly didn't laugh and neither did Bennie. "I'd hang in the apartment, work on my book. It was nicer than the library. The place was loaded. Big-screen TV, nice CD player. Fast computer, a screamer."

Bennie set down her pen. "So, you were cheating on Della Porta."

"Yeah."

"Why?"

Connolly shrugged, her expression impassive.

"I thought you were a woman in love."

"You thought wrong." She laughed abruptly. "You got the degree, but I got the brains."

Bennie didn't react. "Explain Bullock so I can make it credible to a jury, if it comes out."

"I lived with Della Porta but I didn't love him. I told you I didn't like being alone. I didn't love Bullock either. They were just men. I cared about them, but it wasn't like love, in love songs and all."

Bennie thought she sounded adolescent. If songs were the standard, we all were screwed. "When did it end between you and Bullock?"

"A month before Anthony was murdered."

"Did you end it or did he?"

"We both did. He was traveling all the time on business, for a big case out in Arkansas. He just stopped calling."

"You didn't call him?"

"No. I wasn't that interested, and then Anthony got killed."

Bennie felt sick and hollow. For Connolly's life, so empty, and for her defense, in deeper trouble than before. She couldn't prove that Connolly and Della Porta were lovebirds now, and hoped the D.A. didn't know that. Maybe she could try another tack. "Bullock knew about Della Porta, right? Wasn't he jealous of Della Porta?"

"No. Bullock wanted to buy a share of Star. Wanted me to fix it with Anthony. 'Course, I couldn't exactly do that."

"Buy a share? What do you mean?"

"Fighters need backers. Anthony was the manager and he got a group of businessmen to put up money for Star. If Star made money, they made money."

"Could there be a connection between Bullock and Star?"

"No way. Bullock didn't need the coin, believe me."

But Bennie was thinking. There was a problem here and it wasn't that the Bullock theory wouldn't fly. It was that Connolly wouldn't fly. Any jury, given half a chance, will find for a defendant they like, but they weren't going to like Connolly, even if she never said a word in court. The D.A. would be savvy enough to get Connolly's life, morals, and attitude into evidence, and it could kill her, even if she were innocent of the murder.

Bennie's stomach tensed. She had to find some way to sell Connolly to the jury. She looked at Connolly, and the inmate looked back at her with those matching eyes, outlined with eyeliner. It gave her an idea. A gamble, but it was Connolly's only chance.

28

The black plastic hand on the kitchen clock hovered at 5:30, and Mary sat with satisfaction over a plate of steaming spaghetti and bumpy meatballs, with a salad of iceberg lettuce and vinegar-and-oil dressing. The DiNunzio family ate dinner at the same time every night and served pasta four nights a week, except for fish on Fridays, still. Mary felt reassured when things stayed the same, and her parents' home, which she visited every Wednesday for dinner, was the Church of Things That Stayed the Same. She had brought Judy home for dinner because Mary's parents adored her, treating her like the tall child they never had. Judy returned the affection, marveling at each visit that Italians really acted Italian. Mary had no defense for it. Some stereotypes rang true for a reason.

The DiNunzios' brick rowhouse in South Philly was laid out in a straight line from living room to dining room to kitchen, the rooms strung one after the other like the slippery beads on a favored rosary. The sofa in the living room sagged in the center, its shiny green quilting protected by doilies her mother had crocheted decades ago. The room's maroon carpet had been worn in a strip down the middle, a missal's ribbon made by years of walking through the dining room, which was used only on Christmas and Easter. Even as a child, Mary knew something really good had to happen to Jesus Christ for the DiNunzios to eat in the dining room.

The heart of the house was the kitchen, tiny and shaped like a Mass card. A Formica table with rickety wire legs took up most of the room, and the five of them—Mary's mother and father, Mary and her twin Angie, and Judy—had to huddle to fit around it for dinner. Refaced wood cabinets ringed the room and Formica counters cracked at the corners, so near to the kitchen table that Mary's father could stay in his chair and turn up the Lasko fan in the window, which he did. The plastic blades whirred faster but the air remained stifling.

"*Madonne*, it's hot," said Mary's father, Mariano Di-Nunzio. A long time ago, his crew of tilesetters had christened him "Matty," and it stuck. He was a bald, stocky man with large eyes, a bulbous nose, and an affable smile. He wore Bermuda shorts and a white undershirt, his tummy stretching soft as a cherub's under the worn cotton. He had tucked a paper napkin in his T-shirt like a bib. "You gettin' some breeze, Judy?" he asked.

"Yes, thanks." Judy was struggling to twirl her spaghetti.

"Good. You're the guest. We want you to be nice and comfortable."

"I am," Judy said, as steaming strands slipped through her fork for the second time. She tried it again, her tongue to the side in concentration.

"You want help with that?" Angie asked. Her dark blond hair was combed into a short ponytail that curved like a comma; she wore an ivory shirt with short sleeves and khaki shorts. Angie looked like a casual-dress version of her twin, though her manner was far from casual.

Mary smirked. "Don't help her. It's fun to watch her struggle."

"Oh, stop," Angie said. "I'm going to teach her how to twirl."

"But she'll run off and tell all the other WASPs. Then where will we be? Fresh out of state secrets."

Judy fumbled with the spoon as spaghetti slithered off her fork. "I don't get the spoon part."

"You don't need to use the spoon," Angie said, but Mary waved her off.

"Don't believe her, Jude, she's lying. Spoons are key to expert twirling. They don't let you in the Sons of Italy unless you use a spoon."

"You don't need the spoon," Mary's father said, and beside him, her mother nodded, pushing bangs like cirrus clouds from a short, bony brow. Vita DiNunzio was losing her hair from years of teasing, which only made her get it teased more often, at the beauty parlor at the corner.

"But spoons are cool," Mary insisted. "Real dagoes use spoons."

"Why do you use that term?" Angie snapped, and Mary reflected that her twin had left her sense of humor at the convent, with no hope of recovery since she'd taken a job as a paralegal. Nothing about being a paralegal was funny.

"You know, Ange, you used to be a lot of fun."

"Like you?"

"Exactly like me," Mary said, and her meaning wasn't lost on Angie, who averted her eyes.

"Girls, girls," their mother said, her tone a warning.

Mary bit her tongue. Her chest felt tight. She didn't know how to reach Angie, though they'd been so close as kids. Mary had always treasured their twinness, seeing it as unique and special, but the bond that Mary viewed as security, like moorings to a boat, Angie saw as confinement, the tether to the puppy. Angie had spent most of her adult life tugging at that leash, fighting to slip free of it completely. Mary regretted the loss, and the wound had been reopened by the Connolly case; Bennie was embracing a twin she had never known, just as Angie was pushing her away.

"Judy," Angie said, "put the spoon down and pick up some spaghetti on your fork. Pick up just a little and twirl it against the side of the plate."

Judy pierced a few strands of spaghetti with her fork, her expression grimmer than anybody's eating spaghetti should be. "I'm a Stanford grad. I should be able to do this."

"But you can't," Mary told her. "Because you won't use the spoon."

"Mary," Angie warned, in the same tone their mother had used.

Mary's face flushed. She felt suddenly warm in the tiny kitchen. Hot tomato sauce—"gravy" in the vernacular— bubbled in the dented metal saucepan on the stove and residual steam from a pot of spaghetti water curled into the air. The aroma filling the small kitchen—sharp with oregano, sweet with basil, chunky with sausage—that seemed so fragrant when Mary first came home now smelled cloying. "You know," she said, "some people don't eat spaghetti when it's hot out. They think it makes them hotter to eat spaghetti."

Mary's mother looked over, squinting behind her glasses. "What you mean, no spaghett'?"

"No spaghetti in summer. If we ate cold things for dinner, we'd feel cooler."

"Drink your water," said her mother, and beside her,

her father frowned deeply, his forehead fairly cleaving in two.

"What are you talkin', a cold dinner? Cold isn't dinner. If it's cold, it can't be dinner."

"That's not true, Pop," Mary said, not sure why she was pressing such an inane point. She loved spaghetti in any weather. She would've eaten it in a steambath. "In restaurants they have cold dinners, like cold salmon with a salad. Sometimes they serve the salad warm."

"Cold fish, warm salad?" Her father's hand flew to check his hearing aid, a gift from Mary. She'd been so thrilled when he agreed to wear it that she suggested eating in the dining room, but had been roundly rebuffed. "You sayin' *cold* fish, *warm* salad, Mare? Where's this at?"

"Downtown."

"What kinda thing is that? How they make the salad warm?"

"I don't know. Either they don't chill it or they heat it, I guess. It says on the menu, 'A warm salad of wilted greens.'"

"Wilted? Wilted means spoiled. They don't serve it like that."

"Yes, they do. Put it right in front of you."

Her father snorted. "They should be ashamed of themselves! Crooks! Cold fish, warm salad! That's ass-backwards."

"Watch your language, Matty," said Mary's mother, but her father pretended not to hear with alarming accuracy.

"People pay good money for that? That's cocka-mamie!"

Mary caught her twin's eye across the tight circle of the table and to her surprise, Angie was smiling over her water glass. Mary sighed inwardly. She used to be able to read her sister's mind.

"I did it!" Judy yelped suddenly. "Look!" Grinning, she held up a forkful of spaghetti balled like yarn.

Mary laughed, and her father set down his fork and clapped, his dry, rough palms smacking thickly together. "*Brava*, Judy!" he said.

"So tell us about your day, girls," her mother said, and Mary hesitated. She didn't want to tell her parents she was working on the Connolly case, but she didn't want to lie, either. Like a good lawyer, she avoided the question.

"You remind me of when we were little, Ma, and you'd ask what we learned in school that day."

"I'll tell you what we learned," Judy chirped up, finishing her forkful of pasta. "We learned that boxers have bad manners."

"Boxers?" Vita frowned, and Mary looked down at her plate. *Oh, no.*

Matty DiNunzio's face lit up. "You gotta case about boxing? What you gotta do with boxing?"

"We had to question a witness today," Judy answered, launching into what happened at the gym, apparently heedless of Mary's kicks under the table. Matty DiNunzio hunched over the table on his elbows, his eyes widening as his wife's narrowed. Mary knew her mother's suspicions would be slow-cooking like tomato sauce. Thick bubbles popping on a steamy red surface.

"You met Star Harald?" her father said, oblivious in his excitement. "He's a heavyweight. I seen him box a couple months ago. He was on the cable. *Madonne*, whatta jab."

Mary leapt to shift the subject. "You watch boxing, Pop? I thought you were a baseball fan."

"I like the fights. I boxed when I was young. Way back when."

"Tell us about it," Mary asked, but her mother's face told her she was only postponing the inevitable, which was still better than nothing. Every lawyer likes an extension of time.

"Not much to tell. Not like Golden Gloves or nothin'. A lot of us fought, from the neighborhood. Cooch, Johnnie, Freddie. You met them guys, Mare. I could hit hard, take a punch, too. But I wasn't quick enough. My feet."

"Maria," her mother interrupted. She touched her husband's forearm, which was Italian code for shut up now. "What kinda case she got you workin' on?"

Mary didn't have to ask her mother who "she" was. Bennie Rosato had become the Antichrist in the DiNunzio household last year. "Just a case. A normal case."

"What you mean, normal?"

"I just have to do some research, is all. Talk to witnesses, work in the library. Today I met with one of my old classmates, she's teaching handicapped children—"

"Witnesses. What kinda witnesses?"

Mary sipped some water. The kitchen was sweltering. Nobody could cross-examine like a mother. "You know, regular witnesses. Trial witnesses."

"What kinda trial?"

"You know, a trial. It's not my trial. I'm not trying the case or anything." Mary glanced at Judy for help, but she'd become suspiciously reabsorbed in her spaghetti. "I'm also finishing a brief in that First Amendment case I told you about, remember? That's my main case, in federal court. It's for the Third Circuit, the federal court of appeals. Very important stuff, Ma. This is where you say you're so proud of me. That I'm a genius, that they're lucky to have me."

"She got you on a murder case, don't she?" Vita Di-Nunzio set down her fork, and Mary knew she was in trouble.

"Just this one."

"I knew it!" She slammed the table with a palm that only looked fragile. The table wiggled, the plates jumped, and water pooled in the jelly glasses.

"It's not on Bennie, it's on me. If you want to blame anybody, blame me."

"She almost got you *killed*!" her mother shouted, her voice quivering with age and emotion.

"I'm fine, Ma. Everything's fine."

Across the table, Angie looked grave. "Relax, Ma. Mary will be very careful. She'll take care of herself. She won't do anything risky. Will you, Mare?"

"No, absolutely not," Mary said, on cue. "I'm very careful. Not doing anything dangerous at all." Leave it to Angie to know how to handle her mother. Growing up, the twins had worked as a tag team and in the unspoken division of parents, Angie had gotten their mother and Mary their father. "Last year was a one-time thing, Ma. This is just a run-of-the-mill criminal trial. I'll be very careful."

"*Basta!*" her mother said, standing up abruptly. Her face flushed through the thin, broken skin of her cheeks. She fairly shook in her flowered housedress. "I'll go down there right now!"

"What? Where?"

"I'll go down to that office right now and tell that *witch* she's not putting my daughter on no murder case!"

Mary closed her eyes, mortified. "You're not doing that, Ma. The office is closed. Bennie's not even there."

She didn't mention that her mother couldn't drive. It didn't seem like the right time.

"I'll go tomorrow morning. I'll tell her. She'll listen to me, I'll make her!"

"Ma, it's my job."

"Then you *quit!*"

Mary almost laughed. "I can't do that. I have to make a living. My rent alone is—"

"*Move home!*" She threw her arms in the air, her elbows knobby and her underarms slack. "Don't tell me you're too old! Camarr Millie, her daughter lives at home and she's thirty-six!"

"I'm not quitting. I'm a lawyer, I like my job," Mary said, not believing the words even as they fell from her mouth. Who could sell a happy lawyer?

"Matty, talk to her," her mother barked, nudging her husband, and Mary realized for the first time that her parents played on a tag team of their own. She looked at her father, and pain twisted his features as he tugged the napkin bib from the neck of his T-shirt. He didn't say a word, and still a knife of guilt went through her.

"Pop, it's my job," Mary said. "I have to do my job."

"We thought you wasn't doin' no more murder cases, baby," he said softly.

"I can't pick and choose, Pop. You know that, you worked. Could you have one of your crew picking his own work?"

Suddenly her mother pushed her chair under the table, her eyes edged with tears, and hurried from the kitchen. "Ma, wait!" Angie called out, and bolted from the table after her. Judy looked astonished, and Mary tensed in the stifling kitchen.

Her father reached across the table and touched her hand, his palm warm. "Mare, I'm not gonna tell you your business. All I'm gonna tell you is boxing is a mean business, a dirty business. Lotsa people get hurt. Make sure you're not one of them."

"Don't worry, Pop," Mary said, the words hard in coming.

Watching the scene, Judy felt dumbstruck. Her mother didn't cry. Her father didn't call her "baby." Her family preferred their melodrama on a television movie-of-the-week, behind a curve of expensive glass. Or on a stage, at a distance. Yet, as moved as Judy was by the emotion of Mary's parents, she was struck by their words. Matty DiNunzio was right. Boxing was a dirty, dangerous business. Maybe the Della Porta murder had less to do with cops and more to do with boxers. The lawyers had been following Connolly's theory, but Judy didn't trust Connolly the way Bennie did. She decided to follow up, alone. She didn't want to put Mary in harm's way. She didn't want her best friend hurt.

And she certainly didn't want to answer to Vita DiNunzio.

29

B ennie cruised the block in the dark before she pulled up in front of Della Porta's rowhouse, making sure there were no news vans or reporters out front. Trose Street was quiet, with only a few people out. She parked and locked the Expedition, got out with the case file, and plucked through her keys until she found the one to Della Porta's apartment.

Bennie climbed the stoop to the entrance, unlocked the inside door, and went up the stairs to the apartment. She opened the door at the top of the stair, thinking about Connolly. How it must have felt for her to come home to this apartment, to Della Porta. What it was like to find him dead. Bennie had experienced that horror herself, except that she'd loved profoundly the man she'd found. How could this happen to both her and Connolly? Wasn't it too coincidental?

She opened the door, entered the apartment, and flicked on the switch for the overhead light. The apartment looked the same as before, the living area on the left, with the bloodstain. She walked to the faintly rusty outline and flashed on the awful day she saw the pool of blood on her lover's desk. Bennie stared at the bloodstain, deep in thought. She had to admit that she was starting to feel, more than she could logically justify, that Connolly was her twin. Maybe because Bennie had watched Connolly,

observed the way she looked and acted. Noted her manner-
isms and the coincidences in their lives. Yet the more time
Bennie spent around Connolly, the more she felt she understood her, even as she trusted and liked her less. It was
paradoxical, but Bennie was starting to feel *of* Connolly in
some way. It was an uneasy sensation, being suddenly
uncomfortable in her own skin.

Bennie stared down at the stain. Blood. It always came
back to blood. She had to win this case. She had a duty,
not only as Connolly's lawyer, but maybe even as her sister. And there was one way to win. The ethics of it were
arguable, but at the same time, she had an equal ethical
duty to represent her client as zealously as possible. It was
a thorny problem, but most were, in the law, and that's
what kept it interesting.

"Just get on with it, girl," Bennie said aloud, and hurried to the bathroom to save Connolly's life.

Snip, snip, went the scissors. Bennie had bought them at a
drugstore on the way over and they were more suited to
construction paper than hair. She squeezed the orange
handles and tried again, cutting a strand of hair near the
front of her face.

Snip. The honeyed strand fell to the sink, where Bennie
had spread out the day's newspaper from her briefcase.
Her hand moved an awkward inch to the back of her head
and she grabbed another hank of hair.

Snip, snip. A chunk fell to the newspaper, and she
checked the bathroom mirror. The front part of Bennie's
hair was now clipped in layers. She already looked more
like Connolly, even given the difference in their hair colors. Clearing the hair from her forehead emphasized the
similarity in their eyes.

Bennie looked at her reflection and imagined the way she and Connolly would look at counsel table, identical sisters, side-by-side in front of the jury. It would have to affect the jurors. Bennie knew she could get a jury to trust her; it was her greatest strength as a trial lawyer. And if she could get the jury on her side, it wouldn't be much of a leap to get them on Connolly's. Especially if every time they looked at Bennie, they saw Connolly. And vice versa.

Bennie chopped away, preoccupied. Her first approach to the case—hiding the fact that she and Connolly were, or might be, twins—was wrong, and untenable now that the news was live at five. If the media was flogging the story that they were twins, why not go with it? Why not turn it to Connolly's advantage? If Bennie went public with the twin issue, played it up, then every article the press wrote and every story they printed would generate sympathy for Connolly. The buzz had to reach the potential jurors, with the trial only a week away. Suddenly the tight time frame became an advantage, too.

Bennie smiled grimly as she hacked away. It was a great plan, and there was no way the D.A. could counter it. Even if Judge Guthrie issued a gag order, the press would be off and spinning. Every "no comment" would tantalize. *Snip, snip, snip.* Bennie had disguised herself in the past, to look less like herself. This time she was disguising herself to look *more* like herself. A mask, inside out. If Connolly was her twin, the mask was Bennie's true identity.

She made a final cut and set the scissors on the edge of the sink. Snippets of blond hair covered the newspaper and filled the basin. She admired even her crude handiwork, turning her head left and right in front of the mirror. Her head felt lighter; she felt freer.

She dived into her purse for her other new purchases,

grabbed a tube of lipstick and twirled it open, revealing a rosy missile. She raised the lipstick with a schoolgirl's excitement and applied it to her lips. She blotted like she'd seen her mother do as a young child, then reached back into the bag. Liquid eyeliner. She unscrewed the top, took the little brush, and made the first line on her left lid. The goop felt like a cold worm going on and looked worse, but she finished the job.

Bennie looked in the mirror, unsatisfied. The makeup brought a bogus liveliness to her features, but her clothes were wrong. She whipped off her jacket and stuffed it onto the empty towel rack, then opened two buttons of her cotton blouse and tucked her collar under, so that her neckline mimicked the V-neck of Connolly's prison jumpsuit. Bennie rechecked the mirror and was almost satisfied. The clothes underscored the effect of the haircut. At trial she'd dress her client and herself to match; not identically, that would be too obvious, but in the same colors and styles.

Bennie grinned in the mirror, then quickly deflated. Something was wrong. Her smile looked too warm, too happy. Her eyes crinkled at the corners and her nose wrinkled at the bridge. Connolly never smiled that way. Her smile, such as it was, came off as cynical, hardened. Could Bennie make herself look *exactly* like Connolly?

She stepped back from the mirror, tilted her mouth down at the corners, and knit her brow deeply. She checked the mirror. Too much. She stroked her cheeks, smoothing the animation from her features. She needed her face to look slack, vaguely without affect, like Connolly. She closed her eyes and imagined how it felt to be raised with remote parents, never to find a career that satisfied her, and ultimately to be charged for a heinous crime she didn't commit. To be on trial for her very life.

Bennie slipped deeper inside Connolly's mind. She imagined herself discovering that she had been put up for adoption, and that as lousy as her life had turned out, she had an identical twin who became a successful lawyer. Who was chosen over her by their mother; whose success was attained through her sacrifice. Who had taken her very *blood* for her own. Bennie opened her eyes and looked in the mirror. The expression on her face was Connolly's.

Bennie *was* Connolly.

And it terrified her.

30

Mary sat in the conference room in the office, trying to concentrate on the file. It was late; the firm was empty and quiet. Judy had said she had to stop by Jenkins Law Library for research, and Mary felt lonely working on her own. Across the street, a single lighted floor in a dark office building made an illuminated stripe, like a ribbon of Correcto-tape against the black sky.

Mary's coffee went cold as her gaze rolled restlessly over the 911 transcripts fanned out in front of her. She'd read them three times, but they only confirmed her instinct that Connolly was guilty. Mary understood the need for every defendant to have a lawyer, but it was another matter entirely to *be* that lawyer. You couldn't graduate from parochial school and feel otherwise. There was no known cure for a Catholic education.

Her gaze wandered out the window and back again. Not only had she made her mother cry, she was working overtime to help a woman who had committed the worst sin imaginable. Try as she might, Mary couldn't shake the feeling that God floated above the acoustic tiles of the conference room, due north of the fax machine. He was an old white God with a soft gray beard, sitting on an immense throne, like at the Lincoln Memorial. He was flanked by seraphim who had previously taught handicapped children to ride ponies. His wispy eyebrows met in consternation as he gazed down upon the bar association.

Then Mary remembered Bennie's words. *Pretend the Connolly case is just like any other case.* An antitrust case, for example, where the criminals had manicured fingernails and thought a Glock went ticktock. Mary squared her shoulders and picked up the Investigation Interview Record, the notes that detectives took when they questioned a witness at the Roundhouse. It would tell her what the Commonwealth witnesses would say.

Q: I understand that you may have some information about the incident. Please tell me what you know about the events of May nineteenth.
A: Well, it was yesterday, and I was trying to put the baby to sleep.
Q: Go on. About what you heard.
A: I heard a gunshot. It was so loud. After I heard the gunshot, I went to my door and I saw Alice Connolly running from the house.

Mary stared at the sheet and flashed on an earlier question-and-answer, the one she had memorized as a six-year-old. *The Baltimore Catechism,* in a soft blue cover.

Q: Who made you?
A: God made me.
Q: Why did God make you?
A: To represent cold-blooded murderers and various other swine.

Mary gritted her teeth. She grabbed a legal pad, put her head down, and started taking notes. As long as she had this job, she was going to do it and do it right. It was the only way to cope with defending Connolly, and she suspected it was the only way most criminal defense lawyers defended their clients.

Without looking up.

Judy lurked inside the door of the boxing gym, reacquainting herself with the place. The sparring match staged earlier in the day was gone, and a white man pounded the heavy bag in the corner. Two black men worked the speedbags, their muscled arms pumping in deft circular motions. A janitor swept up with a long wooden pushbroom, an unlit cigarette plugged into the side of his mouth. Nobody noticed Judy, or if they did, they didn't bother her.

She watched the boxer on the heavy bag that hung from the ceiling like a dead body. *Womp, womp, womp,* went the sound of leather on thick canvas, reverberating in the gym. The fighter's body swiveled from side to side with each jab. The rhythm reminded Judy of the natural swing of cross-country skiing and the solitude of the boxer was like rock climbing. Odd to find remnants of her two favorite sports in a filthy gym, but Judy had the capacity to romanticize anything. Even really smelly things.

Behind her, in the corner, was a scene she hadn't seen from the door. A short older man in gray sweats was demonstrating a classic boxing stance in front of a lineup of little kids in low-slung boxers. His skin was the color of chestnuts and his eyes a rich, resonant brown, large and lively in a barely lined face. Hair worn natural covered his neatly shaped head, with patches of gray at the temples, and he smiled easily, almost like a kid himself. "Think you can do it? Give it a try!" the man shouted to the group, and Judy walked over to watch.

The kids stepped forward and imitated the stance, their flat torsos and lanky arms ending in puffy red boxing gloves, crisscrossed with duct tape.

"Way to go, boys! That was great!" the man called out, and the kids' chests puffed visibly. "Now, lefts up!" The kids cocked their left fists protectively. "Look like you mean it!" the man shouted. He wiped his brow and grinned at Judy. "They look real good, don't they? They only had two lessons, these boys."

"They look awesome!" Judy said, loud so the kids could hear.

The man returned his attention to the kids. "Now let's see a few jabs, boys." The kids started swinging, imitating moves from TV. "Way to be, way to be!" he called to them as they swung.

"You teach boxing, I gather," Judy called out.

"Sure. Boxin' gives kids somethin' to do, teaches 'em self-esteem. I make 'em do a good deed, too, every day." The man's forehead wrinkled as two kids started shoving each other. "Hey, cut that out, you two. Troy! Vondel! Okay, we're done for the night. Hit the showers!" The kids fell out of line and scampered across the worn Astroturf for the locker room. "Don't leave the towels on the floor! Put 'em in the hamper!" he shouted after them.

"I don't think they heard you," Judy said, smiling.

"They heard, but they don't listen." The man wiped his brow on the sleeve of his sweats and extended a large hand. "I'm Roy Gaines. Everybody call me Mr. Gaines, don't ask why. Not that I won't tell you, jus' I don't remember. Jus' started that way and there's no stoppin' it. So now Mr. Gaines it is."

"Happy to meet you, Mr. Gaines. I'm Judy Forty," Judy said, shaking his hand. It was a false name, but she was undercover. People didn't line up to help lawyers, and she wanted to keep her connection to the Della Porta case under wraps. If she could avoid seeing Star for the next few days, she could pull it off. "You give lessons to adults, too?"

"Ha! I trained half the fighters outta this gym."

"So you must know a lot about boxing."

"Been boxin' since I was a kid. Started out wrasslin' in the schoolyard, down Georgia. Didn't have the height nor the reach to be no professional, though. Been givin' lessons for a long time. Ask the manager of the place, Dayvon Allen, he here in the daytime. Ask him. Ask anybody. Everybody know Mr. Gaines."

Judy nodded. It sounded perfect. "I'd like to take boxing lessons from you."

"Boxin' lessons? Sure." Mr. Gaines looked Judy up and down, appraising her. "You could do it, girl. Got the build for it. Tall, strong. Long arms. Lotsa women boxin' now."

"Really?"

"Christy Martin, the coal miner's daughter? White girl, wears pink shorts, built like a truck. On a card with De La Hoya one time. Helluva boxer. Holds her own, Christy does, and there's that Dutch girl, the real pretty one. What's her name?" Mr. Gaines frowned in thought, then snapped his fingers, an unexpectedly loud sound. "Lucia Rijker! You see her?"

"No."

"Well, you should." Mr. Gaines frowned. "You interested in boxin', you oughta watch it. Watch it all you can.

Watch the men, watch the women, you can always learn somethin'. S'like anythin' else, you gotta study it. Practice. Train. Work. Can't be traipsin' in here lookin' for no diet program."

"How much are lessons?"

"Twenty-five bucks a half hour. Gotta sign me a form, if you serious."

"I am." Judy felt dismayed. A half hour? She couldn't learn much about the gym in half an hour. "Can I take an hour lesson?"

"A half hour be more than enough." Mr. Gaines chuckled, revealing a cracked front tooth that looked like a piece of white bread with a bite taken out of it. "Believe me. Puh-lenty. You got time on your hands, you train. In between lessons, you train. Hear me? Train. Run. Lift. Heavy bag. Reflex bag. I give you a schedule. All my students got a schedule."

"How about three lessons a week?"

"Hoo-ee, you fast. Most people, they do one a week. What the hurry?"

Judy paused. "I already know the basics. My dad boxed. He was a cop."

"A cop, huh?" Mr. Gaines repeated, and Judy nodded, though she was making it up as she went along. Her father was a Stanford professor who would have abhorred boxing if he'd ever deigned to form an opinion about it.

"I think there's something about cops and boxing, don't you?" Judy asked, digging for information. "They seem attracted to it. Isn't there a detective who manages a boxer here?"

"Sure. Star Harald. Great boxer, about to turn pro. You oughta see that fight, at the Blue. Too late to get tickets, gonna be on the USA channel and all."

"Do you know him, this detective?"

"He's dead now." Mr. Gaines clucked. "Good manager. Knew the sport. He got shot. Murdered."

"Shot? That's awful. Did they catch who did it?"

"Sure did. His girl. She's went to jail for it, I think."

"His girl?" Judy echoed, as if she hadn't known. "Did you know her?"

"Nah. Not much. She was mean, you know? Never said nothin' to me, hung with the wives and girlfriends. Figured she was the one who done it, when I heard about it."

"Why? What made you think that?"

"Some people, they jus' bad." Mr. Gaines shook his head. "Wrong numbers, my mama use to call 'em. Now that girl, she was jus' a wrong number."

Judy worried. Everywhere she turned was a completely credible witness who thought Connolly was guilty, and Bennie wouldn't hear any of it. Rather, as Mr. Gaines would say, Bennie heard but she didn't listen.

"Now, Miss Judy, you want to talk lessons or not? You sign me the form, we can start nex' week."

"How about tomorrow morning?" she asked, and Mr. Gaines laughed.

31

Bennie worked in a fever, hauling box after box upstairs from the storage area in the basement of Della Porta's rowhouse. She'd convinced the superintendent that as Connolly's lawyer she had a right to her personal belongings, and he was reliably drunk enough to buy it. Bennie was hoping that reconstructing the apartment would help her to understand the way Connolly and Della Porta lived. Their relationship was the crux of the murder case and its subtleties could lead Bennie to useful evidence or a new angle. And part of her was driven to know more about Connolly, now that she looked more like her with her new haircut and makeup. She was mildly disappointed. The super had been too buzzed to notice her makeover.

Bennie piled boxes late into the night, a wall of almost forty of them in the living room, and surprisingly, the effort reinvigorated her. By the time she had the last box upstairs, it was almost two in the morning and she'd forgotten to call Grady. She tried him on her cell phone but there was no answer. He was undoubtedly sound asleep. She dropped the phone back into her purse, reached into her briefcase for the case file, and located the list of photos taken by the mobile crime unit. The MCU had been thorough, taking grisly but informative photos of the living room.

Bennie set the file down, tore the brown tape from the first box, and began to unpack. It took almost until dawn and left her lower back aching, but by the time she was finished, the apartment was completely reassembled. She walked from room to room, ending up in the doorway to the kitchen, which turned out to be well stocked. Della Porta had evidently been a cook; twenty cookbooks bearing his name inside sat atop the counter next to a Cuisinart. Heavy Calphalon cookware stocked the cabinets: an omelet pan, a middle- and large-size fry pan, even a tiny pan for melting butter. Eyeing the set, Bennie felt a twinge for his loss. Who could have killed Della Porta, and why?

She left the kitchen for the living room. Completely fitted out, it revealed sophisticated taste. The paintings on the front walls were original oils of city scenes by a fine artist named Solmssen: gas stations, storefronts, and a street in Manayunk that had the starkness of Edward Hopper. Over the dining room table hung an abstract watercolor, and a large reproduction of a Lichtenstein dominated the living area, its broad black lines showing a weepy comic-book blonde. Bennie stood staring at it. Interesting taste for a cop, but something about it troubled her.

She walked into the bedroom, which would have been equally classy if she had bothered to rebuild the heavy bed. She'd dragged up only the headboard, of antique brass, and rested it against the front wall according to the police photo. The hue of the brass told Bennie it was genuine, though its lightness suggested it was hollow. Matching pine nightstands flanked the bed, and in the corner stood the most unusual piece of all: an antique stand-up teacher's desk, which looked like a lectern on spindly legs. Bennie walked over to it and ran her fingers along the dense grain of its dark wood. The thing must have cost a fortune.

That was it. She whirled around. The cookware in the kitchen, the art in the living room, the antiques in the bedroom cost major money. That would be in addition to the rent, a thousand a month, which was straining even Bennie's finances. She had read in Della Porta's obit that his deceased parents were middle-class, so there was no family money. Certainly his managing a boxer suggested a man with an interest in making a killing. So how did Della Porta get this kind of money, on the police force? And why spend all the money on the inside, hidden, and not on the apartment itself? Why not move to a better neighborhood, even?

Though the answers would help her defense, they weren't ones Bennie welcomed.

32

"Where have you been, Bennie?" Grady asked, turning from the mirror in the bathroom. The unhappy downturn to his mouth was illuminated by a bare bulb hanging from a wire in the ceiling. His hair dripped from his morning shower and was still soggy at its curling ends. "It's six in the morning. You were out all night."

"I was working on Connolly." Bennie stood in the center dim hall, still awaiting a light fixture. A spray of black wires sprung from the ceiling like an electrical spider, for which Bennie was momentarily grateful. Grady wouldn't be able to see Connolly's haircut in the dark.

"Where were you working? You weren't at the office. I called and got your voice mail."

"I was at the crime scene. Where you off to, so early?"

"I have to be in King of Prussia by eight o'clock." Grady gave the Goody comb a shake and set it down. He was dressed for work in a light gray suit, white oxford shirt, and flowered Liberty tie. "The merger is on again and the venture capitalists want more changes. I don't know when we're gonna close. Also, the plumber never showed to put in the kitchen sink. The key was where you left it."

"Wonderful." Bennie scratched Bear's head as he sat at a floppy heel. "I have no time to call him."

"I'll do it. You get too damn crazy."

"Thanks. You finished in the bathroom? I need to shower. I have to get back to work." Bennie kicked off her pumps and Bear ambled off to sniff one.

"I see the press is smelling blood." Grady looked sympathetic. "You were all over the news on the radio. They're reporting that Connolly is your twin. Who do you think leaked that?"

"God knows." Bennie slipped off her jacket and blouse in the dark, shimmied out of her skirt, and dropped the entire outfit in a pile on the hall floor. "Hang tough. It's gonna get worse."

"Hey, did you get your hair cut or something?" Grady came over, squinting. They stood in the hall together, and Bennie hoped it was dark enough to conceal traces of her Connolly makeup, which she had wiped off. "I thought you liked it long," he said. "I do, too."

"I needed a change."

"Well, I can't see your hair too well," Grady said, fingering a strand. "But the rest of you looks pretty good." He gentled her into a kiss, cuddling her in his jacket. She would have lingered in his arms, but she broke the embrace, feeling vaguely undeserving.

"I have to get going. Sorry." Bennie put her head down and flicked off the light switch to hide her hair before she entered the bathroom.

But Grady stayed at the threshold. "Making any progress?"

"I hired an investigator," she offered, fully aware it was the least significant event of yesterday. Funny how one material omission could lead to another. Maybe not so funny. Bennie bent over the sink and twisted on the warm water, then soaped up her hands with an amber bar of

Neutrogena. "Now, don't you have work to do? Software companies to merge and acquire?"

"Did you see what I left you on the dining room table? I got some information about DNA testing from a lab down in Virginia. I found them on the Internet and they faxed me the application. The test costs about three hundred bucks and it's confidential. I think you should do it."

"DNA?" She lathered up and buried her face in warm water. "I'd feel funny about that."

"Why? It's reliable. I gave 'em a call and a researcher explained the whole process. They cut the DNA from the two blood samples and count the VNTRs, whatever they are. Identical twins have an unusually high number of matches of VNTRs. The test proves if someone is really your identical twin."

"I'm supposed to take Connolly's blood?" Bennie said, then caught herself wondering if she'd done that once already, in the womb. She splashed water on her cheeks.

"Connolly won't mind giving it, if she's really what she claims to be. You'll get an answer in seven to ten days. You'll know the truth."

Bennie twisted off the water and reached for a towel. The truth suddenly struck her as a disruption, a distraction from the case. She'd been trying to keep the personal issues separate from the legal, with less and less success. A DNA test would only make it worse, wouldn't it? She ducked into the clammy towel.

"Bennie?" Grady said. "I think you should do it."

"Maybe I will, but not now." She stuffed the towel onto the rack. "I appreciate what you did, but I don't see the point. I wouldn't have the answer by the trial anyway."

Grady pursed his lips. "I'll leave the application on the table, in case you change your mind."

"Fine." Bennie pushed aside the Plexiglas shower door, circa 1960s, which rumbled in its mildewed tracks. She turned on the water and it sputtered into the brown stain of the ancient tub she used to think was charming. "Christ. Sometimes I'm sorry we bought this house."

"Wait a minute." The light went on in the bathroom, and Grady gasped. "Bennie?" he said, disbelief in his voice. She turned to slip into the shower, but Grady caught her arm. Bennie felt her nakedness fully as he pulled her close, staring at her hair and face. A ribbon of water dribbled forgotten into the tub. "Your hair, it's like Connolly's."

"No, it isn't."

"Yes, it is. I saw her mugshot in the paper. Did you get your hair cut like her? You're trying to see if she's your twin?" Grady looked worried, his gray eyes slightly puffy behind his wire rims. Bennie guessed he hadn't slept well last night and felt a wave of responsibility for that. He deserved a straight answer.

"I'm dressing like Connolly to help her defense. The press has the story that we're twins, and I'm going to exploit the situation to her advantage. That's it. Now I have to take a shower. My new investigator's coming in this morning, I hope."

"So you're *trying* to look like Connolly?" Grady shook his head in wonderment. "When, at trial?"

"Yes, and before."

"Why before?"

"So it's not obvious that I started at trial."

Grady released her arm. "Don't you think that's beyond the pale?"

"Not at all." Bennie wished she could cover herself, even though locker rooms had cured her of any residual modesty. "Any lawyer would do it."

"No, they wouldn't. I'm a lawyer and I wouldn't."

"She's my client. I'm trying to save her life."

Grady set his jaw. "Bennie, this is not about your defense of a client. This is about you, trying to figure out your relationship to Connolly. If that's what you want to understand, take the blood test."

"You have it wrong. I'm doing everything in my power to get her off, and in this case, I happen to have one more weapon than usual."

"That's a rationalization. You're telling yourself you're going through all of this for professional reasons, but you're not." Grady examined her face, determined. "Listen, Connolly walks into your life and you don't know which end is up. The worst thing you can do is to lie to yourself."

"I'm not lying to myself. I'm representing my client."

"Her interests aren't the only ones at stake." Grady held her bare shoulders. "Slow down. It's one thing to walk into a dark room where you're familiar with the furniture. You can wander your own house with safety, navigate the space without seeing. But this isn't just the furniture getting rearranged, the whole landscape is changed. You're in a hotel room, in a new city. And the building's on fire."

"Oh, Christ, Grady." Bennie broke the embrace, more brusquely than she felt. She hated being naked right now and reached for the towel, snapping it from the rack and wrapping it around her body like armor. "Don't be dramatic."

"It's not dramatic, it's realistic. You're getting yourself into a position where there are no foundations for your emotional response. You've taken on the defense of a woman who might be your identical twin. Imagine that at the end of the trial, Connolly is found guilty of murder. Worse, she gets the death penalty."

"I thought of that already. I'm doing everything in my power to make sure that doesn't happen." Bennie turned away and waved a hand under the shower to test the water. It was ready, and so was she. "I won't lose."

"You could. You have to admit, you could. Cutting your hair, dressing like Connolly. You're destroying the emotional distance you need as her lawyer and at the same time telling yourself it was there all along. You're not in control, you're just telling yourself you're in control."

"Grady, I have to take a shower, I really do. I don't have time to discuss this." She dropped the towel, stepped inside the tub, and rolled the shower door shut. Water coursed over her head and she closed her eyes to Grady's wavy outline on the other side of the old Plexiglas.

"Ask Connolly about the DNA test," he called over the sound of the water. "Bet you twenty bucks she won't take it."

"I'll think about it."

"Ask her today. Prove me wrong. We'll talk tonight."

"I won't be home tonight." Water sluiced down Bennie's strong shoulders and down her slim tummy. "I have to work."

"I'm not letting you off the hook," Grady said, then left.

It wasn't until Bennie was toweling off after her shower that she permitted herself to think about whether Grady was right. Something in her resisted the notion and even counseled against considering it for too long, like a jinx. Bennie had to run Connolly's trial and direct her defense.

To win, she'd have to control the courtroom, command the attention of the jury and the respect of the judge. She had to believe in herself absolutely and couldn't afford to have her confidence shaken. She combed out her hair quickly and hurried to dress, but didn't once look in the mirror.

Book Two

So strongly and metaphysically did I conceive my situation then, that while earnestly watching his motions, I seemed distinctly to perceive that my own individuality was now merged in a joint stock company of two; that my free will had received a mortal wound; and that another's mistake or misfortune might plunge me into unmerited disaster or death.

—**Herman Melville,** *Moby-Dick*

33

Joe Citrone wrapped his plaid bathrobe around his lean frame and opened his front door just before breakfast, satisfied to find his newspaper delivered on time for a change. God knows what kept that kid half the time. When Joe was young he got up in the middle of the night to deliver the paper. The *Philadelphia Inquirer* was the morning paper then and the *Evening Bulletin* was what his father read when they sat down to dinner. Now Joe's father had passed and only the *Inquirer* was left. Half the time it didn't get delivered until after Joe's eggs.

He picked the paper off the stoop and straightened up, stiff again. DOUBLE TROUBLE: TWIN DEFENDS TWIN IN COP MURDER, read the headline. Joe shut the door and skimmed the newspaper story until he got to the only paragraph that interested him.

Early reports that Rosato's license to practice law had lapsed were unfounded, sources said today. The attorney was only technically in default on her yearly ethics requirements. According to one well-placed source at the Pennsylvania Bar Association, the lapse "should cast no reflection on Ms. Rosato's ethical standing or prevent her from undertaking any civil or criminal defense."

Strike one. It happens. They'd try again next time up at bat. Joe had options, plenty of them, but he didn't want to resort to them if they weren't necessary. The game had to be played an inning at a time.

Joe flipped to the sports page and scuffed into the kitchen as he read. The new rookie for the Phils was looking good, like he might pull the team out of the basement. The kid's name was on top of the stat sheets in eleven categories, including home runs and RBIs. Joe sat down at the head of the table, the sports page in front of him. In a minute, Yolanda would serve his scrambled eggs, runny the way he liked them, and he could already smell the coffee brewing for his first cup. He could study the stats in peace.

Joe believed in the stats, in numbers. They were scientific, exact. As a young man, he had wanted to be a businessman, maybe an actuary, when he grew up. The old man was against it. Didn't want his kid growing up better than him, the old Italian way. So Joe became a cop instead of a businessman. Then he found out they didn't have to be two different things.

He nodded when he heard the clink of a porcelain plate hitting the table on the other side of the newspaper. The egg smell wafted up, and Joe reached for his fork behind the paper. Next he heard the gurgle of coffee splashing into his cup. The paper said the rookie played like a vet, reminding everybody of Yastrzemski. Shit. Yaz. Suddenly the telephone rang, a jangling sound that disrupted the silent kitchen. Joe heard his wife hurry to the wall phone.

"Yes," Yolanda said. "Hold on. He's right here."

Joe kept reading. He knew who was on the telephone. He was in no hurry to get it. He waved a fork in the air.

"Can he call you back?" Yolanda asked into the receiver.

The phone call would be from Lenihan. He'd be all worked up about Rosato still being on the Della Porta case. Lenihan was too emotional. He would never play like a vet.

"He's in the middle of breakfast, Surf," Yolanda said. "It'll be only ten or fifteen minutes."

Joe shook his head.

"Maybe half an hour," Yolanda added, translating.

Joe frowned at the grainy photo of the rookie making an airborne catch. Kid had legs like a colt and he was tall. Statistically, taller men made better athletes. You name it, any sport. Also, tall men were more successful. It was true. Joe was tall.

"Okay, sorry, thanks. Yes . . . yes . . . I'll make sure he calls." Yolanda hung up the phone. "That was Surf," she said needlessly, and went back to the sink.

Joe nodded. Surf had nothing to worry about, because in the end, the stats held true. Joe always came out on top. He was a vet. He held the sports page to the side and scooped a forkful of buttery eggs into his mouth, where they melted.

Across town in an apartment, Surf Lenihan slammed the phone into its cradle on the nightstand. "Dammit!" he said, so loudly that his girlfriend stirred in her sleep and dragged a pillow over her head. She'd slept like the dead last night, but Surf hadn't caught a wink. He'd watched Howard Stern on the E! channel both times, because the Scores strippers were on, and then he caught a war movie before the early local news. It had the story about Rosato getting her license reinstated on the Connolly case. They had tape of her going in and out of her office.

Surf climbed out of bed and pulled on the navy-blue

pants of his summer uniform. He knew he shouldn't have left it to Citrone. The old man had gone about it all wrong. Got her license taken away. Leaked the twin story to the press. Like publicity would scare off a lawyer.

Surf slipped his shirt on and buttoned it up hastily. He couldn't let Citrone and the others screw this up. He couldn't wait around for them to get it straight. He grabbed his gun holster off the doorknob, looped it around his shoulder, and buckled it on as he headed for the apartment door.

34

Lou Jacobs had done his share of scuba diving, so he figured he knew something about being dropped in the middle of a completely different world. He'd swum with stingrays off the Keys, hung with barracuda during a wreck-dive, and once eyeballed a green-and-black octopus fluttering on the sea floor. But he had never entered a world as foreign as this one; it was all women. There wasn't another man in the joint, not even a messenger.

Lou gave his name to a receptionist with her hair in a tight braid, wondering if women could be as good lawyers as men. Sol Lubar, from the Thirty-seventh, had a woman lawyer for his divorce and she was a bitch on wheels. Lou should have had a lawyer that good when it came his turn. He'd lost the house, half his pension, and the friggin' cat. And it was Laurie who cheated on him. Lou shook his head, still pissed off sixteen years later.

"Is there a problem, Mr. Jacobs?" the receptionist asked, unsmiling.

Lou thought she needed to loosen up. A joke, maybe. "Hey," he said, "you know why divorce is so expensive?"

"Why?"

"Because it's worth it."

The receptionist didn't smile, but Lou didn't give up easy.

"Okay, you don't like that one? Here's another. What's the difference between a lawyer and a prostitute?"

The receptionist blinked at him.

"A prostitute stops screwing you when you're dead."

The receptionist blanched. "That's disgusting."

It was his best joke. Lou thought it was funny as hell, but he decided to clam up and let the fish have the whole damn ocean. Later, when the receptionist told him Rosato was ready for him, he followed his nose to Rosato's office, leaned in the doorway, and tried again. "Rosato. Stop me if you heard this one. What's the difference between a lawyer and a prostitute?"

"A tax bracket?" Bennie said, looking up.

"No, but that's good."

"How about 'nothing?'"

"Better." Lou laughed gruffly. "That was a test. I guess I'm reporting for duty."

"Wonderful!" Bennie eyed him, in his crisp navy-blue blazer, dark pants, and a white business shirt. The only dissonant note was a brown tie of shiny artificial fibers. "What is it with cops and ties?"

"What is it with women and hair?"

"What?"

Lou made a circle with his finger. "You changed your hair. Why do women do that?"

"To confuse cops."

Lou's eyes went flinty. "I'm here to take the job, Rosato, so don't start with me. Bad enough you got a buncha hens up here."

"They didn't bite, did they?"

"No, but they didn't laugh either. It's a great joke, admit it."

"I admit it." Bennie smiled. "Now, let's get started. Why don't you sit down?"

"I like to stand up." Lou folded his arms.

"Suit yourself. I'll begin at the beginning." Bennie gulped some coffee and briefed Lou on the case, holding back her suspicion that Della Porta may have been crooked. She wanted to follow up on that lead herself and didn't know Lou well enough to trust him. In her experience, a cop's sense of loyalty was even worse than an Italian's. "You were a uniformed cop, right, Lou?"

"For forty years, until last year."

"That's quite a career. You just retired?"

"Yep, and hating every minute of it. That's why I got the security job."

"What was your district?"

"The Fourth."

"That's South Philly. So you've canvassed neighbors before."

Lou smiled. "In my sleep."

"Good." Bennie sipped her coffee, which never seemed hot enough. "That's your first assignment. I want you to meet Della Porta's neighbors. Find out what they saw Connolly do that night. Get the details, too, like what Connolly was wearing. I want to know what they'll say on the stand."

"I know the drill."

"Also, find out if any of them saw Connolly throw something in the Dumpster in the alley. That's the D.A.'s story and not all of it jibes. For one thing, no gun turned up. If she was getting rid of evidence, why not dump the gun?"

"Nobody said bad guys were smart. They make stupid mistakes all the time."

"Well, see what you can find out. I'll give you a copy of the file. Read it before you go."

"When you want this neighborhood survey done?"

"Right now. You got a bus to catch?"

Lou shrugged. "No."

"Good." Bennie stood up. "I have to get going, but I want to introduce you to the lawyer you'll be working with. She's only done one survey, but she's one of my best young lawyers." Bennie pressed the intercom button on her telephone. "DiNunzio?" she said into the receiver. "You busy?"

35

"Jesus!" Connolly said. She rose in astonishment on the other side of the Formica counter when Rosato banged into the interview room. "Look at you!"

"Tell me about it."

"You look exactly like me! You haircut is the same, and that eye makeup!"

"I did it myself."

"No kidding." Connolly burst into laughter.

"I'll get better." Bennie did a model's spin-turn and came up smiling. With her new makeover, she felt giddily like an actress playing a role. That the role may actually have been the truth added a thrill Bennie couldn't quite ignore. She shut the door behind her, locking the impostor in with the original and not being absolutely sure which was which.

"How'd you do that, overnight?"

"I got a new haircut and a bad attitude." Bennie swung her briefcase onto the counter. She didn't need Connolly's verification to tell her the transformation had been successful. The prison guards had stared when they patted her down, undoubtedly primed by the newspaper coverage. "It's all part of the master plan."

"Which is?"

"We play twins, at trial," she began, and briefed Connolly on the rationale. Connolly sat down, leaning forward over the counter as Bennie spoke, the story sounding better and better.

"It's amazing," Connolly said when Bennie had finished.

"It's risky, though. You have to follow my rules or it'll blow up in our faces. I control all communication about the trial and about us. At no time do you speak to the press. About anything. You don't even say 'no comment.' I don't want your voice heard. Got it?"

"Yes."

"Don't talk to anybody here about this conversation. Understood? This is confidential trial strategy. If word gets out it's intentional, it'll kill us."

"You mean, me," Connolly said, her expression suddenly grave enough to reassure Bennie.

"Good. Now. We have to talk about Della Porta. I went back to the apartment last night and got it in order the way you two had it."

"You what? My place? Jeez, you're full of surprises."

"So was the apartment. Tell me why everything in it is so expensive."

"What do you mean?"

"The art, the kitchen stuff. Anthony made about fifty grand a year as a detective, right?"

"Right."

"Did he have any source of income other than that? Family, stocks? Or from boxing?"

"No way. Anthony's family is long gone, and Star was a money drain. Anthony spent all his own money on his training, plus the uniforms, the equipment, advertising, the whole thing. That's why he needed the backers."

"What about other sources of income?" Bennie unzipped

her briefcase and tugged out a legal pad. "Did you give him any money?"

"Nothing. I didn't have it."

"Where'd he get all that money then?"

Connolly looked puzzled. "I always figured he made it. I never saw the bills. He handled everything. It was his place and his money, and the stuff was all there from before I came."

"Not on that salary." Bennie edged forward on her seat. "Are you sure Della Porta couldn't have been involved in any kind of corruption?"

"Anthony? No way. I told you before, he was straight as an arrow."

"Isn't it possible that this dispute in the past, between Anthony and the other two cops, Reston and McShea, involved corruption of some kind?"

"Like what?"

"Maybe Reston and McShea were taking money and they wanted Anthony involved and he turned them down. Or maybe Anthony was in with them in the past, before he met you, taking money, and then he stopped?"

"No way. At least, I don't know. All I know is the cops jumped all over themselves pointing the finger at me."

"Did you ever hear or see any kind of unusual discussions between Della Porta and other cops, like at the board meetings you told me about?"

"No. I think they talked girls and boxing."

Bennie thought a minute. The boxing angle troubled her, but she wanted to follow up on the police lead first. She knew the terrain better and something told her it smelled. "Anthony was a homicide detective. Did any of his cases have anything to do with the murder of drug dealers or drug busts?"

"Sure, they had to, but he never talked about work. He didn't like to bring it home."

"Did he ever have any sources or snitches who were involved with drugs?"

"Not that I heard him say. I didn't know anything about his business."

"When he was a uniformed officer, did he bust a lot of drug dealers?"

"I didn't know him then."

Bennie eased back in her chair, momentarily stumped. It was hot in the airless room, and she felt Connolly's confused gaze on her, as well as the vigilant stare of the guard behind the smoked security glass. It didn't fit, but she was slipping into solving the murder instead of preparing the defense. Going to Della Porta's apartment last night had screwed up her focus.

"When do I get outta here?" Connolly asked suddenly. "Trial starts Monday. I haven't seen the outside in a year, except for that hearing."

"They'll move you right before the trial, probably Sunday night or Monday morning. During the trial you'll stay in a holding cell in the Criminal Justice Center."

"I can't wait. Free!" Connolly waved her arms gleefully in the cramped room, and for the first time Bennie caught a glimpse of the child in the woman. She almost felt Connolly's happiness, a thrill flittering through her like a shadow. Could Connolly truly be her twin? Bennie thought of Grady and their conversation in the bathroom.

"You know, my boyfriend thinks we should take a DNA test," Bennie blurted out. "To see if we're twins for real."

"What?" Connolly's face fell, her smile evaporated, and

her arms dropped like a bird shot from the sky. "You still don't believe me? You want to test my DNA?"

Bennie felt a twinge. She'd hurt Connolly at the one moment her guard was down. "I wasn't suggesting it, necessarily. I have some information about a lab that does DNA testing. We send blood samples off and in seven days or so, we know the truth. Apparently they do this sort of testing all the time."

Connolly nodded. "Well, let's do it, then."

"What?" Bennie asked, surprised at the turnaround.

"Let's do it, huh? I'll give my sample today. Will you arrange to get it sent to them, or whatever?"

"I don't get it. What changed your mind?"

"Here's your chance to know the truth," Connolly said quickly, though her tone held no rancor. "You don't have to believe me or take it on faith. You'll have proof, if that's what you need. Set it up. They take blood samples for court in the infirmary. In fact, let's take care of it right now, while you're here."

"Now?" Bennie said, caught off-guard, but Connolly was on her feet.

"Guard!" she called out, turning around. "Yo! Guard!"

Bennie roared away from the prison in the Expedition, distracted. Connolly had given a blood sample at the prison and they'd arranged to send it to the lab to preserve the chain of custody and eliminate contamination. If Connolly would so quickly put it to the test, maybe there was truth to the twin story. There was only one way to find out. Bennie would have to give her own sample. The hospital was on the way back to the office.

She braked at a red light. Cars slowed in the line of noontime traffic and wiggly waves of heat snaked from their hoods. Bennie wasn't sure what to do. She could go back to the office or stop by the hospital. The results would take a week. She felt her heart beating harder and tried to ignore it. Her face felt flushed and she ratcheted up the air-conditioning. She wanted to know the truth, didn't she?

Bennie stared at the traffic light, burning bloodred into her brain. She felt as if she were looking into her own heart. When the light turned green, she yanked the steering wheel to the right and headed for the hospital.

36

The boxing gym was light, with bright sun pouring through its large storefront, though it served only to illuminate every speck of dust and dirt. Judy, in a gray sweatsuit, held out her hands while Mr. Gaines wrapped Ace bandages around her palms and wrists, then stuffed a pair of red boxing gloves on her. They looked like cartoon mittens, except for the duct tape repairing splits at the top. Red headgear covered her forehead and cheeks in cushioned leather, exposing only her eyes. She felt as awkward as the Pillsbury Doughboy when Mr. Gaines began teaching her the fundamentals of a boxing stance.

"Left foot forward, a little out more," he said.

"Sorry." Judy corrected her feet. "I can't twirl spaghetti either."

Mr. Gaines smiled. "Put your right foot back a little. Gotta get your stance right. Gotta get the fundamentals. Gotta bad stance, you like a house gonna fall down. Got it? Like a house gonna fall down when the wolf comes. You know that story?"

"Sure." Judy placed her feet where she thought they should be and double-checked in the mirror. The glass reflected a full gym, with maybe ten men training. Most were shadowboxing, but there was a half-hearted sparring match and men using the equipment. The thumping, thudding, and pounding sounds made a constant drumbeat as glove met bag, body, and headgear. A man on the heavy bag shouted "Hah," "Hah," each time he connected with a jab, syncopating the rhythms. Judy kept an eye on the boxers as she adjusted her stance. "Better, Mr. Gaines?"

"Good. Right. Now, when you gotta move, you keep your feet in that stance. Got it? Gotta have the foundation or the house gonna fall down."

"Okay." Judy obeyed, but it was hard to move in the awkward position and she ended up with her right foot in front. "Damn."

"S'all right. S'all right, you'll get it. You gotta work on this. Gotta get this right. Com'ere, lemme show you what I mean." Mr. Gaines grabbed Judy by her sweatshirt and led her over to a table outside the ring. Paint peeled off the table, which was actually a front door onto which someone had hammered splayed legs, and on the table sat a folded *Daily News*, a bottle of Mr. Clean, and a plastic jug of water with a dirty glass. Mr. Gaines grabbed the jug and glass from the table, then held both over a steel wastecan full of trash. "Pay attention, now. You payin' attention?"

"Sure."

"You gotta be in the right place in the ring. See this?" Mr. Gaines poured water from the jug beside the glass and it splashed into the wastebasket. "See what I mean? Ain't in the right place. Won't work. Not he'ppin'. Not doin' nothin' for you. Now watch." Mr. Gaines moved the glass under the stream of water and it filled the glass. "See now? It's in the right place. All ready. Doin' the right thing. You gotta be in the right place. Got it?"

"Got it." Judy smiled. She had already noticed that Mr. Gaines had a way to explain even the simplest principle. She wished he had a way to catch a killer.

"Now let's get back to work," he said, and led her back to the mirror. "Get your stance, now. Remember what I told you."

Judy stood in position, foot-conscious as a girl at her first dance, and checked the mirror. From this angle she spotted something she hadn't seen before. An attractive young woman sitting against the far wall, knitting. The woman's hair hung in moussed waves around a delicate oval face, with dark and penciled brows. She wore tight jeans and a waist-length leather jacket with black spike-heeled boots.

"What you lookin' at?" Mr. Gaines asked, and Judy snapped to attention.

"That woman, knitting. Who is she?"

"One of the wives."

"Whose wife?"

"Boy on the bag. Danny Morales."

"She's here a lot?"

"All the time. Now, keep your mind on your job here. You come to gossip or box?"

"Box."

"Then box, woman."

Judy didn't have much time. Her boxing lesson was over and she had to get back to the office. She was stretching plausibility with her story of a two-hour doctor's appointment, even with a gynecologist. They overbooked with less guilt than an airline, but there was a limit. Judy crouched next to her gym bag and packed it slowly, watching the young woman with the knitting. Her husband pounded the speedbag next to her. Mr. Gaines had said Connolly hung with the wives. Maybe Mrs. Morales knew something.

Ba-bum, ba-bum, ba-bum, went the speedbag, smacking

the plywood backboard and swinging back for more pun-ishment. Morales punched the bag with the outside of his gloves, his tattooed arms high and his elbows spread side-ways like wings. His wife glanced up from her knitting to watch him, though the boxer concentrated on the drub-bing he gave the speedbag, lost in a trance sustained by the rhythms of his own violence.

Judy zipped her gym bag closed, straightened up, and walked casually in their direction. *Ba-bum, ba-bum, ba-bum*; the sound grew louder. She walked past Morales and stopped next to his wife, who didn't look up from her knit-ting. "I always wanted to learn to knit," Judy said loudly.

The young woman looked up in surprise, her lacquered fingers frozen at her row of tight stitches. Morales stopped hitting the speedbag, which flopped back and forth on the squeaking chain, and glared at Judy. "What did you say to her?" he demanded.

"Uh, nothing really," Judy answered, taken aback. Behind Morales she saw Mr. Gaines, who had stopped coaching another fighter and was watching vigilantly. "I was just trying to learn about knitting."

"Oh, yeah?" Morales blinked perspiration from his eyes, revealing a prominent brow that crumpled with the force of his anger. "Buy a book."

"Danny, Danny," Mr. Gaines called out, shuffling bandy-legged to Morales. He waved an arm in the air as if he were hailing a cab. "Ain't no call for that now. Tha's Judy, Judy Forty. She one of my students."

Morales grinned crookedly. "A chick, takin' lessons here?"

"She a boxer to me, tha's all," Mr. Gaines said. "You should rightly be sayin' welcome to her. He'p bring her along."

Judy felt a guilty pang. Mr. Gaines was standing up for her, and she had lied to him. "That's all right, Coach."

"No, Danny here can introduce himself, he want to be polite. You might like meetin' a famous boxer. Danny has twenty-five fights, twenty-four by knockout, only one by decision. He's comin' up to his first twelve-rounder in a coupla months."

Morales relaxed, apparently soothed by his credentials, and nodded at Judy. "Danny Morales. You a friend of Mr. G's, I'm happy to meet you. Anythin' you wanna know about this sport, you ask. History, pointers, what-not. I don't mind."

"Thank you, Danny. I didn't catch your wife's name," Judy said, and the young woman smiled, apparently pleased at the unaccustomed attention.

"Ronnie, Ronnie Morales," she said. "Anytime you want to know about knitting, you just ask."

Judy took a step closer. "What are you making?"

"A scarf, for Danny." She put a slim finger to her lips. "But don't tell him. It's supposed to be a surprise."

Morales almost smiled. "Like I didn't know. She knit me two scarves and a sweater already."

"You're a lucky man," Judy said, and the conversation stalled. She couldn't talk to Ronnie with her husband there. They had to go where no man could. "Uh, Ronnie, do you know where a ladies' room is? I know they have a locker room, but we can't wash up there, can we?"

"It's around the back. You have to use the janitor's closet."

"I didn't see it. Is it hard to find?"

"Kind of. You want me to show it to you?" Ronnie asked, setting her knitting aside.

"Sure," Judy said, as casually as possible. "Lead on."

37

Bennie hustled into her office with a freshly poured mug of coffee and pushed aside her phone messages, correspondence, and other case notes. Connolly had become the only priority. It was Thursday, for God's sake. Bennie slipped out of her jacket and caught sight of the Band-Aid in the crook of her elbow, then fingered the bumpy red blot in the middle. Her blood; Connolly's blood. In a week she would know if they were the same. The possibility seemed more likely since the test, though Bennie knew her thinking wasn't completely rational.

She sat down in her padded desk chair, and the sun streamed through the window behind her, reminding her like a tap on the shoulder that the day was almost over. She went through her papers to find the police chronology. It was the weakest part of the prosecution's case, and she intended to weaken it to the breaking point.

"Incident Report," read the slip of white paper. These were the papers that Carrier had applied to the court for and which had been released, albeit in severely redacted form. The documents looked as insignificant as newsstand receipts, but were among the most critical documents in a criminal case. Usually they constituted a chronological recounting of the police activity at the crime scene, but in this case they didn't explain how the hell Reston and

McShea got to the scene so fast. There was only one set of documents left to consult, the transcripts of the telephone calls that came into 911.

Bennie pulled the transcripts for that night. The first call had come in at 8:07, with a positive ID. Not so good for the defense, but the caller, a neighbor named Lambertsen, didn't say when she heard the gunshot. Interesting, because Bennie wanted to pinpoint that. She read down further, to the police response. The first response was a minute later, exactly. Bennie made a note and kept reading. There were more calls reporting the gunshot and Connolly running down the street, which Bennie read with increasing dismay. The Commonwealth would parade these witnesses to the stand. The cumulative effect would devastate the defense.

Bennie shook off her fear. She had to find the soft spots in the prosecution, and they were there, she just sensed it. Sunlight moved onto her papers in an oblique shadow that reminded her of her last visit with her mother and she realized she hadn't spoken with her mother's doctor in days. She should call. It would only take a minute. Bennie reached for the phone, punched in the number, and identified herself when they picked up.

"The doctor's been trying to reach you all morning, Miss Rosato," said the receptionist.

Bennie was puzzled. The doctor had wanted to reach her? She hadn't seen his phone message. She tucked the phone in the crook of her neck and thumbed hurriedly through her pink messages. Dr. Provetto, at 9:13 A.M. Dr. Provetto, at 11:45 A.M. My God. Why was he calling? Bennie's heart leapt to her throat the moment she heard the doctor's voice.

38

Judy had discovered that a janitor's closet was really an open toilet near a string mop. The walls were streaked with grime and a gritty Rubbermaid bucket sat under a streaked washbasin. The toilet paper holder was empty and two half rolls of toilet paper were lined up on the tank next to an old copy of *Sports Illustrated*. Judy washed her hands in the basin. "So," she asked, "is knitting hard? It looks hard."

"No, it's easy." Ronnie Morales lingered at the door and checked her hair in a cracked mirror over the sink. She wore light eye makeup but no foundation and her skin was poreless over cheekbones that shaped her face like a Valentine's Day heart. "I taught myself from a book. That's what Danny meant. I could teach you in five minutes. I even have some needles for you, thick ones to start with. I'll bring them for you."

"Thanks," Judy said, surprised at the offer. It struck her that Ronnie Morales was a woman who needed a friend.

"No problem." Ronnie folded her arms against the shiny black of her form-fitting leather jacket. "I knit lots of things. Sweaters for Danny and my mom and sister, some baby clothes for my new nephew, and a vest for my grandfather."

"So you enjoy it."

"No, I hate it," Ronnie said with a giggle. "I'll teach you if you want, but it's totally boring. Doing your nails is more fun than knitting."

"Why do you do it, then?" Judy's hands dripped while she looked around for paper towels.

"For something to do. There's no TV here. I read the new magazines as soon as they come out, then I got nothing to do when Danny's trainin'."

"Do you watch him train every day?" Judy gave up her search and wiped her hands on her sweatpants.

"I have to." Ronnie squinted in the mirror. "Danny says I'm his good luck charm."

"He needs luck with a speedbag?"

Ronnie smiled, then stopped like it was against the rules. "He's a real good fighter. His manager thinks he'll be famous. Be one of the great ones."

"Don't you get bored, though? I mean, even if I loved someone, I might get bored watching him all day."

"Sure I get bored. That's why I knit." Her mouth pursed slightly, wrinkling an upper lip like a Cupid's bow. "Danny is the jealous type."

"Then why does he bring you to the gym? There's nothing but men here."

"He likes to know where I am. Not that I ever cheated on him or nothin'. Not ever. I never would. I mean, *never*." Ronnie watched herself in the mirror as she tossed her head. "You're takin' lessons with Mr. Gaines?"

"Uh, yeah," Judy said, catching up with the abrupt change of subject.

"Not many women in the gym, that's why we don't have no ladies' room. Only women here usually are the other wives. Even they don't come in much anymore."

"Too bad. I'm new in town. It would be nice to meet them. Make friends."

"You ain't missin' nothin'. They're like a group, you know. They think they're all that. There's Juan's wife,

Maria, and Mickey, he's a heavyweight, and his wife, Ceilia. Ceilia is a bitch, I tell you. The only nice one was Valencia, Miguel's girlfriend, but she's gone." Ronnie's smooth forehead wrinkled. "She went to prison."

"Jeez, prison? What for?"

"They said she was selling coke."

"Selling cocaine?" Judy hid her surprise. It was amazing how much you could learn from another woman in a ladies' room, even a crummy ladies' room.

"I don't think Valencia did that, though. She was friendly with the wives. She was friendly with everybody, you know. I always wondered, you know, what's up with them. *They* mighta been doin' business, you know, from *them* I could believe it. But Valencia would never do nothin' like that. She was a wonderful mother."

"You don't think she sold coke?"

"I can't say for sure, you know. I only went out with them once, 'cause of Danny. He didn't like it." Ronnie's voice trailed off. "Not Valencia, though. Valencia was a good person, you know. Now this white girl, she acted like she owned Valencia. She was with the man who managed Star. You know, Star."

"Star?" Judy said, playing dumb, which wasn't easy for a Law Review editor.

"Star Harald. He's turning pro next. He's almost as good as Danny. It was his manager, his girlfriend. I forget her name. This girl, she wasn't even a wife and she acted like she owned everybody, the whole gym." Ronnie's voice grew dishy. "A redhead, dressed like a whore, too. She's in jail now because she killed him."

"She killed her boyfriend? How do you know?"

Ronnie moved a curl from her eyes. "Everybody knows that."

39

Bennie's world lurched to a stop after she hung up the telephone. Her fingers gripped the walnut edge of her desk and she stiffened in her chair. She knew she was breathing but it was soundless, as if she were afraid to draw breath. Or felt she wasn't entitled to, now.

Sunlight from her office window fell on her back but she couldn't feel its warmth. Motes of dust floated through a sunbeam, but she couldn't focus on them. The shadow cast across the Connolly file was her own, but it looked like a cardboard cutout of a human being. Like a silhouette used for target practice, with a hole blown through its heart.

Bennie fought to keep her breathing even, her head clear, her eyes dry. Square buttons lit up on her phone, silently blinking on and off, and beyond her closed door she could hear the secretaries joking with each other. Everything was the same, yet nothing would be the same from now on.

The news confounded her. It seemed astounding that the only inevitable fact should be profoundly inconceivable when it happened. Bewildering that an event Bennie had thought about, even planned for, should take her completely by surprise, especially given her mother's illness. Her depression had been a lethal tug-of-war in which every day of life was a victory, and her mother had finally won.

Her mother had won freedom from a life of torment, of whispers in the night, of fears. Hers was an empty life, a hollow one. That was inconceivable, too. Life was supposed to be full of productive work and of simple pleasures; the laughter of children, the crunch of a fresh apple, the warmth of a soft blanket. Sharp pencils and good, thick books. Life wasn't supposed to be dark with nightmares; brief interludes of clarity in a world of confusion, made blacker because its origins were so unjustified, and unjustifiable.

Bennie felt her throat constrict. It was unfair; unjust. It occurred to her, for the first time, that that's what her own life had been about. A fight for justice where there wasn't any. The urge to set things right when they had gone terribly wrong. Not in courtrooms, though that's what Bennie had always thought until this very minute. Her life was about justice where it mattered. In life. In her mother's life.

She sat still for one more minute, then got up, grabbed her handbag, and walked silently out of her office and through her law firm. She said not a word to anyone, just avoided their curious eyes, even Marshall's, who had taken the doctor's messages and probably guessed what had happened.

Bennie got into the elevator and traveled to the basement garage, then found her car keys in the bottom of her purse and chirped the Ford unlocked. She climbed into the truck, twisted on the ignition, and reversed out of the parking space. A red word lit up on the dashboard, BRAKE, and she yanked up the emergency brake. She acted on autopilot and the only thought in her head was a mild surprise at the number of acts it took to get out of the parking lot and to the hospital:

Insert monthly pass card in slot.

Drive out of garage.

Turn left onto Locust.

Cruise to the corner.

Stop at the red light.

So many tasks to perform, each one discrete and identifiable. Bennie set her mind to performing each task, in the logical order, and so survived the minutes after she learned her mother had passed from the face of this earth.

"She wasn't alone," Hattie sobbed, her coarse, dark cheeks streaked with tears.

Bennie hugged the nurse, holding her firmly, as if she could send strength through her very skin. Hattie had taken care of Bennie's mother for a decade, had been at her side through all of the hospitalizations, the electroshock, and the chemicals. And now this. Bennie, dry-eyed, was grateful to Hattie once again. Her mother hadn't died alone.

"She suffered so much," Hattie said, but Bennie couldn't bear to hear that. She squeezed Hattie closer and buried her face in Hattie's marcelled waves, bleached canary yellow. Her hair was stiff and perfumed from processing, but Bennie took comfort in it just the same.

"My poor baby," Hattie murmured, and Bennie didn't know Hattie had thought of her mother that way. Sobs wracked Hattie's soft, heavy body, and she sagged in Bennie's arms. Bennie walked her over to a chair, gentled her into it, and sat beside her. There was a closed door on the other side of the room. Her mother's body was inside.

"I don't know why they tellin' me she was fine," Hattie said, her tears turning to anger, then back again. Bennie squeezed her until her crying became hiccups and then sputtered to a wheezy stop. The room fell quiet, and Bennie found the silence somehow harder to take. The lump in her throat seemed to calcify. She imagined a plate of bone growing over her chest, shielding her heart from the outside world and sealing her emotions within.

"Are you the family?" interrupted a man's voice, and Bennie turned and looked up. An oily-faced gentleman in a dark suit, with a small mustache and earnest eyes, looked puzzled at the hysterical black woman embraced by the businesslike blonde. "My name is James Covella, from Covella's Funeral Home. Are you the family?"

"Yes," Bennie answered, her voice thick.

"I'm sorry for your terrible loss. We've come for Mrs. Rosato," he said. Discreetly behind him waited a collapsible metal gurney. The sight of it caught Bennie by the throat.

"Not yet," she said firmly. "Not just yet." She halted the man with a large, trembling hand, disentangled herself from Hattie, and rose to her feet to say good-bye. Only after she had slipped inside her mother's room did she permit herself the luxury of breaking down.

40

Alice didn't know what came over her but she felt rammy all of a sudden. She couldn't take it anymore. She had to get out. She had to be free. There was only one skinny window on the unit, and she looked out as she stood, her feet shifting back and forth in the lunch line. "Move up," she said to the inmate in front of her, who obeyed.

Alice felt crazy. It must be the house. It was getting to her today. She couldn't figure out why. She inched forward in the line, trying to keep a lid on it. What was going on? She should have been feeling good; she was that morning when she met with Rosato, but sometime around lunch she got funky. Got a hinky feeling, like something bad was going down.

Alice laughed at herself. Of course she was antsy. Something bad *was* going down. That thing with Shetrell. Somebody trying to whack her. Alice looked around for the eightieth time that morning. Shetrell and Leonia had already gotten their food, they were ahead of her where she could see them. They wouldn't try anything at lunch anyway, in the open. Alice should have felt safe. But she didn't.

She reached the front of the line and grabbed her floppy ham sandwich, strawberry yogurt, and canned fruit, and walked to the table where she always sat, farthest from the others. The tables were bolted to the floor on the common area of the unit, which was ringed by two tiers of cells, fifteen above and fifteen below; most of the bottom tier was double-celled for low-seniority inmates. Inmates spent every minute of every day with the same group of women, for decades.

Alice yanked out a steel chair with a back that said PHILADELPHIA CIVIC CENTER, for some reason. The floor was a washed-out blue-and-white linoleum and the walls were whiter than white, from slave labor. Alice had counted the tiles in the unit's common area several hundred times. She'd come up with eighty-seven tiles each time.

She knew her cage by heart. She could close her eyes and point to where the TV was mounted, high so it couldn't be destroyed. She could see in her sleep the handmade drawings the inmates taped up on the unit walls; DISCIPLINE, TRUST, RESPECT, read the Magic Marker captions. Stick figures held hands under hearts and flowers. Alice wanted to rip them off the wall.

Instead she sipped her coffee, feeling the stiff Band-Aid in the crook of her arm where her blood had been taken. So she'd had her bluff called. It was the only way to keep Rosato cool. The results wouldn't be back until the trial was over. Alice would be long gone. She took a bite of sandwich and hunched over her tray, the way she always did, facing the window. She kept her back to the other tables and so didn't see what was happening between Shetrell and Leonia.

Shetrell sat at the lunch table before her tray, her gaze on Leonia, who sat down in the only empty seat, on the other side of Taniece. *Damn*. Leonia was supposed to sit right next to Shetrell. What a screw-up. Taniece had taken Leonia's seat. Bitch shouldn'ta sat in the way like that. Shoulda known better. "Who tol' you you could sit here?" Shetrell snapped at Taniece.

Taniece looked over. "What I do?"

"Leonia always sit here. You not suppose to be sittin' here."

"I don't have to ax your permission where I sit!"

"Hey!" shouted the guard, and Shetrell shut up. It was Dexter Raveway, Dexter the Pecker. He was a good-lookin' brother but he knew it, standin' behind the guard desk at the front of the room, scratchin' his johnson half the time. She figured he had somethin' goin' with Taniece and that was why Taniece picked lunchtime to mess with her. "Shetrell, that's enough," Dexter shouted. "Don't be bossin' everybody around, now."

Shetrell slunk low in her chair. She couldn't get another write-up, she'd end up in the hole.

"Hmph," Taniece said, like a church lady, and Shetrell glared at Leonia, who nodded.

Shetrell had to think of something. Her eyes rested on her tray, then she spotted somethin' move on the floor under the table, between everybody's sneakers. A cockroach, a big fat brown mother, struttin'. She watched the roach hustle along the linoleum and stop at the table leg. Tryin' to decide what to do. Whether to come up or not.

Come on, baby, Shetrell was thinking. *Come to Mama.* She snagged a piece of bread from her tray and let her hand drop to her side, easy so it didn't look like nothin' was goin' on. Maybe the roach would get the smell. *Come on, sugar. Mama gonna take care of you.* Shetrell watched the roach try to make up its little roach mind. He stopped like a married man, right at the edge. Couldn't go no further. *Come on, baby.*

The roach didn't even have to think twice. It skittered up the table leg, and Shetrell dipped her shoulder, snatched it off, and closed it in her hand. She waited until Taniece turned away, then dropped the roach in the bitch's strawberry yogurt.

Taniece cried out when she spotted a dark bulge moving on her plate. "There's somethin' in my food! A mouse! A rat!" She jumped up and shrieked like she was in a horror movie, and Shetrell woulda laughed her ass off if she hadn't been so worried about gettin' the shank to Leonia.

"A rat! A rat in the food! There's a rat in my food!" Taniece yelled. Her chair fell over, then she stumbled backward and fell on top of it, while Breanna, next to her, leapt away from her tray, knocking into another girl. Shetrell watched everybody jump outta their seats. The white trash shook like they saw a steady job.

"Relax, relax, I'm on it," Dexter the Pecker said, runnin' over like Wesley Snipes to save the day.

Taniece was doin' the freak. "It's a rat, I saw it, it's a rat! It's in my yogurt!" she said, grabbing Dexter's arm. "I was eatin' that!"

Pussy, Shetrell thought. *Get over yourself.*

"Calm down, everybody, calm down," Dexter said, but nobody was listening. "It's just a roach, it's not a rat." He didn't call any other guards, which was just fine with Shetrell. She edged back from the crowd, pretending to be afraid, and saw Leonia backing up, too, meeting her from the other direction. Now was her chance.

Shetrell bumped her way backward, slipped her hand into the elastic of her pants, and slid the shank out. Leonia stood next to Shetrell, grabbed the knife, and acted like she was falling down. Shetrell couldn't see it, but she figured Leonia slipped the shank in her sneaker, under her pants leg. The girl was damn good. She used to snatch wallets at The Gallery.

"Did you get it?" Shetrell yelled, like she was callin' to Dexter about the roach. Out the corner of her eye, she saw Leonia laughin' and knew she got it, all right.

"It's just a roach. It's all taken care of," Dexter said, holding Taniece's tray high over the heads of the women, who were just starting to calm down.

"You better get me another lunch, I ain't eatin' that crap!" Taniece shouted. "I'm gonna *sue* this place!"

Alice turned in her seat to see what the commotion was all about, barely interested. A mouse in Taniece's food. What a lovely hotel. She'd be gone in days. But it didn't leave her much time to take care of Valencia. Alice took a final slug of coffee and crumpled her Styrofoam cup. She gathered her tray, the food unfinished, and walked through the tables to where Valencia was chattering with the other *chiquitas*. Valencia looked up, and Alice leaned down and whispered in her ear, "I heard something from my lawyer. Meet me after head count tonight. The guard will come to you. Don't tell anybody or it won't happen."

"Than' you so much," Valencia said softly.

"You can thank me tonight," Alice told her.

41

For Bennie the next few hours were a haze of acute pain mixed with the oddly mundane business of burying the dead. Tasks had to be performed, and she performed each one. She selected her mother's casket, burial plot, and even last dress, of beige chiffon with tan pumps, with a minimum of tears. She found a valuable ally in the funeral director, with his moussed pompadour and professional smoothness, who scheduled her mother's wake, funeral, and burial in a way that had a pat beginning, middle, and end. In death as in life.

Bennie kept her emotions at bay only because she was so skilled at it. She held tight to Hattie throughout, as much for her own support as for the nurse's, and stopped only to leave a message.

"Hey," Bennie said as the associate answered the call. "I guess you heard."

"Yes, I'm so sorry," Judy said. "Is there anything I can do?"

"Thanks, yes. Draft a letter to Guthrie and tell him what happened. The wake is Friday night, funeral is Saturday, and we'll need a week postponement of the Connolly trial. If we ask for a week, he'll probably give us three days. I'll stop in and sign the letter tonight, then you get it hand-delivered tomorrow."

"No, I meant, is there anything I can do for you? Not about the case."

"Do for the case, you'll be doing for me. Any updates?"

"Yes. Mary talked to her classmate about Guthrie and Burden. She thinks Burden got Guthrie his judgeship, in return for his billings."

"A costly judgeship. Tell her to follow up and find out where Burden is. They said he was out of the country at the emergency hearing. I want to know if he still is, and where. Like that. That all you got?"

Judy hesitated. "I did find out something you should know."

"Give me the headline."

"I think Connolly was selling drugs and using a group of boxers' wives to do it."

Bennie leaned against the cheap paneled wall of the lounge. "Is this true? How do you know?"

"I talked to one of the wives today, at the gym."

"Selling drugs? Connolly?" Bennie let herself slide into one of the brown folding chairs that ringed the room. It was hard to think. "What were you doing at the gym? That wasn't what I asked you do."

"I know, I was following a hunch."

Bennie rubbed her forehead. Was Connolly involved in drug dealing? Was Della Porta? Had Connolly lied to her again? "Do you have proof of this, Carrier, or is it just talk? Did this wife name names?"

"It's not gossip. There's a Maria, a Ceilia, I didn't get last names but I will. Oh, and there's a Valencia something, who may have sold for Connolly. She's in prison now for possession. For what it's worth, the consensus is our client is as guilty as they come."

"Bennie?" Hattie called out suddenly from the adjoining room. Her voice sounded shaky.

"I have to go, Carrier. Find out where this Valencia is." Bennie took a breath. "Start at county prison, with Connolly."

Judy hung up the telephone, her young face falling into grave lines. "Bennie doesn't sound so good," she said, and looked across the conference room at Mary, who had just come in from canvassing Connolly's neighbors with the investigator, Lou.

"Marshall told me," Mary said, with sympathy. She set her boxy briefcase on the table and wiped sticky bangs from her forehead. "It must be tough, losing your parents."

"Yeah." Judy dropped into a swivel chair. "My parents are so healthy. They climb, ride bikes, travel. I always think they'll live forever."

"I think my parents will live forever, too, and all they do for exercise is pray." Mary wanted to change the subject. "We going for an extension?"

"Yes, a week."

"We need a year to get Connolly off." Mary rolled out a swivel chair and sat down. "Lou is still out there looking, but we didn't find any witnesses that would help the defense. Plenty of neighbors saw Connolly run down the street, however. I think she did it, Jude. I think she killed him."

"Of course she did. She deals drugs, too. A well-rounded felon." Judy told Mary about her secret boxing lessons and what she'd learned from Ronnie Morales, to Mary's growing astonishment.

"I can't believe this," Mary said when she was finished.

"What? The drugs? The murder?"

"No, the boxing lessons." Mary felt hurt. "You told me you went to the gynecologist."

"I lied. I'm sorry, I had to."

"Why?"

"Because if I told you, you'd come with me, and your mother would kill us both."

"Silly." Mary smiled. "My mother would only kill you."

42

Because it was after the prison's business hours, Bennie had to wait in the interview room for Connolly. She couldn't remember feeling so drained. She had rowed in regattas, powered single sculls with sheer muscle and grit, and still never felt this enervated. Fatigue after a race always produced a vague, if drowsy, euphoria and a feeling of accomplishment, but this tiredness was of a darker sort. A bone-deep weariness that came partly from grief and partly from having to contain grief. She straightened up in the plastic chair, folded and unfolded her hands on the smooth Formica counter, then finally clasped them together in her lap.

Bennie startled at a loud *ca-chunka* and she looked up to see Connolly being led into the secured hallway to the interview room. The inmate's stride was strong as she walked down the corridor, and Bennie realized that the usual noise level had prevented her from ever hearing those footfalls. Connolly walked like Bennie, fast and slightly duck-toed. It had always bothered her mother, who used to say, "Walk with your legs together, like a lady."

"What did you say?" Connolly asked, her expression puzzled as she walked through the door into the inmate's half of the room.

"What?"

"You said something about the way I walk."

"No, I didn't. I said . . ." Bennie's voice failed her, then she took a deep breath. "You'd better sit down. I have bad news."

"About my case? Is something wrong?" Connolly took a seat and leaned forward over the counter. "I knew it. I knew something was going on. I could feel it."

"No, your case is fine. It's worse than that. My mother has, well, passed on. In the hospital. She wasn't in any pain, and she wasn't alone."

"That's a relief," Connolly blurted out, then froze when she saw Bennie's stunned expression. "I mean, it's a relief she didn't suffer," Connolly added quickly, but Bennie fell against the back of her chair as if pushed.

"That's not what it sounded like. It sounded like you were relieved that she—"

"Died? Of course I'm not relieved that she died. Why would I be? That's not what I meant."

"No? Do you even care?"

"Oh, Christ." Connolly raked a hand through her coppery hair. "Oh, all right, I was relieved it wasn't about my case, okay? They wake me up and tell me my lawyer's here after hours. What else would it be about? You said we don't talk about personal things, like our mother, so the last thing I expect is that you'd come up to talk about her. I didn't even know she was that sick. I thought she was mental or something. You can't die from that, can you?"

"Evidently."

"Well, that's too bad. I'm sorry. For both of us." Connolly nodded, though Bennie couldn't help but notice that her tone was matter-of-fact. Maybe everybody was right about Connolly. Maybe she was heartless, a killer. A drug dealer, like Carrier suspected.

"You know," Bennie said, "I did have something come up

in your case today. One of my associates thinks you were involved in selling drugs, with the wives of the boxers."

"Give me a break." Connolly laughed ruefully, and Bennie's gut twisted.

"That's not a denial. Your line is, 'That's not true.' 'That's absurd.' 'I'm surprised you would even suggest such a thing.'"

"It's *not* true." Connolly's stony glare met Bennie's dubious one. "I swear, I didn't have anything to do with dope. I knew the boxers' wives, but I certainly didn't sell drugs with them."

"One of the wives was named Valencia. I don't know her last name. I understand she's here, in this prison. Do you know her?"

Connolly's eyes flickered. "No. I don't know any Valencia and I didn't have anything to do with any drugs. Neither did Anthony, no matter what your little associate says."

Bennie sagged in the chair, spent. Confused. Angry, hurting, and screwing up a major case. Every day she was finding out another way Connolly had lied to her. First, Bullock. Now this drug thing. Bennie faced up to something she had been thinking on the drive to the prison tonight. "I told you not to lie to me and you did, and I can't trust you anymore. I can't go forward, especially now . . . with my mother. I'll get you another lawyer, the best in criminal practice."

"You're pulling out on me?"

"Not completely. I'll be there watching you from the front row, but I can't be trial counsel, not now. My mother died. She deserves to be mourned."

"And what do I deserve?" Connolly spat back, and Bennie leaned forward, angry.

"This isn't about you. This is about a woman who you claim bore you. How come your own mother's death doesn't even faze you?"

"Please forgive me for not crying." Connolly's mouth twisted bitterly. "My mother never gave a crap about me. She abandoned me as soon as she saw me. You're the one she cared about. You're the one she kept. So you'll understand if my only concern is my own ass. I'm selfish as sin. I get it from my mother."

Bennie flinched, shaken to the core. She couldn't bear to hear anybody talk that way about her mother, especially now. Suddenly she felt no more like Connolly's twin than she had the day they met. She rose stiffly and went to the door. She wanted Connolly out of her sight.

"You're not getting out of this case now, Rosato," Connolly shouted. "I read the papers, I see the news. We're the lead story. The media is eating it up and the jury will, too. Nobody can pull off the twin defense but my twin."

Bennie felt sick inside, trapped. "Guard!" she called through the door, though she knew the guard would be watching her.

"Go to hell!" Connolly shouted as the guard appeared, and the curse reverberated inside Bennie's skull all the way back to the office.

Bennie switched on the lights in her firm's reception area and walked past the empty secretaries' desks. The printers and fax machines had been turned off, as had the associates' office lights, and Bennie could see from the brushed nap of the carpet that the cleaning ladies had come and gone. It was good to know that her law firm took care of itself, because right now she couldn't take care of another thing.

She entered her office and sat down at her desk. Her business correspondence was covered by a pile of sympathy cards in shades of pink, lavender, and gray. The sight made her throat feel thick, and she set them aside without opening any. She didn't want to feel sympathy right now. She didn't want to feel anything.

Under the cards lay the letter to Judge Guthrie that Carrier had drafted, requesting a continuance. Bennie crumpled it up and pitched it into the waste can, shaking her head. Never had her decision-making been so screwy on a case. She shouldn't have undertaken the representation in the first place. She had been wrong, terribly wrong, and she had to straighten it out.

Bennie punched a key on her computer and started drafting a motion, requesting that she be permitted to withdraw from the representation and also argued an alternative, as most lawyers did, for a postponement of a week because of a death in her family. She'd leave it with directions for Carrier to file ASAP and explain to the associates later why the boss had flip-flopped. After she finished the motion, she drafted and faxed letters to the two best criminal defense lawyers in Philly, offering them the Connolly representation. Both would jump at the chance to take on the high-profile matter.

But Bennie felt nothing like relief as she handed Connolly's fate to another.

Almost as soon as Bennie opened the front door to her house, Grady swept her into his arms. He had clearly waited up for her, still dressed in his work clothes, a rumpled white oxford shirt and wrinkled suit pants. "Jeez, babe, I'm so sorry," he said softly. "I've been trying to reach you everywhere. Are you okay?"

"I guess," she said, though the words sounded hoarse, even to her. She remained in his embrace only reluctantly, not so much because she didn't want to be held by him, but because she didn't want to be held at all. "I think things are pretty much under control now."

"I should have been there. I'm so sorry." Grady squeezed her tighter and she could hear him groan. "I was in a meeting over this stupid merger. I didn't get to make any calls and I didn't get your message until late."

"It's okay, there wasn't anything you could do anyway. I picked out what I had to, and Hattie was with her, at the end." Bennie squirmed in Grady's arms but he held fast.

"It's good Hattie was there."

"Yes," Bennie said, having suddenly run out of conversation. She didn't want to talk. She didn't want to be touched. She wanted only to go upstairs, lie down, and feel miserable. Maybe treat herself to another good, long cry. "Can I go now?" she blurted out, and Grady laughed abruptly and released her.

"Sure, honey, I'm sorry."

"I'm just tired. I need to lie down." She felt a nudge against her leg and looked down at the golden retriever leaning into her, his tail down. Bear's body warmed her thigh, and she scratched the flyaway hair behind his ear. "Dogs are good," she said, her voice thick.

"Let's go upstairs. I'll tuck you in."

"I can tuck myself in."

"Whether you know it or not, you need me now. I'm taking you upstairs and putting you to bed. Understand?"

Bennie smiled, though somehow even that hurt. "Okay," she said, and permitted herself to be led upstairs to bed and tucked in like a very small girl.

43

Early next morning, Judy stood in the sunny conference room and read the faxed order again and again, as if that would change the result: "IT IS HEREBY ORDERED that the Defense Counsel's Motion for Withdrawal and, In the Alternative, for a Postponement is hereby DENIED." "I don't get this," Judy said. "How could he deny it?"

"Guthrie denied our motion, in its entirety? No withdrawal? Not even a continuance?" Mary, standing next to her, flipped over the top page of the order. "There's not even an opinion. There's no explanation at all."

"He doesn't have to explain anything, he's a judge."

"This is a sin. Bennie can't possibly work this case. Her mother just died, for God's sake. He can't give her a week off, even three days?"

Judy shook her head. "I guess he's figuring that she got the standard three days, if you count from Thursday. That would be Friday, Saturday, and Sunday. Jury selection is set for this Monday, with opening arguments right afterwards."

"Can we file an appeal?"

Judy looked over. "No, whiz. It's an interlocutory order, not appealable until the case is over."

"I knew that. It was a trick question."

Judy smiled, thinking. "I suppose we could file some kind of emergency order or maybe a petition for misconduct, but that wouldn't help. The Superior Court wouldn't intervene on an emergency basis for something within a judge's discretion. Even if we filed a misconduct petition, the only remedy is a reprimand."

"I knew that, too."

"What did you know?"

"What you said."

Judy smiled, then it faded quickly. "I hate to bother Bennie with this. Do I have to call her at home?"

"Of course. We have no choice. She can work at home if we feed her the information we have." Mary gestured at the papers on the conference table. "I found out Burden's still out of the country, I can write her a memo. I can dictate my notes on the neighborhood survey and send her a copy by messenger. Then I could draft a cross-examination of the Commonwealth witnesses."

"That should help."

"I'm a fountain of helpfulness. What are you going to do?"

"Correct your work, as always," Judy said, and reached for the phone to call Bennie.

At home, Bennie sat on the edge of the bed in her white terrycloth bathrobe, holding the phone after the associate briefed her fully and hung up. Bennie couldn't think of a single judge who would have denied that request, at least for the postponement, and it was out of character for the well-bred Harrison Guthrie. Stunned, she held the telephone receiver in midair, and Grady plucked it from her hand and placed it on the cradle.

"Why did he deny it?" Grady asked. He was dressed in jeans and a gray T-shirt, and he'd gotten up early, brewed fresh coffee, and made French toast that Bennie hadn't touched.

"We don't know. There was no opinion, just the order."

"He denied the postponement, too? What could he be thinking?"

"God knows." Bennie shook her head. Her temples throbbed and her eyes felt dry and sticky. She sagged with exhaustion after a sleepless night. Bear trotted over, setting his large head on her thigh, and she scratched it idly. "Maybe my motion wasn't good enough. Maybe I should have found a case, some precedent."

"No." Grady folded his arms. "That wouldn't make the difference. He's on solid grounds legally, but as a matter of custom, you think at least he'd give you a postponement. It's common decency."

"Maybe it was the press coverage. Maybe he wants it over with."

"That can't be it. This decision will cause more criticism, won't it? When it gets out that your mother has passed and he wouldn't even grant a week's extension? Hell, everybody's got a mother. Guthrie's got to run for reelection some day."

"He's getting on, maybe he's not worried about reelection," Bennie said, but even as she spoke she knew it didn't make sense. All judges worried about reelection, if not their reputation. "It's like he's hell-bent on screwing me."

"That's possible. You're not the most popular lawyer in town, except with me."

"Wait a minute," Bennie said, her brain waking up suddenly. Maybe it was personal, but maybe it wasn't directed at her. What had Connolly said, that first day they met? *I think the judge is in on it, too.* "Maybe Judge Guthrie is in on it."

"In on what?"

"A conspiracy against Connolly."

"A what?"

"Think about it, Grady. Who gets hurt most by this decision? Connolly." Bennie's thoughts cleared like fog. It all fell into place. "I'm sitting here, all wrapped up in myself, but it's Connolly's life on the line. With this ruling, she gets stuck with a lawyer who doesn't have the time or the energy to prepare for trial. What does that do to her chance of winning?"

"But a conspiracy, involving Guthrie?"

"It's not impossible. Somebody's taking aim, and I'm not the target, she is. Think back. First, somebody leaks to the press that Connolly's my twin. Second, somebody at the bar association starts screwing with my license. Third, I don't get the extension the first time I apply, even though it was reasonable. Now I don't get an extension even after my mother passes. It stinks, Grady, and it goes all the way up to Judge Guthrie."

"Bennie." Grady grabbed a chair, yanked it across the plywood subfloor toward the bed, and sat down. "Listen to yourself. You're saying that a Common Pleas Court judge is plotting against a criminal defendant. How likely is that?"

"It's possible," Bennie said, alert for the first time in what seemed like years. "Guthrie got his judgeship because of Henry Burden. Burden was the D.A. and knows everybody in law enforcement. Connolly says the cops framed her for this, and the police response to the scene—the timing—is suspicious. Even if Connolly was selling drugs—"

"Connolly was selling drugs?" Grady interrupted, and Bennie realized she hadn't told him that.

"Grady, assume the cops killed Della Porta and framed Connolly for it, why can't a judge be involved, too? You never heard of judicial corruption? On the Common Pleas Court bench? Please. Years ago the roofers were paying cash for cases, Grady. *Cash*."

"Connolly is a liar. She's lying about being framed and she's lying about being your twin. Now you're telling me she's a drug dealer? She's manipulating—"

"We don't know she lied about any of that, Grady. She agreed to the DNA test, did I tell you that? We both gave blood yesterday. Or the day before that." Bennie rubbed her eyes. Her mother's death had chased every other thought from her head.

"No, you didn't tell me, but don't infer so much from the fact she agreed."

"Why not? You'd infer an awful lot if she refused. So would I."

Grady cocked his head. "She could have agreed to string you along. Or maybe she believes she's your twin. Who knows?"

Bennie sighed, exasperated and confused. She couldn't put her finger on it, but something was definitely fishy about Judge Guthrie's order. She sprang up from the bed, jolting the golden retriever from her lap. "I have to get dressed."

"What? Why?" Grady asked, startled. "You going to work?"

"Not exactly," she answered, and hurried to shower.

44

"My goodness! Ms. Rosato, you, eh, don't have an appointment, do you?" The judge's aged receptionist looked startled behind her bifocals and double-checked the appointment book lying open on her desk. Her slim hand bore an Irish wedding band, and Bennie could smell her lemony hand lotion from across the desk.

"This is an impromptu visit. Judge Guthrie wasn't in his courtroom, so I assume he's in chambers."

"Why, yes, but one can't simply *visit* Judge Guthrie."

"Oh, he'll be thrilled to see me." Bennie winked, and the secretary rose to her feet, waving a hand.

"Please, no. You can't go in there. The judge is working."

"So am I," Bennie said. She strode to the office door, knocked briefly, and opened it. The judge's chambers were decorated in Shaker style, and antique cherry furniture circled an elegant silk Oriental in front of a large mahogany desk. Certificates blanketed the paneled walls, and ginger lamps lent an understated glow to casebooks and legal treatises that filled cherry bookcases. Judge Guthrie stood across the carpet reading a chubby United States reporter; its stiff, ivory pages open in a fan. He peered over his tortoiseshell reading glasses at the intrusion.

"Ms. Rosato," he said, turning from the bank of cream-colored volumes. The judge made a frail, stooped figure without his judicial robes. "Please accept my condolences in the death of your mother."

"I got them this morning. 'It is hereby ordered,' I think it said."

"Ah, quite. I thought you might be disappointed."

"That, too. Puzzled is more apt, Your Honor."

"Ms. Rosato, please call me Judge. Lawyers who barge into my office always call me Judge."

Bennie couldn't find her smile. "I need to know why you didn't grant my motion, Judge. I should have been able to withdraw, especially in these circumstances. I can't represent the defendant anymore. I'm too close to her, too emotionally involved, and with my mother—"

"I can understand your predicament," Judge Guthrie said, his voice calm even as the door behind Bennie opened and his secretary peeked in worriedly, with a male law clerk cowering behind her.

"Judge," the secretary interrupted, in a tremulous voice, "I telephoned the sheriffs, and they're on their way." She glanced at Bennie, who thought she read a twinge of regret behind her bifocals, but the judge only laughed.

"Call off the dogs, Millie. Get back to work, Ronald. I can handle Ms. Rosato on my own. She's not the first lawyer unhappy with one of my rulings and she's not quite so terrifying as she thinks."

"Yes, Judge." The secretary nodded, withdrawing and closing the door after her.

Judge Guthrie cleared his throat. "I anticipated your displeasure with my order. It wasn't an easy decision, given my sympathy for your recent loss, and we do have history, you and I, don't we?"

"Yes, we do."

"I'm fond of you, Ms. Rosato. I tell you that directly. However, I had to deny your motion to withdraw. Recall that I granted your earlier motion to step in as defendant's counsel. Less than a week later, you move to step out. I can't sanction that sort of conduct. It would create havoc, not only with my calendar but with the rights of criminal defendants."

"But, Judge, you read the papers. Surely you've seen that there are extenuating circumstances in this case. I admit it, I was wrong. I shouldn't have gotten involved in the first place."

"You mean the 'twin murder case.' I would prefer to avoid tabloid journalism, though it's impossible these days." Judge Guthrie shook his head, his wispy white hair bright in the light of chambers. "No, it was imprudent of you to become involved in the Connolly matter. But you did, and that's where we find ourselves. I don't recall your asserting in your brief that the defendant wishes you to withdraw, do I?"

"No. She wants me to remain her counsel."

"I assumed as much." Judge Guthrie nodded. "I couldn't very well grant that withdrawal motion then, now could I?"

Bennie swallowed. Ever since this case began, she'd been arguing the wrong side. Still. "But why no extension, Judge? It's routine in the case of death in the immediate family. The trial hasn't started yet. You know I'm right on the extension."

Judge Guthrie stiffened. "I'm not in the habit of sched-uling my cases around counsel's availability. That's the cart before the horse, my dear. I told you in open court we couldn't have further delays in this matter, and we cannot. I have a breach-of-contracts matter scheduled for the following week with out-of-town counsel and that should take a full month. Now. You have my order." Judge Guthrie snapped the casebook closed, and the soft *thunk* punctuated his sentence.

"I don't believe that's the real reason, Judge."

"The *real* reason? My then, what's the *real* reason, Ms. Rosato?"

Bennie hesitated. She was accustomed to busting cops, but judges were another matter entirely. "I believe there's a police conspiracy against Alice Connolly and I think you're a part of it. I think you're protecting the police, in return for the old favor of getting you this judgeship. I think that's why you gave Connolly's defense to Henry Burden in the first place, so he'd sit on it. And how convenient that Burden is out of the country so nobody can question him."

"My, that's quite a theory." Judge Guthrie smiled faintly and replaced the book. Only when it was completely ensconced did he turn and face Bennie. "Corrupt judges, corrupt police, corrupt lawyers. Who is behind all this, and why?"

Bennie found his reaction odd and noted he hadn't denied her charge, even reflexively. "I don't know yet, but it's not who, it's what, and the answer has to be money. It always is. I think a lot of people stand to make a lot of money if Connolly gets railroaded. They want Connolly to have a lawyer so preoccupied she can't think straight or work hard. Which only makes me want to work harder, by the way."

"I see. Well. If you suspect these terrible things, why don't you go ahead and file a charge?" Judge Guthrie eased his glasses off his nose and cleaned them by blowing softly in one lens then the other, two shallow puffs of breath. "Why storm in here like gangbusters, to no result?"

Bennie paused. Strange. Was he making a suggestion? "I came to give you the benefit of the doubt."

"Ah." The judge held up a bony hand, from which his tortoiseshell glasses dangled. "You mean you have no proof. You have only your suspicion, unsubstantiated, and that's what motivates you. You disagree with my order, so you charge into my office. You come without opposing counsel. You make scurrilous allegations. Lawyers lose their licenses for such conduct, you know."

"They tried that already. It didn't work."

"You are in quite a state, aren't you?" Judge Guthrie rolled out his leather desk chair and eased into it. His desk was dotted with gift gavels in malachite and crystal, anchored by a large porcelain lamp. Its light glinted on a lacquered set of brass scales, an award from the bar association. "I remember how I felt when my mother passed away. It fell to me to make the arrangements for my mother's funeral. Yet I worked throughout, at the firm, for I had clients depending on me. It wasn't a responsibility I took lightly, nor was the responsibility I bore my family. I never take my responsibilities lightly, whether they be to my clients or to my family."

Bennie struggled to read between the lines. Was someone threatening him or his family? "I am looking out for my client, Judge. I believe she's being set up for a crime she didn't commit. I'm not about to let that happen. Neither should you."

"My, my." Judge Guthrie replaced his glasses as he gazed out his office window. The Criminal Justice Center was located on a side street in a city struggling to keep business from escaping to the suburbs. There was no view except for the shadowy windows of the vacant office building across the way. The judge seemed momentarily lost to Bennie, and she sensed that if he was involved in a conspiracy, he was being coerced.

"Who are you protecting, Judge? What do they have on you?"

"My, my, my," Judge Guthrie said, tenting his fingers as he focused outside the window. "Grief is a funny thing. It plays tricks with the brain. It's an emotional time for you, but you will have to set your emotions to the side. You're at sixes and sevens, in a tizzy, owing to your terrible loss, but it is time for you to get along now. You have lots of work to do, Ms. Rosato, and very little time to do it in."

Bennie sighed, torn. "Your Honor, if I'm going to try this case, I'm going to take your friends down. Don't make me take you down with them."

"I do hope you feel better, Ms. Rosato. I did send your mother some lovely flowers, you know. Lest you think me a wicked man." Judge Guthrie swiveled to face Bennie and opened his hands slowly. "I am not a wicked man," he repeated.

"We are what we do," she said, and left the judge hiding behind his awards.

"Bennie, any comment on the ruling?" "Bennie, what do you think about Judge Guthrie's decision?" "Will you appeal the judge's decision, Ms. Rosato?"

Bennie barreled through the reporters at the courthouse and later outside her office building. They followed her from one place to the next, plaguing her with questions, jostling her, sticking videocams and tape machines in her face. She realized how much her world, at least her inner world, had slowed down since her mother died. She felt oddly like an invalid forced outside, into light and movement, and it disoriented her. She fended the press off with a jittery hand and prayed the cameras wouldn't broadcast her anxiety.

"No comment," she murmured as she pushed through the revolving door into her lobby and crossed to the elevator bank. The doors opened, and Bennie took the elevator to her floor. The reception area was as quiet as an oasis, except that everyone was staring at her. Bennie avoided all eyes but Marshall's, sitting at the reception desk. "Any messages?" Bennie asked simply.

"Yes, sure," Marshall said. She slipped a strand of hair behind a pierced ear, gathered the mail, and handed it over. "I'm so sorry—"

"Thanks," Bennie said, accepting the work, if not the expression of sympathy. She had to block it out if she was going to be effective and she'd meant what she told Judge Guthrie. If somebody wanted her paralyzed, then her only response was to move faster. She tucked the papers under her arm and hurried to the conference room.

"Bennie, I'm sorry," Judy said, her young face soft with sorrow, and Mary looked positively teary.

"I'm really—"

"Sorry," Bennie supplied, then added, "I know. Thanks. But we're all up a creek if we don't get back to work." She tossed her papers on the conference room table, where they landed with a slap. "Tell me where we are in this case. I got your notes. Mary, you start with the details."

Mary filled Bennie in on the dismal results of their neighborhood canvassing. When she finished she added, "And Lou's still out there, so maybe he'll find out something."

"Maybe," Bennie said, and turned to Judy. "Tell me about this drug thing. I got your message about Valencia.

Connolly says she doesn't know her and denies selling drugs."

"I'm not surprised," Judy said, and reiterated the details of what Ronnie Morales had told her. "I can go back to the gym to learn more, if you want. I'd like to try to meet some of the other wives, see what I can find out."

"No, we're in high gear now. You have to get the paper-work done. Jury instructions, motions *in limine,* questions for voir dire. It all has to be done right away, and whatever has to be filed has to get filed." Bennie grabbed her papers. "I'm going to get my copy of the file and work at home for an hour or two before the viewing."

"Tonight is the viewing?" Mary asked. "We'd like to go."

"Thanks, but neither of you can come. We've got a defense to stage."

Judy frowned. "But we'd like to. We can work after-wards."

"No." Bennie headed for the door. "If you're there, you're fired. Don't file anything without my seeing it first. Fax it to me at home or send it by messenger. Call if you have any questions or need anything."

"Sure," Judy said, mystified, and Mary nodded as Ben-nie slipped out the door and hustled to her office to pack her briefcase.

45

Fleur-de-lis of ersatz gilt flocked the wallpaper and the room was long and narrow, almost a coffin itself. Sound from another wake traveled through the thin walls and the cheap nap of the rug betrayed that it was indoor-outdoor carpeting. Covella's Funeral Home wasn't the first tier of Italian funeral homes, where the mob wakes were held, but Bennie thought it suited. It was unpretentious and small, like her mother, and if it had bowling trophies displayed on a shelf in the back of the room, so be it. It didn't matter to Bennie where she mourned her mother. She'd be mourning her the rest of her life.

Bennie sagged in an overstuffed chair in the front row between Hattie and Grady. Her head throbbed dully and her eyes were sore and dry. She was all cried out and hollow inside. The press thronged outside, but they'd been kept at bay by a ring of streetwise morticians. At least it remained quiet inside the funeral home.

Grady squeezed her hand, and Hattie sat on Bennie's other side. Her yellow hair was the only bright spot on her; the dark skin around her eyes was swollen, and she wore a black pantsuit with short sleeves and a pointed collar that she kept tugging into place. The three of them— Grady, Bennie, and Hattie—constituted the sum total of her mother's mourners, but Bennie shrugged off any shame about it. She'd been to political wakes, business wakes, and school-reunion wakes, all jam-packed with people who cared little for the body lying amid the flowers. This loss was greater, somehow undiluted, because it was just the three of them huddled together, their heads bent.

Bennie's thoughts turned to Connolly and she felt pleased that Connolly wasn't there. Even if Connolly was a blood relative, her presence would have been an insult to her mother's memory, considering how little the death had affected her. Bennie shifted in the armchair and wondered if she should have tried to notify her father. Winslow wasn't her mother's husband, but he might have wanted to be here, if the saved note was any indication. Still, he could read the obituaries as well as anyone. Maybe he'd come, suddenly appear out of nowhere. How many times had Bennie wished that as a child? And how many times did it happen?

She didn't bother to look for him and realized that she felt about him the way Connolly felt about her mother. He had missed her life, and whether or not it was his decision at the outset, he hadn't tried to correct it. Hadn't once tried to contact Bennie, so why should she bend over backward to contact him? How would she feel at his passing? Would she care as little as Connolly did at her mother's?

Bennie's feelings were jumbled, her thoughts disoriented. She sank into the chair, with Grady's arm at her back. She felt so distant from him, from everyone, in willed isolation. She hadn't invited anyone from the office to the wake or even her oldest friend, Sam Freminet. She didn't want anyone to see her like this, or know her this way.

"Father Teobaldo is here," said the funeral director, who materialized from nowhere. Behind him stood a slight Catholic priest, with a damp forehead, a long bony nose, and a face too gaunt for a young man.

"I'm sorry, Ms. Rosato," he said, extending a slim hand and shaking hers. He eased into the seat beside Hattie, who introduced herself and shook his hand. "Pleased to meet you, too," he said, and sounded to Bennie like he actually meant it.

"S'nice you took the time to come," Hattie said, a hoarse lilt to her voice. She grew up in Georgia and like Grady, had an accent that surfaced when she was tired or upset. This evening she was both. "I know you didn't know Missus Rosato. She wasn't a well woman. She couldn't get out to church."

"That's all right. I'm not here to judge her. God won't judge her. He'll welcome her."

"I know he will, Father," Hattie said, her voice sonorous. "Jesus loves all of us."

Bennie looked away. She never had much use for religion and wasn't about to start with the thought of her mother's death being welcome to anyone, even God. Her gaze fell on the front of the room and she realized that she hadn't once looked at the bier where her mother lay. It had been hard enough to see her, back at the hospital. Bennie made herself look at the front of the room and try to absorb it. An act of will, almost against her will.

It was easier to look first around the casket, rather than at the casket itself. White wrought iron sconces flanked her mother's coffin, their light insignificant. Tacky flower arrangements ringed the front: pink-sprayed chrysanthemums and paint-covered daisies wrenched into the shape of hearts, banners, and, improbably, a horseshoe. Bennie had ordered dozens of long-stemmed white roses, but elegance and simplicity were apparently unheard of at a

South Philly funeral. White satin sashes spanned the flower hearts, one reading *Beloved Mother* in handscript of Elmer's glue and glitter, and the other saying *Mom* in crimson. Bennie decided to let it go. The flowers mattered as little as the bowling trophies. Her mother was gone.

She made herself look at the coffin and the vision wrenched her heart. A rose-colored light had been mounted inside the satin upholstery of the casket, bathing her mother's face in a pink glow. Brownish foundation had been sponged onto her mother's skin and her lips sealed in a matching pink lipstick. That bothered Bennie more than anything, the unnatural closing to her mother's lips, and she wondered uneasily how it had been accomplished. She swallowed hard and bit back her tears. Her gaze traveled down her mother's side. In one rigid hand had been placed a pair of wire-rimmed reading glasses. Bennie had no idea how the mortician had gotten the glasses; she'd forgotten that her mother had even worn glasses. Her mother had been so ill the past few months, she hadn't been able to read.

"Excuse me," said the funeral director, returning and leaning down to Bennie. His moussed hair was by now familiar, though he smelled tonight of lemon-lime Barbasol. "Should we begin, or wait for the other mourners?" he asked.

"Begin, please," Bennie answered, testy. She had explained it to the man twice. *Just the three of us,* she had said, but still he'd set up the room with ten rows of folding chairs, as if the lack of mourners was somehow shameful. Coming from a tradition that actually paid mourners, it probably was.

"But there was another mourner. What happened to him?"

"What mourner?"

"A gentleman," he said, raising a hand, and Bennie turned around. There was nothing there but the trophies, their fake gold angels elevating bowling balls like Communion wafers.

"Who was he?"

"I don't know, I didn't ask. He was here early, before you came. Before the reporters."

"What did he look like?"

"An older gentlemen, with a tweed coat, I think."

Bennie couldn't believe what she was hearing. It was Connolly's description of Winslow. "What did he want? Did he say anything?"

"I gathered he wished to pay his respects. I suggested to him that the service wasn't for several hours, but he said he knew that. He left flowers."

"What flowers?" she asked, a lump in her throat, and the funeral director pointed toward the sprayed white carnations.

"I set them behind that last arrangement. They're . . . different."

"I want to see them," Bennie said, rising. She went to the last arrangement and pushed it aside, then knelt down. In back of the stiff crysanthemum concoction sat a clear glass vase and from it sprung a fresh bouquet of leggy pink cosmos, white daisies, blush roses, and black-eyed Susans. At the fringe were pink snapdragons and foxglove with velvety purple pockets. She recognized the flowers. They were from Winslow's garden. She bent down and cupped the blossoms in her hands.

"Bennie?" Grady said, appearing behind her, but she was breathing in the fresh perfume of the flowers. Her father had been here. He had brought her mother flowers. He had cared. He was real.

"Bennie?" Grady said again, but she was rising to her feet, without thinking. Her heart was pounding. Maybe he was still here. Maybe he hadn't gone. She got up and hustled down the aisle of folding chairs to the back of the room and hurried out to the entrance hall. She didn't know why, he was probably long gone, but she looked for him anyway.

It was dark, but reporters mobbed the sidewalk. One spotted her and pointed for his cameraman. Flashes popped in Bennie's eyes; two, then a dozen. They seared like lasers into her brain and still she couldn't stop searching, even though it was so hard to see. Maybe he was behind the crowd. Bennie stood there, her hands to the glass in the dark, and didn't leave until Grady came to take her back inside.

After the wake, Bennie stopped at the office to pick up some papers, then walked home to clear her head while Grady dropped Hattie at her house. She had a defense to prepare and almost wanted to get to work. Let it occupy her thoughts and chase her emotions away.

Once home, she changed into jeans and a workshirt, padded into her home office, and got to work with her ritual props at her side: fresh coffee and a crinkly bag of M&M's. Though her comfort foods were in place, she had little luck with her first task, drafting her opening argument. Her head hurt. She ached at the core. Still, she sat at the computer and willed herself to peck out the first sentence. *Ladies and gentlemen of the jury, you see before you* . . .

Each keystroke sounded in the empty room. The night was quiet, its stillness broken by intermittent police sirens. Bennie sipped coffee, curiously tasteless. *Ladies and gentlemen of the jury, before you* . . .

No.

Good morning. Before you, ladies and gentlemen of the jury, sits . . .

Suddenly Bennie heard the front door open and close downstairs, then the heavy clunk of shopping bags hitting the floor. It would be Grady, home from picking up some groceries. Bear leapt to alertness and skittered downstairs, toenails sliding on the bare floors, but Bennie didn't feel quite as welcoming. She'd wanted the house to herself.

"Honey?" Grady called upstairs. "Ya home?"

"In my office," she called back, but he had already reached the top of the stairs with the dog. He wore the clothes from the wake, but his print tie was loosened into a crooked V and his oxford shirt wrinkled.

"Hot as hell out there." Grady walked to Bennie's desk, leaned over, and gave her a dry kiss on the cheek. His eyes looked bleary behind his rimmed glasses and his gaze found the monitor. "Your opening?"

"Yep."

"Can I help?"

"Not really."

"I got fresh cream and a lifetime supply of M&M's. Nothin's too good for my girl."

Bennie forced a smile, but her thoughts kept straying. Her mother. The purple foxglove. Then, *Good morning. Before you, ladies and gentlemen . . .*

"You want to talk? Cry some more?" Grady smiled with sympathy. "I got a shoulder. Two in fact. We can lie down together, take a break."

"Thanks, but no. No time."

"You want to talk about the case, then? Try your opening argument out on me?"

"No, I'm not there yet. Got to write it first."

Grady pursed his lips. "Want fresh coffee?"

"Got some." Bennie turned to the monitor. *Good morning. Before you, ladies and. . . .* "Grady, I'm sorry, I have to concentrate."

"Okay," he said, giving her another peck on the cheek. "I'm outta here."

Bennie stared at the screen as he left the room, the dog sashaying behind with his characteristic slip-slide. She couldn't focus. Her coffee cooled as she found herself listening for Grady's comings and goings around the house. She smelled the popping of frying chicken and anticipated the kitchen growing humid with boiling potatoes. Later he'd mash them with bacon. Grady was a terrific cook, particularly of Southern fare, and he was making one of Bennie's favorite meals.

She heard the clink of dishes as he set the plywood table. She could almost taste the cold beer he'd undoubtedly uncap. She couldn't remember the last time she'd eaten anything. The aroma of sizzling bacon wafted up from the kitchen and into the hallway. It was driving her nuts.

Bennie closed the computer file. She had to get out of here. She had to go where she could be away from everyone. She had to concentrate on the case, on Connolly.

She knew just the place.

46

Surf Lenihan sat low inside the black bucket seat of the black TransAm. He wore a white polo shirt and jeans and tugged on a carton of strawberry milk. He'd parked down the street a safe distance from the house. Watching, in the dark.

Surf slugged another gulp of strawberry milk and felt good for the first time in a long time. Maybe it was because he was finally doing something about the situation himself, instead of waiting for Citrone to get off his ass.

Surf was young and moving up in the department. He'd already started to network, just like in business, and was just beginning to know the right people. He wasn't going to let Rosato screw him up. He wasn't going to let anybody screw him up. He had too much ahead of him.

Surf kept an eye on the house. Red-brick, a dumpy three-story. You'd think she'd buy a nicer house with all the money she made off the department. Surf had followed Rosato home from work, tracking her at a distance in the car, which was his girl's. The TransAm was more obvious than he would have liked, but at least it was black. It did the job.

As soon as Rosato had left her office building, Surf figured she was going home. He knew where that was. He'd looked up her address in the phone book and had almost beaten her here, slipping into a parking space and slinking low in his seat as she turned the corner, moving fast on foot. She was strong and not bad-lookin' if you liked big girls. Surf didn't. Her stems were okay, but her boobs weren't big enough. Plus, she was a lawyer. Who would want to screw a lawyer? Later Surf got his answer—another lawyer. A tall, skinny dude with a flowered tie had gone inside the house after her. Pussy had a shopping bag.

Surf peeked up at the second floor window. The light had gone on there a while ago but he couldn't see in the window, the blinds were closed. He took a last slug of milk and stowed the empty carton in back of the seat. He'd wait for Rosato to come out, then choose his time. He'd do what he had to to stop her.

Wait. A light went on outside the house, to the right of the front door. Maybe it was on a timer. Surf stayed low in the driver's seat. The front door of the house opened and closed. Rosato came out and walked down the stoop. She had a briefcase in one hand and a dog on a leash in the other. Nice pooch, but didn't look like much of a watch-dog. Good. Surf watched her walk up the street, alone, without the boyfriend. Better. Tonight would be the night. Now would be the time. He twisted on the ignition, pulled out of the space, and cruised up the street after her.

Surf slowed as he watched her get into a car, a big blue Ford, and when she took off, closed the gap enough to see the dog hanging out the back window. He wondered where Rosato was going—maybe back to the office, maybe she forgot something. With the dog? No. They passed the number street closest to the office.

The Ford ended up traveling down South Street. A tough break. South was clogged with traffic, as usual. The sidewalks were full of losers. Couples out for a walk after dinner, frat boys on the make, chicks from South Philly with big hair. Too many citizens. Surf couldn't do anything here. He braked sharply at the light and his gun slid from under the front seat. He edged it back with the heel of his boot.

Where was Rosato going? Surf realized he should have known, when they got there.

He parked at the corner of Trose Street, halfway down the block from Della Porta's apartment, and watched as Rosato got out of the Ford with the dog and crossed the street to Della Porta's building. Surf had been there many times, when they were in business with Della Porta. The street was skinny and dark. No streetlights. No one on the street. It was a go.

Surf palmed his gun, stuck it into the back of his jeans, and climbed out of the TransAm. He left the door open slightly so the noise didn't tip off Rosato. She was at the front door of the building, messing with keys. Her back was turned. The dog's tail was wagging like crazy.

Surf quick-stepped across the street and had almost reached the stoop when Rosato unlocked the door. He could've pushed her inside and capped her there, but stopped himself. The light in the entrance hall was too bright. Surf ducked behind a skinny tree near the curb. Rosato locked the door behind her. He watched her through the window as she went up the stairs.

Surf waited behind the tree until the light went on in Della Porta's apartment. He lingered another minute, to be sure, then darted to the rowhouse and unscrewed the lightbulb over the front door. It flickered to black and the stoop was bathed in darkness. Surf crept back down the stoop and stationed himself in the shadows by the front door. He could be patient, if he had to. Citrone never appreciated that, he underestimated Surf.

So had Rosato.

47

L *adies and gentlemen of the jury, before . . .*
    No.

Good morning. Before you, ladies and gentlemen of the jury, sits . . .

Damn. It still wasn't working. Bennie's attention kept wandering, even in Connolly's apartment. She felt exhausted, listless. She yawned and leaned back in Connolly's chair, in the home office that was a replica of her own. Bear had come along, though that decision had proved predictably regrettable. The dog was scratching at the floor in the living room, bothering the bloodstain. The sound of his toenails broke Bennie's already shaky concentration.

"Bear, no!" Bennie called out irritably, but the scratching didn't stop. She tried to ignore it, but couldn't. She felt bollixed up. *Grady would say I told you so.* He'd told her she was crazy to go to the apartment. Damn him. Bennie rested her chin in her hand, staring at the bright white screen of the monitor.

Bear was scratching again. *Scritch, scritch, scratch.*

"Bear, no! *No!*" Bennie shouted, but the scratching didn't stop. The dog would destroy the floor. Bennie stood up, rolled back the chair, and stormed into the living room. Bear was tearing at the stain, his ears flopped forward and his back humped with effort. An unpleasant adrenal scent filled the air.

"Bear!" she yelled, but the dog couldn't be distracted. She went over and yanked him back by the collar. The floorboards were scored with nailmarks, crosshatching over the blood. Still the dog pawed frantically at the floor, scraping and scratching to get back, and finally lunged from Bennie's grasp. He attacked the stain, clawing the floor in a rhythmic motion, one paw after the other. She had never seen him do that before. What was it about the blood that got the dog so riled up? He had scratched it away and was destroying the floor's finish. He wasn't scratching at the blood anymore, he was almost digging like a dog in a yard. The retriever seemed to think something was under there. Maybe something was.

Bennie got up and went to the kitchen, looking for a tool. She pulled open a drawer and rummaged through the knives, serving forks, and wooden spoons. She grabbed a small knife and hurried back to the living room, where her co-counsel had succeeded in destroying the top floorboard.

"Good dog," Bennie said, in a change of heart. She dropped into terrier position beside him, wedged the knife like a crowbar under the floorboard, and pulled it back. The floorboard bent up, offering more resistance than she expected from an old floor. Then she realized that the floorboard and the others next to it were slightly brighter than the rest of the floor. Newer. These boards had been cut and replaced, very carefully. Something was under there.

Bennie yanked with all her might and the floorboard splintered and snapped off. Bear leapt at the open hole and began pawing feverishly. Bennie worked beside him, driving the knife back into the floor, then prying off the rest of the floorboard until it came free. She dropped the knife and peered into the hole. Bear stood beside her, tail wagging with excitement. Nestled underneath the floorboards sat a package wrapped in brown paper.

Bennie reached into the hole for the package, wrenched it out with difficulty, and plunked it on her lap. It was a heavy square of brown paper crisscrossed with coarse white twine. The size of a suitcase but Bennie knew it didn't contain suits. She tried to untie the string, then broke it when it wouldn't give way. The package didn't smell like anything and she wasn't tempted to shake it. She ripped away the paper, almost afraid to learn what it contained. Peeking through the paper's jagged tear was a stack of money.

My God. Bennie pulled out a packet fastened with a blue rubber band. It was a six-inch pack of one hundred dollar bills, about one hundred of them. $10,000. There were packs of fifties, twenties, and more hundreds; ten neat stacks across, three front to back, and the package four packs deep, wrinkled and soiled. Bennie was looking at about $500,000 in cash. Jesus. That kind of money, in cash, came only from one place. It even smelled dirty.

Drug money.

Bennie felt sick inside. She had suspected Della Porta was corrupt, and here was proof. And what Carrier had found out, that Connolly was dealing drugs with the boxers' wives, had to be true. Connolly had played her, had probably been playing her from the beginning. Bennie's heart felt like a stone wedged in hard ground. She shoved the money back into its hiding place, yanked the blanket chest over it, and tore out of the apartment.

48

Alice lingered at the door to her cell, standing away from the window in the dark. It was just before the last head count, at 12:00 midnight. The prison was silent and still; the radios and TVs had finally ceased their endless noise. Alice would have no problem with the guard, a little money went a long way with Dexter the Pecker. The problem in the house wasn't the guards, it was the snitches. Lowlifes would do anything, even finger one of their own.

Alice watched as Dexter sauntered down the hall, right on time. The lights were off in the unit and only a small tensor light shone at the security desk near the unit door, where the other guard thumbed through a hunting catalog, waiting for his break. Regs required him to stay at the desk during the head count, but that didn't mean he actually paid attention.

Dexter approached Alice's cell, dipping his head to check each door on the way. There were five head counts a day in the house, including one at 3:00 A.M., but what they called last count was at midnight. It was the best time to execute step one of her plan.

The guard drew closer to Alice's cell. She shifted in the shadows and double-checked that the screwdriver she'd boosted from the computer shop was still in place. It was. Dexter was only two doors away. Her cellie was in her bed, pretending to sleep. Alice wasn't worried about the kid. She knew enough to keep her mouth shut.

Dexter was one door away, tilting his head toward the cell. Alice moved directly in front of her door. Dexter reached her door and coughed. At the same moment, he slipped his key inside the knob and extracted it smoothly. She shoved her hand in the door to keep it open, and he passed silently, moving on to check the next cell as if nothing had happened.

Alice stood motionless at her door, watching the other guard in the lamplight below. Through the open door she could hear Dexter's footsteps as he walked along the concrete balcony, pausing at rhythmic intervals to check a cell door. Her hand began to throb in the heavy door but she didn't open it wider. She didn't want that hunter looking up at the wrong time.

Alice watched the other guard turn the pages, then close his catalog and look up expectantly. Dexter reached the last cell door on the tier, then walked down the wire steps to the floor of the unit, his electroplated badge catching the light of the lamp as he reached the security desk.

"Ready, Jake," Dexter said, his voice faint, and the other guard left the unit. After he had gone, Dexter unlocked the unit door and yawned theatrically, the signal to Alice, then walked toward the outdoor area. As he stood in front of the window, his back to the unit, Alice slipped out the door of her cell, flattened her back against the cinderblock wall, and bolted. She sprinted in a crouch under the windows of the cells, hurried down the stairs in her sneakers, then darted out the unlocked door of the unit.

She was on her own. The hallway was quiet, dead-still, and dim. A line of low-wattage lights down the middle of the corridor lighted her path like a runway. She scooted along the wall, running a finger along the cinderblock, her heart pounding. Not with fear, with excitement. The guards' break room was down the hall to the right, but nobody would come out now. Dexter had brokered the deal. Alice sprinted around the corner into the corridor that led to the computer room. She arrived at the door and stuck a finger into her sneaker for the key. She fished out the key, shoved it in the lock, and slipped inside, breathing hard.

The computer room was dark and empty, but Alice felt right at home. The monitors were lined up against the wall, their dustcovers sloppy, and the seats in a row in front of them. She'd have met Valencia in this room but for the security camera behind the curved mirror. She couldn't fix everything. It was probably too dark for the camera to pick her up, but Alice wasn't taking any chances.

She hurried through the lab to the adjoining storage room and let herself in with the same key. The room was full of dusty cardboard boxes that contained ancient 286 machines, castoffs that ended up here for a rehabilitation that would never happen, like the inmates. Sticking out were some Gateway boxes, with those stupid cow-spots in black and white. They were new computers that some rich bitch donated to make herself feel good, and Alice had been mickeying with the inventory to disappear them. She knew two guards who wanted them for their kids and was about to barter them when the Rosato thing happened.

Alice hunched behind the boxes. The plan was for the guard to let Valencia enter through the other door, off the hall, not the one off the computer room. Valencia would probably be worried, wondering why a meeting about her case had to be held in the dead of night, but she'd come anyway, like a sheep to the slaughter. The weak needed only an excuse. They agreed to their own death.

Suddenly the doorknob twisted open on the other side of the room. Alice edged out of sight, flattening against the boxes at the sound. Valencia would be shuffling through the door in the next second, and Alice knew exactly what she had to accomplish. Put her at ease, then kill her. Alice peeked around the box.

But the silhouette in the doorway wasn't Valencia's. The outlined shoulders were massive, the hands huge. The form was Leonia's. Alice recovered from her surprise a second too late.

Leonia charged like a Brahma bull. Her heavy hand arced through the air and a homemade knife glinted in the light from the hallway. Alice grabbed Leonia's wrist in midarc and squeezed. The two women wheeled around the room, crashing into cardboard boxes as they fought for the shank. Alice's arms spasmed with effort. It wasn't enough. Leonia threw her backward.

Alice fell against the boxes and slid down. Leonia was on her in a split second. The shank hovered above Alice's chest. Her heart thundered. Adrenaline poured into her bloodstream. She forced herself to think. To act. "No!" she shouted, and kneed Leonia brutally in the pubic bone.

"Ugh," Leonia grunted in pain and released her grip. Alice rolled to the side, whipped the screwdriver from her waistband, and whirled around.

"You bitch!" Leonia shouted, getting up, and Alice grabbed Leonia by the hair, wrenched her neck backward, and stabbed the sharp screwdriver into Leonia's throat.

Leonia's eyes flared wide in shock. Her mouth opened

but no sound came out. Blood welled around the screw-driver. Leonia struggled to stand up, still alive.

It was harder to kill somebody than most people real-ized, especially a bull like Leonia. Alice shoved the screwdriver deeper, wedging it into the soft tissue near the jugular. She couldn't pull it out or she'd be covered with blood. Tough to explain to the prison laundry. Sud-denly the door opened and Alice turned.

Valencia stood shocked in the doorway, and Alice knew instantly what to do. "Help me!" she whispered, and Valencia stepped forward, already starting to whimper.

"Díos!" she said, more a cry than a word.

"Take her knife!" Alice ordered, and Valencia bent over and took the shank from a stricken Leonia and handed it to Alice.

"Thank you," Alice said, taking the knife. "Now hold the screwdriver."

"Hol' *what*?" Valencia asked, horrified.

"The screwdriver! Now!" She grabbed Valencia's hand and placed it on the screwdriver. Valencia turned her head away, like a kid at the dentist, which was convenient. Alice raised the knife and brought it down into Valencia's chest, burying it deep.

Valencia emitted a baby's squeak and collapsed to her knees, falling heavily to the floor. It was a solid hit. Alice stood over them both, panting hard, waiting until they'd bled enough. It had gone well. Two birds with one stone. It would look like a prison fight with the inmates killing each other. Alice even took the extra step of wrapping Leonia's hand around the shank, just to be sure. Her tracks were covered. All the prints were right. The guards would stay quiet or they'd incriminate themselves.

Alice waited until she was sure they were dead, then left the room and slipped back into her cell with Dexter's help. She undressed in the dark to the sound of her room-mate's bogus snoring and eased silently into the saggy bed. Later she'd deal with Shetrell, pay her a little visit. It was too risky to do right now, and Alice felt tired. She was fake-sleeping by the time the sirens went off much later, signaling that they'd found the bodies.

49

Surf was hiding by the entrance to Della Porta's row-house when Rosato ran out like a bat out of hell, the dog bounding beside her to the Ford. She hadn't turned out the light upstairs so he didn't know she was coming. He'd missed his chance to get her in the entrance hall. Damn! Rosato was running so fast he didn't run after her. She would've made him easy, maybe screamed.

Surf stepped behind the tree as the Ford roared out of the space. Then he darted to the TransAm, climbed in, and twisted on the ignition. He stopped abruptly. Hold on a minute. What was going on? Rosato hadn't been in a hurry to get to Della Porta's but she was in a real big hurry to leave. Why?

Surf peered over the rumbling hood of the car at Della Porta's apartment. Rosato had left the light on. What was she doing up there anyway? Why did she run out?

Surf switched off the ignition and got out of the TransAm.

50

Bennie pulled up, confused by the sight. It was the dead of night, but the prison was alive with activity. Light blasted through its slitted windows into the night and alarms screamed from the watchtowers. Vehicles of all sorts clogged the entrance: black cruisers from the Department of Corrections, white squad cars from the city cops, news vans with tall poles for microwave transmission, and three fire rescue trucks. What had happened? An escape? A fire? Bennie steered into the parking lot with an excited Bear running back and forth on the backseat.

A Philadelphia cop came toward her. "Back it out!" he shouted over the din, waving her off with a black Maglite.

Bennie stuck her head out the window. "My client's in there. I have to see my client. Lawyers on trial have twenty-four-hour access."

"Not tonight, lady."

"What's going on? Has there been a fire?" Fright gripped her stomach. As furious as she was at Connolly, she didn't want anything to happen to her.

"I said, back it out, lady!" the cop shouted, but Bennie pulled beside the entrance, yanked up the emergency brake, and leapt from the car. "Hey, wait!" the cop bellowed after her, but she ran toward the hubbub. Her breath came in ragged bursts and she realized she was afraid. She didn't know why, or how, but she was afraid. There could have been a fire. The rescue trucks. Or a fight, a riot. She raced toward the crowd of officials and reporters, then shoved her way to the entrance.

"Whoa, there," said a tall prison guard, blocking the front door with another guard in a black shirt. "Nobody's going in here tonight."

"But my client, my twin, is in there," Bennie heard herself say.

"Sorry. We have orders not to let anyone into the facility. Even family."

"What? Why? At least give me some information. What's going on? Is it a fire, a riot?"

"A problem," the guard said, glancing at the other.

"What kind of problem? Come on, tell me. Jesus, it's all over the news, right?" Bennie gestured at the news vans, and the guard softened reluctantly.

"Knife fight. Two women inmates killed."

"No!" Bennie cried. "Who? Do you have names?"

"Next of kin ain't been notified, right, Pete?" He looked at the other guard, who shook his head. "Can't tell you nothin' 'til then. It's procedure."

"Just tell me, was Alice Connolly killed?"

"Connolly?" The guard shook his head. "That's not one of the names. You're okay."

Still the news struck Bennie like a deadweight. She couldn't understand the dull pain at the core of her chest. She should have been relieved, but she wasn't. A knife fight. Something felt very wrong. "Who was killed? Tell me."

"That's all we can tell you. You want to see your twin, call in the morning and arrange it with the warden. They'll be in lockdown all night. Open for business as usual tomorrow morning."

Bennie turned away without a word. She couldn't speak. She couldn't see. Television klieg lights were everywhere. Sirens blared. Reporters yakked into microphones. Bennie's gut torqued with emotion. It was hard to breathe. She found her way to the fringe of the crowd. She gulped cool air and regained her footing.

A double murder, the night before Connolly's trial. The same night after she and Connolly had talked. Holy God. Bennie squinted up at the brick of the maximum security institution. Red, white, and blue lights flashed on its façade like a carnival. THE OPPORTUNITY TO CHANGE glinted in the kaleidoscope of colors, and she remembered the day she met Connolly.

And then Bennie knew. Deep within, the knowledge grew without notice or warning and spread beyond logic and rationality. Her bones told her, rattling with the news, then Bennie's very heart confirmed it. Connolly had killed tonight. Bennie knew it, sure as she lived and breathed. Her mind reeled and she found herself caught behind a TV crew. White lights flashed on, and she slipped from the glare as she heard a cameraman say, "Okay, Jim, on in five, four, three, two, one."

"Jim Carson reporting, this just in," said an anchorman's voice. "The dead in tonight's fatal stabbing have been identified as Valencia Mendoza and Leonia Page. Prison officials are investigating how . . ."

Valencia Mendoza. *Valencia*. Bennie didn't need the report to confirm what she already knew. Connolly had killed Valencia. Bennie had raised Valencia's name and only hours later Valencia was killed.

Bennie spun on her heels, TV lights blinding her and sirens screaming through her brain. She stormed back through the crowd, keeping her head low to avoid being recognized, and charged to the main entrance, where the same two guards stood in front of the main door, regarding her wearily.

"I have to see Alice Connolly," Bennie said, finding her voice.

"Told you, lady. They're in lockdown."

"She's my client and she's on trial on Monday. She has a right to consult with her attorney, a constitutional right." Bennie wasn't certain of the legalities but she wasn't about to be stopped. "You won't let me in, I want to see the warden now."

"He's busy."

"You're refusing to let a criminal defendant consult with her attorney? You want to be responsible for that?" Bennie's fierce gaze flicked from one guard's black nameplate to the other's. "Officer Donaldson and Officer Machello. Those names will look good in the caption. You guys ever been sued for infringing the civil liberties of inmates? Depositions, trial, it's a lot of fun. Costs a fortune, too, but you gentlemen probably have trust funds."

"We got orders," the guard said flatly. "It's not our decision."

"Then why are you deciding?" Bennie asked, and the guards exchanged looks.

Bennie had never met with Connolly in the secured "no-contact room," but the warden had ordered it given the crisis. The room was smaller than the standard interview rooms, telescoped down to cell size, and a dense bullet-proof window divided prisoner from lawyer, for the lawyer's protection. Bennie gave the scratched plastic a sharp rap with her knuckles. Tonight it would protect the inmate from her lawyer.

The room smelled rank and its white cinderblock walls were scuffed. A metal grate with chipped white paint ran under the bulletproof panel, to allow voices to go through but not contraband or weapons. Bennie stood on her side of the room, waiting for Connolly to be brought up. She'd waited for over an hour already, but the time hadn't cooled her off. Instead she grew only more horrified. Connolly was a killer, and on Monday Bennie would be defending her on a murder charge. The thought turned her stomach. She paced the tiny room behind the plastic chair bolted to the floor on her side of the window. She was trapped in this case, against everybody's better judgment. Someday she hoped for better judgment of her own.

Bennie's head snapped around as the guard unlocked the door on the inmate's side of the no-contact room and let Connolly in. Then he closed the soundproof door and stood directly outside it. Inmates weren't left unguarded for no-contact visits and especially not tonight. Bennie faced Connolly, who plunked down in her chair, her cuffed wrists slipping between her legs. She looked sleepy and less attractive than before, since her makeup had worn off. Or maybe because Bennie knew the truth about her.

"Now what?" Connolly said. The metal grate under the window drained the humanity from her tone, though Bennie was becoming convinced she had none anyway.

"Busy night up here, isn't it?"

"Shit, yeah. Sirens. Assholes everywhere. Lockdown. They keep waking us up. I can't get any rest."

"The only ones who can are Valencia Mendoza and Leonia Page."

Connolly blinked. "This is true."

"That's a good start. Let's talk about what's true." Bennie sat down and glared through the plastic at Connolly. "You killed Valencia."

"No."

"You killed Leonia."

"No."

"Tell the truth."

"I have."

"I'm sick of your lying," Bennie said through clenched teeth, and Connolly grinned crookedly.

"Nobody's sicker than me."

It took Bennie aback momentarily. "I found out Valencia was dealing for you and told you that the last time I saw you."

"I'm not a dealer."

"Yes, you are. You and Della Porta were in it together. I found your nest egg tonight. Half a million bucks under your living room floor. You killed Valencia to shut her up."

Connolly's head flopped to the side and she covered her eyes with her cuffed hands, but when she moved her hands to the side, she was grinning. "Peekaboo."

"This isn't a game. I asked you a question. You killed Valencia, didn't you? And you killed Della Porta, too."

"No," Connolly said. "I didn't kill Anthony, I told you that."

"I don't believe a word you say, not after this. You're a liar, you're a cheat. You sell drugs for money and you murder without remorse. You just stabbed two people to death and you're pissed because we're keeping you up."

"I didn't kill Anthony, I swear."

"Fuck you."

"Fuck you back," Connolly said evenly, then rose and pressed her face to the bulletproof glass. Her eyes loomed cold and furious, though her expression had hardly changed. "Get up. Stand up."

"Why?"

"You want the truth, stand the fuck up."

Bennie stood up and leaned close to the glass, almost eye-to-eye with the inmate who looked exactly like her. With their matching haircuts, tense and exhausted expressions, and lack of makeup, they could have been a single woman leaning close to a mirror. None of this was lost on Bennie, who fought to maintain emotional control.

"Fine," Connolly said, "I lied before. I sold coke and rock for a living. Lyman Bullock, who I fucked silly, laundered the money and socked it where nobody will ever find it, for a very healthy cut. I had a good organization, with good workers, the boxers' wives. I ran those girls like you run yours. *Better*."

Bennie struggled to contain her thoughts, in tumult.

"I capped Valencia and that black bitch. You have to, doing what I do. It's a cost of doing business." Connolly's gaze bored into Bennie. "But the truth is, I did not kill Anthony."

"I don't believe you."

"You should. That went down the way I told you. The cops did it, I swear to God. That's the truth."

"The cops? Why?"

"Money, of course. We started out in business with them, Anthony did, but I could see we could do better without them. They were deadweight, and we didn't need them for distribution, we had the girls. So we went solo and started cuttin' in on their action. We were gettin' bigger and bigger, and they musta got wind of it. I think they killed Anthony because of it and set me up for the murder.

Anthony always said they had friends in high places, but I have no way to prove it. That's where you come in."

"You expect me to prove it," Bennie said, her mouth dry as bone.

"You're goddamn right I do. You have to prove those shits did it. I didn't kill Anthony, they did. It goes all the way to the top. The D.A., the judge. They're all in on it. They have to be."

Bennie's head throbbed dully. That much of it rang true, after the way Judge Guthrie had acted in his office. But could it be true? Could Connolly be guilty of everything *but* Della Porta's murder?

"Now you're my lawyer, you can't get out, and you have to prove me innocent."

"Innocent is the last word I'd use."

"Whatever. And while I'm spilling my guts, everything I told you about Winslow was true, except I made up that blood syndrome and the dream shit." Connolly's hands pressed against the glass. Her manacled wrists made her fingers look like the jointed legs of a wolf spider. "Fact is, I don't know if I'm your twin and I don't care. I don't need a sister, I don't need anybody. As soon as you get me off, I'm outta your life. Got it, *sis*?"

"Don't ever call me that," Bennie snapped, and withdrew from the divider.

51

Bennie spent the night driving around the city in the dark, with the dog asleep in the back. She didn't know where she was headed; she had nowhere to go. She didn't want to go home and she couldn't bring herself to return to Connolly's apartment. She didn't belong anywhere anymore. She had lost herself.

At dawn she drove home and slipped into bed beside a deeply snoring Grady. The sound used to make Bennie smile, but tonight nothing could do that. She didn't sleep, just lay there, and finally got up to work in her home office, since it was Saturday. Then she showered, dressed, and avoided her lover's inquiries until it was time to go and bury her mother.

Bennie's shoulders sagged in the smooth oak pew as she sat through the Mass at the Catholic church in her mother's old neighborhood. The church was shabby and small; though neat and well kept, with brown marble arches and walls the color of cantaloupe. Red votive candles flickered in stepped rows to the right of the altar, before a statue of the Virgin Mary, which Hattie prayed to before the Mass began. Bennie didn't bother, on the assumption that her previous prayers had been ignored. The facts spoke for themselves, as lawyers say.

Her mother's casket remained in the aisle, draped in a white cloth, dignified except for the steel gurney peeking from under the cover. Bennie avoided looking to the left, and still couldn't completely comprehend that her mother was gone, entertaining a child's doubt that her mother was in fact in the coffin. Then she remembered: They'd held a brief service at the funeral home, where Bennie had said a final good-bye and lightly rubbed her mother's hand. She hadn't even minded that the hand felt cold, even hard, because it was the last time. Then she held Hattie when the funeral director asked them to leave the room, and Bennie knew that they were going to close the casket then and seal her mother inside. So of course her mother was *in there*. Of course.

Bennie chased the thoughts from her head as the Mass began, with heavy organ music and a lone tenor who sang "Ave Maria." She had always regarded "Ave Maria" as the Church's trump card at funerals, but resisted tears by concentrating on the goings-on at the altar. Two young girls were assisting at the ceremony, which Bennie noted as a political matter, and she chose not to focus on the words of the old priest. At the end of the Mass, the priest stepped from the altar, his white robes swaying, swinging a large ball of incense that trailed dark and pungent smoke. The smoke filled her nose and brought tears brimming to her eyes, as the priest said something about how her mother was surrendering her body and spirit to Jesus Christ. Bennie knew her mother had surrendered her body and spirit to something quite different, a long time ago, with no choice in the matter. And it wasn't anything half as benevolent as Jesus Christ.

She tried to think back to before her mother's illness had taken over, gradually at first, then completely. Bennie knew her mother had loved her long after she was well enough to say so, though she barely remembered her mother's caring for her as a child. Bennie guessed her mother had performed the routine functions that mothers do every day, for there had been evidence of it. Bennie had won awards in elementary school, tiny pins like tie tacks that lay ignored in her jewelry box, for getting good grades and having good penmanship. She had stumbled across one of the tacks this morning, dressing for her mother's funeral, and it jarred loose a single memory: her mother teaching her cursive writing at the kitchen table, a fleeting picture of the rounded circles and elongated loops of the Palmer method as they swooped above and below the dotted lines.

Like this, Benedetta, her mother would say. *Loop the loop, like an airplane.*

Sitting in the pew, Bennie found herself inferring her mother's acts from the evidence, almost like exhibits in a trial. In school photos, Bennie's hair was always in braids, which she loved, with matching barrettes at the ends. But Bennie didn't braid her own hair at age six. Somebody had braided her hair every morning. Somebody must have matched those silly barrettes. It had to have been her mother, because there was no one else around. Her mother had done those simple things and undoubtedly more, even as she was struggling with the darkness overcoming her. She had been a mother. Bennie's mother.

Suddenly pallbearers appeared from nowhere, genuflected in unison, all six of them, three on either side of the casket. Then they stood up and slid the drape from the casket with a discreet flourish, revealing a name engraved on a brass nameplate. CARMELLA ROSATO, it said, and Bennie wiped her eyes and forced herself to think of nothing but ordering that plate and being pleased that the funeral director had been able to obtain the one she wanted, in a modern font. The pallbearers walked the casket down the marble aisle, rolling it behind the priest and altar girls. Grady took Bennie's arm and walked with her and Hattie behind the casket, through the smoke that lingered in the air like streaks of gray silt in the earth, burning Bennie's eyes and heart.

After the Mass was over, Bennie sat in the back of the gray limo, sandwiched between a somber Grady and a weepy Hattie, and only then did function return briefly to her brain. She remembered her father and wondered if he'd be at the cemetery, then the thought vanished into the chilly swoosh of the limo's robust air-conditioning. "Cold in here," Bennie said, which gave her something to say and think about until they reached the cemetery. Grady held her hand loosely, his profile to the overwide window of the limo, the passing scenery distorted in the convex lenses of his wire-rims.

The three traveled wordlessly to the cemetery, passing through its wrought iron gates, and Bennie looked outside the window for the first time with any interest. Hattie merely grunted. To Hattie's disapproval, Bennie had rejected the parish cemetery for a suburban memorial park. Hard to quarrel with a rolling lawn dappled with sunlight and a pond with Canada geese, which took leisurely flight, honking against a cloudless sky, as the limo cruised past. No stone angels, granite crucifixes, or mausoleums marred the natural view; the monuments were tastefully recessed, flush with the ground. Bennie knew her mother had never seen this much open land in her life, much less an actual Canada goose, yet something told Bennie her mother deserved to be here, among natural beauty. She was entitled to it, at least, in death.

The grave had been prepared as the limo pulled up, and

mounds of rich, clay-veined earth lay heaped around a concrete vault. The entire affair had been set up under an incongruously cheery yellow canopy, which Bennie considered uprooting and shredding with her bare hands. One of the funeral directors waved to her with a gesture more appropriate to an airport runway, and Bennie was propelled toward him and given a single red rose. She stared at it in her hand, and it felt frosty from a florist's refrigerator. Bennie flashed on her father's fresh-cut cosmos and looked around reflexively. The memorial park was green and quiet. A warm breeze flickered through the distant trees. Winslow was nowhere in sight, and there were no monuments for him to hide behind. He had not come.

She thought it would matter, but it didn't. She thought she'd want to see him, but she didn't. She felt satisfied he wasn't there, and neither was Connolly. After last night, Connolly's presence would have profaned this place. In the end it was as it should be, as it had been in the beginning and throughout, just she and her mother, only the two of them, alone together.

Bennie stood beside the glossy casket, trying to stand up straight while the priest droned away, and when he was finished and it came time for her to place the red rose over the brass nameplate, she realized that there was no other person in the world she truly needed, except one. And, oddly, it was someone who could offer her nothing but her own needs, and somehow that had been enough.

CARMELLA ROSATO.

Who rested, finally, in peace.

52

"**Y**ou *jerk*! You little *jerk*!" Star shoved the squirrelly dude against the alley wall. It was dark, but Star could see his head bounce off the brick. "You little prick!" Star shouted at him.

"No! Don't kill me! Please, God!" The dude's hands flew up to where his head got hit and he crumpled in half like a paper doll, falling to his knees on a pile of rotted wood and greasy drywall. The corner was filled with garbage spilling out of Hefty bags. "No, please. Star! It's fixed, it's fixed! It's already fixed!"

"You screwed it up, dumb ass." Star came at the man, grabbed him by his skanky-ass hair weave, and slammed his head back against the wall. The man screamed in agony. "You think you're gonna get a second chance?"

"I said, we fixed it," the dude whispered, his voice weak with pain. "It's a done deal. T-Boy and me, it's all square."

"T-Boy? T-Boy?" Star tightened his grip on the hair weave and started to pull. "T-Boy was the one said he'd get it done. Said nothin' would go wrong, remember? Well, somethin' went wrong, real wrong! I can read the newspaper! You think I wouldn't see? The fight is next week!"

"Wait. No. Please. Listen." The little bitch clawed at Star's hands as he pulled the weave. "No, oh, no. Please. My plugs, that kills. Please!"

"Everything went wrong, didn't it? Con'ly whacked your bitch, bitch." Star kept yanking on his hair weave. The dude squirmed like a catfish so Star pulled harder. "Con'ly's alive and your bitch is dead!"

"We'll fix it, you'll see. We'll get her after the trial, inside or out." The dude went up on tiptoe. His scalp stretched like salt water taffy.

"You gonna look like Don King, bro!" Star shouted, and felt the plugs start to come free in his hands. "How you gonna get to Con'ly in the courthouse?"

"Aah! Stop! No!" Tears rolled down the dude's cheeks. "My hair! You're *pulling it out!*"

"No kidding!" Suddenly Star yanked with brute force and a fistful of hair came out. Bloody scalp, hair, and skin stuck to it like glue. "You and T-Boy get to Con'ly! Finish the job you started! I'll call you and tell you 'xactly what you're gonna do. You'll do her and bring me proof!"

"God help me," the man moaned. Blood bubbled out of his head and dripped over his forehead. He lost consciousness and slid down the brick wall.

"Don't forget your wig-hat, mama," Star said, and slammed the rat hair on the dude's bloody head.

53

"Bennie, I'm real sorry about your mother," Lou said, riding in the passenger seat of Bennie's Ford, heading with her to Connolly's apartment. She had called him at home after the funeral. She told him they had something important to do, despite the hour.

"Thanks. Sorry I called you so late."

"Don't matter. It was just me, with a beer and sunflower seeds in front of the Phillies game. They're losing anyway." Lou loosened his tie, looking suddenly uncomfortable in his navy-blue jacket and khaki slacks. "You sure you feel up to working?"

"I'm fine." Bennie steered through Saturday-night traffic, heavy because of the suburbanites heading to the restaurants. They'd drive in from Paoli and other ritzy neighborhoods to gawk at the pierced nipples and purple haircuts. Take a look at the gritty city through the tinted window of a Jag. "Trial's Monday."

"But you just had the funeral—"

"I know that, Lou."

"Gotcha," he said, and looked over at Rosato, still dressed up in a black suit. Her eyes looked red, but they stayed straight ahead over the steering wheel. She had a job to do, she was doing it. The broad was tough, but Lou respected that. She'd make a good partner, in a way.

"The canvassing went bad, I hear?" Bennie asked.

"For the defense."

"That's what Mary said. I read her notes. DiNunzio's a good lawyer, isn't she?"

"Whiny, but okay."

"She gave you a hard time?" Bennie smiled. "For that she gets a raise."

"You know, if you weren't having such a bad day, I'd make it worse."

Bennie laughed, for the first time in years, it seemed. "So what else you doin' for me?"

"I'm gonna finish canvassing around the block tomorrow."

"That was my thought. Winchester Street, where the alley comes out. See if anybody saw the arrest. Anything."

"I know." Lou looked out the window at the mirror on his side of the Ford. A line of traffic crawled behind them like a caterpillar, and two cars back cruised a black TransAm. Lou had seen it behind them before, around the office. Funny it should be going down South Street, too. He kept an eye on it out of habit. Once a cop, always a cop. Lou couldn't drive a highway without checking license plates, trying to pick out which car was stolen or had drugs in it. He kept his eyes on the TransAm. "I been thinking about your case, Rosato."

"What do you think, champ?"

"I think Connolly killed a cop and she's goin' down for it." Lou watched as a navy Town Car behind them peeled off to the right, leaving only a sky-blue BMW convertible between them and the black TransAm. The BMW was a nice little car, a two-seater. "The neighbors I met, they knew what they saw. They're eyewitnesses, and she ran from the collar."

"She was afraid of the cops. She had good reason."

"Only bad guys are afraid of good guys." Lou's eyes stayed on the outside mirror. The BMW was sweet, and behind it he could almost make out the driver of the TransAm in the streetlights. A blond kid, good-looking. Lou remembered when he was that young. He owned a used Chevy Biscayne, two-tone, turquoise and white, with a push-button shift on the dash. They didn't make cars like that anymore. Tanks.

"I agree. Connolly's as bad as they come, badder than bad, but I don't think she killed Della Porta. Too much else is going on. Too much I can't explain."

Lou didn't say anything. He'd heard about the twin thing. He figured Rosato was getting manipulated by a con. She wasn't the first lawyer; she wouldn't be the last. Somebody like Rosato, she wanted to believe, inside. The Ford turned onto Tenth Street, and the blond kid in the TransAm turned, too. Keeping his distance, farther back than he had to. It was standard surveillance procedure, Lou recognized it instantly. "Take three right turns, Rosato," he said quickly.

"What? That's a circle."

"Old cop trick. Humor me."

Bennie blinked, but steered the Ford right at the next street. "We being followed?"

"Tell you in two right turns."

She took a right and glanced in the rearview. A convertible sports car. Then a black TransAm. "The sports car?"

"The other," Lou said, eyeing the TransAm as it followed them to the next corner and turned right. "It's still on us."

Bennie's fingers tightened on the wheel as she coasted to the corner and took another right. The BMW stayed straight and so did the TransAm, behind it. Her mirror went clear. "They're both gone," she said, relieved.

"There you go. It was nothing. So why are we going to the crime scene?"

"You're my investigator. You gotta investigate." Bennie was choosing her words carefully. She was taking Lou to the apartment so he could find the money under the floor. She couldn't testify about finding it because she was a lawyer, but Lou could. She didn't want to corrupt his testimony, so she had to let him find the money on his own.

"You want me to investigate the crime scene, almost a year later?" Lou frowned. "Should be clean by now."

"Should be."

"Shouldn't be anything there."

"Shouldn't be."

"For this you got me in a tie? On a Sunday night? I'm *shvitzing*."

"I'll turn up the air." Bennie racheted up the Ford's air-conditioning and pretended she was paying attention to her driving, and Lou laughed softly.

"You're a lousy liar, Rosato."

"The worst in the bar association."

"I wasn't born yesterday."

"I could tell, from all the wrinkles," Bennie said, and turned onto Trose Street. She double-parked and Lou got out, checking for the TransAm. It wasn't in sight. Kid was probably cruising for girls. Oh, to be young again, he thought, and followed Bennie to the rowhouse.

"So what do you want me to see?" Lou asked, once they were upstairs. His eyes narrowed as he entered the apartment and looked around, appraising it with a professional eye.

"I can't tell you that."

"Where am I supposed to see it?"

"Can't tell you that either." Bennie closed the door and leaned against it, getting her second wind. It felt almost good to be out with Lou. Doing something; not thinking about her mother. "That's why you make the big bucks."

"Ha." Lou stepped into the center of the room. "Am I warm?"

"No. And I thought you were so smart."

"No, just handsome." Lou walked to the left side of the room, where the blanket chest was askew, the way Bennie had left it, to conceal the hole in the floor. "I'm getting warmer, aren't I?"

"You tell me," Bennie said. She felt a shiver of excitement as Lou bent over and slid the chest aside with an audible grunt. His testimony would be terrific at trial. He was so credible, so clearly loath to find evidence that pointed away from the accused cop killer. Bennie could only imagine the jury's reaction when Lou testified about the money he found under the floor of a highly decorated detective. It would be enough evidence of illicit dealing to permit Bennie to prove that Della Porta was killed by competing drug dealers, whether they were police or not. Bennie suppressed her excitement.

"I think I'm getting warmer," Lou called back as he squatted and pulled up the floorboards Bennie had replaced.

"It's entirely possible." Bennie remained at the door, keeping her distance. She wanted his testimony absolutely pure. "Not just another pretty face, are you?"

"Not me." Lou tossed a strip of stained floorboard aside and it landed with a clatter. "Here we go."

"Did you find anything?"

"I think so."

"What is it?"

"A hole."

"What's in the hole?"

"*Bupkes.*"

"What?"

"It's Yiddish. It means 'nothing.'"

"I know what it means." Bennie hurried to Lou's side and stood stricken over the open floor. The hole in the floor was completely empty. The money was gone. Her mouth dropped open. "I left a package of money there. Five hundred thousand dollars, at least."

"*Five hundred grand?*" Lou squinted, astonished, from his haunches. "Here? You gotta be kiddin'."

"No, I found it. I swear." Bennie's thoughts raced ahead. What would she do without the money? She couldn't prove police corruption at trial now, not without Connolly's testimony, and there was no way she'd put Connolly on the stand. What would Bennie do for a defense?

"Rosato, you feelin' okay?" Lou rose and brushed down his khakis, wrinkled at the knee like an elephant's knees. "Your mom, and all. It's a tough—"

"No. There was money there. I found it and then put it back."

"When?" Lou asked, and Bennie told him the whole story, everything she knew and everything she had learned. Her defense was falling apart, and it was time to trust someone. Lou's face fell into grim lines as she spoke, his expression changing from surprise to suspicion. When Bennie finished the account he said nothing, but walked to the wall and flicked off the light overhead, plunging them both into darkness.

"What are you doing?" she asked, as Lou crossed the living room to the window.

"Come here," he said urgently, and Bennie joined him. A line of cars was parked at the curb on the other side of Trose Street, and she followed Lou's finger to the one at the end.

A black TransAm.

BOOK THREE

Kill the body and the head will die.

—**A boxing maxim**

54

The Criminal Justice Center was built as a replacement courthouse for City Hall because the City of Brotherly Love had so many criminals, City Hall couldn't try them all. A slim column of blond sandstone with modern art deco touches, the new Criminal Justice Center stood like the pretty younger sister across the street from the Victorian dowager that was City Hall. Courtroom 306 was the largest courtroom in the Justice Center, and the only secured one. A wall of clear plastic, bulletproof and soundproof, spanned its width and divided the bar of court from the gallery, which was packed with reporters and spectators. A trio of sketch artists sat together in the front row, one armed with tiny brass binoculars.

Bennie waited at counsel table for trial to begin, hating that the lawyers, judge, and court personnel were behind glass. It made her feel uncomfortably as if she were on television and the gallery were a studio audience; not that she could point a finger, considering her trial strategy of the "twin defense." Since the other night, however, Bennie had discarded any plan of looking like Connolly at trial. She wore her hair unstyled this morning, had on no makeup, and her suit was the navy one she always wore to court. Except for the haircut, she looked almost like her breezy, confident self again, though she didn't feel that way inside.

Her mother's death was a pain that Bennie felt more acutely, like a wound that grows more sensitive to the touch. She had never been so aware of her aloneness in the world, and it made her vulnerable, shaky. The thought would cross her mind to call her mother's doctor, a reminder sent for so many years from the tickler file in the back of her brain, and each time Bennie got the message, she recalled anew that it was a phone call she no longer had to make.

Her gaze fell on the blank legal pad in front of her, refocusing her on the task at hand: Try this case and win. Bennie had come to believe that Connolly, though hardly innocent, hadn't committed the murder for which she stood trial. Somebody else had, and that person was getting away with murder. It was wrong, and that Connolly deserved to be punished didn't make it right, because the next defendant wouldn't. For Bennie, justice was always about the next defendant. And in this case, it could also be about saving her mother's other daughter, as loathsome as she was.

"Let's get started, ladies and gentlemen," said Judge Guthrie, taking a quick sip of water from a tall glass. The judge wore a bow tie of Stewart plaid with his robes and slipped off his tortoiseshell reading glasses. His sharp eyes focused on the courtroom deputy, and if he recalled his meeting with Bennie at all, it didn't show. "Please bring in the defendant, Mr. Deputy."

The deputy hurried to a door on the side of the modern courtroom, which was concealed behind a mahogany panel. The judge looked expectantly at the closed door, and the spectators turned their heads as one. The district attorney, Dorsey Hilliard, sneaked a glance, and Bennie arranged her face into a professional mask. The paneled door opened and a cop in a black windbreaker entered the courtroom, followed by Alice Connolly.

Bennie almost gasped at the sight.

Connolly had performed a makeover in reverse, to look like Bennie. She had dyed her hair a pale blond color that matched Bennie's and it hung as unstyled as Bennie's. She wore no makeup, uncharacteristically; and her royal-blue suit and white shirt complemented Bennie's own navy suit and white silk shirt. No wonder Connolly had opted not to be present for jury selection; she had wanted to preserve her surprise. Connolly must have realized that after the prison murders, Bennie would lose heart for the twin defense, and had evidently decided to stage it herself, with a vengeance. When Connolly crossed the courtroom, it was as if Bennie were watching her reflection in a true mirror, seeing herself walk in her own direction.

She felt blindsided, suddenly thrown off-balance. The defendant had become the lawyer; the twins had traded places. It was as if Connolly were trying to steal her position, her reputation, her very self. Bennie had created a monster and it was her. Looked like her. Walked like her. Then the monster sat in a seat next to her at counsel table, faced the front of the courtroom, and awaited the beginning of the trial like a seasoned litigator.

Bennie looked quickly around. At the prosecution table, Hilliard was reading papers, undoubtedly hoping not to draw attention to the similarity, but everyone in the courtroom had eyes. The deputy nudged an already surprised court reporter. Judy and Mary, sitting at the bar of court behind counsel table, were exchanging looks. Judge Guthrie peered over his glasses at Connolly and Bennie, then frowned deeply at the gallery.

Crack! Crack! Crack! "Order, ladies and gentlemen," the judge said into a black stem of a microphone, which would carry his warning through hidden speakers to the gallery. "There must be order in this courtroom throughout these proceedings. We may not be able to hear you through the glass, but the same rules of decorum still apply. Anyone who doesn't abide by them will be ousted." *Crack!* Judge Guthrie banged the gavel. "Kindly escort the jury in, Mr. Deputy, and let's begin."

Bennie forced herself to relax, preparing for the only opinion that mattered: the jury's. The twelve people who would have Connolly's miserable life in their hands. She recrossed her legs, then noticed that Connolly was recrossing her legs the same way. Bennie would have said something, but the jurors began filing in, shuffling through the door. She watched them with a stony face, waiting for their reaction. Jurors always looked cowed when they entered a courtroom for the first time and this jury was no exception. They walked into the jury box with their heads down and found their seats as self-consciously as late theatergoers.

Bennie pushed herself back into her chair. She knew the jurors would steal glances at defense table and absorb the visual impact of her sitting next to Connolly, like bookends. She wished she could hold up a sign that said, THIS WAS ALL HER DOING, but then realized that it wouldn't be true. It *was* Bennie's doing. She had devised the twin defense and set it in motion. She was locked in a prison of her own making. And the murderer was on the outside, with the key.

Bennie felt like apologizing to every juror. They were a smart jury, with a higher education level than most. She and Hilliard had picked them in record time for a death-qualified jury, because Judge Guthrie had presided over voir dire and permitted only the most routine questions. It wasn't her favorite way to pick a jury, but Bennie had relied on her instincts, biases, and judgment to wind up with a good, fair crew.

Crack! "This is *Commonwealth v. Connolly,* Docket Number 82634," Judge Guthrie said. "Good morning, ladies and gentleman of the jury. We met earlier during voir dire and now it's time to begin our work in earnest. Mr. Hilliard, are you ready for your opening argument?" His graceful tone sounded more like a question than an order, and Hilliard reached for his crutches, placed them expertly under his elbows, and rose from his seat.

"I am, Your Honor." The district attorney nodded curtly in his dark, pinstriped suit, sharply tailored around his large, muscular frame. The jurors eyed him as he walked to the podium, grunting slightly from the effort of movements they all took for granted. Bennie watched their gaze lingering on the contradiction of a huge, strong body that couldn't power itself even a single step forward. Well-meaning people, the jurors' faces showed a sympathy they couldn't help but feel. It was an open secret that Hilliard's disability gave him a politically correct edge with them, though it clearly wasn't intended. His disability was a nonissue for him.

"Ladies and gentlemen of the jury," he began, "my name is Dorsey Hilliard and I represent the people of the Commonwealth of Pennsylvania against Alice Connolly. The defendant has been charged with the crime of murder for the death of her lover, Detective Anthony Della Porta. I do not believe in lengthy arguments. I let my witnesses do my talking for me. So I will keep this brief."

Hilliard raised his voice, his bass tones resonant and his cadence no-nonsense. "The Commonwealth will prove that on the night of the murder, the lovers argued, as they did with increasing frequency. After the argument, the defendant shot Detective Anthony Della Porta point-blank in the head with a handgun. The Commonwealth will prove that the defendant did intentionally, and in a premeditated manner, murder Detective Della Porta, one of the most respected and decorated detectives in the Philadelphia Police Department."

Bennie shifted in her chair, thinking of the money she'd found under the floorboards. How the hell would she get it in?

"The evidence will show that neighbors heard the lethal gunshot and saw the defendant fleeing the scene of the crime. Police arrived at the scene and also saw her fleeing, holding a plastic bag. They saw her run into an alley to escape them. They were able to arrest her only by chasing her and finally tackling her to the ground. Even then, the defendant fought to escape, and what she told them when they arrested her will not only shock you, it will prove to you beyond any doubt that she is guilty of this crime."

Back at defense table, Bennie tried not to squirm. She could only imagine what the cops would make up. At her shoulder, Connolly was shifting in her seat, though Bennie couldn't tell if it was artifice or nerves.

After a pause, Hilliard continued. "Once the defendant was in custody, police conducted a complete search of Trose Street, including the alley that the defendant had run into. You will hear evidence that there was a Dumpster in the alley, and in the Dumpster, authorities found that plastic bag, which contained clothes belonging to the defendant. Experts will tell you that the clothes were soaked with the still-warm blood of Detective Della Porta." Hilliard paused again, as if for a moment of silence. "By the last witness for the Commonwealth, each of you will be absolutely certain that the defendant killed Anthony Della Porta and is guilty of murder. Thank you for your attention, for your service to the Commonwealth, and to our country." Hilliard eased into his crutches and returned to his seat.

"Ms. Rosato," Judge Guthrie said, "we're ready for your opening argument." He moved some papers on the dais, without looking up. The black marble backdrop behind the dais glistened darkly and the ersatz gold disk of the Commonwealth shone like a tarnished sun.

Bennie rose to her feet, her expression only apparently confident. She walked straight to the jury, bypassing the podium. She always delivered her arguments standing directly in front of the jury, talking to them eye-to-eye. Usually Bennie knew exactly what she'd say.

Not today.

55

Bennie slipped her hands in her skirt pockets and stood silent for a minute, head down, trying to compose herself. She thought of her mother, and Connolly. Then the black TransAm, for which she looked every trip to and from the courthouse, and the murdered inmates. The rarest thing in a courtroom was a lawyer not talking, and Bennie felt, more than heard, the courtroom fall quiet and the jury waiting, their eyes on her. She looked up, cleared her mind, and did another remarkable thing. She decided to tell them everything, and all of it the truth.

"My name is Bennie Rosato, and I represent Alice Connolly, who is accused of murder in this case. I remember selecting you for this jury, and you were an intelligent group, so I will address you as such. You have undoubtedly noticed that Alice Connolly and I look alike. We look like identical twins, in fact."

"Objection, Your Honor," Hilliard said, pushing himself out of his seat with two solid arms. "Ms. Rosato's familial relationships are absolutely irrelevant to this case."

Judge Guthrie slipped his glasses from his nose. "Please approach the bench, counsel."

"Yes, sir." Bennie swallowed hard and strode to the dais, where Hilliard met her, standing next to a court reporter.

Judge Guthrie leaned forward. "What is going on here, Ms. Rosato?"

"I'm making my opening statement, Your Honor. I want to deal up front with a matter the jury has to be wondering about, as you must be."

"Your personal relationships have nothing to do with the guilt or innocence of this defendant." Judge Guthrie shifted unhappily and the rich folds of his black robing caught the overhead light. "Your twinship is a collateral issue at best."

"Of course it's collateral," Hilliard agreed, his tone angry even at a whisper. "It's more than collateral, in fact. It's completely irrelevant and prejudicial."

Bennie held up a slightly shaking palm. "That's precisely my point. It is collateral, but it has the power to distract the jury so much they can't focus on the evidence. If I don't deal with this issue at the outset, the whole trial they'll be thinking—are they twins or aren't they?"

Hilliard's shaved head snapped toward the judge. "Your Honor, does defense counsel really expect us to believe that she didn't dress her client for court today? That she didn't hide her for jury selection? Ms. Rosato wants the jury to make the connection between her and her client. Their hair and their clothes are the same. She's managed to personally vouch for the defendant without saying a word."

Bennie grasped the dais more urgently than she wanted to acknowledge. "I'm trying to defuse this situation, Your Honor, by putting it on the table. Ms. Connolly is on trial for her life, and as defense counsel, it's an error not to afford me the latitude to dispose of any issue that will obviate her ability to get a fair trial. I have every right to finish my opening, Your Honor. I . . . have no choice."

Judge Guthrie frowned. "I'm going to overrule the objection for the present time. However, Ms. Rosato, rest assured that if there is case law that governs this type of trickery, my law clerks will find it. In addition, any attempts the defense makes to personally vouch for the defendant's innocence will subject you to contempt. You may continue, Ms. Rosato, but proceed with the utmost caution."

"Thank you," Bennie said, though she felt as if she'd been mugged. Hilliard walked back to counsel table, and she returned to the jury, eye-to-eye with an older black woman who sat front and center. Belle Highwater, age sixty-two, librarian; Bennie remembered from the jury sheets. The librarian's straightened hair was graying and frizzy at the temples and her brow was divided by a furrow Bennie hoped she hadn't caused.

"What I was about to tell you," she continued, "is that there is an issue we have to deal with right now, before it gets in the way of this trial. It's obvious to all of us, it's staring us right in the face. Take a good, long look at my client, Alice Connolly. Go ahead, ladies and gentlemen, don't be shy. Look now and take her in. Look at Alice Connolly's face, body, clothes, and makeup, or lack thereof. Notice even the way she sits."

The jurors' heads turned obediently, and Connolly stiffened in her seat at the unexpected scrutiny. Bennie enjoyed her discomfort. Exposing Connolly's stratagem to the jury would rob it of its power. Bennie was regaining control of the case. She couldn't have planned it better. She hadn't.

Bennie cleared her throat to get the jury's attention. "Now, if you would, look at me. Compare my face, body, and clothes with my client's." Her arms rested at her sides as fourteen pairs of curious eyes swept her form. "Notice anything? It's obvious, isn't it? Alice Connolly looks like me, even dresses like me, doesn't she?" Bennie paused, and the black librarian nodded. "When she walked in this morning, I was amazed at how much we look like twins. She even sits like me and will probably use some of the same gestures I use at counsel table. But the truth is, I have no idea if Ms. Connolly is my twin or not. I didn't meet her until this case, so it's as much a mystery to me as it is to you."

A juror in the front row, a young white man with a goatee and tiny Ben Franklin glasses, edged forward on his seat, intrigued. Bennie remembered him from the jury sheets, too: William Desmoines, age twenty-six, Temple grad, videographer.

"I am raising the issue only to answer as honestly as I can a question you must have. I cannot change the way I look, and I cannot change the way Alice Connolly looks. I cannot help that we look alike, nor will I hide it from you. All I can do is ask you not to focus on the similarity between me and Ms. Connolly, but concentrate only on the evidence and the testimony in this case."

Hilliard's eyes narrowed. At the bar of court, Judy stirred restlessly, hiding her confusion. Either it was the coolest opening argument she had ever heard or Bennie had lost it completely. Next to Judy, Mary prayed the rosary in her head. *Pray for us lawyers, now and at our last billable hour. Amen.*

Bennie walked to the corner of the jury box. "The prosecutor and I agree on only one fact: this is a court of law, and your job is to find the truth. You must determine whether Alice Connolly is guilty or innocent of the murder with which she has been charged. The prosecutor can parade witnesses at you, but at the end of the day, remember this: all they have is a bare, circumstantial case. No one saw Alice Connolly commit this crime, no one could have. By the end of this trial you will be convinced that not only can the Commonwealth not prove its case against Alice Connolly beyond a reasonable doubt, but that Alice Connolly is completely innocent of the murder of Anthony Della Porta. Thank you."

Bennie walked to her chair and sat down, avoiding Connolly's eye. She had no idea how she'd prove what she said. She just knew that it was true and she was the one meant to prove it. Here and now.

56

Wind sent discarded newspapers rolling along the grimy city curb. It was a blustery, gray morning, teetering on the edge of a summer thunderstorm. If the weather couldn't make up its mind, neither could Lou Jacobs. He stood on the stoop of the rowhouse and hesitated before he knocked. His fist hung in the air, hovering clenched before the front door. He felt damn uncomfortable helping get a cop killer off. Then again, he felt damn uncomfortable that the cop may have been dirty. Lou had spent the past few days asking everybody he knew about the black TransAm. Nobody knew the car. Lou had even cruised around, trying to pick up the TransAm on a tail, but no soap.

Lou stood at the front door like a sophomore on his first date. He was starting to think the TransAm meant zip. As for the money under the floorboards, that was touchy to bring up with his friends, and Lou would never slam another cop without proof. That money could have come from anywhere. The lottery. The slots. Savings. Anywhere. Then he thought again. Yeah, right. *Half a mil?* Hot damn!

Lou knocked on the door but no one answered. He had to finish the job he'd started, canvassing the neighbors. It was the only way he knew to do a job. Slow and steady wins the race. The address of the rowhouse was 3010 Winchester Street, the street in back of Trose; it was the first house where the alley came out and where McShea and Reston had collared Connolly. Lou had to believe he'd find something on Winchester if he just took it methodical.

Half a mil.

Lou thought about knocking again, then lowered his arm and stood there like a stupid ass. Couldn't even decide whether to knock. Half of him wanted to know what was going on; the other half would just as soon let it lie. The neighbors had IDed Connolly running down Trose, then Winchester. They all said the same thing. Lou could feel it to his marrow: Connolly was the doer. Whatever Della Porta had been into, she was into deeper, and he was the one who got dead in the end. Lou didn't like helping her walk.

Hell with it. Screw her. He turned from the door and climbed back down the stoop, buttoning his blazer around his waist so it wouldn't fly around. He strode down the street, trying not to think about the money. He woulda loved to have even five thousand in the bank for a cushion, but he didn't, not with his alimony payments. The economy was through the roof and his ex-wife was the only one who couldn't find a job. She was a welfare queen, and he was the Democrats.

Lou put his head to the wind. He'd never taken a bribe as a cop, not a nickel, though he had plenty of opportunities, all small-time. If Della Porta was dirty, shame on him. Now that he was dead, his shame should die with him.

Lou reached his brown Honda and dug in his pants pocket for his keys. He didn't need this aggravation. It wasn't what he signed up for when he went with Rosato. This kind of crap was up to Internal Affairs, not to him. He was just a beat cop, retired, and though he had always done careful police work, he'd realized a long time ago that he wouldn't be one of the great ones. Didn't have the head for it, or the taste. The killer instinct some of them had or that politician's touch.

Lou got inside his car and was about to turn on the ignition when the guilt got to him. He always thought of himself as a man of his word. He had given Rosato his word and he couldn't let her down, especially not now, with her mother gone. He could see it broke her up, more than she let on. Maybe more than she knew. Lou understood, he was like that when his mother passed. Besides, he always kept his word as a cop, even though he wasn't a higher-up. He was proud of the integrity he brought to the badge.

With a sigh, he switched off the ignition, got out of the car, and went back to 3010 Winchester Street.

57

On the witness stand, Officer Sean McShea wore a navy-blue uniform that strained at its double seams to accommodate his girth, and his peaked cap rested next to a worn Bible with red-edged pages. He spoke into the microphone with authority and warmth in equal measure. "How long have I been with my partner, Art Reston?" McShea asked, reiterating the prosecutor's question. "Seven years. Not as long as my wife, but she's a better cook."

The jury laughed, but Bennie simmered at counsel table. She hadn't been at all surprised to hear that McShea played Santa Claus at Children's Hospital, a fact he managed to slip into his early testimony. McShea was everybody's favorite neighborhood cop and the perfect choice for the Commonwealth's first witness, like a legal warm-up act.

Hilliard was smiling, leaning on his crutches at the podium. "Now, Officer McShea, let's turn to the events of the night in question, May nineteenth of last year. Did there come a time when you and Officer Art Reston received a radio report about a gunshot fired at 3006 Trose Street?"

"Yes. The report came over the radio when we were a block away, traveling north on Tenth Street. We happened to be in the area when we heard the report. Since we were so close, we kept driving on Tenth Street to Trose."

"Did you formally respond to the call?"

"No."

"And why was that?"

"As soon as I heard the report, I just hit the gas and reacted. I knew the address was Anthony's, uh, Detective Della Porta's, and I knew we were close enough to do something about it."

"In retrospect, should you have radioed in that you were responding to the report?"

"Yes, but I was concentrating on saving a cop's life."

Hilliard nodded, approvingly. "Officer McShea, what did you and your partner do next?"

"We drove to the corner of Trose Street and stopped the car."

"Did you see anything on Trose Street?"

"Yes. We saw the defendant. She was running down Trose Street from the scene of the crime."

Bennie shot up. "Move to strike, Your Honor. That's speculative and misleading."

"Overruled. The witness is expert enough to make such conclusions, Ms. Rosato," Judge Guthrie said, his lower lip puckering. It etched two tiny lines at each corner of his fine mouth and wrinkled his chin wattles into his bright bow tie. "Please proceed, Mr. Hilliard."

"Officer McShea, how did the defendant appear to you when she was running? Emotionally, I mean."

"Objection," Bennie said, half rising, but Judge Guthrie gave his head a wobbly shake.

"Overruled," Judge Guthrie said, and Bennie added a silent hashmark to the tally of the objections she'd lost.

She was only two for ten. Any time Judge Guthrie could rule against her without arousing suspicion or annoying the jury, he would. Trial judges had carte blanche on evidentiary rulings, and appellate courts didn't throw out jury verdicts unless the evidentiary errors made a difference in the trial's outcome. Otherwise, they were legally considered "harmless error," although Bennie believed no errors were harmless when a life was at stake.

McShea cleared his throat. "She looked panicky, stressed. My kids would say she was 'freaked.'"

Hilliard walked to a large foamcore exhibit, a black-and-white diagram of Trose Street, which had been set up on an easel and faced the jury. "Referring to Exhibit C-1, would you show the jury where you first spotted the defendant that night?" Hilliard gestured to the exhibit resting on the easel's ledge, raising his crutch like a personal pointer.

"Sure," McShea said, wielding the pointer with practiced motion. "We saw her right in front of the day care center, which is 3010 Trose Street. She ran past the day care center, westbound, past 3012 and 3014, to the alley."

"Officer McShea, would you tell the jury what you and Officer Reston did after you saw the defendant run west on Trose Street?"

"We pulled the patrol car up to Trose Street and just as we were about to turn the corner, we saw the defendant running toward us. The defendant ran past the houses, then took a left into the alley. I put the car in reverse and reversed back to Winchester Street, which is where the alley empties out. The defendant ran out the other side of the alley and down Winchester Street. We drove down Winchester Street, then we exited the vehicle and pursued on foot."

"Describe for the jury, if you would, what you refer to

as your pursuit of the defendant. Use the exhibit if you need to."

"The defendant was running down Winchester, heading east. I kept running down the block after her and so did my partner. My partner outstripped me right here," McShea pointed to a spot on the middle of the diagram of Winchester Street, "and he reached the defendant first. He had to use force to subdue her. She resisted arrest."

"Did either of you identify yourself as police officers during this pursuit of the defendant?"

"Yes, it's procedure."

"How did you identify yourself as a police officer?"

"I shouted, 'Freeze, police.' I know my lines."

Hilliard smiled. "Did the defendant stop running?"

"No, she ran faster. My partner subdued the defendant by tackling her to the ground. She was struggling pretty bad, and he was trying to hold her down. I arrived on the scene and ordered her to get down, so I could cuff her."

"Officer McShea, when you say the defendant was 'struggling pretty bad,' what exactly do you mean?"

"She was kicking, biting, and punching with her arms. She struggled on the ground and kept kicking upward at my partner, in the groin area. I was shouting, 'Get down, get down,' but she wouldn't listen. Before I got her cuffed, she tried to get up and run away again."

"Did the defendant say anything to you while you were handcuffing her?" Hilliard asked, and Bennie's ears pricked up.

"Objection!" she said, rising quickly. "The question calls for hearsay, Your Honor."

"It's not hearsay, it's coming in for the truth, and it's an admission anyway," Hilliard said, and Bennie knew she couldn't discuss this in front of the jury. *Connolly had made an admission?* When had the cops dreamed this up? There wasn't any testimony about an admission at the prelim.

"May we approach, Your Honor?" Bennie asked, and Judge Guthrie motioned them forward. She hustled to the bench and waited until Hilliard reached it. "Your Honor, this is hearsay."

"If it's an admission, it comes in, Ms. Rosato. You know the rules."

"There was no testimony about any admission at the preliminary hearing. Whatever this admission is, it should have been supplied to the defense, and it wasn't."

"Your Honor," Hilliard piped up, "the Commonwealth was under no obligation to offer each and every statement to the defense, and Ms. Rosato has total access to her client. She could have asked her."

Bennie gripped the beveled edge of the dais. "But, Your Honor—"

"I've already ruled," Judge Guthrie interrupted, shaking his head. "The statement is admissible."

"Thank you, Your Honor," Hilliard said, and returned to counsel table. Bennie did the same, her face betraying none of the anxiety she felt as she sat down next to Connolly. An admission could be lethal to the defense.

Hilliard walked over to the witness stand. "Officer McShea, what did the defendant say to you when you arrested her?"

Officer McShea spoke clearly into the microphone. "While I was cuffing her, she said she did it, and she offered us money to let her go. She offered us thirty thousand dollars apiece and when we said no, she upped it to a hundred."

Silence fell in the courtroom, as if the trial had suddenly stalled in a pocket of dead air. An older juror in the front row leaned back in her chair and a young woman next to her blinked. The black librarian scowled at Connolly, who was scribbling a note to Bennie on her legal pad. Connolly wrote, I BEGGED THEM NOT TO KILL ME. Bennie skimmed the note without comment. All she could think was, they just did.

"Officer McShea," Hilliard continued, "is it your testimony, then, that the defendant confessed and attempted to bribe you not to take her into custody?"

"Yes."

"And you refused?"

"Of course. When we didn't accept, she demanded a lawyer."

Hilliard paused to let it sink in. "Officer McShea, permit me to take you back a minute, in the events of that night. When you first saw the defendant running down Trose Street, did you see anything in the defendant's hand?"

"Yes, she was holding a white bag. Plastic, like you get at the Acme. Or, I should say, my wife gets at the Acme. I can't take the credit when she does the work." McShea smiled, as did the women in the front row of the jury. Connolly shifted next to Bennie, but didn't say anything.

"Now Officer McShea, fast-forward to when you and Officer Reston were arresting her. Was she still carrying the white plastic bag?"

"No. The defendant had nothing in her hand when I cuffed her."

"So the white plastic bag vanished when the defendant came out of the alley, is that correct?"

"Objection," Bennie said. "The district attorney is testifying, Your Honor."

"Overruled," Judge Guthrie barked, and addressed the

witness. "Officer McShea, would you answer the question, please?"

"The plastic bag was in her hand when the defendant ran into the alley and it wasn't there when we arrested her."

"When did you next see that bag, Officer McShea?" Hilliard asked.

"We took the defendant into custody, locked her in the squad car, and went looking for the plastic bag. We both saw her go into the alley with it and come out without it, so we knew pretty well where it had to be. I'm smarter than I look."

Hilliard smiled and leaned on the witness box, so close to the cop he was practically in his seat. It wasn't Hilliard's handicap, it was his way of vouching for the cop, so common Bennie thought of it as the D.A. lap dance. "Officer McShea," he said, "tell the jury the results of your search."

"Officer Reston and I searched the alley in the middle of the block, toward the west end. In the alley was a Dumpster, from the construction across the street. We searched the Dumpster and in it we found a white plastic bag, like the one I saw in the defendant's hand."

"Did you find anything inside the bag?"

"Yes. A woman's gray sweatshirt. It had blood all over it. It was still wet and warm."

Hilliard picked up a tagged white bag from the evidence table and moved it into evidence. Bennie watched as the jurors craned their necks at the dark streaks on the crumpled sweatshirt, which could only be blood. "Officer McShea, I'm holding Exhibit C-12 and C-13. Is this the white bag and the sweatshirt you found?"

The cop stretched out a hand for the clothes bag and examined it through the plastic, turning it over. "Yes."

"Now, Officer McShea, you testified that you found the sweatshirt, C-13, in the Dumpster in the alley. Was the Dumpster full or empty?"

"Pretty full, lots of construction trash. Boards, rubble, and whatnot."

"Did you have to dig in the trash to find this sweatshirt?"

"No. It was right on top of the other trash."

"Was it concealed there?"

"Not at all."

Bennie eyed the jurors. To a one, they were engrossed in the story. McShea's testimony was easily understood, absolutely incriminating, and totally false. She'd have to handle him with care on cross.

"Officer McShea," Hilliard asked, "by the way, did you or your partner find the murder weapon in the alley?"

"No, we didn't. To the best of my knowledge, the murder weapon was never recovered."

"I see." Hilliard paused. "Did there come a time when you and your partner took the defendant down to the Roundhouse, the police administration building, in the squad car?"

"Yes, sure."

"When you took the defendant to the Roundhouse, was she visibly upset or crying over the death of her lover, Detective Della Porta?"

"Objection, Your Honor," Bennie said. "Does Mr. Hilliard mean other than the witness has already described? People show their grief in many different ways." Her mother's face materialized suddenly in her mind's eye.

"Rephrase the question," Judge Guthrie said, leaning back again. He arranged his robe around him and patted the gathered stitching that ringed his robe like a yoke.

"Officer McShea," Hilliard asked, "was the defendant crying when you took her to the Roundhouse?"

"No, but a couple of us were," McShea said, bitterness tainting his tone, and Bennie knew instantly that the jury would be reminded that the murdered man was a fallen policeman. She had to find a way to let them know what their hero had hidden under his floor.

"I have no further questions. Your witness, Ms. Rosato," Hilliard said, his tone grave. "Thank you."

Hilliard gathered his papers at the podium as Bennie stepped from behind counsel table, buttoned her suit jacket, and shook off her mother's image. She had to prove to the jury something that adults should already have known. There really was no Santa Claus.

58

Bennie took a second to frame her first question. She'd tried enough cases to know that some of the jurors had already decided she was representing a cold-blooded cop killer and would regard her with the same loathing as her client. But most of them would reserve judgment, and she saw them casting an inquisitive eye on her and Connolly's complementary blue suits and identical hairstyles. She hated the scheme she'd set in motion and wished she could wriggle from her own skin, like a common snake.

"Officer McShea," Bennie began, walking to the podium, "what is your district?"

"The Twentieth."

Bennie didn't use the map of the city she'd had made because it would slow the exam. "Now, just to simplify things, your beat is the western segment of the city, is that right?"

"Yes."

"Isn't it true that Detective Della Porta's apartment is located in a different district, the Eleventh?"

"Yes."

"The Eleventh is on the other side of the city from the Twentieth, isn't it?

"Yes." McShea appeared unfazed, and Bennie walked around the podium, to the edge of the microphone's range. The gallery wouldn't be able to hear well, but she was no longer playing for the studio audience.

"You and your partner were the first patrol car to respond to the Della Porta murder, isn't that right, Officer McShea?"

"Yes."

"You were not responding to a radio call, were you?"

"No."

"You couldn't be, because the first call came into 911 after that, isn't that right?"

"If you say so. Right."

"And you were on duty that night, were you not?"

McShea cocked his head. "We were."

"Now, you testified that you just happened to be in Detective Della Porta's neighborhood at the time. If you were on duty, why were you out of your district?"

"We, uh, went down to get dinner." McShea looked frankly sheepish.

"You went out of your district to get dinner? Where?"

"A cheesesteak, at Pat's. A Cheese Whiz, to be specific."

The jury nodded and smiled. Every Philadelphian got a "Cheese Whiz," a steak sandwich with Cheese Whiz, at Pat's Steaks. Not only would the story strike a hometown chord with the jurors, it was impossible to verify, and so human it sounded believable. Bennie agreed with McShea; he was smarter than he looked.

"So you went to Pat's for a cheesesteak that night?"

"Yes."

"How much time would you say it takes to drive from your district to Pat's Steaks, on Tenth Street?"

"Probably half an hour, if you don't take South Street.

You know how the song goes. That's where all the hippies meet," McShea joked, and the jury laughed with him again. Bennie was aware she was coming off like a killjoy, but she failed to see the humor.

"Let's do the math, Officer McShea. If it takes half an hour to get to Pat's from your beat, it would take a half an hour to get back, right?"

"Sure."

"So far that's an hour. Now, did you eat the cheesesteak at Pat's, at one of the tables outside, or did you take it out and go back to your district?"

"We ate at Pat's. Outside, standing up, next to that big counter with the peppers and ketchup." McShea turned to the jury in appeal, palms up. "I mean, you have to eat at Pat's. It's tradition." The jury smiled, and so did McShea, who let his gaze slip toward the back of the gallery. Bennie didn't turn to see whom he was looking at, with the jury watching her. She assumed it was his captain, since this testimony wouldn't look so good in McShea's personnel file. The cop was entering damned-if-you-do, damned-if-you-don't territory, and Bennie intended to lead him there and buy him a house.

"Now, since this was in early summer, on May nineteenth, I bet Pat's was hopping that night, wasn't it?"

"Sure. Pat's was busy. Pat's is always busy."

"So there was a line out front of the window, where you get the cheesesteaks, is that right?"

"Yes."

"Did you and Officer Reston wait in line to place your order or did you go to the front of the line?"

"I don't remember."

Bennie folded her arms. "I don't get it. You remember

you were there, you remember what you ate, you remember where you ate it, but you don't remember whether you went to the front of the line or not?"

"Objection, asked and answered, Your Honor," Hilliard said.

Bennie faced Judge Guthrie. "Your Honor, this is cross-examination. The defense has a right to understand the events of the night of the murder."

Hilliard rose on his arms. "Your Honor, anything Officer McShea ate for dinner is irrelevant to the commission of the crime in question. He was merely the arresting officer."

Bennie had to bite her tongue. "Your Honor, the issue isn't what Officer McShea had for dinner. It concerns the timing of his arrival at the scene of the crime and how he and his partner 'just happened' to be there."

Judge Guthrie put up a hand and leaned back in his chair. "I'll allow it, in a very limited scope."

"Thank you," she said, as Hilliard eased back into his chair and Bennie faced the witness. "Officer McShea, you were saying you don't remember if you went to the front of the line to order your cheesesteak."

"Probably if it was a busy night, we'd go to the front of the line. If it was a slow night and we didn't have jobs, we'd wait in line."

"Was it a slow night the night of May nineteenth?"

McShea hesitated. "I don't recall."

"Well, if it were a busy night in your district, you wouldn't have left for a cheesesteak, would you?"

"Objection!" Hilliard said, rising. "Your Honor, defense counsel is asking this witness to speculate."

"Is it just speculation that this police officer would do his duty?" Bennie asked, suppressing a smile, and noticed with satisfaction that the juror with the goatee grinned with her. She hoped he'd end up as foreman. She remembered him as bright and articulate from voir dire.

"Sustained." Judge Guthrie nibbled the calico stem of his glasses. "You need not answer the question, Officer."

"I'm pretty sure it wasn't a busy night on the job," McShea said anyway.

"Thank you," Bennie said. "So, Officer McShea, let's assume that on the night in question you waited in line at Pat's. Do you remember how long it took to get to the front of the line?"

"Five, ten minutes at most."

"By the way, how much did dinner cost that night, for you and your partner?"

"I don't remember."

Bennie cocked her head. Either somebody hadn't taken McShea through the details of his story, or he had forgotten them. "You don't remember that either?"

"No."

"Did you pay for dinner or did Officer Reston pay?"

"Uh, I think Reston did. He's always got dough on him. He's single."

Bennie didn't smile. "Do you remember or are you making it up as you go along?"

"Objection, Your Honor!" Hilliard called from the prosecution table, and Judge Guthrie frowned deeply.

"Sustained. Ms. Rosato, I caution you to temper your questions with civility."

Bennie took it on the chin and faced the witness. "Getting back on track, Officer McShea, how long did it take you and Officer Reston to eat your cheesesteaks?"

"Inhaled is more like it. It doesn't take too long, not the way I eat. Fifteen minutes, a half hour, at the most."

McShea glanced again at the back of the gallery, and the look wasn't lost on Bennie, who walked around her table to check the back pew of the gallery. To her surprise, it wasn't any police brass who McShea was looking at, but a uniformed cop. A young, blond-haired cop who looked like a surfer. *Oh, no.* He fit Lou's description of the driver of the black TransAm. Bennie's pulse quickened.

"Let me understand your testimony, Officer McShea." Bennie turned to make a note on her legal pad and passed the pad casually back to Judy. It said, GET THE NAME OF THAT BLOND COP IN THE BACK ROW.

She continued. "Officer, taking your estimate, that's an hour and a half to get and eat dinner that night. How's my addition?"

"Better than mine."

"How many other cars cover your district of the city?"

"One."

"So when you're not there, the other patrol officers are left with maybe sixty city blocks to cover by themselves?"

McShea looked sheepish again. "Hey, I'm not proud of it. It was a onetime thing."

"Nevertheless, how would you characterize your district, Officer McShea, as a high-crime area or low-crime area?"

"It depends."

"If I told you the *Philadelphia Inquirer* characterizes it as high crime, would you be surprised?"

"I'm not surprised by anything in the *Inquirer*," the witness shot back, but Bennie saw that the front row of the jury had lost its sense of humor. They would recognize the neighborhood and were listening with concern, especially the black librarian. As Bennie recalled, her branch was in a rough city neighborhood, and she plainly disapproved.

"Fine." Bennie decided to leave it alone. "So other than the cheesesteak, there was no other reason you were in Detective Della Porta's neighborhood?"

"No."

"You didn't have a meeting with Detective Della Porta that night?"

"No."

"You didn't have a score to settle with Detective Della Porta?"

"Objection!" Hilliard said, half rising. "There's no foundation for that question, Your Honor. What is defense counsel even talking about?"

"Sustained," Judge Guthrie ruled, sliding his chair forward so quickly that a banging noise reverberated through the courtroom's microphone system.

Bennie backed off, for the time being. "You testified that Alice Connolly confessed and tried to bribe you not to take her into custody, is that right?"

"Yes."

"And you testified she did this while you were arresting her, on Winchester Street, is that right?"

"Yes."

"Rowhouses line Winchester Street, do they not?"

"Sure."

"And you arrested Alice Connolly in front of which house, I don't recall you testifying."

McShea looked heavenward for a moment. "I don't know. It was at the end of the block, the east end."

"Was there anybody else who heard this except you and your partner?"

"Nobody else was there."

"Did Ms. Connolly shout this confession?"

"No." McShea snorted derisively. "People don't usually

shout murder confessions in public. Her voice was lower than normal."

Bennie tried to visualize it. "Help me understand this, Officer McShea. You testified that you and Officer Reston had to subdue Alice Connolly, is that right?"

"Yes."

"So I assume her face was down on the pavement and her hands were behind her while you were attempting to handcuff her, is that right?"

"Yes."

"And you testified she was struggling and kicking, right?"

"Yes."

"And you testified you were standing above her, struggling with her, correct?"

"Yes."

"And you were shouting, 'Get down, get down'?"

"Yes."

"So how did you hear Alice Connolly make this so-called confession, if her voice was lower than normal?"

McShea paused. "Okay, it was a little louder than that."

"How much louder?"

"Loud enough to hear."

"Loud enough for the neighbors to hear?"

"Not that loud."

Bennie scratched her head, for effect. "Officer McShea, I'm confused. A minute ago, you testified that Alice confessed in a lower tone than normal. Now you're saying it was a normal tone of voice. Which is it, Officer McShea?"

"Normal."

"Normal enough for you to hear, but not normal enough for anyone *but* you and your partner to hear?"

"Objection, Your Honor," Hilliard said, and Judge Guthrie leaned forward.

"Sustained."

Bennie couldn't do any more with it on cross. She'd have to bring the Winchester neighbors in, in the defense case. "Officer McShea, were you friends with Detective Della Porta?"

"We knew each other."

"How well did you know each other?"

"Saw each other at police events and whatnot. Before he got promoted out, to detective."

"You said 'promoted out.' Do you know which district Detective Della Porta was promoted from?"

"The Eleventh, I think."

"Officer McShea, did you ever serve in the Eleventh District?"

"No, I was always in the Twentieth. It's the neighborhood I grew up in."

"Was your partner, Officer Reston, friendly with Detective Della Porta as well?"

"Yes."

"To your knowledge, has Officer Reston always served in the Twentieth?"

"No."

"He was transferred to it?"

"Yes."

"From where?"

"From the Eleventh."

Bennie thought about it. "So Detective Della Porta and your partner, Art Reston, both served in the Eleventh?"

"Yes."

Bennie hesitated. It was folly to try to root out a conspiracy in open court, in real time, but she had no choice. Whatever dirt they were into started in the Eleventh District and probably stayed there if the pattern held true. "Officer McShea, did you ever visit Detective Della Porta at his apartment?"

"Maybe once or twice."

Bennie's heartbeat quickened. She needed to pin down the specifics of any connection between the two men. "What were the occasions that you visited Della Porta's apartment?"

"He gave a party, I think. Coupla parties. It was a while ago."

"How many parties?"

"I don't remember, it was a while ago."

"You testified that you recognized Detective Della Porta's house number when it came over the radio, isn't that right?"

"Yes."

"So it had to be a lot of parties for you to remember the house number and the house, didn't it?"

"Objection," Hilliard said, but Bennie raised her palms in appeal.

"This is cross-examination, Your Honor."

"Sustained," Judge Guthrie ruled, and began reading papers on the dais.

Bennie glanced at the jury. The librarian looked concerned again and the videographer shot a veiled look at the judge. Judge Guthrie was playing a risky game. If the jury sensed the bias in his rulings and felt that they weren't getting the truth, they'd side with Bennie. She decided to emphasize it to them. It was the only way to combat the judge. "Your Honor, the jury is entitled to understand the connection between Detective Della Porta, Officer McShea, and Officer Reston."

"There *is* no connection!" Hilliard protested.

"I'll rephrase that," Bennie said. "The jury is entitled to understand what, if any, connection exists between these three police officers."

"Sustained," Judge Guthrie ruled again. He leaned over the open index on his desk and for the first time since the cross-examination began, met Bennie's eye directly. She sensed he was trying to warn her off. For her good? For his? In any event, she wasn't listening.

"Thank you, Your Honor," Hilliard said, taking his seat, and Bennie turned to the witness.

"Officer McShea, I'll change the subject for you. Please tell the jury what your job duties are as an active uniformed police officer."

"What do you mean?" McShea asked, wary now, and Bennie slipped her hands into her pockets.

"I mean, what do you do as a cop?"

"I protect citizens from crime and enforce the law."

"What kinds of law?"

"Robbery, murder, auto theft."

"Laws against the use and sale of drugs, as well?"

"Objection," Hilliard said, half rising on arms braced against counsel table. "What possible relevance do Officer McShea's duties have to a murder case?"

Bennie faced Judge Guthrie. "Your Honor, in his direct, the prosecutor established Officer McShea's credentials as a police officer, a father, a husband, even as Santa Claus. The defense is entitled to explore that once he's opened the door. It's a simple question, Your Honor."

"I just don't see any point to it, Your Honor," Hilliard said, glancing at the jury.

Judge Guthrie peered over his glasses. "You may explore this in a very limited scope, Ms. Rosato."

"Thank you, Your Honor," Bennie said, and faced the witness. "Officer McShea, do you enforce drug laws in your district?"

"Yes."

"What type of drugs?"

"Marijuana. Cocaine, crack cocaine, heroin. Meth-amphetamine. PCP. Ecstasy. Shall I go on?"

Bennie shook her head. "That's plenty. Officer McShea, have you ever arrested anyone for use or sale of any such drugs?"

"Yes."

"Have you ever confiscated any drugs in connection with those arrests?"

"Yes."

"Have you ever confiscated any cash in connection with those arrests?"

"Objection!" Hilliard said, rising and reaching for his crutches. "This is far beyond any relevant inquiry, Your Honor."

Judge Guthrie nodded. "I agree, the objection is sustained. Ms. Rosato, please move on to your next line of questioning."

"Yes, Your Honor." Bennie addressed the witness and prepared to let it rip. "I have one final question, Officer McShea. Were you aware that Detective Della Porta was involved in a conspiracy of police officers to sell confis-cated drugs?"

"Objection!" Hilliard thundered, grabbing his crutches and leaping to his feet.

"Sustained!" Judge Guthrie ruled, the stem of his reading glasses almost falling from his mouth. His eyes flared as he looked past Bennie to the jury, then to the gallery on the other side of the bulletproof divider. Spectators chattered to each other, courtroom artists drew at speed, and reporters dashed off notes. "Order! Order!" he shouted, rooting through the papers for his gavel, then forgoing it altogether. "Order in the Court! Order!" The judge turned to Bennie. "Ms. Rosato, if you ever ask a question like that without laying a proper foundation, I'll hold you in contempt. Do you understand?"

"Yes, Your Honor," Bennie said, her chin high. She knew what she'd found under that floor. There was only one way to get it into evidence. She was one step closer.

Judge Guthrie swiveled toward the jury. "Ladies and gentlemen, please disregard that last question. Merely because defense counsel asks a question does not make it so. There hasn't been any evidence presented in this trial that the decedent, Detective Della Porta, had any involvement whatsoever in any illicit drug dealing." Judge Guthrie grabbed his reading glasses from the dais and stood up. "We'll break for lunch and readjourn at one-thirty. Mr. Sheriff, please escort the jury out."

Bennie watched the prosecutor slap his legal pad closed in anger, and she sat down in the midst of the havoc she had created, oddly satisfied.

"Meet with me at lunch," Connolly whispered. Her voice echoed Bennie's own, and the lawyer's satisfaction evaporated in the blink of an eye.

59

Judy, on a mission, shot from her seat as soon as the court session ended. She pushed through the locked door in the bulletproof divider and slipped into the gallery, getting a bead on the blond cop as he headed out the double doors of the courtroom. The cop was at the front of the throng, one of the first to leave. Judy went after him, keeping her head down and charging ahead so the reporters wouldn't bother her. The marble hallway outside the courtroom was mobbed, and Judy lost sight of the cop's blue shirt in the sea of blue shirts. Cops were always around the courthouse waiting to testify.

The blond cop resurfaced near the elevator bank, waiting with a circle of others. There was usually a stampede to get out of the Justice Center at lunchtime and tacit courthouse decorum demanded that cops get priority to the elevators. But Judy was never one for decorum anyway. She threaded her way through the crowd and ended up only one cop away. Underneath the shiny patent-leather bill of his hat, she could see that the cop's blue eyes were large and bright, his nose short, and his teeth bright against his tan. He was a hunk, but too Hitler Youth for Judy's taste. She tried to get a look at the black nameplate on the far side of the cop's broad chest, but he was turned away.

Judy reached for his sleeve. "Excuse me, may I speak with you for a minute, Officer?" she asked, and the cop's eyes hardened.

"I'm late for my tour."

"Maybe I can help you, miss," offered one of the other cops, with a broad smile.

"She's one of Connolly's lawyers, Doug," interrupted the third cop, but Judy's eyes stayed on the blonde. The elevator door had opened and he was slipping inside, wedging himself between the already uncomfortable passengers.

"Wait a minute, comin' through!" Judy said. She barreled into the elevator by bending her knees and plowing ahead, just like Mr. Gaines had taught her. Interesting that boxing lessons came in handy for trial lawyers.

"Hey, look out!" groused one of the passengers as Judy squeezed in the cab and the elevator doors closed behind her. "What you think you're doin', steppin' on my foot?"

"Sorry." Judy looked past the passenger to the blond cop, who kept his gaze averted. She still couldn't read his nameplate; it was blocked. "Officer, I do need to speak with you," she said, but he ignored her. The passengers looked at her like she was crazy, since she had already established that she was ill-mannered. "Meet you in the lobby, Officer."

The elevator doors opened behind her and the crowd in the cab pressed forward, flowing around Judy like a river. The blond cop brushed past her, but she fell into step beside him and glanced at his nameplate. LENIHAN.

"Is there a reason you're avoiding me, Officer Lenihan?" Judy asked, practically running to keep pace. "Why were you in the courtroom today?" The cop plowed through the courthouse lobby, passed the line at the metal detector, and shoved the courthouse door open. "What possible interest do you have in the Connolly case, Officer Lenihan?" Judy called out, brash as a reporter, but he charged ahead.

It was raining outside the Criminal Justice Center, a full-fledged summer thunderstorm, and people crowded for shelter under the entrance in front of the courthouse, talking and smoking until the rain broke. Frail beech trees in aluminum cylinders rustled in the downpour, and people opened umbrellas like new blossoms. A group of lawyers scurried into the rain, and Lenihan bolted between them and across Filbert, heedless of the storm.

Judy dashed after him, beginning to anger. She spent her waking hours asking questions people didn't answer. "Officer Lenihan, stop!"

Lenihan picked up the pace. Heavy droplets pounded on his hat and epaulets, turning them a darker blue in quarter-sized spots.

Judy sprinted to catch up with him, blinking raindrops from her eyes. Her shoulders were getting drenched. "You can't run away from this, Lenihan," she shouted, as she dogged his thick, black heels. They passed an empty office building in a controlled run, its granite façade slick in the storm. The crowd wasn't so thick here, though one old woman peered at them from under a pink ruffled umbrella. "I have your name and badge number!" Judy yelled after the cop. "We'll subpoena you, Officer Lenihan! We'll ask you on the stand!"

The cop whirled around suddenly, his handsome face red with anger. "Did you threaten me?" he said through clenched teeth. "I thought I heard you threaten me."

Judy stepped back in the downpour, feeling a sudden chill she knew wasn't the rain. "What do you know about Della Porta's murder? What are you hiding?"

"Who do you think you are?" the cop demanded, his eyes flashing under the wet brim of his hat, but Judy stood her ground. Stance was her specialty.

"What do you know about Della Porta's dealing drugs? Do you have information for us? Talk to me now and we can make a deal."

"Don't mess where you don't belong," the cop whispered, leaning close. Then he turned and hurried into the lunchtime throng of bobbing umbrellas, their bright colors a cheery counterpoint to a conversation that left Judy shaking.

What the hell had that been about? What did he mean? Rain soaked Judy's smock, and she bounded back to the courthouse, clip-clopping in her clogs like a spooked colt.

60

There wasn't time to go back to the office during the lunch recess, so the defense team staked out a war room in a courthouse conference room, a sterile white cubicle off the courtroom. Light from a fluorescent panel filled the tiny room, which felt crowded with only four chrome chairs with tan wicker backs encircling a round table of fake wood. At the moment, the table was cluttered with deli sandwiches, pungent canoes of kosher dills, and copies of the police activity sheets. Bennie was making notes and wolfing down a tuna fish on rye when Carrier burst in and told her what had happened.

"You did *what*?" Bennie asked, scanning her soggy associate in alarm. She set down her sandwich. "You *threatened* him?"

"Not really." Judy wiped damp bangs from her forehead. "If you don't count the subpoena part."

"That counts," Mary told her, from behind an unfinished tossed salad. She wore a paper napkin bib over a black linen suit and her hair was pulled back into a businesslike twist. "Subpoenas count, definitely."

Bennie frowned. "You were supposed to find out his name, that's all. Lenihan. Good work. I didn't want you to talk to him, much less threaten him."

"He threatened me back, and he's a cop."

"Carrier, if Lenihan was involved in the drug business, he'll be panicking. Your threat could flush him out, make him do something dangerous." Bennie had told the associates about the money under the floorboards, but hadn't told them she was being followed by the black TransAm, to protect them. "From now on, do what I say. No more and no less."

Judy stiffened at the rebuke, and Mary looked down at her salad.

Bennie regretted her sharpness and tried to explain. "The cops are keeping an eye on us, to see how close we're getting. If Lenihan heard the cross of McShea, he'll think we're a lot closer than we are. That's good. I'd like the rats to run scared and see what they do. It'll give me more leads to follow. But I want to do it, not you. Or DiNunzio."

Judy sat down, mollified. "You think Lenihan took the money?"

"Probably. I don't know why he's not halfway around the world by now."

"The bonehead factor?" Judy offered, and Mary shrugged.

"Maybe he just can't imagine leaving Philadelphia."

Bennie shook her head. "Or maybe there's more where that came from. In any event, I'll call Lou and turn Lenihan over to him. Let's us handle the lawyering and Lou handle the investigation, okay?"

"Fair enough," Judy said, unwrapping her sandwich. A roast beef special, with extra Russian spilling out the sides. "Got it. Kill the body, the head will die."

"What?" Bennie asked.

"It's a boxing expression. Mr. Gaines, my coach, taught it to me. It means, you don't have to go for the head, for the knockout. If you keep whaling away at the body, you'll win the fight. Same thing here. If we keep pounding on the bottom of this conspiracy, the top will come tumbling down."

"You're taking boxing lessons?"

"For the case."

Bennie's face fell. "Well, quit. Leave the punching to me, child. It's not a game, and it's not lessons." She stood up. "I have to go. We're on in ten minutes, and I have a date with the devil."

"Hilliard?" Judy asked, but Mary knew who she meant.

Bennie met Connolly as she sat handcuffed in her royal-blue suit on her side of the courthouse interview room. It was cleaner and more modern than the interview room at the prison, but a variation on the same theme: two white plastic chairs on either side of a white counter, and a shield of bulletproof glass that separated client from lawyer.

"I have one question for you," Bennie said, and Connolly scowled. Her skin looked pallid without makeup, or maybe because Bennie wasn't used to the new blond color that seemed to wash out her features, close-up. In any event, the strain of the morning was plain on Connolly's face.

"I don't care about your question. I've been trying to meet with you all lunch," she spat out. "Didn't you get my note? I gave it to the deputy."

"I got your note." Bennie folded her arms and stood beside the empty chair on her side of the glass. "You know a cop named Lenihan? A blond guy, young."

"No. I wanted to talk to you about—"

"Lenihan wasn't in your drug business?"

"If he was, I don't know it, but—"

"You have no idea what cops were in on the drug business?"

"I told you already, no."

"Bull."

"The cops took care of the supply, with Anthony. He didn't tell me, I didn't want to know."

"Bull."

"I never heard of Lenihan. I sold the product, I didn't care where it came from. There was no reason for me to know, so I didn't want to know." Connolly edged forward, a pitchfork of wrinkles appearing above the bridge of her nose. She looked just like Bennie when Bennie was antagonized in the extreme. "What, are you cross-examining me? I'm trying to talk to you. What the hell did you think you were doing in that opening argument?"

"Saving your worthless life," Bennie said. Then she turned on her heel and walked out of the interview room.

61

On the witness stand, Officer Arthur Reston made a more conservative picture than his partner had. He was trim through the waist and collected in his pressed uniform. His neat, dark mustache had been newly trimmed under a straight nose, and his brown eyes were slightly lifeless, which telegraphed as professional from the stand. "No, I did not hear the testimony given by my partner, Sean McShea," Reston answered.

Hilliard nodded. "And that was because you were sequestered, is that correct, Officer Reston?"

"Yes, sir." The witness sat tall in front of the microphone and held his prominent chin high, as if the collar of his uniform were a bit too tight. "I waited outside in the hall until I was called to testify."

"Would you consider yourself a diligent patrol officer, Officer Reston?" Hilliard asked.

Bennie almost gagged but didn't object. Self-serving questions were obvious to jurors, and she knew where this was going anyway.

"I take my job very seriously, if that's what you mean," Reston said.

"You have served for how many years?"

"Fifteen."

"Have you received any decorations because of your performance as a police officer?"

"Yes. I've received several commendations for certain arrests and for bravery. I was Police Officer of the Year last year. I've been lucky."

"Permit me to take you back, if I may, deeper into your career history."

Bennie half rose. "Objection, Your Honor, as to relevancy."

Judge Guthrie nodded. "I'll overrule it for now, but let's not travel too far afield, Mr. Hilliard."

"Certainly, Your Honor." Hilliard squared his shoulders. He seemed energized since lunchtime, not from food, but adrenaline. Bennie had thrown down the glove with her question about drugs and she could almost see Hilliard's juices flowing.

"Officer Reston," Hilliard said, "isn't it true that your former partner was killed in a shoot-out in the line of duty, in which you were also grievously injured?"

"Yes, sir."

One of the jurors coughed, several looked moved, and even Bennie felt a twinge at the tragedy of an officer killed in the line of duty. She had nothing against honest police, only crooked ones, and the thought of death sobered her. She knew what death looked like, had felt its chilly touch in the hand of her mother. She realized now that she had seen death coming in her mother's eyes that afternoon at the hospital, though Bennie didn't want to acknowledge it then, as if greeting death were to invite it.

Hilliard continued, "You were shot in the cheek and spent four months in the hospital and another five in rehabilitation?"

"Yes, sir."

"Officer Reston, you have been partners with Officer McShea for seven of your fifteen years on the force, have you not?"

"I have."

"And you were on duty with him on the evening in question, May nineteenth, is that correct?"

"Yes."

Hilliard checked his notes at the podium. "Please tell the jury why you were in the vicinity of Anthony Della Porta's apartment, at Tenth and Trose Street."

"We stopped down there for dinner, at Pat's Steaks."

"You left your district to do this, is that correct?"

"Only this one time, and because we could get cover."

"So the district is never left unprotected, isn't that correct?"

Bennie half rose. "Objection, Your Honor. The prosecution is mischaracterizing prior testimony."

"Overruled, Ms. Rosato." Judge Guthrie nodded in the direction of the jurors. "The jury can hear for itself."

"It's a minor point, Your Honor, and I'll move on," Hilliard said, waving in an offhand manner. "Officer Reston, you knew Detective Della Porta, did you not?"

"Yes."

"Were you friends?"

"Yes. We both like boxing. Liked. Went to the Blue together, once."

"What is the Blue, Officer Reston?"

"The Blue Horizon, up Broad Street. Anthony, Detective Della Porta, used to get me tickets, ringside."

"Officer Reston, what kind of man was Detective Della Porta?"

Bennie stood up. "Your Honor, I object on relevancy grounds. Officer Reston purports to be a fact witness, not a character witness."

"I beg to differ," Hilliard said, stepping toward the dais. "Ms. Rosato has maligned Detective Della Porta's character and reputation. I think the jury has a right to know what kind of a man Anthony Della Porta was."

Judge Guthrie leaned back in his chair and tented his fingers the same way he had in chambers. Bennie noted that the overhead lights made him look older than his years, or perhaps he'd had a few sleepless nights since their meeting, too. "Overruled," he said. "Mr. Hilliard, I'll allow the question."

Bennie took her seat, frustrated. She could feel Connolly beside her, equally unhappy, but didn't look over.

"You were going to tell us something about Detective Della Porta, Officer Reston."

The cop nodded. "Detective Della Porta was a good man and a fine police officer. He worked his way up to Detective. He got one of the highest scores ever on the exam, which tests general knowledge, you know. Intelligence. It's not about police procedure."

"Do you know if Detective Della Porta was active in civic groups?" Hilliard asked.

"He surely was. Detective Della Porta donated his time to civic groups in his area of interest, which was boxing. He was like a big brother to plenty of boxers, and even managed Star Harald, who's about to turn pro, if any of you heard of him." Officer Reston turned to the jury and scanned their faces for verification. In the middle of the back row, a young black man raised thin eyebrows in recognition. He was Jamell Speaker, thirtysomething, shoe salesman; Bennie remembered him from voir dire.

"Officer Reston, I must ask you an uncomfortable question, one that will come at you from left field, as it did me. Was Detective Della Porta involved in drug dealing, in any way, shape, or form?"

The shock on the cop's face was evident. His dark eyes

flared in disbelief, then anger. His tight lips remained pursed, and the effect was that Officer Reston was too mortified to answer.

"Officer Reston, to the best of your knowledge, was Detective Della Porta involved in drug dealing?" Hilliard asked again.

"Of course not," Reston snapped finally, his voice ringing with anger.

"To the best of your knowledge, did Detective Della Porta ever use illicit drugs himself?"

"No, sir."

"Officer Reston, you have attended parties at Detective Della Porta's apartment, haven't you?"

"Yes."

"How many?"

"I don't recall, but there were several, and they were more like get-togethers, not parties. Detective Della Porta had a lot of friends and we used to go over there after the tour, or after a match, to unwind. He liked to cook. He'd cook omelets for everybody on the three-to-eleven."

"Did you ever see drugs of any kind in use or available at these get-togethers?"

"No, sir."

"I thought as much," Hilliard said quickly, with a pointedly contemptuous glance at Bennie. "Now, to May nineteenth of last year. Can you please describe how you came to arrest the defendant for the murder of Anthony Della Porta?"

Officer Reston testified, telling a terse version of the story his partner had, corroborating Connolly's panicked flight, the sighting of the white plastic bag in her hand, and her confession at capture. Bennie listened without objection, sizing Reston up as a strong witness whose testimony would have to be attacked with some skill. But she wouldn't go over the same ground as she had with McShea; she'd have to get tougher and Reston was the right witness to do it. He was less likeable than McShea, and she wouldn't look like she was picking on him.

"I have no further questions at this time," Hilliard said, and Bennie was on her feet.

62

Bennie began her cross-examination of Officer Reston at the podium, but wouldn't stay there long. She wanted to get in the cop's face, literally. "Officer Reston, you testified that you were a friend of Detective Della Porta's, isn't that right?"

"Yes."

"Hadn't you been to get-togethers at his house?"

"Yes."

"So you knew, didn't you, that his apartment was on the second floor?"

"Yes."

Bennie walked to the jury box and faced the cop. "And you had to be familiar with the layout of the apartment, am I right?"

"Yes."

"So you knew that you entered into a living room, walked to the left through a bedroom, and at the end was a spare room used as a home office, isn't that right?"

"Yes."

"So you knew the clothes closet was in the bedroom?"

"I assume."

"You assume?" Bennie leaned on the jury rail. "The bathroom is in the bedroom, isn't it?"

"Yes."

"If you'd been to several get-togethers at Detective Della Porta's apartment, having omelets and coffee, you probably used the bathroom."

Reston paused, his eyes squinting slightly in thought. "Yes. Once or twice."

"The closet is the only other door in the bedroom, isn't it?"

"Yes, now that I think about it."

"So you were familiar with where the clothes closet was in Detective Della Porta's apartment, weren't you?"

"I guess so, yes."

Bennie leaned against the polished rail. "Officer Reston, weren't you also familiar with the location of the house?"

"Yes."

"In your visits to Detective Della Porta's apartment, did you ever see that there was construction directly across the street?"

"Yes."

"They're building a very large apartment building?"

"Yes."

"Were they building it a year ago?"

"Yes."

"Didn't you see, as well, the Dumpsters out in front for construction debris?"

"I guess, yes."

Bennie braced herself. "Officer Reston, isn't it true that you planted the bloody clothes in the Dumpster on Trose Street, to frame Alice Connolly for this murder?"

"Objection!" Hilliard shouted, rising and reaching for his crutches. "Your Honor, there's no foundation for this question. Again, it comes out of left field, and is irrelevant and prejudicial."

"Sustained," Judge Guthrie said, as Bennie knew he would. She had gotten the statement before the jury, and they were rustling in their seats.

"Move to strike the question and answer, Your Honor," Hilliard added, but Bennie faced the judge.

"Your Honor, there are no grounds to strike the question. It's important for the appellate court to see this exchange, should we need to appeal this matter."

"Motion to strike granted," Judge Guthrie ruled, his blue eyes flashing behind his glasses. "Move to your next question, counsel."

Bennie bore down. "Officer Reston, you testified that Detective Della Porta had many friends on the police force. Who were his other friends on the force, if you know?"

"Objection," Hilliard said from a sitting position at the prosecution table. "The question is irrelevant, Your Honor."

"Your Honor," Bennie said, "it is highly relevant to the defense of this case that Detective Della Porta, Officer Reston, Officer McShea, and other members of the Philadelphia police were involved in a drug conspiracy."

"Objection!" Hilliard barked. "Your Honor, that's slander! Defamation of the rankest kind, and an obvious attempt to distract the jury from the real issues in this case."

"Approach the bench, right now, both of you!" Judge Guthrie snapped, snatching his reading glasses from his nose and gesturing to his court reporter. "Kindly place this on the record."

Bennie approached the bench, sneaking a glance at the jury on the way. The videographer looked worried for her. He was young and urban, and Bennie knew from experience that a juror's willingness to believe police misconduct varied with generational, racial, and even geographic factors.

"Ms. Rosato," Judge Guthrie whispered hoarsely, "the Court has warned you not to follow this line of questioning. There is no evidence of a police conspiracy in this matter, none at all."

Hilliard nodded vigorously. "In addition, Your Honor, the very insinuation is prejudicial. The jury is already looking for proof of a conspiracy that doesn't exist. The only evidence of a conspiracy is counsel's own testimony."

"Your Honor," Bennie said firmly, "it's axiomatic that conspiracies, particularly official conspiracies, are difficult to prove." She fought the irony of arguing the point to a judge who himself was a co-conspirator. "Cross-examination has always been the engine—"

"Please don't argue Justice Holmes to me, Ms. Rosato." Judge Guthrie strained to lean over the dais. "The Court recalls the quotation and though we find it compelling, it is not entitled to precedential weight. You transgressed with that drug reference within the jury's hearing. The Court has already warned you about such references and it is within this Court's powers to hold you in contempt."

"I have to cross-examine this witness, Your Honor." Bennie met his eye. "This is standard cross-examination in a conspiracy case."

"This isn't a conspiracy case, Ms. Rosato."

"It's a conspiracy case to me, Your Honor. Conspiracy to commit murder. The wrong person is on trial here, and I'm entitled to pursue and develop the defense theory of the case. It's part and parcel of Ms. Connolly's right to a fair trial."

Hilliard scowled. "Smoke and mirrors aren't a fair trial, Your Honor. It's the antithesis of a fair trial. Evidence that is irrelevant, such as the kind of innuendo she's peddling as theory, is absolutely inadmissible, for the very reason that it misleads and confuses the jury. This is a smear job, without any proof or specifics."

"I have specifics, Your Honor," Bennie argued, and Judge Guthrie's wispy eyebrows arched behind his glasses.

"Specifics? Kindly let the Court hear them, Ms. Rosato. We'd like an offer of proof."

Bennie gripped the dais. An offer of proof meant that she'd have to show her hand to Guthrie and Hilliard. "Your Honor, case law is clear that I can cross this witness in these circumstances without an offer of proof. I have a right to ask the question, then Mr. Hilliard can object if he wants. But I don't have to offer the question first."

"Well, well." Judge Guthrie puckered his mouth, the slack tissue of his cheeks jiggling with consternation. "You're refusing to make an offer of proof?"

"To you? With all due respect, sir." Bennie shifted her focus to the court reporter, earnestly tapping out her statement on the steno machine. "I want it clear on the record that it is in the best interests of my client for the witness to hear the question before this Court does."

Hilliard exploded, his large mouth agape. "What's she insinuating, Your Honor? Is she accusing you of misconduct? Has Ms. Rosato lost her mind?" He looked genuinely shocked, and Judge Guthrie's hooded eyes flickered with anger, then with something Bennie recognized instantly: fear.

The judge eased back slowly in his chair. "Ms. Rosato, the Court will not respond to what the prosecution so accurately calls an insinuation. Additionally, the record will show that the Court did not impede any exploration of putative official corruption. Please, go ahead and ask your question, but only if it contains such specifics. Mr. Hilliard, kindly take your seat."

Bennie turned from the judge and knew without looking that the jury was anticipating her question, as was the gallery behind her. She blocked them all from her mind. This was between her and Reston. The cop straightened his tie and watched Bennie walk to the spot in front of him with wary interest. She wouldn't get another shot. She had to aim for the heart.

"Officer Reston," Bennie said, "when Officer Lenihan of the Eleventh District testifies that you, Officer McShea, and Detective Della Porta were involved in drug dealing, will he be lying?"

"Objection, Your Honor!" Hilliard thundered. "Move to strike that question! It's irrelevant, prejudicial, and utterly without foundation! Who is Officer Lenihan? What does any of this have to do with Detective Della Porta's murder?"

"Sustained," Judge Guthrie said. He replaced his glasses, then addressed the jury, his mouth quavering faintly. "Strike the question from the record, and ladies and gentlemen, please strike the question from your mind. Ms. Rosato has no right to ask such a question without proof or evidence. Please remember that a question by an attorney is not testimony from a witness stand, and you may not consider it as such."

The jurors looked grave, and a black man in the back row nodded in understanding. But Bennie could see their eyes trained on Reston, whose expression was dull with restrained fury. She had engaged the enemy. She didn't know how far the conspiracy went or who was at the center of it, but she understood that she had provoked it, poked it like a tiger in a pen. But no cage could contain this beast, and sooner or later, it would strike back, defending its own survival.

If Bennie didn't kill it first.

"I have no further questions," she said. She turned her back on the witness, walked back to her chair, and sat down.

63

Surf caught up with Joe Citrone outside the Eleventh, just as he was pulling away. The asphalt of the parking lot behind the station house was a slick black and almost empty. Everybody on tour was out now or at lunch. Citrone had his new partner in the car, so Surf had to play it cool. He couldn't rip Joe's throat out, which is what he really wanted to do. "Joe, we need to talk," he said casually.

"Can't." Citrone looked out the window of the patrol car, his hands resting on the steering wheel. The engine rumbled, jiggling beads of rainwater that warmed on the cruiser's hood. "We just got a job."

From the passenger seat, Citrone's partner Ed Vega ducked his head, smiling under his mustache. "How's it hangin', pal?" Vega said.

"Good, good, Ed," Surf said, drumming his fingertips on the wet roof of the car. "Gotta delay you for a minute, my friend. Your partner owes me some cash, and I'm seeing my girl tonight."

"Gotcha, big guy," Vega said, and Citrone frowned.

"Need it now?" Citrone squinted against the last of the rain that dripped through the window. The storm was dissolving to a fine, chill mist.

"Yeah, I need it now," Surf insisted with a fake laugh, and opened the door. "Cough it up."

"Relax, kid." Citrone unfolded his long legs from the driver's seat and got out of the car. Gravel crunched underneath his shoes, their patent polished to a high shine, and he slammed the car door closed. "Be right back, Ed."

"This way." Surf took Citrone's arm and led him a distance from the car, out of Vega's earshot. Vega could be undercover, for all Surf knew. That was how they got those cops in the Thirty-seventh, with a sting. Took down the whole district. Surf didn't trust anybody anymore, least of all other cops.

"Get your hand offa my sleeve," Citrone said when they were alone. He tugged his arm from Surf's grasp. "I've had it up to here with you."

"*You've* had it?" Lenihan's temper flared. "You messed this up so bad, none of us are going to get out of it."

"You got a fresh mouth, Lenihan."

Surf glanced at the patrol car and flashed a Boy Scout smile. "I told you this would happen. I told all of you, but you thought it was a big joke. We're made, Citrone. Rosato was askin' questions in court this morning. She's on to us."

"Tell me somethin' I don't know. You think you're the only one with people in the courtroom?"

"I don't need *people*. I was there myself." Surf didn't mention the bitch catching up with him outside the courthouse. He didn't want Citrone to give him crap. "I heard it all."

"Then you heard Rosato say you'd be testifying against Art."

"*What?*" Surf looked at Citrone, shocked. "Me, flip on Art?"

"That's not true, is it, kid? She's bluffin', isn't she?"

"Of course she is." Surf's mouth felt dry. "I mean, of course it ain't true. You kiddin'?"

"You shoulda stayed away." Citrone shook his head as he reached into his back pocket, retrieved a slim calf billfold, and plucked out a new twenty from the neatly ordered bills. "Take this in case my partner's watchin'. Then get lost."

"Sure, I'll get lost." Surf snatched the bill from Citrone's hand and pocketed it. "I'll get lost when I get my cut of the half a mil."

"It's comin'."

"Yeah, when is it comin'? I coulda taken my cut off the top. I coulda taken the whole pile, but I didn't. I brought it to you like a good boy and you said to wait. What am I waitin' for?"

"The right time."

"What's that mean? Why can't we divvy it up now? Then we can all get outta Dodge."

"No."

"Why not, Joe? Explain it to me, old man. You might have to say a whole sentence."

Citrone's eyes went flinty. "Every time there's a meet, there could be a witness. Every time there's a phone call, there could be a tap. Be patient 'til the situation is under control."

"Like it was in control last week and the week before that? Della Porta was takin' money from us, and you didn't know about it. He was settin' up that bitch."

"All along, I knew."

"So what, you knew? You knew." Surf's temper gave way and he raised his voice. "You didn't do anything about it, Citrone. That's your MO. You know everything, but you don't *do* anything."

"Calm down," Citrone said quietly, which only made Surf angrier.

"Screw you. You act like you got muscle, but you got nothin' goin' on. *Nothin'!*"

Without another word, Citrone turned around and walked away, leaving Surf standing there in the rainy mist, alone with his fear and his rage.

64

Back at her office, Bennie's associates yammered away while her tired eyes meandered over a print on the wall of the conference room: *Max Schmitt in a Single Scull*, Thomas Eakins's portrait of the rowing lawyer who was the painter's idol. She found herself looking at Eakins himself, unidentified in his own painting and sculling with effort in the background. Eakins had lived in Bennie's Fairmount neighborhood, only a block from her, and his mother had had manic depression most of his life, too. Funny.

Bennie's gaze wandered to the window. She wondered how Eakins felt when his mother died. Why didn't he paint that? Or her? The night offered no answers, only darkness, and clouds obliterated the stars. Bennie had rowed on nights like this night, when the river flowed as black as the sky, carved into onyx ripples by the wind across its surface. On those nights she felt herself at the very center of a black sphere, suspended above and below a darkness without density.

"Bennie, do we have a blood expert yet?" DiNunzio asked, reading from notes on a yellow legal pad. Carrier sat to her left, swiveling side-to-side with nervous energy. To the right of the associates sat Lou, listening carefully, his chin grizzled gray and wrinkling into his hand.

Bennie came out of her reverie. "I'll cross their blood expert. It's a matter of logic, not expertise. I can get him to say what I need."

"Then that's it," Mary said. "There's only twenty-five things left to do, without the blood expert."

"By tomorrow morning?" Judy asked. Her Dutch-boy haircut had gone greasy from a day of raking it with her fingers, and her face, usually so game and honest, looked wan.

"No, not tonight," Bennie said. She stood up and gathered her papers. "All of you are going home, including you, Mr. Jacobs. I'm going to look over my notes for tomorrow one more time, then get out of here. None of us can do good work if we're dead on our feet."

Lou stood up, too, and shook his khaki pants down to his loafers. "That makes sense. I'll finish the two neighbors I have left in the morning, then follow up on Lenihan."

Bennie looked over. "You really think the neighbors will yield anything? If we can work up something on Lenihan, the neighbors won't matter."

"You never know, neighbors see a lot." Lou flattened his tie with an open hand. "I think I got all the scuttlebutt I can on Lenihan."

"That he's a loner who likes the ladies? That he's in the Eleventh and moving up in the department? Then it's time to follow him. I need to know where he goes and what he does the next few days. Take pictures, too, Lou. I want proof so I can cross him on it when he denies it."

Judy nodded, pursing her lips. "If he's smart, he'll lay low. Take a vacation."

Lou shook his head. "It ain't that easy to get vacation time on the force. You have to apply way in advance."

"Let's table this for now," Bennie said suddenly. "We're all tired, and two of us are very old. Carrier, DiNunzio, leave your stuff here, you can start fresh in the morning.

Vamoose!" She waved the associates out of the conference room, and they stood up and shook off their cramped
muscles, giddy at being set free.

"Trial fever," Bennie explained to Lou, who smiled as
they got up from the conference table and left the room.

"I woulda guessed PMS," he said, and Bennie laughed.

"A related syndrome." She followed the associates into
the empty reception area, where they hit the elevator button. The offices were empty except for the hallway. "Lou,
hang with me a minute."

"No problem," he said, as the elevator arrived and the
associates got inside.

"Good night, Mom and Dad," they chimed, and the
elevator closed smoothly, whisking them downward.

"Pieces of work," Lou said, as the elevator rattled
down the shaft. The building was so quiet they could hear
the associates laughing on the way down and the *ping* of
the cab when it reached the lobby floor.

"Yeah, they are." Bennie folded her arms. "So here's
the problem, Lou. You don't want to take it to Lenihan,
do you?"

"I admit, I ain't in love with it."

"Fair enough. Then don't do it. You stay with the
neighbors, do as complete a job as possible. I've worked
with other investigators, I'll call one of them."

"I'm just not convinced it's what you think, is all. I
mean, money under a floor?" Lou shrugged, his hands
deep in his pockets. "That wouldn't be enough to charge a
cop with nothin'. The only thing you're goin' on is Connolly's word, and she has no credibility in my book. She's
rotten to the core."

Bennie flashed on Connolly's confession to the inmate
murders. "She sure is, but she didn't kill Della Porta."

"I don't get you, Rosato." Lou shook his head, exasperated. "You goin' to all this trouble to save Connolly, and here she is, dressin' like you, playin' to the press, the whole nine yards. You're even willing to smear a cop, work all night, do everything for her. Why? Because you feel like her twin?"

"No, I don't." Bennie couldn't shake her memory of Connolly's confession at the prison.

"Then what? You've been around, you gotta know. Somebody like Connolly, even if she didn't kill Della Porta, she killed somebody else, and she'll kill again, sooner or later. She's scum. She belongs right where she is."

"That's not the way it works, Lou. Connolly's not in jail for being bad, she's in jail for killing Della Porta. We can't start putting people away because they're bad. That's not justice."

"Justice?" Lou smirked. "So if she kills three hundred people but not this one, she walks. That's justice?"

"Sorry to say, yes."

"Talk to me after the next murder, lady," he said, and Bennie couldn't think of an immediate reply.

Bennie was halfway up Broad Street when she noticed a dark car following her, half a block down the street and in the right lane. It looked a lot like a TransAm, but she wasn't sure. She drove with her eyes glued to the rearview. She couldn't make out the car's driver or its color, either. The only streetlights on Broad Street were old-fashioned and cast almost no light.

The street glistened from the rainstorm and was deserted except for a boxy white delivery van behind Bennie. The van accelerated and filled her entire rearview mirror. It had blacked-out windows in the back, so she couldn't see through it. The TransAm, if it was the TransAm, slipped into line behind the van.

Bennie cruised to the traffic light in front of City Hall, lit with purplish lighting that cast harsh shadows on its Victorian vaults and arches. Gargoyles screeched silently from the arches, but Bennie hadn't been spooked by gargoyles for a long time. Tonight it was the cops that worried her. One cop in particular.

The traffic light turned red, and she looked at the outside mirror. Behind the van she could see the slanted grille of the car, but it was still too dark to identify it as a TransAm. Maybe it wasn't. She'd thought she had seen a black TransAm four times yesterday and had been mistaken each time. She was getting paranoid.

Still, Bennie hit the gas. The white van trailed her at a slow speed and she could see the dark car following close behind, almost tailgating. The three vehicles snaked around City Hall, traveled past the Criminal Justice Center, and headed for the Benjamin Franklin Parkway. Bennie lived in the neighborhood that surrounded the Art Museum at the west end of the parkway. She had chosen the location because it was affordable, unpretentious, and close to the Schuylkill, for rowing; the same reasons Thomas Eakins had picked it much earlier. Though it wasn't far, Bennie found herself worrying if she'd make it home safely.

She accelerated, and her Ford moved onto the four-lane boulevard that was the Ben Franklin Parkway, slick and wet from the storm. Her tires splashed through a puddle in the gutter, spraying water onto the truck's siders, and the Ford rumbled under the multicolored flags of all nations that flapped in the wind. NIGERIA, KENYA, TANZANIA, read the labels as Bennie sped past. The white van hung back, and after a moment the dark car popped from behind it and charged aggressively up the right lane, directly under a streetlight. It was a TransAm. Blue or black, Bennie couldn't tell, but she wasn't splitting hairs.

Her fingers gripped the steering wheel. The TransAm was thirty yards behind her and coming on strong. Her heart began to pound and she steered her truck around Logan Circle, struggling to remain upright as she whirled around Swann Fountain, which shot illuminated arcs of water into the night. The TransAm sped up, closing the distance between them, and Bennie saw its color as it passed by the lighted fountain. Black. *Oh, no.* The silhouette behind the wheel was of a man. It had to be Lenihan.

Her chest constricted. She thought fast. She had no weapon but she had a car phone, a hands-free model. Her fingers fumbled for the keyboard and she pressed the coded button for 911.

"Emergency operator," said a professional voice when the connection crackled to life.

"I need help. I'm being followed, in a car. A black TransAm." She plowed through another puddle and checked the rearview. It was only her and the TransAm. "I just passed Logan Circle and I'm heading for the Art Museum. What do I do?"

"Are you in your car, miss?"

"Yes! It's a blue Ford."

"And this car is following yours?"

"Yes! Yes!" Bennie struggled to steer and shout at the same time.

"What makes you think this car is following you, ma'am?"

The TransAm was closing in. It was twenty yards behind,

then fifteen. Bennie stiff-armed the steering wheel. "Take my word for it! He's a police officer named Lenihan."

"Did you say a police officer is following your car, miss? Why don't you flag him if you need help?"

"I need help *from* him. Put out a bulletin. I'm traveling west, up Ben Franklin Parkway. Should I drive to a station house?" Bennie had no sooner asked the question than she realized she had whizzed past the street that led her to her district's station house. The TransAm was so close. Then it switched into her lane. Right behind her.

"Help!" Bennie shouted. She trounced on the gas pedal and the Ford rocketed forward, careening up the parkway. The streetlights blurred to bright lines. The flags were streaks of color. It was all Bennie could do to keep the truck stable. She aimed right for the Art Museum.

"Miss, are you there? Miss?"

"Help!" Bennie shouted, her own cry reverberating in her ears. She checked her rearview mirror and squinted against the light. The TransAm blasted its high beams into the Ford. The black car was right on her bumper. She could see the face behind the wheel. His expression, grim. His hair, blond. Lenihan.

A bolt of fear shot through Bennie's body. The Ford barreled down the slick boulevard. Eakins Oval, the rotary in front of the Art Museum, lay just ahead. The traffic light turned red at the cross street but Bennie roared through it. She held tight to the steering wheel and took the curve around the Oval at speed. Light filled her truck and the TransAm jolted the Ford from behind. Bennie hung on to the steering wheel for dear life.

"Miss? Miss?" the operator asked. "Did you say the police are there?"

"No! Help!" Bennie cried, then gave up. The Art Museum loomed dead ahead, looking like an amber-colored temple to the ancient Greeks. Lights at its base set it glowing gold in the night and it stood high atop a promontory. A huge set of stairs led to its columned entrance. They gave Bennie an idea. She had to go where Lenihan couldn't. She drove a truck; Lenihan had a TransAm. It was no contest.

Suddenly Bennie cranked the steering wheel hard to the right and the Ford skidded left. Its back end fishtailed, throwing her against the driver's side door. The impact sent an arc of pain through her left shoulder but she hung on to the steering wheel, frantic. The Ford ended up facing the direction it came from. Bennie spotted the TransAm. It screeched into a full three-sixty, spraying water from its tires like a pinwheel. It would take Lenihan time to recover.

Bennie slammed on the gas and twisted the Ford onto the sidewalk. Her back wheels churned in grit and rainwater. She pointed the Ford at the steps of the Art Museum. There was nowhere to go but up. If Rocky could do it, so could Rosato.

She engaged her four-wheel drive and the Ford bounded onto the pavement and charged up the granite staircase. She bounced in the driver's seat despite her shoulder harness, taking each step to the landing, then racing skyward. Fountains flanking the Art Museum steps spurted water into the air, misting onto the truck. Cast iron gaslights lit her way.

Bennie hit the gas. The truck bobbled like it was racing over railroad tracks. Its suspension squeaked in protest. Her jaw rattled in her skull. Her front tooth sliced through her lower lip. She felt her own warm blood bubble into her mouth. The truck hit the next landing and lurched forward.

Bennie checked the rearview. The TransAm had recovered from its spinout and tore onto the sidewalk after her, but it stalled at the bottom of the staircase. It took three steps up, then lost traction and slid backward. Bennie's heart leapt with relief. She kept the gas flowing and the Ford climbed the next set of steps. Only one set to go to the plaza and the huge circular fountain in front of the museum. The Corinthian columns of its façade stretched before her, five stories high, bathed in golden light. At the top of the tiled roof, Greek gods and goddesses gazed with serene indifference into the dark sky.

The Ford surged forward. Bennie lost sight of the TransAm. She was five steps from the museum plaza. Around the back of the museum was a route she used to run on her way to the Schuylkill, which flowed on the far side of the museum. She wasn't far from Boathouse Row, home of her own fiberglass scull. This was Bennie's turf. She was nearly home free.

She took another jolt as the Ford climbed onto the granite flagstone of the plaza. The lighted fountain misted the Ford's windshield. The Art Museum blazed before her. Bennie careened right, almost crashing into the stanchions that kept traffic from the plaza, then turned left onto the narrow road around the back of the museum. It led to a parking lot and a cobblestone road that returned to the parkway. She'd take the parkway to the nearest police station, back at Twenty-second Street. The voice of the 911 operator sounded far away.

Bennie glanced in her rearview. The TransAm was nowhere in sight. Then she realized it could come around the back. She had to get away before Lenihan came after her. She navigated the narrow road between the museum and a low stone wall. Cast-iron lamps lined the road and Bennie spotted a security camera mounted under one. She prayed museum security would come.

Out of nowhere, Bennie heard the roar of an engine. Her windshield filled with light. She threw up her hands. There was a deafening crash that drove her back into the seat, then snapped her body forward into the shoulder harness. Dazed, she opened her eyes.

Her windshield was a network of broken glass. Her hood had buckled in the middle. The TransAm had slammed into the Ford and sat facing her, its hood crumpled and leaking steam. A split second later, Lenihan staggered out of the car. In his hand was a black nightstick.

Oh, God. Bennie tried her ignition but the Ford was dead. She looked around wildly. The phone was out. Lenihan was coming at the truck. He would kill her. She screamed, the sound thundering in her head. Her vision went foggy.

A cracking sound shattered her driver's side window. Bennie looked over in terror. Lenihan was pounding the glass with the baton. His face was bloodied, contorted with a lethal fury. *Oh my God.*

Bennie stopped screaming. She had to act, to go. To run. She snapped off her shoulder harness and scrambled to the passenger side of the truck. She wrenched open the door and almost fell onto the wet flagstone. She hadn't hit the ground before she heard heavy footsteps behind her. Lenihan was upon her.

"You bitch!" the cop bellowed. Lenihan grabbed Bennie by the neck from behind and jammed the nightstick under her chin, cutting off her windpipe. Her throat exploded in pain. Her eyes filled with tears. She clawed the nightstick, struggling to wrench it off.

"You're dead, bitch!" Lenihan dragged her to the edge of the stone wall. A panel of lights at the foot of the wall blinded her. She gasped for breath. She tore at his hands, then his nylon windbreaker.

"Get over there!" Lenihan shouted, then slammed Bennie onto the hard edge of the stone wall. The rough stone scraped her cheek. Her ribs seared in agony. She dangled over the wall. She could barely see for the pain and the darkness. It was fifty feet down to a concrete delivery ramp. "Get over the wall!"

Bennie forced herself to think, but she was losing consciousness. She couldn't breathe. Lenihan shoved her higher onto the wide wall and tried to push her over the side. *No, God.* Her head flopped over the other side of the wall. A ballpoint pen from her blazer pocket rolled onto the wall. That was it!

With her last breath, Bennie grabbed the pen and stabbed blindly backward. Lenihan's surprised gurgle told her that she had hit something. The nightstick eased at her throat. Her body shuddered as her lungs gulped air. There was no time to lose.

"Aaargh!" Lenihan cried. He dropped his nightstick and it clattered to the asphalt.

Bennie torqued in his grasp. The ballpoint hung from the base of Lenihan's neck and he yanked it out. Blood spurted from the wound. His eyes blazed with renewed fury. He grabbed Bennie by the throat and slammed her back against the wall, banging her head against hard rock. She fought back on the edge of consciousness, hanging on his shirt so as not to fall over the side.

They struggled up and onto the wall, their shadows

commingling in a grotesque lover's dance, their silhouettes magnified in the lights. Lenihan's blood drenched them both. Bennie felt its hot spray on her cheek. Its primal smell filled her nostrils. Her nails raked Lenihan's windbreaker as he rolled her to the edge of the wall. The sky went black around her.

"Hey, you! Hey, cut that out!" came a shout, and Bennie felt Lenihan's grip release her throat. She coughed for breath and opened her eyes long enough to see a museum security guard running toward them both. "Cut that out, you two!" the guard yelled.

Lenihan startled at the sight, then wobbled, losing his balance at the wall's edge.

"No!" Bennie cried, and reached for him. His windbreaker brushed her fingertips, but she closed her fist too late. Lenihan slipped from her fingers, his eyes sick with terror as he dropped over the side of the wall. The last sound Bennie heard before she collapsed was Lenihan's final shriek, joined by the screams of approaching police sirens.

65

Bennie hadn't realized how much the police hated her until she walked into Two Squad that night, after Lenihan's death. The squad room was a dirty light blue, crammed with battered gray desks, lined with dented file cabinets, and encircled by water-stained curtains. It seemed to Bennie that everyone was on the night tour as she walked through their silent ranks and was led into the interview room for questioning. It wouldn't help to tell them that she was sorry. It wouldn't help to tell them she felt worse than they did. Nor would it help to tell them that Lenihan was trying to kill her. Bennie Rosato, who had built a career suing the department, had now killed one of their own. That was all that mattered to them.

"Take a seat, Ms. Rosato," said one of the detectives, though Bennie had been here many times. The room was tiny, its institutional green walls unscrubbed, and she sat down in the steel Windsor chair that was bolted to the ground, reserved for murder suspects. The room smelled faintly of stale smoke, and flush against the grimy wall was a rickety wooden table, half the size of a card table. Scattered across its uneven surface were blank statement forms and an ancient Smith-Corona.

Bennie wasn't worried for herself. She knew the police couldn't charge her in Lenihan's death; they hadn't even cuffed her on the drive to the Roundhouse. The museum guard would tell what happened, there'd be 911 transcripts to support Bennie's story, and Lenihan's baton was in plain sight. God knew if his original plan was to make Bennie's death look like a mugging or a carjacking, but neither ruse would work now. The attack was proof positive of a police conspiracy, one ruthless enough to kill to protect itself. The gloves were off. The war was on and had claimed its first casualty.

"Your lawyers are here, Rosato," the detective said, and Bennie looked up.

Judy and Mary stood in the doorway behind Grady, their expressions strained with fear. Grady rushed forward and gathered Bennie in his arms, lifting her almost bodily out of the chair. Pain arced through her ribs. "I'm all right," she said, but Grady turned to the detective.

"Leave us alone, please. We need five minutes."

"Five minutes, counselor," the detective said. He had a runner's build and a trim haircut. He opened the door and left.

"Grady, wait," Bennie said, holding up a palm. "There's something I have to do. DiNunzio, Carrier, sit down." Grady stepped aside as the associates, in jackets over their street clothes, sank into chairs. Judy looked worried, and Mary positively stricken, the three wrinkles across her young forehead now permanent as the earth's strata. "Are you okay?" Bennie asked her.

"Are *you* okay?" Mary answered, her voice hushed. "Your lip is all bloody."

"I'm fine." Bennie ran her tongue over a sore bottom lip. "But listen, what happened tonight is no joke. You guys are off this case. No more court appearances, no more signing any papers that get filed."

"Bennie, no," Judy protested, but Mary remained silent, which Bennie noted.

"Carrier, you have no choice. First thing tomorrow, you file a withdrawal of your and Mary's appearance. I want it as high-profile as possible. Tell Marshall to send a press release about it, too. I want you two off this case and I want everybody to know it."

"How's that gonna look?" Judy raked her tousled hair with her hand. She was wearing jeans and a football jersey that stuck out under a short Patagonia jacket. "It'll look like we quit, like we got scared."

"You can't worry about what people think. Your safety is more important."

"Than my reputation as a lawyer? Than my responsibility to you?" Judy shook her head and her hair swung around her ears. "I'm not quitting. I'm showing up tomorrow in court. That's my choice."

"No, it isn't. It's my law firm, I make the case assignments. We need an associate on the Burkett case. You're it. Both of you."

"I won't do it," Judy insisted, and Bennie rubbed her forehead. Her head throbbed from the bump she'd taken in the back. Her cheek had stopped bleeding but her jaw ached, and all this arguing didn't help.

"Carrier, just once, could you do what I say? Just once, could you listen?"

"I'm listening, I'm just not obeying. What would my getting off the case solve? What about you? You're the one they're after. This cop tried to kill—"

"Yes, what about you, Bennie?" Grady chimed in, and Bennie looked up from her chair to see the fear on his face. His skin, fair to start with, was an unhappy shade of pale, and his eyes red from work and worry. Blond nubs dotted his chin and his old DUKE T-shirt was on inside out, tugged on in a hurry. "I know you won't quit, but you can't go on without some security. Either I'm in that courtroom or you hire protection."

"Protection? You mean a bodyguard?"

"I mean three bodyguards."

"We can't afford three."

"I'll settle for two, but that's my final offer." Grady turned to the associates and managed a smile. "Is that agreeable to you, counsel? Two bodyguards?"

"Yep," Judy said. "That means I'm still in. Okay, boss?"

"No, not okay."

Grady touched Bennie's shoulder. "It should be her choice. Look at all the stupid choices you make, and nobody stops you."

Bennie smiled. "Stop. It hurts to laugh."

Judy laughed. "It's a settlement, then. I'm still on the case."

Bennie sighed, too shaken to fight. "All right, I'll settle for Carrier, but, DiNunzio, you're on Burkett starting tomorrow. File your withdrawal of appearance in the morning, then take the rest of the day off. Got it?"

Three heads suddenly turned, and all of a sudden Mary felt as if she were the one in the chair for prime suspects. "I don't know," she said.

"It's not up to you," Bennie told her. "You did wonderful work on this case, with the neighbors, and now it's over."

"But the neighbors haven't been called yet, as witnesses. How will you cross them? I haven't prepared you."

"I'll be fine. I have your notes. I know what to do."

There was a sharp rap on the door and Bennie stiffened, wincing as her ribs protested the change in posture.

"Rosato?" said a man's voice, and the door to the interview room opened.

But it wasn't one of the detectives. Standing at the threshold, his grizzled face lined with regret, his familiar khaki pants and navy blazer a wrinkled mess, stood Lou Jacobs.

It had gone as Bennie had expected at the Roundhouse, with Grady acting as her attorney, though he was barely needed. The detectives listened to Bennie's account of Lenihan's death with civility and professionalism, and credited it almost immediately. They had no alternative, given the supporting evidence. DiNunzio and Carrier perched on folding chairs and managed to keep their tears in check, but it was Lou who surprised Bennie.

He hovered at her shoulder opposite Grady during the entire questioning, taking her side against the police without having to say a word. When she was finished, he rested a warm hand on her shoulder, which she found more comforting than she could rightly account for. Bennie hardly knew the man, but she sensed something benevolent in him. A goodness not found in the young; a tenderness that came only with years. Lou would be her bodyguard. In a way, he already was.

Bennie remained quiet in the car ride home with Grady, who was as kind and as solicitous as he could be. At the house, he made her fresh coffee, understanding that Bennie didn't feel like talking. He put an ice pack on her head, which remained sore in the back, and gave her a tablespoon of honey to make her throat feel better. It helped, even though it was less than scientific. Her lip had swelled where she'd cut it and her jaw was shaky from being bounced around, and for that Grady prescribed a night's rest. Beside him.

Bennie was grateful to him, but oddly found herself unable to say so. She lay sleepless, awake until dawn. She couldn't think, but could only feel. If she had met death firsthand with her mother's passing, Bennie was on an intimate basis with it now. She couldn't help but feel partly responsible for Lenihan's death. She kept replaying the fight on the wall in her mind. If she had just closed her fingers around the windbreaker a second earlier.

Bennie closed her eyes in the dark bedroom. Her thoughts wandered to the prison murders. Connolly had driven a screwdriver into Leonia Page's throat, almost the same spot where Bennie had stabbed Lenihan with the pen. Was there such a thing as the killer instinct? Did Bennie have it, too? Tears slipped from beneath her eyes, one after the other, coming as uncontrollably as her questions. Was her heart as dark as Connolly's? Did she have that level of hate in her nature, subsisting deep in her bone and fiber, residing within her very cells?

The bedroom remained still. The night was deep and silent. The only sound was the low electrical hum of the alarm clock, its squared-off face glowing a fraudulent orange. Grady's breathing came soft and even. The dog snored from a curl on the plywood subfloor at the foot of the bed. This room, this man, and even this animal used to make Bennie feel safe, used to fill her with love. She used to think of her mother, sleeping as peacefully as she could, in the hospital, watched over by the best doctors money could buy. The thought would comfort her, complete her somehow. Bennie's life was full then, and sweet. She was happy.

But right now, Bennie couldn't even remember what happiness felt like.

66

The early rays of the morning sun fought their way through the skyscrapers into chambers, and Judge Guthrie sat almost slumped behind his elegant mahogany desk. His reading glasses lay folded beside a hunter green blotter, and he gazed at Bennie with hooded eyes, sloping downwards. "I was so terribly sorry to hear of what befell you last night, Ms. Rosato."

"Thank you, Your Honor," Bennie said. Freshly showered and dressed in her standard navy suit, she crossed her legs in the leather chair across from the judge's desk. She and Hilliard had received an early morning call from Judge Guthrie, in inevitable response to the media accounts of Lenihan's death. KILLER TWINS, read the worst of the tabloid headlines, along with the subtler DOUBLE JEOPARDY.

"How are your injuries, my dear?" Judge Guthrie asked. He sounded sincere and almost looked it, in a red paisley bow tie with a white oxford shirt that hadn't been on long enough to wrinkle.

"I'm alive, thank you." Bennie's lip remained sore and her shoulder and side ached. Her jaw still felt rattled, though the scrape on her cheek had been concealed by foundation. Nevertheless, she was determined to put last night behind her. Letting it get to her was letting them win.

"It's terrible," Hilliard chimed in, his voice grave. His beefy frame looked as if it had been clothed hastily, in a tan pinstriped suit and a cream-colored shirt that contrasted with the darkness of his skin. His gray tie had been knotted sloppily, unusual for Hilliard. "I spent most of the night trying to get to the bottom of it."

Judge Guthrie turned. "What did you learn, Mr. Hilliard?"

"We understand that Officer Lenihan was very upset by Bennie's cross-examination in court the other day, when she mentioned his name in connection with official corruption. They tell our office that Lenihan reacted badly, thought it was an embarrassment, a disgrace. We believe he went to talk with Bennie, perhaps confront her about what she'd said, but he lost control. Our office will be issuing a statement this morning. We regret deeply what happened, of course."

Bennie said nothing. Behind Judge Guthrie's frail shoulder, his court reporter tapped on the long black keys of the steno machine. This conference would be on the record, and Bennie was mindful that any transcript could find its way into the news, COURT-TV, or even the Internet. She wouldn't say a word that wouldn't be for public consumption.

Hilliard shook his head. "Frankly, Officer Lenihan was a renegade, a loose cannon. You might as well know, both of you, that we understand he went drinking last night. His blood alcohol level was double the legal limit."

Bennie listened, her face impassive though her thoughts were in tumult. She hadn't smelled alcohol on Lenihan's breath last night and she would have if there had been any. Somebody either injected him with alcohol postmortem or falsified the lab results. She wondered who had signed off on the blood work.

"My, my," Judge Guthrie said quietly. "That's quite a shame, quite a shame."

"It certainly is," Hilliard agreed. "You never think anything like this happens, then it does."

"Such a young man, too," the judge mused. "So sad, so sad."

Hilliard nodded. "Lenihan had so much going for him. Was on his way up. Except for his personality problems, he was a good cop. His personnel record was clean as a whistle."

Bennie thought their conversation stilted, as programmed as a dialogue in a high school language lab. She could read between the clichés. Lenihan's personnel record had been altered. Any infraction had been magnified to a personality problem, to support their "loose cannon" spin. She looked at the prosecutor and wondered again if he was in on the conspiracy.

Hilliard turned to Bennie, shifting his weight with difficulty in the chair. Beside him on the floor lay his crutches. "The police department is also going to issue you a formal apology for what happened. I know it doesn't sound like much, but it's the best we can do under the circumstances."

"Thank you very much," Bennie said, choosing her words carefully. "I'm very sorry about Officer Lenihan's death myself. No apology by the department is necessary."

"On a personal note, I don't hold you responsible for the questions you asked in court. I understand that you had to cross-examine on something. I've been in your position, Bennie, when you don't have a case."

Bennie bristled. "My cross-examination was entirely appropriate."

"You can't really be serious about this drug corruption theory, can you?" Hilliard scoffed, and Bennie permitted herself a tight smile.

"The defense will do its theorizing in court."

"But you don't have a shred of evidence."

Judge Guthrie picked up his reading glasses and unfolded them. "Let's not argue, counsel. The question for us is, what effect should this terrible occurrence have on the trial? I surmise, Ms. Rosato, that you will be requesting a few days' time to recover from your injuries and distress. In view of the recent loss in your immediate family, the Court will grant you a reasonable continuance. I gather, Mr. Prosecutor, that you would agree."

"Within reason, of course," Hilliard said quickly, but Bennie had anticipated the move.

"Thank you, both of you, but I won't be needing any continuance, Your Honor. I'd like to keep the case on track. I expect that Mr. Hilliard will call his next witness"—she checked her watch—"in one hour."

The court reporter looked up in surprise, her mouth a perfectly lipsticked circle. There was no way Bennie wanted an extension now. She had the conspirators in disarray and she had to keep the heat on. She was closer than ever to bringing to justice whoever was behind the conspiracy. Besides, nothing pissed her off like attempted murder, especially her own.

"My, this is unexpected," Judge Guthrie remarked, easing his glasses onto his nose. "Surely you will be needing some time to collect yourself and prepare your case. A day or two, perhaps?"

Hilliard's dark brow furrowed in confusion. "Bennie, don't push yourself like this. Nobody could live through what you're living through and still try a case."

Bennie smiled politely. "Thanks for your concern, but I'm perfectly able to go forward. We have a sequestered jury, and I'd hate to keep them from their families any longer than necessary."

Judge Guthrie made a familiar tent of his fingers. "The Court doesn't quite understand, Ms. Rosato. Before this tragic event, an extension of time was your most fervent desire."

"That's true, Your Honor. But since what happened last night, I think it's more important than ever to conclude this case. Delay makes it more likely that the jury may be tainted by the publicity, precluding the defendant's ability to receive a fair trial. In fact, the defense finds itself in the position of opposing any extension at this critical point."

Judge Guthrie's finger tent collapsed. "Well, then. The Court will see both of you next door at the previously scheduled hour, counsel."

"Thank you, Your Honor," Bennie said. She picked up her briefcase, hiding the discomfort that shot through her ribs, then left chambers ahead of Hilliard.

Sitting in Judge Guthrie's waiting room was Judy Carrier, flanked by two extraordinarily muscular young men. Lou had made sure the guards were at Bennie's house when she left for court that morning. He'd called them "Mike" and "Ike" because they looked so much alike: brown hair buzz-cut into oblivion, navy polyester suits, and regulation Ray-Ban aviators. Yet it wasn't their presence that surprised Bennie, it was Mary DiNunzio's, at the near end of the sofa. She rose to her feet with Carrier and the bodyguards.

"How'd it go?" Mary asked as they left chambers and entered the corridor. The floor was of black-and-white marble and the white vaulted ceiling towered over their heads. The press was momentarily at bay, obeying orders not to come within fifty feet of the judge's chambers.

"What are you doing here?" Bennie looked at Mary, whose brown suit hung on her form, as if she'd lost weight. "Why aren't you back at the office, withdrawing from this case?"

"I want to stay on," Mary answered. She had thought about it all night. "I have to. You need me."

Bennie smiled. "I have tried cases without you."

"I'm not a quitter." Mary hustled to keep pace down the corridor. "I thought about this and I've made a decision. It's firm. If I'm a lawyer, I'm going to lawyer."

Bennie frowned. "*If* you're a lawyer? You are a lawyer, and a far better one than you know."

"Thank you." Mary felt blood rush to her face. She'd never heard Bennie praise anyone.

"But I still want you off this case."

"No. I'm going to court with you."

"Take a compromise, then. It's a research mission on this case, purely factual. Do it from your desk, and out of trouble."

"Sure, what?"

"Find out if our friend Dorsey Hilliard has any connection to Judge Guthrie or Henry Burden, or both."

"Both Burden and Hilliard were in the D.A.'s office, obviously."

Bennie shook her head grimly as she bustled forward. "More specific than that. See if they worked the same case, like that. I don't know what I'm looking for, but I want you to find it."

Mary smiled crookedly. "Gotcha," she said, and Judy glanced at her friend.

"What are you going to do about your parents, Mare?"

"It's time I grew up," Mary said, and for a second, she almost believed it.

67

The next witness for the prosecution, Jane Lambertsen, perched on the stand, well dressed in a flowered spring dress, chic gold jewelry, and a sweater the color of Granny Smith apples. Her raven hair had been gathered back into a thick ponytail, emphasizing her youth and freshness. Lambertsen contrasted in every way with the cops who had testified the day before, and Bennie figured that Hilliard had reshuffled his batting order after Lenihan's death.

The courtroom was quiet, the court personnel occupying themselves with official duties, and the jury presumptively ignorant of the events swirling outside the courthouse walls. If they thought Bennie looked a little puffy around the face, they'd ascribe it to a late night at the office. Only Bennie knew open war had been declared, as she and the entire courtroom sat fully focused on the next witness for the Commonwealth.

"Yes, I did hear them arguing that night," Mrs. Lambertsen testified.

Hilliard straightened at the podium. "That is, you're testifying that you heard Alice Connolly and Anthony Della Porta arguing before his murder on the night in question?"

"Objection," Bennie snapped. "The prosecutor is testifying again."

Judge Guthrie fiddled with a bow tie that was already straight. He seemed completely preoccupied to Bennie since their meeting in chambers. Perhaps the knowledge that his cohorts weren't fellow Quakers had sobered him. "I'll allow it," the judge ruled. "You may answer, Mrs. Lambertsen."

"That's right," the witness said. "I heard arguing that night, a little before eight o'clock. I was trying to put the baby down. To bed, you know. Her bedtime was at seven forty-five then, and I was watching the clock."

A woman juror in the front row nodded, and Lambertsen caught her eye and smiled back. Bennie thumbed through her papers for her notes; her head hurt too much to remember the jury sheets. The juror was Libby DuMont, age thirty-two, homemaker, mother of three.

"Mrs. Lambertsen," Hilliard said, "you've already testified that you lived in the rowhouse next door to Detective Della Porta and the defendant. Does that mean you shared a common wall?"

"Yes, and it's a thin wall, too. You can hear sounds, kind of muffled. I used to worry all the time that they'd hear the baby crying. I did hear them argue, a lot."

"How often would you say the defendant and Detective Della Porta argued, Mrs. Lambertsen?"

"Well, she moved in in September, I think. I would say the arguing started in October."

Beside Bennie, Connolly shifted unhappily in her seat. She was wearing the same blue suit as yesterday, which matched Bennie's, and looked like a lawyer with her cultured pearls. Bennie hadn't spoken to Connolly since Lenihan's attack and had to assume she didn't know about it. As much as she loathed Connolly, Bennie had to admit that Connolly had been telling the truth about the police conspiracy. It made Bennie credit Connolly's story, even if, paradoxically, she couldn't abide sitting with her.

"Did their fighting have a pattern you could discern?" Hilliard asked, and Bennie didn't object. Judge Guthrie would permit Hilliard to lead, on direct.

"It seemed like they fought at night, mostly," Lambertsen answered.

"Could you make out anything they said during these fights?"

"Objection, hearsay," Bennie said, half rising. Her side hurt but she ignored it. "The question is vague, irrelevant, and assumes facts not in evidence. There's been no proof that these voices belonged to the defendant or to Mr. Della Porta."

"You may want to rephrase that, Mr. Prosecutor," Judge Guthrie said after a moment, which Bennie regarded as a small victory.

Hilliard paused to act exasperated. "Without telling the jury what the words were, Mrs. Lambertsen, could you make out who was speaking?"

"Only sometimes, when they really yelled. I tried not to listen, I didn't want to invade their privacy. I just heard voices shouting at each other."

"In general, again without telling us the words, whose voice was generally louder during these fights, the defendant's or Detective Della Porta's?"

"Objection, Your Honor," Bennie said, half rising again.

Hilliard held up a hand, flashing a large class ring of garnet and gold. "I'll rephrase. Mrs. Lambertsen, when you heard arguing coming from the apartment shared by the defendant and Detective Della Porta, whose voice was generally louder, the woman's or the man's?"

Bennie objected on the same grounds but Judge Guthrie denied it. Mrs. Lambertsen testified, "The woman's voice was usually louder."

"Thank you," Hilliard said. "Now, going back to the night of May nineteenth, how long did the argument last?"

"Fifteen minutes, at the most."

"Do you recall what happened after the argument?"

"I heard a noise. Sometimes after they argue I hear a door slam. This time it was a gunshot."

Two of the jurors looked at each other and several stiffened in their seats. Hilliard paused to let it register. "What did you do after you heard the gunshot?" he asked.

"I went to the door to see what was going on. I have one of those chains on the door, so I left it on and peeked out."

"Wait a minute, why did you go to the door, Mrs. Lambertsen?" Hilliard asked, apparently spontaneously, and Bennie reflected that the question demonstrated why he was such a good lawyer. Hilliard asked witnesses the questions that would occur to jurors, reinforcing his logical nature and aligning him with the jury.

"I'm not sure exactly," Lambertsen admitted. "The gunshot came from next door, but I couldn't go next door, so I went to my door and opened it a little. Just to see what was going on. Like, a crack."

"What did you see when you went to the door?"

"I saw Alice, Alice Connolly, running by. She ran right by my door."

The jury shifted, though Connolly remained still. Bennie willed herself to stay calm. She'd known this testimony was coming. It would only get worse, as each of the neighbors corroborated. Hilliard looked grave. "Mrs. Lambertsen, how did the defendant appear to you as she ran by?" he asked.

"Worried, scared, kind of in a panic. Like you'd look after a fight, but worse."

The jurors listened to every word, caught up in the story. Bennie wished she could break it up with an objection, but it would cost her more in credibility than she'd gain. She glanced uneasily over her shoulder at the gallery, which looked rapt. Directly behind her sat Mike and Ike, solid as fence posts at either end of the front row. No cops watched from the back row, where Lenihan had sat. It was hard to believe he was there only yesterday, watching her. Bennie flashed on him falling in horror over the wall and found herself wondering when his funeral would be. She knew just how his family would feel, picking out the casket. Sick. Horrified. Dazed.

"Mrs. Lambertsen, after you saw Alice Connolly run by, what did you do?"

"I called 911 and told them what I had seen, and the police came."

Hilliard continued by eliciting the details of the 911 call and found an excuse to take Lambertsen again through the gunshot and Connolly's running down the street, to emphasize it to the jury. It was a slam-dunk direct examination of an appealing and critical witness.

Bennie rose to her feet, wincing from hidden injuries and knowing that she had to attack Lambertsen's testimony without attacking the witness. And she had to do it without getting bollixed up by what had happened last night. Near-death experiences didn't make for productive workdays.

But she couldn't think about that now.

68

Bennie stood beside the podium and addressed the young mother. "Mrs. Lambertsen, thinking back to the night of May nineteenth, you say you heard arguing, is that right?"

"Yes."

"Did you hear male and female voices arguing, or did you just hear voices raised in argument?"

Lambertsen thought a minute. "I guess I just heard voices."

Bennie sighed inwardly, with relief. Funny thing about the truth. It enabled a lawyer to ask a question she didn't know the answer to, because she knew what the answer had to be. "Now, Ms. Lambertsen, there came a time when you saw Alice Connolly running down the street. Do you remember what she was wearing?"

"Uh, no."

"Do you remember what type of shirt she had on?"

"I didn't notice, or if I did, I don't remember."

"And you didn't see what she was wearing on the bottom, jeans or shorts, did you?"

"No."

"Was she carrying anything?"

"I don't know. I didn't notice that either."

Bennie nodded. No white plastic bag? She had almost

made the point and sensed not to push it. "Now, you testified you were trying to put your baby down at seven forty-
five that night, isn't that right?"

"Yes. It was always a fight then, it still is. She doesn't
want to miss anything." Mrs. Lambertsen smiled, as did
the young mother in the front row. It was a warm
moment, and Bennie decided to prolong it. There was pre-
cious little warmth in the world, of late.

"Mrs. Lambertsen, how old was your baby on May
nineteenth of last year?"

"About two months old. She was born on March
twenty-third, so she was a newborn."

"And what is her name, by the way?" Bennie asked, to
loosen up the witness, who obviously welcomed talking
about her child. Bennie's only point of reference was her
dog and she could talk golden retrievers for hours.

"Molly's her name."

"Okay, Molly. You were with Molly. Now, what time
was it when you heard the gunshot?"

"Eight o'clock."

"You know that how?"

"I looked at the clock. Molly hadn't napped that afternoon and she needed to go down. On days like that, you
have an eye on the clock."

"Now, when did you look at the clock, in relation to
when you heard the gunshot?"

Lambertsen thought a minute, pursing lips lipsticked a
light, feminine pink. "I looked at the clock right after I
heard the gunshot."

Bennie paused. It was a crucial point. She had to
prove that more time had elapsed between the sound of
the gunshot and when Lambertsen saw Connolly running

past her door. If Bennie's theory was true, whoever shot Della Porta had gotten out just before Connolly arrived home. "What kind of clock do you have? Is it digital?"

"No, it's a small, round one on the oven front. You know those?"

"Sure. So you have to read it, like the old days?"

The witness smiled. "Yes."

"Mrs. Lambertsen, what did you do after you looked at the clock?"

"I went to the door, opened it, and looked out."

"Did you? Let's go back over the exact sequence of events." Bennie walked around the front of the podium and leaned on it, wincing as her shoulder flexed. If she had to develop her defense as she went along, so be it. She'd always thought that was the worst trouble a lawyer could get into, but that was before last night. "Mrs. Lambertsen, where in your house were you when you heard the gunshot?"

"I was in the kitchen."

"What were you doing in the kitchen?"

"Rocking the baby, trying to get her to settle down."

Bennie nodded, wishing she had done the interview of Lambertsen herself and finagled her way into that house. "Where is your kitchen in relation to the front door?"

"The kitchen's in the front of the house, to the left of the front door."

"How large is the kitchen?"

"It's long and skinny. About twenty feet long."

"So, Mrs. Lambertsen, you walked through the kitchen, about twenty feet, to get to the front door?"

"Yes."

"I see." Bennie visualized the scene and imagined a

mother's instinct. "You didn't take the baby with you to see about the gunshot, did you?"

"God, no. I put her down."

"Where did you put Molly?"

"In her baby chair, on the counter. One of those portable chairs, with a handle. It was in the kitchen."

"So you put Molly in her chair. Did you strap her in?"

"Yes. I always do. She's wriggly. Wiry."

"Did she sit in the seat willingly?"

Mrs. Lambertsen burst into light laughter. "Molly doesn't do anything willingly. She has a mind of her own." The jurors laughed, too, relishing the baby talk, which Bennie knew was only apparently a frolic and detour.

"Did Molly cry in the chair?"

"A little, and kicked. Fussed, you know. Molly was kind of clingy at that age. She didn't like it when I left the room. She'd kick and cry."

"So you had to settle Molly before you went to the door, right?"

"Yes."

"What did you do to settle her?"

"Gave her a pacifier, then patted her. Smoothed her hair, she likes that."

"Did she settle down then?"

"No. I think I gave her a toy, too. Her favorite toy then was Rubber Duckie. I gave her Duckie."

Judge Guthrie smiled benevolently from the dais. "You're a very good mother, Mrs. Lambertsen," he said, and the witness blushed at the praise.

"I agree," Bennie said. She suppressed thoughts of her own mother. "Let's see, Mrs. Lambertsen, before you went to the door, you put Molly in her chair, fastened the strap, gave her a toy duck and a pacifier, and you patted her and smoothed her hair, is that your recollection?"

"Yes."

"Where was the rubber duck, by the way?"

"It was in a plastic bin on the kitchen counter."

"Were there other toys in the bin, Mrs. Lambertsen?"

"There are toys everywhere in my house. Fisher-Price is our decorator," she answered, and the jurors laughed again.

"So you had to root through the toy bin to find the rubber duck, is that right?"

"Right."

"How long would you say it took for you to do all those things that good mothers do—that is, put Molly in her chair, fasten the strap, find her a toy duck, give it to her with a pacifier, and pat her and smooth her hair?"

"How much time? Uh, maybe five minutes, maybe more."

Bennie guessed the witness was underestimating, albeit unintentionally. "How much more? As much as ten minutes?"

"Maybe, but more like seven."

Bennie had made progress. Seven to ten minutes was almost enough time for a killer to escape and Connolly to arrive, but close. "And that was before you went to the door?"

"Uh, yes." Mrs. Lambertsen glanced regretfully at Hilliard, taking notes at counsel table.

"Mrs. Lambertsen, after you got Molly the duck, did you walk or run the twenty feet to the door?"

"Walked."

Bennie reconsidered the scenario. It was hard to think,

with her jaw aching. She should have taken more Advil. "Wait a minute. You said Molly's chair was on the counter in the kitchen. Can you see the baby from the front door?"

"No."

"So you had to leave Molly out of sight, on the counter, while you went to the door?"

"Yes."

"And she was kicking and crying, in one of those baby chairs?"

"Yes."

Out of the corner of her eye, Bennie saw the young mother in the front row frown just the slightest bit. It gave Bennie her cue and she walked stiffly from the podium to the witness stand, instinctively closing in on a point even she didn't understand yet. "Mrs. Lambertsen, when you left Molly on the counter to go to the door, kicking and fussing, weren't you worried she would fall off the counter?"

"Objection!" Hilliard shouted, his voice booming from the prosecution table. The sound had the intended effect of interrupting the good vibes Bennie was nurturing. "What could be the possible relevance of these details?"

Bennie faced the judge. "This is an entirely proper exploration of the events of the night in question, Your Honor."

Judge Guthrie leaned back in his chair, touching his teeth with the stem of his reading glasses. "Overruled."

Bennie turned to the witness. "Mrs. Lambertsen, weren't you worried about Molly when you left her on the counter to go to the door?"

"Yes, I was. I should have put the chair on the floor, but I didn't. I was so distracted by the gunshot and all. It was like two things happening at once." The witness paused, thinking. "Now that I think of it, I ran back to check when I was halfway there."

Bennie nodded. It was a break. "Considering that, how long do you think it took you to get to the door? Maybe three to five minutes?"

"Yes, probably."

"So would it be fair to add three to five minutes to the time you saw Alice Connolly run by?"

"Yes."

"Would that bring us to a total of ten to twelve minutes between the time you heard the gunshot and the time you reached the door and saw Alice Connolly?"

"Well, yes."

Bennie paused, pleased, then thought back through Lambertsen's testimony. It always surprised her that information witnesses volunteered during their testimony assumed significance in context. "Mrs. Lambertsen, you mentioned earlier that Molly needed a nap. When was the last time that day that she had slept?"

"Objection, Your Honor." Hilliard half rose from his chair. "This line of questioning is totally irrelevant and calls for the witness to speculate."

"Your Honor," Bennie said firmly, "the relevancy of the questions will become clear, and I don't think Mrs. Lambertsen is speculating. She's obviously very attentive to her child, as you yourself noted."

Judge Guthrie frowned. "Mrs. Lambertsen, please don't speculate or guess at your answers. Feel free to say so if you don't remember."

"Thank you, Your Honor," Mrs. Lambertsen said. "I know Molly's schedule. Even then, she kept to a schedule."

Hilliard sat down heavily as Bennie sent up a prayer of

thanks. "Mrs. Lambertsen, the question was, when was the last time that day that Molly had slept?"

"She had been awake since her morning nap. She woke up at about six in the morning, then went right back to sleep. She woke up at about ten-thirty, in those days. She didn't even take an afternoon nap, or if she did it lasted like an hour."

"So on May nineteenth, she was up from about ten-thirty in the morning until when she eventually went to sleep, is that right?"

"Right."

"Take us back a bit, to the day before May nineteenth. You said Molly was two months old at the time. If you can recall, what was her schedule then?"

Hilliard sighed audibly, but refrained from making an objection. His cranky growl got him the interruption he wanted anyway.

"Oh, God. It was hell, sheer hell," Mrs. Lambertsen said, rolling her eyes. "She would start fussing late in the day, when she was really too tired to stay awake. She would fall asleep at about nine o'clock, then wake up at about midnight. We'd watch Jay Leno together."

"If you remember, did Molly go right back to sleep after the Jay Leno show on the night of May eighteenth?"

"She never went right back to sleep," Mrs. Lambertsen shot back, so flatly that the jurors laughed. "She always wanted to play after she'd nursed. She was happy, well fed, and had my attention."

"When was the next time Molly did go back to sleep, the night of May eighteenth?"

"She didn't go back down at all. We were both up all night."

Bennie couldn't imagine it. She thought of her mother's

devotion, with a pang of fresh grief. She paused a minute and hoped the jurors attributed it to her next question. "Mrs. Lambertsen, had you napped that day, on May nineteenth?"

"Not since the morning. I always napped when Molly napped or I wouldn't have survived her first year. Somebody in my playgroup told me to do that and it was good advice."

"So in the night before May nineteenth, you had a total of three hours sleep?"

"Yes."

Bennie thought about how she felt without a good night's sleep for a week. "Doesn't sleep deprivation affect your concentration?"

"For sure. I'm one of those people who need a lot of sleep, nine hours a night. Once I took Molly to the doctor, she had an ear infection, and I couldn't remember whether the doctor told me to put drops in her ears or mouth. Another time I bought diapers and left them on the counter."

The jurors smiled, and Bennie waited before her next question. "Did you ever think you read something, and read it wrong?" she asked.

"Objection!" Hilliard said as he rose and reached for his crutches. He knew where Bennie was going and it wasn't baby talk anymore. He slipped strong forearms into the aluminum handles of his crutches. "The question calls for speculation and is vague. I think this entire line of questioning is totally irrelevant and a waste of the Court's time."

Judge Guthrie was caught cleaning his reading glasses. "I think not, Mr. Hilliard," he ruled, and Hilliard took his seat heavily.

Bennie glanced at the judge, thankful. If Judge Guthrie

had been ruling against her yesterday, he was playing fair today. Too bad she almost had to get killed to get his attention. "Mrs. Lambertsen," she said, "you may answer the question."

"I guess I remember reading the directions on the bottle over and over. Even out loud."

"Thinking back to the night of May nineteenth, recall that you're trying to get Molly to calm down, you're working on three hours of sleep and you hear a gunshot. Then you run to the door, come back, and read the clock. How can you be sure you read the clock right?"

Lambertsen looked away, apparently reconsidering. "I think I did."

"You're sure your perceptions were correct that night, even though you were working on three hours' sleep?"

"I am."

Bennie slipped her hands into her pockets. Maybe she was pushing it, but she couldn't help herself. She wanted to know what had happened that night. "But other perceptions of yours were off that night, weren't they, Mrs. Lambertsen?"

"Like what?" the witness asked thoughtfully, and Bennie could feel the jurors faces as they turned toward her. If she could come through, she sensed they'd shift to her side. Bennie felt it like an undertow tugging at her ankles, threatening to drown her if she didn't swim hard.

"Well, Mrs. Lambertsen, when you looked out your front door, you didn't perceive what Alice Connolly was wearing for a shirt, did you?"

"Uh, no."

"And you didn't perceive what Alice Connolly was wearing on the bottom, jeans or shorts, did you?"

"Well, no," she answered, a tremor of doubt in her

tone, and Bennie felt the tide begin to turn. Mrs. Lambertsen was an intelligent, reasonable person, bending over backward to be honest in her testimony. In Bennie's experience, they made the worst witnesses ever.

"So isn't it possible, Mrs. Lambertsen, given how tired you were and all that was going on, that you're not exactly sure what the clock said when you read it? Police records show you didn't call 911 until 8:07."

Mrs. Lambertsen straightened in her chair. Bennie held her breath, and Hilliard his objection. Judge Guthrie craned his neck over his papers as the silence lengthened. The jury focused completely on the young mother, waiting for her answer.

Finally Mrs. Lambertsen said, "I guess I can't really be sure if it said eight o'clock."

Bennie's body sagged suddenly with the release of tension. "I have no further questions," she said, and returned to her chair behind counsel table.

"Your Honor, I have redirect," Hilliard said, rising and holding up a finger, but Bennie relaxed in her chair. She knew he couldn't erase Lambertsen's testimony.

Connolly leaned over and tapped Bennie's sleeve. "Way to go, counselor. There's not many lawyers who could kill a cop, then kick ass in court the next day."

Bennie's face flushed with shame. She looked over, stung, but Connolly had turned away, a smile playing at the corners of her mouth.

69

It was the lunch break at trial, and Bennie faced Connolly in the courthouse interview room. Bennie was so angry she couldn't feel her assorted aches and pains. "How did you know about Lenihan?" she demanded.

"How could I not know?"

"You're incarcerated, for one thing."

"That never stopped me before. Impressed?"

Bennie folded her arms. "Who are you in contact with on the outside? Is it Bullock?"

"Relax." Connolly sat back and smiled. Her wrists lay handcuffed in her lap, incongruous with her suit and pearls. "One of the guards showed me the newspaper. I told you the cops were behind it. Lenihan, McShea, Reston, they're all out to get me. Now do you think I'm telling the truth?"

"About them, yes."

"So you know I'm innocent."

"You didn't kill Della Porta. We'll leave it at that. Did you know Lenihan or not?"

"No, I told you that."

"You never heard anyone mention him? He almost killed me last night. What's his connection to you, or them?"

"No idea."

Bennie grew only more determined. "Why does the judge want me disabled on this case? Do you know?"

"So I'll get railroaded."

"Why? How's he connected to this conspiracy?"

"I don't know how, I told you."

"What about the D.A., Hilliard? What about him?"

"I don't know what the connection is, I said."

"You don't know anything that can help us out?"

"Us? I'm touched."

"Us is me and my associates."

Connolly laughed. "Can't help you, girlie. It's your show."

"Show's over. See you in court." Bennie reached for the doorknob and walked out. But it wasn't as easy to turn away as it should have been.

Bennie left Connolly upset and walked into the courthouse conference room while DiNunzio and Carrier finished eating. The associates were seated in the same chairs as at the last break, like a family at a dinner table. Mary was having her customary Greek salad, and the crust of an impossibly large sandwich lay in waxed paper in front of Judy. The scene almost managed to soothe Bennie's spirit.

"We got you some chicken soup," Judy said, pushing a plastic container across the table. Her eyes were bright, her hair shiny, and her large frame jittery with energy in a loose-fitting navy smock. "Mary thought you could use it, for medicinal purposes."

"I'm fine."

"Nobody's fine after a night like last night."

Bennie slipped into her seat and didn't move to uncap the soup container. "How'd we do with Lambertsen?"

"Awesome."

"That a term of art? How'd the jury take it?"

"They got it, I think."

"Good. You guys figured out the next witness? Another neighbor, to shore up Lambertsen? What are their names?" Bennie struggled to remember, but Mary jumped in.

"There's Ray Munoz, Mary Vidas, and Ryan Murray," she said, her answer firm. "Also a Frederick Sharp. All of them saw Connolly running by that night."

Bennie nodded, pleased. "Good for you, DiNunzio."

"I studied," Mary said with a wry smile. "Munoz is the main neighbor we have to worry about. But something tells me Hilliard won't put up another neighbor after Lambertsen."

"I agree," Judy said. "Hilliard just put up a girl and got killed. Babies, pacifiers, neighbors—it's girl testimony. Also, he doesn't have anybody to address the time issue. He needs something objective, harder to impeach. Boy testimony."

Bennie thought it was an odd way of looking at the world. "So who is it? The coroner? A blood expert?"

"That's my bet. Can you handle it? You feel okay?"

"I'm fine," Bennie said, but she had hardly finished the sentence when Mary began clearing her throat, loudly.

"I could take a witness," the associate said. "If you want."

Judy's mouth dropped open. "Mare?"

"You would?" Bennie asked with a smile.

Mary nodded. "I could try. I'm good on boy stuff, whatever that means. Math, science, bicycles with bars down the middle. I think I could do it."

Bennie shook her head. "Before last night, I would have let you, but not now. I don't want you on the firing line." A soft knock sounded on the conference room door, and Bennie looked over. "We expecting anybody?"

"Mike and Ike?" Mary offered.

"Ooh, I feel safer already," Judy said. "Big, strong men protecting me."

Mary smiled. "They're gay, you know. Ike told me."

"For real?" Judy asked.

"If I'm lyin', I'm dyin'."

Judy laughed. "What did you say? You never say things like that."

"Sometimes I do."

Bennie was opening the door onto a short, elderly couple, standing close enough to each other to be huddling against a blizzard. They smelled faintly of mothballs in their cloth coats and looked vaguely familiar. "I'm sorry, this is the attorney's conference room," Bennie told them.

"I can read English!" the old woman snapped, though an Italian accent flavored her words. She glared through thick glasses that magnified milky brown eyes. "We come to make sure our daughter is safe!"

"Oh, no," came a loud moan from the conference room, and Bennie turned to see DiNunzio leaping to her pumps.

Lou flipped up the collar of his dark-blue windbreaker and kept his head down against the drizzle. The sidewalk was wet and raindrops dotted the pebbled surface. Soggy trash clumped in the gutter, blocking the sewer. Lou couldn't remember the last time it had been sunny in this goddamn city. Maybe the last time somebody had cleaned up South Philly. He was in a foul, foul mood. Investigating one of his own. A killer.

Lou shook his head, jingling the change in his pockets. He'd told Rosato last night he'd follow up on Lenihan, and he had started as soon as he got home, making phone calls. Lenihan was in the Eleventh, and Lou used to have buddies in the Eleventh. One of his buddies had died, prostate cancer, and the other, Carlos, had moved to Tempe, Arizona. *For the air,* Carlos had said, when Lou called him long-distance last night.

What, we don't have air in Philly? Lou said.

Lou and Carlos shot the breeze awhile, dime a minute, and it turned out Carlos's kid joined the force, also the Eleventh. Maybe the kid could give him the skinny about Lenihan and drug dealing. Lou had asked Carlos to set it up, and Carlos had said yes. Lou lowered his head and watched unhappily as rain pelted his leather loafers, making a wavy water line around the edge of the toe. The back of his collar felt clammy. He tried to shake off the drops, but couldn't. It wasn't the rain bothering him anyway.

It was Rosato. She'd almost got whacked right under his nose. He hadn't seen it coming. What was the matter with him? He was a *cop.* Maybe he really was getting old.

Lou reached the corner and looked down the street, blinking against the drizzle. A patrol car was coming on, a half block away, probably on its way to the precinct house. The car looked like a new one with a factory-fresh white paint job. Red, white, and blue lights shiny on the roof, like the flag.

Lou jogged across the street, trying to jump the gutter and falling short. He was getting old. He remembered the first time he got into a squad car, he twisted the wheel back and forth like a kid. But what he felt like was a man. *Responsible.* Not just for himself, for his wife and family, but for everyone. To protect and to serve. It had meant a lot to Lou.

The drizzle came heavier, and Lou picked up the pace. A bank of rowhouses lined the cross street, then a corner bakery. Nobody was inside the bakery, but its shelves were full. Old glass display cases heaped with butter cookies that were covered by pink cellophane hay. Trays of soft pinwheel cookies with sticky red jam in the middle. Lou shook his head, hurrying by. All those old-time bakeries would be gone soon. Everybody wanted everything new nowadays. Good-bye, little white boxes tied with string.

Lou spotted the precinct house straight ahead, on the left. You'd never know it was a police station from the outside. The sign was small and the yellow brick poorly maintained for a municipal building. Steel cages covered the windows and the flag was at half-mast. It was because of Lenihan, though the kid wouldn't be getting the hero treatment. The Department would want the whole thing to blow over, and so would the mayor.

Lou got closer. Squad cars were piled like cookies around the place. Never enough parking around any precinct house; never enough cops, never enough cars. Nobody could keep up with the scumbags, the drugs so plentiful they blanketed everything, cheap as baker's flour. Not a soul in the world could stop it. Lou knew that in his head, but it didn't stop him from trying. He was stupid that way. He climbed the front steps of the station house and went inside.

Behind the desk was a young black woman with her hair tucked up under her hat and a smile covered with braces. She asked if she could help him, like it was a bakery shop, and Lou smiled. "Lookin' for Ed Vega," he said.

"You just missed him. He'll be right back."

"Damn," Lou said. "I'll wait. He was supposed to meet me for lunch."

"You're not a reporter, are you?" she asked, her eyes narrowing, and Lou laughed.

"Hell, no. I'm—I *used to be*—a cop."

70

The witness, Dr. Liam Pettis, was bald, with a silver-white tuft of hair above each fuzzy ear, and his smile was flanked by the softest of jowls. He wore a seersucker suit of sky-blue stripes that fit his small, pudgy frame as if it had been bought many years ago. In response to Dorsey Hilliard's questions, Dr. Pettis recited a laundry list of expert qualifications—degrees, publications, and awards— yet still managed to sound slightly surprised when Judge Guthrie qualified him as an expert.

"Dr. Pettis," Hilliard continued, "in addition to being a professor and a licensed physician, you are also an expert in blood spatter analysis, are you not?"

"I am."

"Briefly explain what blood spatter analysis means, in layman's terms, if you would."

"Blood spatter analysis, or bloodstain pattern analysis, means simply that when blood is acted upon by physical forces, it will deposit itself on items at a crime scene or on the clothing of a perpetrator in a certain pattern. By understanding these patterns, we can learn much about the manner in which the murder was accomplished."

Bennie caught a glimpse of the gallery. Sketch artists rushed to get a drawing and reporters made rapid notes. Mike and Ike remained in position and behind them huddled the DiNunzios. Mrs. DiNunzio glared at her, and Bennie wondered who were more protective, bodyguards or Italian parents. Still, she didn't resent Mary's mother, who reminded her of what her mother could have been, had she been well.

"Dr. Pettis," Hilliard asked, "could you describe for the jury the type of injury Detective Della Porta sustained in relation to the blood spatter you examined?"

"Certainly. In this case, a gun, a .22 caliber weapon, was fired into the decedent's lower forehead. Here." Dr. Pettis pointed a furry finger at the middle of his brow. "The skin over the bone exploded, the cranium was pierced, and blood and matter in the cranial vault were blown forward. The bullet lodged in the back of the skull and made a small hole in the forehead. Its geometry was quite round, which suggests that the weapon was fired directly at the victim, point-blank. Considering the blood spatter on the walls and furniture of the apartment, which I examined through photographic evidence, I would say the weapon was fired from a distance of three to four feet."

Hilliard crossed to the evidence table and picked up the plastic bag containing the bloody sweatshirt. "Dr. Pettis, have you had a chance to examine the blood on the sweatshirt that constitutes Commonwealth Exhibit 13, which we admitted earlier into evidence?"

"Yes, sir, I have."

Hilliard rested on a single crutch, extracted the sweatshirt from the bag, and walked to the stand with the sweatshirt, which flopped at his side like a blood-soaked battle standard. "These spots on the sweatshirt are what you are referring to as blood spatter, is that correct?"

"Yes. That is a very typical pattern of blood spatter. In addition, I performed a number of tests on that blood, the conventional blood work for typing and so forth, as well as DNA testing. PCR testing. I could elaborate, if you wish, on the PCR process."

Hilliard shook his gleaming head. "That won't be necessary," he answered, glancing at the jurors. "PCR testing is accepted in the scientific community as reliable and valid, is it not, Dr. Pettis?"

"Oh, yes, of course. PCR testing is used for plant and animal research around the country. In the human biology context, PCR testing may be used to determine paternity and twinness."

Bennie flushed instantly, thinking of the DNA test she and Connolly had taken. She had completely forgotten about the test because of all that had happened in the interim. When would those results be in? She caught one of the jurors, the videographer with the goatee, looking over at her.

"Dr. Pettis, did you test the blood on the sweatshirt and compare it for identification purposes with a sample of Detective Della Porta's blood supplied you by the Commonwealth?"

"I did," Dr. Pettis said, nodding.

"And is it your considered expert opinion, to a reasonable degree of medical certainty, that the blood on this sweatshirt is that of Detective Della Porta?"

"Yes, it is."

"Thank you, sir. I have no further questions of this witness, Your Honor," Hilliard said, gathering the sweatshirt and dropping it back at the evidence table, bloody side up before the jurors. They fell silent, gazing at the stains. Even Bennie imagined the blood on Della Porta's forehead, then the blood spurting from Lenihan's neck. The blood of Valencia Mendoza. Then hers and Connolly's, squinted at through microscopes, cell-size.

"Will you cross-examine, Ms. Rosato?" Judge Guthrie asked, and Bennie rose without looking at her client.

71

"It's Vega the Younger," Lou said when he saw Carlos Vega's kid bounding out of the rain and through the glass doors of the precinct house.

"Sorry I'm late, sir," the young cop said. He palmed his dripping cap and brushed it dry. A flock of uniforms flowed into the station house, talking and shedding wet slickers when they got inside. They all looked like babies to Lou, none as robust as Carlos's kid, who crammed his hat under his arm and extended a large hand. "I'm Ed Vega. Pleased to meet you, Mr. Jacobs."

"Who's Mr. Jacobs?" Lou said. He shook the kid's hand and held on to it for a minute, marveling at his broad, earnest face. The kid had dark hair, a small mustache, and the bedroom eyes his father had at twenty-three. "Call me Lou, okay? Your dad, now he has to call me Mr. Jacobs."

Vega laughed. "Okay, Lou. Sorry I'm late. You buyin' me lunch, I hear?"

"Depends on how hungry you are."

"I could eat a horse," the kid said, and Lou shot him a look.

"Drink water. I'm on Social Security."

"Deal."

Lou fell in step with the kid and they headed back outside, but were stopped at the door by a flood of uniforms coming in from the rain. Lou counted eight of them, including two broads who cursed worse than the men. "It's a brave new world, ain't it?" Lou said, without elaborating, as an older, taller cop hurried up the steps.

"Hey, Lou," Ed said, grabbing the older man by the elbow, "wanna meet somebody even older than you? Lou, this is Joe Citrone, my partner. Joe, Lou Jacobs, a friend of my dad's."

"Hey," Citrone said quickly, nodding like he was too busy to shake hands. He tried to pass but the boisterous crowd blocked the door.

"You look kinda familiar," Lou said, his crow's-feet wrinkling as he appraised Citrone. A fit guy, with hard eyes and no laugh lines. "When'd you graduate the academy? Class of—"

"Don't try to make conversation," Ed interrupted with a grin. "Joe Citrone is a man of few words."

Lou laughed. "Most cops yap like yentas."

"Lou, you want to know about Lenihan, you oughta be talkin' to Joe," Vega said, and Lou's ears pricked up.

"You knew Lenihan, buddy?"

"No, I didn't," Citrone said, and confusion creased the younger cop's forehead.

"Sure you did, the other day . . ." Vega started to say, but his sentence trailed off.

"You're mistaken, Ed." Citrone looked at Lou. "Good meeting you."

Vega fell silent as his partner walked away, then he slapped his cap on and gave it a twist. "Where we goin' to lunch?" he asked.

"Where else?" Lou said, and after a backward glance at Citrone, he ventured into the storm.

Debbie's Diner, with its aluminum sides, train-car shape, and familiar doughnut sign, had become a fixture in

South Philly. The food was good, the prices cheap, and the only drawback to the diner were the mob killings that took place in its front parking lot, generally in odd-numbered years. The murders were of the old-fashioned variety; a single, accurate gunshot to a target selected by an organized crime family, not the scattershot drive-by that shredded kids in the crossfire and left Lou asking what had the world come to, whenever the killers acted so inhuman. But rather than scare the patrons away, the murders served only to authenticate Debbie's, fazing neither the made men nor uniformed cops who ate there. Lou knew that as long as there was scrambled eggs with ketchup, there would be Debbie's. And he was glad.

"Let's sit here," Lou said, and showed Vega to his favorite booth. He sat down and grabbed some paper napkins from the steel dispenser, leaving it rocking. "You wet, kid? You want a napkin to dry off?"

"No, thanks." Vega shook his hair dry like a New-foundland puppy, and the waitress came over, cute with a short haircut and a black uniform that fit just right.

"You guys ever hear of umbrellas?"

"No," Lou said. "We hate umbrellas."

Vega grinned. "It's a cop thing."

The waitress shook her head. Her lapel pin, in the trade-mark doughnut shape, read TERESA—THREE YEARS, her name and years of service at Debbie's. Teresa was an infant by Debbie standards. "Two coffees, right away?" she asked.

"You're a genius," Vega said with a grin.

"Yeah, right. I should go on *Jeopardy*," she said, and took off.

Vega ran his hand over his hair and it popped back up like porcupine quills. "So, Lou, I don't know anything about him. Never even met the guy. It's an effin' shame, what happened."

"You hear anything about him? What's the scuttle-butt?"

"There isn't any."

"Hard to believe."

"Lou, I don't know what my dad told you, but I only been in the district two months. I just got paired with Citrone."

Lou nodded. "Citrone knows Lenihan, though?"

"You heard him. No."

"I heard *you*. You said he did."

"I musta made a mistake."

Lou blinked. "I don't think so, son, and I gotta know what you know. Lenihan got dead tryin' to kill somebody I care about. I want to know why."

"I don't know. I don't know anything."

"You said Citrone knows Lenihan. What made you say that?"

Vega swiped his hair again and squinted around for the waitress. "Where's that coffee?"

"Why'd you think Citrone knew Lenihan?"

Vega waved a hand, caught the waitress's eye, and made a drinking motion. She nodded, grabbed the pot by its brown plastic handle, and scored two mugs on the fly.

"Ed, why did you think Citrone knew Lenihan?" Lou asked again, but the kid kept squinting at the waitress, avoiding his eye. "Ed?"

"Here's the brew," Vega said, turning around as the heavy mugs arrived and the waitress set them on the table with a harsh clatter.

"I was gettin' the menus for you, Skippy." She poured the coffee into one mug, then the next. Lou noticed a dark tattoo on her forearm, a Chinese symbol, and wondered when girls started getting tattoos. Right after they joined the police force, but before they started law firms? Lou watched the waitress walk away and saw with satisfaction that some things still remained the same.

Vega gulped his coffee and hunched over the table. "Mr. Jacobs, Lou," he said, in a low voice. "My dad says you're a great guy, so you're a great guy, but I'm not about to go up against Joe Citrone for you. You understand?"

"I'm only asking for information."

"Information is going up against Citrone, and I don't know anything anyway, I swear."

Lou sipped his coffee and looked at the kid's face. "You're afraid."

"Bull."

"Don't work in clothes, kid. They'd make you in a minute."

"I'm not afraid, there's nothing to be afraid of. That I don't want to mess with Citrone? Nothing wrong with that, I'm new on the job."

Lou edged over the table. "What's the big deal? Citrone the President of the United States? Did I miss something when I was in the can?"

"Citrone's the old man. He knows everybody."

"Then he must know Lenihan, like you said the first time." Lou held his coffee cup. "Kid, Lenihan was in business with two guys from the Twentieth. They were in it together, with a detective, Della Porta, who got it last year and who used to be in the Eleventh. You think Citrone knows something about it? He's an old-timer, like you said."

Vega stood up abruptly, reached in his pocket, and flipped open his wallet. "Don't call me, don't find me, don't bother me." He threw a creased five on the table. "Stay away from me. Stay away from my father."

Lou rose, his knees creaky. "Listen, I just want to talk."

"You heard me," Vega said, and lumbered from the booth and out of the diner.

Lou watched him jog across the parking lot to his patrol car. *Running scared*, Lou thought.

"What happened to your friend?" she asked. The waitress appeared and tugged a pad and a stubby pencil from a black apron.

"My friend? He had to see a man about a horse."

"Wha?" The waitress scratched her head with her pencil.

"It's an expression. Don't you know that expression?"

"No. You wanna order?"

"Gimme three scrambled eggs and answer me this. You see a lot of cops in here, don't you?"

"Yeah."

"You ever see a cop in here named Lenihan? He was from the Eleventh."

"Lenihan? Isn't he that blond babe from the newspaper?"

Babe? Lou thought he heard her wrong. Maybe he did need a hearing aid. "Babe? When did men become babes?"

"Wha?"

Lou wiped his forehead, still damp. "Forget it. Did Lenihan eat here?"

"Sure."

"Who'd he eat with?"

"Other cops."

"Which other cops?"

The waitress shrugged. "How would I know?"

"Cops wear nameplates, for one thing."

"I don't read their nameplates. Besides, I don't talk about my customers."

"It's just a question. Who'd he eat with, usually?"

"You a cop? I thought you were a cop."

"No, I'm just a guy. An old guy who wants to know."

"Well, you're out of luck, old guy who wants to know," the waitress said, and shifted her weight. "You still want those eggs?"

"You got ketchup, right?"

"'Course."

"Then yes," Lou said, and sipped his coffee as she sashayed off.

72

Bennie faced the blood expert on the witness stand. "Dr. Pettis, you and I have met before, so I won't introduce myself."

The professor nodded, with a jowly smile. "Good to see you again, Ms. Rosato."

"And you, sir," Bennie said, hamming it up. The jury liked Pettis and she wanted them to know that Pettis liked her, too, so she wasn't the enemy. It was the best tactic with a reasonable expert put up by the other side: make him your own. "Dr. Pettis, the Commonwealth has provided you with various items to examine in this matter. It has provided you with photos, a complete file, blood samples, and a sweatshirt, is that right?"

"Yes."

"The Commonwealth did not provide you with a weapon to examine, did it?"

"No."

"Is it your understanding that the police have not recovered the murder weapon in this case?"

"Yes."

Bennie was watching the jurors' faces. They looked attentive, and she guessed they were already wondering about the absence of the murder weapon. She walked calmly to the witness stand. "Dr. Pettis, what kind of forensic evidence can be found on a gun used to commit a murder?"

"Objection," Hilliard said, half rising. "This is beyond the scope of direct examination. Dr. Pettis didn't discuss murder weapons on direct."

Bennie faced Judge Guthrie, who sat listening behind his tented fingers. "Your Honor, Dr. Pettis has been qualified as a forensics expert, and I'm asking him some basic questions about forensics."

"I'll permit it," Judge Guthrie said, and his mouth disappeared behind his finger steeple.

Bennie returned to Dr. Pettis. "Please tell us the type of evidence you usually find on a murder weapon, such as a .22 caliber gun, for example."

"Obviously, one would find fingerprints on the gun, which may result in a positive identification. There may also be flakes of skin, hair, or other trace evidence that could help identify the person who shot the gun."

Bennie raised a hand. "But in this case, there was no weapon, so no suspect can be identified or eliminated on that basis in this case, is that right?"

"Yes."

"Dr. Pettis, are you also aware that a sweatshirt was found in a Dumpster in an alley, is that right?"

"I was told that by the prosecutor, yes."

"No gun was found in the Dumpster, that you know of?"

"Not that I know."

Bennie took a moment to look at the jurors' faces, one by one. If they were wondering, let them wonder. "I have another forensics question, Dr. Pettis. When a person fires a gun, from any distance, aren't certain residues deposited on their hand?"

"Yes, provided there's no intermediate barrier, such as a glove."

"Can you test for the presence of such residues in your lab?"

"Yes, of course."

"Were you asked to perform any such test on Alice Connolly's hands?"

"No."

"You have no knowledge if any samples of residues were taken from Alice Connolly's hands, do you, Dr. Pettis?"

"I do not."

"Thank you. Let's move on." Bennie crossed to the evidence table and plucked the large baggie containing the sweatshirt from the evidence table. "Dr. Pettis, I am showing you what is marked as Commonwealth Exhibit 13. Do you recall testifying about the spatter pattern on this sweatshirt?"

"Yes."

Bennie extracted the sweatshirt and unfolded it, releasing a stale, distasteful scent. The blood dotting its surface was caked and dried, but she couldn't help feeling vaguely nauseated. "Dr. Pettis, blood spatter analysis is well accepted in the law enforcement community, isn't it?"

"Yes."

"And most law enforcement professionals, such as the police, are familiar with its principles, are they not?"

"Objection, calls for speculation, Your Honor," Hilliard said from his chair.

"Overruled," Judge Guthrie said. "Dr. Pettis may so testify."

Dr. Pettis faced Bennie. "Law enforcement professionals, such as police, would be familiar with blood spatter analysis. I myself lecture on it at police academies around the country."

"Do you lecture on blood spatter to the Philadelphia police, as part of their training?"

"I do, and on other forensic principles as well."

Bennie cocked her head, still holding the sweatshirt. "Do you have an estimate of how many police officers you've trained over the years in principles of blood spatter analysis?"

"I'm so long in the tooth, God only knows," he said, and the jurors smiled with him. "Thousands, easily."

"Thank you." Bennie held up the sweatshirt. "Dr. Pettis, didn't you testify earlier that the blood spatter pattern on this sweatshirt is typical?"

"Yes, I did."

"You teach this in your lecture course to the police, is that right, sir?"

"Yes."

Bennie faced the jury, still holding the sweatshirt against her own chest. She didn't need hair or skin analysis to tell her it was Connolly's; it would have fit Bennie exactly. "Tell the jury, Dr. Pettis, do you ever re-create spatter like this in your lab?"

"Yes. All the time. I do it to test my hypotheses and confirm my conclusions."

"So you *create* blood spatter, all the time? How do you do it?"

"I simply spray blood, I use pig's blood, at different garments. If it's at a distance I use a spray gun. But short of that, I simply flick the blood onto the garment, as Jackson Pollock did with paint. It isn't difficult."

Bennie smiled inwardly. Thank God for the expert's modesty. "So isn't it true that an individual familiar with blood spatter principles can *create* blood spatter?"

"Yes."

Bennie tossed the sweatshirt aside to signal to the jury how useless it was. She never was one for subtle cues. "I have no further questions," she said, but Hilliard was already reaching for his crutches.

Dr. Marc Merwicke was the most respected of the city's medical examiners, and Bennie wondered as Hilliard qualified him if his signature was the one on Lenihan's false blood alcohol levels. But Dr. Merwicke's appearance belied the suggestion that he could be capable of anything as exciting as a criminal conspiracy. Dressed in a gray suit and a solid tie of platinum color, Merwicke was about forty years old, with wet-down hair prematurely gray and a pallor that belonged in a morgue. Bennie felt a cold chill looking at him, thinking of her mother, then Lenihan. So much death; it was all around her. Her life was thick with it, as were her thoughts.

Hilliard asked a series of questions that took Merwicke through the autopsy he performed on Della Porta. Over Bennie's objections, Merwicke launched into a complete and painstaking examination of grisly autopsy photos, wound site photos, and magnifications of exit and entrance wounds. They were projected on a large screen pulled down from the wall, like a macabre movie, and Bennie watched the librarian turn away and the back row of the jury shudder almost collectively.

Merwicke finally testified that the "shooter"— borrowing the term from police lingo—could have been a man or woman, but was a tall person. Bennie watched nervously as several of the jurors turned to size Connolly up. The jurors frowned further when Merwicke testified that hair and skin samples from the defendant matched several found on the sweatshirt, linking the blood-spattered exhibit to Connolly.

"I have one last question, Dr. Merwicke," Hilliard asked, returning to the podium. "Does your office routinely perform tests for gunshot residue on the hands of murder suspects?"

"Yes."

"Did you perform a residue test on Alice Connolly's hands in this case?"

"No."

"Why was that, Dr. Merwicke?"

"Lawyers," the witness said flatly, and the jury laughed.

"Move to strike, Your Honor," Bennie said, standing up. She didn't understand the answer and she wasn't about to lose the residue point. "A lawyer joke isn't responsive, Your Honor."

"Your Honor," Hilliard said from the podium, "I was about to ask the witness to explain his answer." Judge Guthrie nodded, and Hilliard asked the witness to elaborate.

Dr. Merwicke's mouth tightened. "I meant that we can't always perform the tests we need to because criminal defense lawyers obstruct our efforts."

"Objection!" Bennie said, angry. "Move to strike that question and answer, Your Honor. There has been no evidence in this case that defense lawyers obstructed efforts to test Ms. Connolly's hand and—"

"But they did," Merwicke broke in, pointing a finger. "Alice Connolly's first lawyers did. They filed a motion. They made such a stink, my office couldn't get a sample. We had to take it to court, and by the time we could get a judge to rule, your client's hands were clean."

"Move to strike the testimony!" Bennie said, though it shocked her. There hadn't been any motion about it in the Jemison file and she had been too busy to check the docket sheets herself. "Your Honor, the witness may not testify as to any decisions or filings by previous defense counsel in this matter. Ms. Connolly has a right to assert all protections due her under the Constitution."

"Your Honor," Hilliard argued, "defense counsel opened the door, with Dr. Pettis. The Commonwealth is entitled to elicit why a gun residue test wasn't performed on the defendant's hands, now that defense counsel made it an issue in her examination."

"Quite right, the objection is overruled," Judge Guthrie said. "I'll not strike the testimony."

"Thank you, Your Honor," Hilliard said. "Permit me a minute while I determine if I have any further questions."

Bennie sank into her seat, her eyes on the jury. They had heard the whole exchange and it was devastating to the defense. She had screwed up the residue point. What had Jemison, Crabbe done? Opposed the residue test? Why? Because it would prove that Connolly *hadn't* fired the gun? And why hadn't their briefs or motion been in the file?

"I have no further questions, Your Honor," Hilliard said, his tone ringing with confidence as he gathered his papers and took his seat.

Bennie rose, hiding her unease. She had to set it right, if possible. "Dr. Merwicke, I have only a few questions for you. You testified that no residue test was performed in this case, is that right?"

"Yes."

"That test could have just as easily have shown that Alice Connolly did *not* fire the gun that killed Detective Della Porta, couldn't it?"

"Well . . . yes."

"In fact, isn't it true that if the residue test had been

performed, and no residue was found on Alice Connolly's hands, that would be proof positive that she was not the murderer of Detective Della Porta?"

"Then why would she oppose the test?" Merwicke's eyes flashed with anger, and Bennie bore down.

"It's a yes or no question, Dr. Merwicke. If no residue was found on Alice Connolly's hands, it would prove beyond the shadow of a doubt that she had not fired that gun. Yes or no?"

"Yes. But then why—"

"Dr. Merwicke, do you know for a fact that Alice Connolly opposed it or do you know only that her previous *lawyers* opposed it?"

"I assume she would know—"

"You assume wrong," Bennie spat back, and Hilliard half rose.

"Move to strike, Your Honor. Defense counsel is testifying."

Judge Guthrie nodded quickly. "Sustained. Please strike that comment, Ms. Reporter."

"No further questions," Bennie said. She'd said it for the jury anyway. She could only hope it would mitigate the damage she'd just done. She sat down and caught Connolly's expression. She looked as stricken as Bennie felt, and it wasn't contrived. Connolly's features, so like Bennie's without makeup, were limned with the stark, cold fear of a woman who had glimpsed her own execution. It was as if Bennie were looking at her own death mask.

And she couldn't turn away.

73

The defense team, including Lou, huddled back at the office over a dinner of take-out ribs at a walnut conference table dotted with crumpled paper towels. A paper clip tray had been converted to a water bowl and droplets of saturated fat floated on the water like oil in a gutter. "How'd we do today, Coach?" Judy asked, licking her fingers.

Bennie wiped her mouth with a napkin. "We took a big hit, thanks to me."

"It wasn't so bad," Mary said. Her eyes were tired from a predinner session at her computer, running down her assignment about Dorsey Hilliard. So far she'd had no luck. Hilliard had no unusual relation to Judge Guthrie, at least on reported cases online. He'd been before him in six cases; won three and lost three. "We just have to keep at it," Mary said, more to herself than Bennie.

"Cheer up, Rosato." Lou rolled his chair back and crossed his damp loafers. "At least we got a lead on Lenihan. Tomorrow I find Joe Citrone."

Bennie shook her head. "Lou, we discussed this already. You're not seeing Citrone. It's too dangerous."

"Oh, I forgot." Lou saluted. "You order, and I obey."

"Don't do it, Lou."

"I won't, Ben."

Bennie suppressed a smile. "I mean it. Go back to the

neighbors, finish canvassing the neighbors. Find me one that saw a tall cop go into that apartment."

"Whatever you say, lady, but Joe Citrone is tall."

"Then show 'em pictures of Citrone. Find me a defense witness. It would make a nice change."

"First thing in the morning, dear."

"Lou, I mean it. That's an order."

Lou took another slug of Rolling Rock from a green bottle. His was the only beer on the table with all the diet Coke cans. Lou loved beer, always had. It was his one vice, going back to when he was thirteen and his father gave him his first one. Ortleib's, in the brown bottle, which they didn't make any more. Ortleib's was his favorite, classier than Schlitz, a real Philly brand. And Frank's soda, too, that was from Philly. "If it's Frank's, thanks," Lou said aloud, faintly buzzed, and Bennie laughed.

"Snap out of it, Lou."

"I can't. I saw a girl with a tattoo today." Lou took another slug. "I've had all I can stands and I can't stands no more."

Judy laughed. "That's Popeye, isn't it? Popeye the Sailor Man. That's what Popeye always says before he eats the spinach."

"Good girl!" Lou raised his bottle in silent tribute. To Popeye. To Ortleib's. To old-fashioned bakeries and his well-loved ex-wife.

Bennie smiled. "I remember Popeye." Black-and-white cartoons flickered through her brain like a dime-store flip book. "He squeezes the spinach can and it pops open, right?"

Judy laughed again. "The spinach flies into the air with a really loud squirt, and Popeye catches it in his mouth.

Then you see it go down his throat and his arms turn into anvils. Or they, like, inflate."

Lou imitated her. "Right, they, like, inflate."

"Shut up, you," Judy said, and threw a straw at Lou, who ducked.

"Plus, girls shouldn't have tattoos," Lou shouted. "You hear me? No tattoos for girls! Only for sailor men!"

Mary clapped, suddenly lighthearted. Being a lawyer wasn't so bad, at least one night a year. "Sailor men? *Sailor* men?"

"What'sa matter with sailor men?" Lou asked, and they all laughed, suddenly giddy.

Bennie grinned, looking around the conference table, watching them all relax for the first time in days. It felt good to her, too, to laugh and forget about postmortem reports and spattered blood and even about her mother. About Lenihan and Della Porta and Grady. Bennie had called him twice but he wasn't at home and she guessed he was working late. She couldn't remember the last time they'd seen each other, talked, or made love.

"Sing it!" Lou was shouting, and the associates began warbling the Popeye theme song, complete with fighting to the finish and eating spinach. Singing filled the conference room, and Bennie didn't hush any of them. Let them get it out of their system. Then, like all sailor men, they'd have to take on the Blutos of the world.

Toot toot!

74

The next morning, Alice dressed for court in the small holding room. She hadn't slept at all last night. Rosato wouldn't return any of her calls and she had no contact with Bullock or the outside. She couldn't tell which way the trial would go, but yesterday went terrible. Rosato should put her up on the stand. Alice could sell the story. She could sell anything.

She slipped into a gray skirt and yanked on a silk blouse. It would be a big day in court, the last day of the prosecution's case. Alice had saved the gray suit for today on a hunch that Rosato would be wearing hers. In the photos Alice had seen, Rosato wore the gray suit for her most important appearances, with matching gray shoes. Connolly slipped her feet into an identical pair and clicked her heels together three times, like Dorothy in the Emerald City. "Get me out of this, sis," she said aloud.

She started brushing her hair. Rosato's hair would be freshly washed, so Alice had made sure her own hair was clean and hung limp like Rosato's. If Alice did her job right, she and Rosato would look exactly identical today. The guard knocked on the door. "Wait a minute," Alice called out.

A few minutes later, she was walking handcuffed behind the guard, led through one locked door, then another, and through the narrow hallway to the courtroom. "Like a lamb to the slaughter, huh?" Alice said, but the guard shook his head.

"Trust in the Lord, Miss Connolly."

Alice snorted. "Why? Will he work on contingency?"

The guard opened the door to the courtroom, and the first thing Alice saw was Rosato, sitting at defense table. And she was wearing her best gray suit.

Bennie ignored Connolly's gray suit and scrutinized the Commonwealth witness as the court session got under way. Ray Munoz was short, about fifty years old, and muscular, a bricklayer before a back disability ended his working years. His brown eyes were set deep above heavy cheekbones and his demeanor was garrulous and unpleasant, as if the world hadn't heard enough about his disintegrated disk. Hilliard brought the witness to the particulars. "Mr. Munoz," he asked, from the podium, "please show the jury where your house is located on Trose Street. Use the pointer, if you would."

"I'm right here, at 3016," Munoz said, pointing at the exhibit of Trose Street. His black knit shirt matched his hair, which sprung coarse as a scrub brush from his scalp. "Lived in that house for three years. Since I came from Texas."

"Mr. Munoz, are you indicating that you live five houses west of number 3006, on the same side of the street that the murder of Detective Della Porta took place?"

"Yeah, right." Munoz pointed to the sidewalk in front of his rowhouse. "Now, it was right here that I saw the lady run by. I could see right out the window."

"I didn't ask you that question yet, Mr. Munoz," Hilliard said, his tone reproachful, and Munoz frowned.

"Get to the point. I don't get paid by the hour anymore,

like you lawyers." The jury laughed until Hilliard began coughing loudly.

"Excuse me," Hilliard said. "Mr. Munoz, where were you before you looked out of your window?"

"I was readin' in my living room." Munoz set the pointer down. "I like to read the form after dinner."

"The form, Mr. Munoz?"

"The racin' form, son."

The jurors laughed again, and Munoz sat taller in his chair, encouraged, like a bad boy acting out in class. Bennie would have laughed with them, but Hilliard stayed with his stern principal role. "Mr. Munoz, where were you while you were reading the racing form?"

"In my BarcaLounger, I was sittin'."

"And where is your BarcaLounger, Mr. Munoz?"

"In front of the TV. Where else?"

Hilliard stiffened. "Where is your chair in relation to the living room window?"

"I got the BarcaLounger right next to the window. The window faces on the street. I sit by the window, for the light. Also the breeze. I don't have air-condition."

"So you were sitting in a chair by the window on the night in question. Was the window open?"

"That's the only way I know to get the breeze." The jury laughed, and Munoz grinned, fully playing to them now. "I ain't kiddin'. You can sweat like a pig in this town. Worse than south Texas and that's sayin' somethin'."

"Please, Mr. Munoz. Was there a screen in the window? And when you answer, please address me and answer the question by saying yes or no."

"I was answerin' yes or no."

"No you weren't, Mr. Munoz. Please say either yes or no, understood?"

Munoz cocked an eyebrow.

"The question is, was there a screen in the window?"

"'Course there was a screen in the window. That's how I heard the noise. Sounded like a firecracker. I thought it was some kids, outside. You know, kids gettin' ready for Fourth of July." He glanced again at the jury and an older woman in the front row nodded in agreement. "You know, kids," Munoz said again.

Hilliard looked up at the judge. "Your Honor, could you please instruct the witness to answer the question in the manner indicated? It would make the record much clearer."

Judge Guthrie nodded curtly and turned to the witness. "Mr. Munoz, if you don't mind, for the record."

"If you say so, Judge," Munoz said, glowering at Hilliard so fiercely that Bennie realized the prosecutor had made his first, and probably only, mistake of the trial. He had just turned a direct examination into a power struggle. The jury looked uncomfortable in their seats, a captive audience to the exchange.

"Mr. Munoz, do you know what time it was when you heard the noise you mentioned? As I said, please face me and answer yes or no."

Munoz stared at the prosecutor. "No."

"You didn't look at your watch?"

"No. How'm I doin', counselor?"

"Fine, Mr. Munoz," Hilliard said, consulting his notes. "Now. There came a time when you looked out the window. Mr. Munoz, do you know how long after you heard the shot that you looked out the window?"

"I'm suppose to answer yes or no?"

"Yes. Answer yes or no, please."

"Yes."

"How long was it between the time you heard the noise and the time you looked out the window?"

"Yes or no?"

Hilliard inhaled audibly. "Obviously not."

"Okay, you gotta tell me how you want my answer, or I don't know. I'm not as brilliant as you. For the record." Munoz smiled, and so did two of the jurors, but Hilliard gripped the podium and stood straighter.

"Mr. Munoz, how long was it between the time you heard the firecracker noise and the time you looked out the window?"

"A little while."

"Mr. Munoz, can you describe the time any better than 'a little while'?"

"You want me to answer yes or no?"

"Yes, please!"

"No."

The jury stifled smiles, and Hilliard wiped a hand over his lumpy scalp. If he had hair, he'd be pulling it out. "Mr. Munoz, tell this jury exactly what you saw when you looked out your window."

"I tol' you, I saw a lady runnin' by. I saw her face and her hair, goin' right by my window."

"So you got a good look at her?"

"Objection," Bennie said, half rising. "The prosecutor is testifying, Your Honor. The witness didn't say he got a good look. In fact, the witness hasn't even said who 'her' is."

"Sustained." Judge Guthrie peered over his glasses. "Mr. Hilliard, the Court understands that you are trying to clarify the record, but please use care in how you phrase your questions."

"Yes, Your Honor." Hilliard squared off against the witness from the podium. "Mr. Munoz, just so the record is clear, would you identify the woman you saw running by your window?"

"Identify? What's that mean?"

"Point her out in the courtroom," Hilliard snapped, but Munoz was already squinting at Bennie and Connolly. His thick arm rose and he pointed a stubby index finger at the defense table, but his aim wavered.

"I saw one of them, I don't know which one," he said. "They look like twins."

Bennie sat bolt upright in her seat, realizing what would happen the split-second before it did. Munoz couldn't make the ID of Connolly, not with them dressed and looking so much alike.

"Mr. Munoz," Hilliard said hastily, "you're pointing at the defendant and not her lawyer, correct?"

"Objection!" Bennie said, rising to her feet. "That's not what the witness did or said, Your Honor. Mr. Munoz testified he could not identify the defendant as the woman he saw running that night."

"Your Honor!" Hilliard fairly shouted from the podium. "For God's sake, the witness pointed right at the defendant."

Bennie approached the bench. "Your Honor, Mr. Munoz pointed between me and my client. He *said* he couldn't identify the defendant."

Crack! Crack! Judge Guthrie banged the gavel, his brow creased with concern. "Order, please. Counsel, please, and in the gallery. This Court has previously admonished you, you must maintain order!" Judge Guthrie swiveled his high-backed leather chair to face the witness. "Mr. Munoz, permit me to clarify the record. Did you identify, by that I mean point to, the defendant?"

"I don't know what the defendant is, I pointed at those

ladies. They look like each other. The one I saw had red hair, anyway. Neither of them have red."

"Move to strike as unresponsive and prejudicial," Hilliard barked, and Bennie couldn't restrain herself.

"Your Honor, there's no grounds to strike the answer! The witness's testimony is clear and he just confirmed it. Mr. Hilliard just doesn't like the answer he got."

Munoz pumped his head. "She's right! He don't like the answer, so he tells me I'm wrong. I know what I'm sayin', Judge. I know what I saw. I saw a redhead."

"Your Honor, please," Hilliard said, scrambling for his crutches and shoving them under his elbows. "Let me rewind the tape a moment. Mr. Munoz, do you remember being shown a photo array by the police and picking out the defendant's picture?"

"Objection, Your Honor!" Bennie said, but Judge Guthrie waved her into silence.

"Overruled."

Munoz looked confused. "Photo *what*?"

Hilliard plucked an exhibit from the podium, hustled with it to the stand, and set it down in front of the witness. "Let the record show that I am supplying Mr. Munoz with Commonwealth Exhibit 21, a photo array. Now, Mr. Munoz, have you seen this set of photos before?"

"Yeah."

"And when you were shown it, didn't you pick out the left middle picture as the woman who you saw running past your window?"

"So what?" Munoz tossed the photo array to the side, and Bennie couldn't have done it better herself. "You asked me who is the lady I saw out my window. You said answer yes or no. You said point to the lady in the courtroom. I can't do that and swear to God. You don't like my answer, that's too damn—"

"Your Honor," Hilliard interrupted, "may we continue this discussion in chambers?"

"Objection, Your Honor." Bennie stood as if rooted to the spot. "The prosecutor interrupted the witness's answer. Mr. Munoz was in the middle of completing his answer."

Judge Guthrie slammed the gavel to its pedestal. *Crack!* "Silence! In chambers, *now*, Ms. Rosato! Mr. Deputy, dismiss the jury! Mr. Hilliard, the Commonwealth's outstanding motion to strike is granted. This colloquy is not for the record."

"Place my running objection on the record, please," Bennie told the court reporter, a young woman who had lifted her hands from the keyboard. "I want the record to show that Mr. Munoz's testimony is being silenced by prosecutor Dorsey Hilliard and the Honorable Harrison Guthrie."

"*Ms. Rosato!*" Judge Guthrie shouted, whirling around in his leather chair. "Don't you *dare* give orders to my court reporter! Court is in recess! Counsel, in chambers! Deputy, *move!*"

75

Judge Guthrie stood behind his desk chair, his black robe unhooked at the top and his starchy white shirt exposed. His lined hands clutched the top of his leather chair, and Bennie wasn't surprised that his fingertips made deep indentations in its buttery burgundy hide. The trial had veered out of his control and any guilty verdict he'd guaranteed hung in jeopardy. He didn't look at Bennie as he spoke and he could barely keep his tone civil.

"Ms. Rosato," he said, "I was shocked by your conduct this morning. The accusations, the innuendo, in open court!" The judge glanced at the court reporter. "But my personal feelings are of no consequence at this juncture. We must settle a legal issue of grave importance. Please state your position, Mr. Hilliard."

"Your Honor, Ms. Rosato is intentionally confusing and manipulating the jury. She came to court today dressed identically to her client, in a gray suit with gray shoes, and she looks exactly like her client. Her scheme has succeeded in confusing a vital fact witness. Ms. Rosato cannot continue as defense counsel, Your Honor. The Commonwealth is requesting she be removed."

Bennie almost exploded. "There's no grounds for—"

"Quiet, Ms. Rosato!" Judge Guthrie ordered.

Hilliard edged forward on his seat. "Ms. Rosato's conduct has been outrageous and unethical. She should be replaced by one of her associates. There would be no prejudice to the defendant, because Ms. Rosato's associates have been in the courtroom every day."

Judge Guthrie faced Bennie, his expression cold. "Ms. Rosato, what do you have to say for yourself?"

"Judge, I did not plan to dress like my client today. I had no idea what my client would wear. I look like my client, that's true, but it's unprecedented to remove me as trial counsel merely for my physical appearance. There's no case law that holds that a client on trial for her life may not retain her lawyer of choice because that lawyer looks like her."

Hilliard's smooth pate snapped around. "There's no precedent because it's never happened. How many times you think a twin represents her twin, in a murder trial?"

"Excuse me." Bennie talked over him, directly to Judge Guthrie. "In addition, if the Court recalls, I did attempt to withdraw my appearance in this matter after my mother's passing, partly because of my difficulty in representing Ms. Connolly, and the Court denied my motion."

Judge Guthrie stiffened. "This Court did not, and could not, have anticipated that you would attempt to so boldly exploit the situation."

"I didn't do that, Your Honor. The courtroom ID was requested by the prosecutor and the testimony was given by Mr. Munoz, the Commonwealth's own witness. I merely acted to protect the record and the witness's testimony, and was under a legal and ethical duty to make a mistaken identity argument at that point. The record is clear that Mr. Munoz could not make a positive ID of my client in court. The jury is entitled to weigh that testimony, as any other, and we should all be back in court right now, starting on my cross."

"What?" Hilliard was so frustrated he banged his crutches into the soft rug. "After that stunt you just pulled? You should be held in contempt!"

"There's no basis for a contempt citation," Bennie shot back. "I haven't violated a judge's ruling."

Judge Guthrie held up a cautionary finger. "Not so fast, Ms. Rosato." He paused and sighed. "The Court finds itself between a rock and a hard place, counsel. The question is where we go from here. My law clerks tell me that Ms. Rosato may stay on as counsel regardless of the physical similarity between her and her client. The cases suggest, and they are scant indeed, that if the Court were to *sua sponte*, or on the Commonwealth's oral motion, ask her to withdraw in these circumstances, at this point, it could constitute reversible error and create a colorable issue for appeal."

Hilliard addressed the judge. "But going forward with Ms. Rosato prejudices the Commonwealth. We can't do redirect on Munoz and we can't put up the other neighbors to say they saw Connolly running from the scene, because they'll be confused by Ms. Rosato's appearance. It eliminates my afternoon witnesses."

Bennie edged forward. "Your Honor, if his witnesses can't make the ID, they can't make the ID. If his people can say only that they saw a woman who looks a lot like me running by, then that's not proof of identity beyond a reasonable doubt."

"Save your closing for the jury," Hilliard snapped, but Bennie was speaking for the record.

"Your Honor, the prosecution already has Mrs. Lambertsen's ID. The rest of the witnesses are cumulative, and there's no prejudice to the Commonwealth."

"They were corroborative witnesses!" Hilliard shouted. "Don't tell me how to try my case!"

Judge Guthrie walked around to the front of his chair and sat down slowly, his eyes avoiding both lawyers. "Mr. Prosecutor, I understand your frustration, but there are no other options at this point. We find ourselves in a quandary. The only alternative is a mistrial, and the Court doubts the Commonwealth will request that."

"Absolutely not," Hilliard said. "The Commonwealth can't take the chance on double jeopardy attaching. Then we couldn't retry Connolly."

Judge Guthrie nodded slowly, his gaze straying from both lawyers to the window. "Then we must go forward, after lunch. Court resumes, at one-thirty."

"Thank you, Your Honor," Hilliard said, almost sarcastically, hoisting himself to his feet, and Bennie followed him to the door, without a word to Judge Guthrie. The judge's mood mirrored Hilliard's. They were both trapped and hated her for it. It gave Bennie no satisfaction. She hadn't acted to confuse Munoz, Connolly had, and Bennie no longer wanted to cheat to win. Worse, the victory she'd gained was only temporary, and the forces behind the conspiracy would redouble their efforts.

Having a tiger by the tail wasn't all it was cracked up to be, especially in a murder case.

76

Lou glanced at the sky through the windshield of his Honda. The sun struggled through the thick gray clouds that blanketed the red-brick skyline in this part of town. At least it wasn't raining; he'd worn his good loafers again. He was parked catty-corner to the parking lot in back of the Eleventh, waiting for Citrone to report back. So far he'd had more luck waiting for the sun to come out. The girl at the front desk told him Citrone was expected around ten in the morning, but that was two hours ago.

Lou drained his coffee cup and bided his time, watching the uniforms come and go. No sign of Citrone or Vega. He went inside the precinct house and checked, but the girl kept saying Citrone should be coming in soon. Lou tried calling him at home from a pay phone on the corner, but Citrone's phone was unlisted. There were two other Citrones in the book and Lou called both. One never heard of Joe Citrone and the other no speaka de English. Nobody bothered to learn the language anymore. Even the immigrants were better in the old days.

Lou considered it, watching the uniforms and looking for Citrone's patrol car. Number 98, the girl said it was. America was full of people who didn't want to be American. Lou's parents never felt that way. They were proud of being German Jews, but they came to America because they wanted to become Americans. They didn't want Lou and his sisters to speak Yiddish like the other Jewish kids, or God forbid, like Russian Jews. They were looking to the future, not the past.

Lou checked the clock again. 12:18. Anybody else woulda been antsy, but not Lou. Careful police work, step-by-step, would pay off. Sometimes you just had to wait. Not everybody had the patience for it, but he did. It wasn't always a good thing. It kept him in a bad marriage for way too long. Like a cup of coffee, it just turned cold, and nobody knew where or when.

Lou's stomach growled. It was lunchtime. Another patrol car pulled into the last space left in the lot. He squinted to read the number. 32. A single uniform got out of the car and started examining the side door, like he'd caught a dent there. Lou scanned the lot. More cars would be coming in now, checking in around lunch.

Another car pulled into the lot, and Lou looked for its number. 10. Son of a bitch! The car parked sideways behind the row in front, blocking them in, and two uniforms got out, talking. They walked over to the cop looking at the dented door and started talking to him, standing around the car. It looked like they were razzing him about the dent. Lou looked at the clock. 12:32. When he looked up, patrol car 98 was turning into the lot. At the wheel was Joe Citrone, with Vega beside him.

Hot damn! Lou waited until Citrone pulled up and parked sideways next to the last patrol car. After Citrone had cut the engine, Lou got out of the Honda. He crossed the street, keeping an eye on Citrone. Citrone had stopped at the threesome gathered around the dent, and Lou hustled onto the lot and made his way between the parked patrol cars. Vega saw Lou coming before Citrone did, and Lou caught Vega warning Citrone by touching his elbow.

"Joe," Lou called out. "Joe Citrone."

The tall cop didn't respond, just stayed cool as Lou approached.

"Remember me? I'm Lou Jacobs, from yesterday."

"No."

"We met on the steps, you don't remember?"

"No," Citrone said with a poker face, and Lou laughed, taken aback.

"Come on, sure you do. We met. I was with Ed here." Lou looked at Ed Vega, who was shifting his feet as he stood in front of the other cops. "Hey, kid, tell him."

"I don't know you, pal," Vega said coldly, and Lou's mouth went dry. They had gotten to Carlos's kid.

"You kiddin' me, Ed? We went to Debbie's, you don't remember?"

"I don't know what you're talking about." Vega shook his head and his eyes turned hard. "You must have me mixed up with some other guy." The three cops behind Vega looked Lou up and down, then backed off like he had a disease.

"Come on, Ed." Lou considered pressing him, but didn't want to get the kid in dutch with Citrone. If Vega ended up dead, Lou would never forgive himself. He turned to Citrone. "Look, Citrone. Stop screwing around. We both know you knew Lenihan. You're senior in the same district. You want to talk to me about it in private or you want to do it in public?"

"I'm not talking to you at all." Citrone turned his back and walked away, as did Vega. They passed through the group of cops to the back door of the station house.

"Citrone!" Lou called out after him, on impulse. "Where's that half a mil? You got it stashed somewhere safe?"

Citrone didn't stop moving, though Lou thought he

saw Vega freeze, then move on. The other three cops looked shocked, which was just what Lou wanted. Get them all asking questions. Talking. Whispering. More got traded in the locker room than the New York Stock Exchange. Lou felt suddenly inspired.

"Citrone!" he shouted again. "You were in business with Lenihan and we all know it. You, Lenihan, and God knows who else, making a fortune, pushing drugs. You sent Lenihan to kill Rosato, Citrone. You're worse than the scum you bring in, Citrone!"

Citrone and Vega disappeared inside the station house, but Lou's audience wasn't Citrone anymore. It was the other cops in the district and there were more of them pulling up by the minute. One by one, they got out of their cars and listened. "You're made, Citrone! Your cover is blown, baby!"

The three cops stood rooted to the spot, and Lou couldn't tell from their expressions whether they were crooked or clean. The clean ones would agree with him. They would be tired of the crap Citrone was pulling, disgracing them all, for dough. The clean cops were the only weapon Lou had, and he had to reach them before more people got killed. So much for slow and steady police work; somebody had to blow the lid off these crooks. Who better than him, Lou Jacobs from Leidy Street?

"You're goin' down, Citrone!" Lou bellowed, making a liver-spotted megaphone of his hands. "You and every single crook in this house! Because you're dirty, Citrone! You're dirty as they come! You ruin it for all of us! You give good cops a bad name! You're a disgrace to the Eleventh, you sack!"

Lou's words echoed in the chill air. Every cop standing around heard them. Cops on the second floor of the precinct house gathered at the windows.

"I served in the Fourth, where crooks like you didn't exist, Citrone! Crooks like you weren't tolerated! Any cop in this house, any cop here who won't tolerate this, should call me, Lou Jacobs! I'm in the book, in town!" Lou had to catch his breath. "You hear that, Citrone? You hear me? I'm gonna take you down! *I'VE HAD ALL I CAN STANDS AND I CAN'T STANDS NO MORE!*"

With that last shout, Lou stopped and looked around. The parking lot was stone silent. Cops stood like statues between the cars. One stared, stricken, but a relieved smile spread across the face of another. Lou figured it wouldn't be long before he got a call from one of them. Or from Internal Affairs. Or from Citrone himself. Whatever it would be, Lou would be ready for it. He turned on his best loafers and walked back to his Honda like a much taller man.

I yam what I yam.

77

"The prosecution calls Shetrell Harting to the stand," Dorsey Hilliard announced to the waiting courtroom, and Connolly emitted a low moan.

"Here comes trouble," she said under her breath.

"What?" Bennie whispered, vaguely remembering the name buried in the Commonwealth's lengthy witness list, disclosed before trial. There'd been so many witnesses, Bennie hadn't had time to run them all down and she figured Harting wasn't important since she hadn't testified for the Commonwealth at the prelim. Now Bennie worried she'd called it wrong. "Who's she?"

Connolly leaned over. "Leonia Page was her girl, if you get my drift."

"Please approach the stand, Ms. Harting, and the deputy will swear you in," Judge Guthrie said, peering over the dais. The jurors' heads wheeled expectantly to the back of the courtroom, but the witness entered from the side, through the door that led to the holding cells.

"A prisoner?" Bennie said under her breath, and Connolly nodded yes. "What's she gonna say?"

"She's gonna lie her ass off," Connolly whispered back.

Oh, no. Bennie shifted to the edge of her seat as Harting walked to the witness stand. She was tall, black, and too thin to be healthy, and her coarse hair had been ironed into a paintbrush ponytail. She was dressed in blue jeans with bell bottoms and a red nylon top that caught the eye. An inmate who could incriminate Connolly, with revenge as a motive to lie. No wonder Hilliard had saved her until last. Bennie gestured backward to DiNunzio, who left her seat and came over.

"What?" Mary whispered.

"Go, now. Find out everything you can about this woman. Take Lou with you. Tell him to get the dirt from his cop buddies."

"Lou's not here."

Bennie's eyes flared. "He was at the office this morning."

"He left when court started. Said he'd be back tonight."

Bennie fumed. So Lou had gone to see Citrone. "Then take Carrier. I want everything you can get on this witness. Go!"

DiNunzio took off, and Bennie watched Harting place her long fingers on the Bible, take the oath, and ease into the witness stand. She could have been a model but for her eyes. A dull, sulking green, they didn't bother to please and engaged no one directly, least of all the prosecutor. "Ms. Harting," Hilliard began, his tone almost stern, "please tell this jury where you have been living for the past year."

"County prison, sir."

"That same prison that housed Alice Connolly until this trial?"

"Yes, sir."

"Please tell the jury why you were incarcerated, Ms. Harting."

"I'm doin' time for possession and distributin' crack cocaine. Also some weapons violations, I think."

The jurors in the front row sat engrossed, while the videographer stifled a smile. The court reporter typed away, the steno machine spitting a white paper tape into a tray, in folded strips.

"Ms. Harting, did I contact you and ask for your testimony, or did you contact me?"

"I called up your office from the house, I mean, prison."

"Ms. Harting, have I or anyone else representing the Commonwealth made any threats or promises to you in return for your testimony today?"

"No."

"So, Ms. Harting, it's your testimony that you came here today on your own initiative?"

"Yeah. Yes, I called you and axed could I come."

"Fine." Hilliard nodded and thumbed through a folder on the podium. "Now, would you please tell us how you know the defendant?"

"We on the same unit. We friends, her an' me, and she teaches the computer class I take."

At defense table, Bennie was gauging the jury's response. Each juror was listening carefully, many of them seeing a felon for the first time. Connolly passed Bennie a legal pad. On it was written, LIES!!! SHE HATES MY GUTS. SHE'S TRYING TO BURY ME.

"Ms. Harting," Hilliard continued, "did there come a time when the defendant had a conversation with you alone, after computer class?"

"Yeah."

"Do you remember when that conversation took place?"

"It was sometime last year is all I remember."

Connolly scribbled, NEVER, NEVER HAPPENED, but Bennie waved her to stop writing. The jury was watching Connolly's reaction to the testimony.

Hilliard checked his notes. "Ms. Harting, please tell the

jury about the conversation you had with the defendant on the day in question, if you would."

"Well, Alice tol' me—"

"Objection," Bennie said, on her feet. "Your Honor, this is hearsay."

Hilliard shook his head. "Your Honor, it's not hearsay. It's not offered for the truth and again, it's an admission."

"Overruled, Ms. Rosato." Judge Guthrie waved Bennie into her seat and nodded in the direction of the prosecutor. "Please continue, Mr. Hilliard."

"Ms. Harting, please face the jury and tell them what the defendant said to you."

The witness turned her chair toward the jury. "Well, Alice tol' me that she capped her boyfriend, Anthony. That she killed him. She said that nobody would never catch her. Said she was too smart for the cops, too smart for everybody."

A juror in the front row gasped, and two others exchanged looks. Bennie forced herself to sit stoic, though Connolly glared straight ahead at the witness. Harting crossed her legs, seeming to relax into her new role as star witness for the Commonwealth, and faced Hilliard.

"Ms. Harting," he said, "what did you say to the defendant when she said this?"

"I tol' her you kill a cop in this town, you pay with your life."

"And what did she say in response?"

Bennie half rose. "I have a running objection to this line of questioning."

"Duly noted," Judge Guthrie said dismissively.

Harting nodded, shaking off the interruption. "She said she'd get away with it, 'cause she was about to hire her the best lawyer in Philly. Was gonna try and convince the lawyer she was her twin, so she'd take her case on."

On the dais Judge Guthrie cocked an eyebrow and looked over, and at defense table Bennie felt her face flush with embarrassment. Connolly, next to her, was writing hastily, DON'T BELIEVE A WORD OF IT.

"Ms. Harting, did you believe what the defendant told you about her plans?"

"Yes, sir, I did."

"Why was that?"

"Because I seen her. Alice was the computer teacher, like I said, and she got in the computer room all the time. She studied about that lawyer on the computer, looked up pictures of her, got all kind of information. She had it all planned out."

Bennie struggled to control her emotions. It explained Connolly's accuracy in matching her wardrobe, down to her shoes. She'd been had; it had all been a carefully devised scheme from the outset. Her thoughts raced ahead. Still, even if Connolly had planned to dupe her, Connolly didn't kill Della Porta. Lenihan had tried to kill Bennie for a reason, but the jury would never know about Lenihan's attempt on her life. They would credit Harting and convict Connolly.

Hilliard skimmed his notes. "I have no further questions, Your Honor."

Judge Guthrie nodded at defense table. "Ms. Rosato, do you wish to cross-examine?"

Bennie stood up, slightly weak at the knees. "Your Honor, my associates are busy gathering valuable information for the defense's cross-examination of this witness. They will not be finished until the end of the day, if that. I request that we begin my cross first thing tomorrow morning, Your Honor."

"Your Honor," Hilliard said, raising his chin, "the

Commonwealth objects to recessing right now. My office promised the warden of the county prison we would return Ms. Harting tonight."

"Your Honor," Bennie argued, "this testimony comes as a surprise, as Ms. Harting did not testify at the preliminary hearing. The defense questions the reliability of her testimony. Surely the court wants to ensure the reliability of all of the testimony before the jury."

Judge Guthrie paused, undoubtedly aware that the jury awaited his ruling. "You may have your night, Ms. Rosato," he said finally, reluctance weighing his tone. "Be in court in the morning at nine, sharp. Mr. Hilliard, please have Ms. Harting returned tonight and brought back tomorrow morning. Make my apologies to the warden." The judge turned to the witness. "Ms. Harting, you may step down."

"Thank you, sir," the witness said, and climbed out of the stand while the jury was led from the mahogany box. Harting avoided Connolly's eyes while she walked to the paneled door, but Bennie shot Connolly a warning glance. It didn't help the cause that Connolly looked ready to kill.

Bennie packed her briefcase. She had her work cut out for her and no time to lose. "I'll be there in five," she said as the deputy came for Connolly.

"I *told* you all I know about Shetrell," Connolly said from the other side of the bulletproof plastic. "I got nothing to do with that bitch."

"Jesus." Bennie paced the interview room, but it was barely wide enough for five steps up and back. "She sent someone to kill you and you don't know why?"

"It was the cops, I'm telling you. Any idiot can see it. They put a contract out on me. They tried to kill me and when they messed up, they tried to kill you."

"Why use Harting?"

"Why not? She's connected on the outside, she'd be easy to reach. Plus, she's a gangbanger and she had people to do it for her. Shetrell's a good choice, a great choice. If I was gonna put out a contract, I'd use her, too."

"It was very damaging testimony." Bennie reached the blank white wall and turned around. "I have to cross her with something."

"You want to put me up? I'll sell it, believe me."

Bennie glared at her. "It was true, what Harting said about the pictures and the computer. You researched my life, my clothes. The twin story, it was all bullshit."

"I told you, she's lying."

"Then how did she know it?"

Connolly's eyelids fluttered. "Okay, okay. Some of it's true. I did research you on the Web. Your clothes and shit. Your website. She musta spied on me. Bitch has spies everywhere. Half the gang sells for her."

"She runs a drug business, in prison? How is that possible? How is any of it possible?"

"Money," Connolly said with a grim smile. "You know how much money is in drugs? You can buy girls, boys, guards, and cops. Judges and lawyers. Police and deputy mayors. Anything and anybody, tax-free. How you think the cops bought Hilliard and Guthrie?"

Bennie's heart sank, and for the first time since the trial started, she saw that the defense was going to lose. Connolly would go onto death row for a crime she didn't commit. Bennie would be invited to witness the execution. As much as she loathed Connolly, she couldn't bear that sight. "I have to get to the office," she said, ashamed at the thickness in her throat, and left the interview room.

78

"All we got is this?" Bennie said, reading the documents back at the office. The conference room table was blanketed with sheets of Shetrell Harting's prior convictions. It was after hours, so the office was empty except for the three lawyers working on Connolly. The air smelled faintly of hazelnut coffee and leftover pizza. Bennie would have felt good to be back on her own turf if her case hadn't been sliding down the tubes. "But drugs, prostitution, it's not enough. It's standard cross of a jailhouse snitch."

"It's the best I could do," Mary said, and Bennie waved her off, her hand reflected in the dark windows.

"I'm not criticizing you. We need something more. Something better."

Judy came around and read over Bennie's shoulder. "Don't underestimate its impact on a jury. You think those old ladies are gonna like that Harting sold herself for money? You just gotta play it up."

"I agree," Mary said, reaching for the jury diagrams. "The librarian, she wears a crucifix. The Asian woman in the back row, Ms. Hiu, she was frowning the whole time Harting testified. They don't like her."

"Damn." Bennie gulped coffee but couldn't wait for it to kick in. "We have to go forward. We were in decent shape until Harting, we have to get back on track. We'll counter Harting with a good defense case."

Ping! went the elevator, and they all looked through the glass wall of the conference room to the elevator bank. In the other conference room across the hall, Mike and Ike came to attention over their dinners and newspapers. The elevator doors opened and out came Lou, stepping nimbly toward the conference room, waving his hand like he was hailing a cab.

"Hey, Rosato!" he shouted, so loud they could hear him though the glass.

"Somebody's excited," Bennie said, hopeful. She'd been worried about him, too, though she hadn't realized it until he burst grinning through the conference room door.

"Go ahead, ask me how was work." Lou flung his arms wide. He couldn't remember when he'd felt this good.

"You were supposed to be canvassing the neighbors. You went to see Citrone."

"You could say that." Lou yanked out a chair and told them the whole story, about seeing Citrone and the Popeye in the precinct parking lot. "Then I went home, had myself a beer, and waited."

"For what?" Bennie asked, nervous.

"For a phone call."

"Did you get one?"

"Naturally," Lou answered, obviously enjoying the suspense.

"From who?"

"From a cop who says he has the goods on Citrone. We arranged a meet."

"Wow!" Judy hooted, and Mary looked astounded. Only Bennie's expression showed dismay.

"You're gonna meet him, Lou? How do you know he's for real? What did he say?"

"I know what you're worried about, and you don't have

to worry." Lou patted her hand, but Bennie wasn't comforted.

"What's his name?"

"He wouldn't tell me, he was afraid. Said he couldn't trust me yet, and I don't blame him. He's from the Eleventh, though. He saw me having conniptions in the lot."

Judy leaned over. "So we gonna meet him?"

Lou smiled. "Not you, sailor man. Me. He wants me alone."

Bennie shook her head. "I don't like this, Lou. If he has evidence of police corruption, he should go to the D.A., to the FBI. We can meet him there, even take him there."

"He ain't goin' to the D.A. or the feds. He doesn't want to be a crusader, he just wants to get it done. He trusts me because I'm a cop. He gives me the skinny, I'll take it forward."

"He told you all this?"

"No, but I can tell."

Bennie shuddered. "If this guy was setting you up, that's just what he'd say. You made yourself a target today, Lou. You declared open season on yourself. These cops are killers."

"It's not a setup. He's a cop, sounds my age. He wants to meet with me, and I'm going to do it. You don't have to worry, I can handle myself." Lou stood and smoothed down his jacket. "I know the mentality better than you do. You do the courtroom bit. I'll handle the cops."

"Where's the meeting? I'm going with you."

Lou's lips set firmly, his grizzled jowls soft. "The hell you are."

Bennie stood up. "I'm going. If I don't go, I'll follow you. I'll take Mike and Ike with me."

"We'll be right behind her, Lou," Mary said, and found herself standing up. She wasn't about to let Lou get hurt. She'd grown to like him when they canvassed together. "I'll bring my parents, too. My mother, Lou."

Judy rose, too, beside Mary. "I'm standing up only because everybody else is. I don't have anybody to bring, but I can box."

"You can't box," Mary said.

"I can, kind of. I watched people boxing. I know how to stand while someone else is boxing."

Lou shook his head. "I knew I shouldn't have said anything."

"But you did," Bennie said, "so we make a deal. You and I meet the cop, and Mike and Ike back us up in a car. The associates stay here in case we get killed, so there's somebody left to try the case."

"Damn!" Mary said, and Judy looked over with a surprised smile.

The night got blacker outside Mary's office window, but the associates huddled at the computer. Mary sat the keyboard, chewing Doublemint like a demon. It was the only time she treated herself to sugared gum, at trial. A lawyer's is a fast and dangerous life. "See, Jude? Nothing." She hit the ENTER key and a message appeared. The search yielded NO MATCHES.

"Let me think about this." Judy squeezed her eyes shut. "You searched cases that Hilliard tried before Guthrie and you got six. Henry Burden, most recently vacationing in Timbuktu, was in none of those cases."

"Yes."

Judy opened her eyes. "Any cases at all that Burden had with Hilliard, whether they were before Guthrie or not?"

"No, I tried that. I checked their birthdates in *Martindale-Hubbell*. Hilliard is thirty-five and Burden is fifty-five. That's twenty years' difference, for you math-phobes. Burden and Hilliard didn't even overlap at the D.A.'s office, much less try cases together."

"Rats." Judy thought harder. "You're searching cases with Hilliard as a lawyer. Try cases with Hilliard as a party."

"In a criminal case? There are no parties."

"I meant as a complainant. When did you get so smart?"

"Since Bennie told me what a superb lawyer I was. Didn't you hear?"

Judy smiled. "We've created a monster. Plug in Hilliard as a complainant, whiz."

Mary searched the program's libraries for complainants. "Can't. They don't index it that way, maybe for privacy reasons."

Judy sighed. "The government concerned about our privacy? Impossible. There must be another way."

"Hold on." Mary tapped out "Hilliard" in the ALL CASES category, as if it were a standard word search. The screen read, YOUR SEARCH WILL YIELD 1,283 CASES. ARE YOU SURE YOU WANT TO CONTINUE? Y/N. Mary pressed Y. "You betcha," she said, champing her gum.

"Are you nuts?"

"Clearly."

"A thousand cases. It'll take all night."

"Also true."

"Where did you get this energy?"

"Drug of choice," Mary said, and passed her the Doublemint.

79

Drizzle darkened the night, and Bennie and Lou stood next to the concrete stoop of a closed luncheonette. The cop showed up in a makeshift disguise, a Phillies cap and sunglasses, and Bennie could make out only some of his features in the calcium-white halo of a distant street-light. His silvery sideburns were shorn close to his head and his laughlines were pronounced. His mouth, set low above a receding chin, twisted with suspicion when he saw Bennie with Lou.

"Why'd you bring her?" the cop asked with contempt.

"I told her not to come," Lou said. "She don't listen."

"I'm the one Lenihan tried to kill," Bennie told the cop. "I'd like to know why, if you don't mind."

"I don't know why," the cop said. He wore a black nylon jacket with the collar turned up. His pants were dark, as were his shoes. "Either of you carryin'?"

"I am," Lou said, and the cop stepped forward and patted him down.

"Checkin' for a wire," he said, and when he was finished, turned to Bennie. "Lady, you're here, you're gettin' patted down."

Lou groaned. "That ain't necessary, buddy. I vouch for her."

The cop shook his head, a single swivel of the baseball cap. "Sorry, I can't take chances."

"Fine," Bennie said uncomfortably. The cop's hands quickly traveled her body and she talked her way through it. She did the same thing at the gynecologist's. "What do you know about Anthony Della Porta's murder?"

"Nothin'," the cop rasped. Bennie smelled cigarettes on his breath as he finished the pat-down and turned to Lou. "Why is she askin' me questions? I thought I was talkin' to you. You're Jacobs, right?"

"Sure, buddy. Lou Jacobs."

"You're the one from the parkin' lot. Shootin' your mouth off. Looked like you was havin' fun." The cop emitted a snort, and Lou laughed with him.

"Time of my life."

"You got it. We ain't dead yet." The cop's smile faded. "I asked around about you. They say you're okay."

"I'm more than okay. Who are you anyway? What's your name?"

"You gotta know that? Maybe we're all better off I don't tell you."

"Have it your way. Why'd you call?"

"There was this job, last year. It was at the projects, in town. A small-time rock dealer named Brunell, nothing special. A snitch told me about Brunell, so I ran it down. My partner and I get there, we're makin' the collar. Brunell is comin' along, no problem. We got him unawares and the dope is in plain view. Ziplocs on the coffee table, pipes and paraphernalia all around. You know, Lou."

"Sure."

"So we're about to take him in and the door opens and in comes Citrone and his partner. Not the new one, Vega. Latorce, the old partner, a black guy. You know him?"

"Never met him, but the name sounds familiar."

"So Citrone comes in and throws us out, just like that.

'Get the hell out,' he says. Latorce don't look too happy about it."

"What did you do?"

"We got the hell out. I figured Citrone wanted the collar, I know he's got seniority, but my partner, he was scared. He said he'd heard talk about Citrone, we should get out and shut up. So we did." The cop paused to wet his lips. "Then we get out, and I figure the report will come in any day. Only it never comes in. There's no report, no collar. Brunell wasn't booked and that's not the worst of it." The cop looked around, making sure they were alone. The street was black and still, the drizzle steady. "A week later, Latorce gets killed."

"Bill Latorce?" Lou remembered the name then. He'd seen it in the obits. "He was killed in the line of duty. He responded to a 911 call, a domestic."

"Bull. Latorce goes in first, figures it's hubby knockin' the wife around. No report of a gun, nothin', so Citrone, he's takin' his time gettin' out of the car, which already ain't procedure. Latorce knocks on the bedroom door and catches one in the head, point-blank. What's the odds a cop that experienced would screw up a domestic like that?"

"Cops make mistakes," Bennie said, and the cop's head snapped in Bennie's direction.

"What do you know, honey? I know, I'm a cop, thirty-two years on the force. You learn a lot over time on this job. Latorce was no dummy. If he thought somethin' was goin' down, the hubby had a gun, he wouldn'ta gone in by himself. Latorce got killed because he didn't like what went down with Brunell the week before. Somethin' went wrong, with me and my partner bein' there. So Citrone set him up."

"Jesus," Lou said. A bad feeling started in his stomach and seeped into his blood. "His own partner."

"You got it." The cop shifted his feet as if it were a winter night. "Listen, I gotta go."

"Sure," Lou said, but Bennie spoke up.

"Do you know anything about Della Porta's murder?" she asked.

"No."

"You know anything about cops named Reston or McShea?"

"Never heard of McShea. Reston, he used to be in the Eleventh."

"Was he dirty? You ever hear anything about that?"

"No, I wasn't in the Eleventh when he was there. I transferred from the Thirty-second." The cop glanced over his shoulder. "I gotta go. Don't screw me, Jacobs. I'm givin' you this to get those suckers. Don't name me, man."

Lou nodded. "Got you covered."

"See you." The cop walked off stiffly, his pants legs flapping, his Phillies cap down, and in the next second he'd disappeared into the darkness of the slick city street.

80

S everal hours later, Judy had fallen asleep in the chair beside Mary, who had skimmed almost three hundred cases, each going back in time earlier than the last. Though she hadn't read each one completely, Mary had gotten a thorough overview of Dorsey Hilliard's career as a prosecutor. He had won many more than he lost and his legal arguments were right on the money. He'd never been found ineffective as a lawyer, the most common grounds for collateral appeal, and many of the judicial opinions referred to the clarity of his closing, which didn't bode well for the Connolly case.

Mary had found endless cases that Hilliard had tried and several in which he had appeared as a witness, to testify about the effectiveness of other counsel. She had even found a civil case he had brought against an insurer on his own behalf, for expenses relating to physical therapy for his handicap. The insurer had balked at reimbursing Hilliard, and at twenty-one years of age he had sued them for it and won. Mary found herself cheering inside. Hilliard hadn't even been to law school at the time. How long had he wanted to be a lawyer? How long had he lived with his disability?

Mary remembered the little boy on the white pony, being taught to ride by her classmate. His dark eyes, waiting for her answer. *He understands more than you and me*, Joy had said. Mary sensed that she had let him, and Joy, down, but part of her wasn't ready to let go of the law. It wasn't that she enjoyed being a lawyer, but she had become intrigued in this case after they'd attacked Bennie. It was that part of Mary that made her punch the ENTER key and read on, into the night.

81

"Mike and Ike still behind us?" Bennie asked, boosting herself up in the passenger seat to check Lou's rearview mirror.

"Sit down, they're back there." Lou braked at the light in his Honda. Rain pelted the windshield but the wipers didn't clear the view, and he switched on the defroster. "Told you it wasn't a setup. Cop spilled his guts."

"You don't know that, Lou. It could still be a setup."

"How?"

"It could have been bad information to throw us off. Or get us killed."

Lou looked over. "Come on, it was legit."

"Also, somebody could have been watching us."

"Nobody was watching us. We woulda seen it, or the cop would have."

"Oh, yeah?" Bennie snorted. "We had Mike and Ike following us, and your cop friend didn't pick them up."

Lou moaned, even over the sound of the defroster. "Rosato, check it with Mike and Ike. They woulda seen if somebody was watching us."

"Somebody could *still* be watching us."

"You drive me nuts. You're gettin' paranoid now."

"Maybe because a cop tried to kill me, and my Ford is dead."

Lou didn't say anything for a minute. "I think we got some good info there. He was a real stand-up guy, that cop."

"Yeah, but it won't help the case."

Lou glanced over. "Nothin' you could use? Latorce was killed the same way Della Porta was, a shot to the head."

"That doesn't get you far, you know that."

"What about the fact that the Brunell collar never happened? Can't you use that, to show evidence of corruption?"

"By Citrone, who, on this record, has nothing to do with Della Porta's murder? No, in a word." Bennie peered through her window, watching the traffic. Windshield wipers flapped on overtime and the asphalt street glistened. The rain was endless, and since Harting's testimony, Connolly was lost.

"You're worried."

"An understatement."

"I'll run down the Brunell lead."

"No, it's dangerous."

"What if there's a connection between Brunell and Reston? That would be likely, since Reston was in the Eleventh."

"It's too dangerous. It'll come too late anyway."

"I'll make something happen."

Bennie looked over. He sounded like her. "You can't fix everything, Lou."

"Rosato, shut up." Lou sighed, and the Honda accelerated smoothly. "Where you goin', back to the office?"

"No, I'll work at home.

"Your boyfriend will like that."

Bennie felt a twinge. "If he's awake, which I doubt," she said, and looked out the window into the rain.

82

Mary checked her desk clock. It was five-thirty in the morning, almost dawn. The sky was a grayish-blue outside her window and she could already see the beginning of the city's stirring. She kept her eyes on her computer screen. She was down to the last ten cases. Judy had gone home a long time ago to get ready for court, but Mary would shower and change at the office. She hit the key and skimmed the ninth case from the last.

Hilliard trying a case for aggravated assault. It had to be his first major case. A barroom fight. One guy slashing another, too close to the jugular for a lesser charge. Nothing untoward about the case, and Hilliard won. Good. By now, Mary was on the prosecutor's side, picturing him as a handsome young black man, arguing from the heart, propped up by crutches that scarcely seemed necessary. She hit the key for the eighth case.

Almost fifteen years ago. A simple assault. Hilliard wins. Nothing strange in the case. Nothing connected with Guthrie, Burden, or Connolly at all. Mary sighed. She'd been here before. Fruitless all-nighters. She was even out of gum. She hit the key for the seventh case, then skimmed it. Then the sixth, and the fifth, and so on down.

LAST CASE, read the screen.

Mary blinked. It was hard to believe she was at the end. The last of a thousand-odd cases. Only an idiot would come this far. She hit the key and the case popped onto the screen. Its date was in the sixties, a full twenty years before the previous case. Hilliard would have been a toddler then, if not a kid.

Mary shook her head. A computer glitch. Dorsey Hilliard would have nothing to do with such an old case. *"Commonwealth v. Severey,"* read the caption, and Mary skimmed the headnote summary with disappointment. The defendant, Andre Severey, had been convicted of murder in the death of a kid stepping off a SEPTA bus. Severey had been aiming at a rival gang member on the street, and a stray bullet had killed one child and wounded another.

Mary sat up in her seat, her body tensing as she read. The bullet had cut the spinal cord of the wounded child, who had lived only a block away. Mary's eyes raced to the end of the sentence. The child's name was Dorsey Hilliard.

Mary sat still at the keyboard. My God. That was how Dorsey got his injury. She hit the key for the next page, though she guessed what she'd find. Under the prosecution was a single name:

Henry R. Burden, Esq.

Mary read it over and over but it didn't change. It had to be Burden's first case in the district attorney's office; he was only an assistant then. What did it mean? Burden had convicted the man who put Hilliard on crutches. Gotten a life sentence, without parole.

Mary thought about it. Severey was convicted of murder, though it smacked of overcharging. It was a heinous crime, but not premeditated enough. Was Hilliard beholden to Burden for the conviction? Mary felt she would be. Was there a connection here that was germane to the Connolly case?

Mary reached for the phone to call Bennie. Then she thought a minute. It was early to wake Bennie up, and Mary had one short assignment to go. It was a legal research question, slightly off the point, but Mary had a hunch it might come in handy. Fueled by adrenaline, she let the receiver go and hit the key to begin a new search.

83

The courtroom fell silent as Shetrell Harting entered, took her seat in the witness box, and was reminded by the judge that she was still under oath. "I understand, Your Honor," Harting said, settling her slim form into the black bucket seat.

"Ms. Rosato, you may begin your cross-examination," Judge Guthrie said, without looking up, and Bennie strode to the podium, instinctively wanting to keep the inmate at arm's length.

"Ms. Harting, you are currently an inmate at county prison, is that right?"

"Yeah." Harting had changed her outfit and wore a light, white cotton sweater with her blue jeans, but her expression remained as remote as yesterday.

"And you testified yesterday that you were serving time for possession and distribution of crack cocaine, is that right?"

"Yeah."

"That conviction wasn't the first time you've broken the law, was it?"

"No."

"You have another conviction, two years before that, also for drug dealing, is that correct?"

"Yes."

"And several before that, for solicitation."

"Uh, yes."

"In fact, three times in a two-year period you were convicted for solicitation, is that right?"

"Yes."

Bennie checked the jury, alert this morning, listening tensely. The videographer had edged to the front of his seat, as had the librarian. They wanted to see what Bennie could do to Harting, which only confirmed the lawyer's theory about the impact of her testimony. "Now, Ms. Harting, you testified yesterday that you and Alice Connolly were friends, didn't you?"

"Yes."

"And you testified about a conversation you had with Alice Connolly after computer class one day."

"Yes."

"And you testified that Alice Connolly told you that she had killed Detective Della Porta, is that right?"

"Yeah, I said that, but I'm thinkin' I should tell the truth today."

Bennie blinked. "Pardon me?"

"I'm goin' to tell the truth today."

Bennie thought she'd misheard. "The truth?"

"I mean, that was wrong, what I said yesterday."

Bennie fumbled for her bearings. "You mean that Alice Connolly did not tell you that she killed Detective Della Porta?"

"Yeah." Harting's eyes flickered a flat green. "Alice never tol' me nothin' like that."

Bennie hid her bewilderment. Out of the corner of her eye, she could see Judge Guthrie cocking his head, his reaction restrained, and most of the jurors looked confused. Dorsey Hilliard's face morphed into a horrified mask. She remembered what DiNunzio had told her this morning about Burden's prosecuting the man who had injured him, and concluded that Connolly was payback for the conviction.

"Ms. Harting," Bennie asked, "do you mean that your testimony of yesterday, that Alice Connolly told you that she had killed Detective Della Porta, was false?"

"Yes. I lied on her yesterday."

"Objection!" Hilliard said, snatching his crutches and rising to his feet almost before they were completely supporting him.

"On what grounds?" Bennie asked.

Hilliard looked over, his mouth open slightly. "The question was leading."

"It's your witness," Bennie shot back. "This is cross, remember?"

"Order!" Judge Guthrie barked, reaching for his gavel. "Mr. Hilliard, please take your seat. Ms. Rosato, please address your questions to the witness."

"Thank you, Your Honor," Bennie said. She had no idea why Harting was recanting, but she had to pin down this testimony. "Ms. Harting, were you lying when you testified that Alice Connolly told you she killed Anthony Della Porta?"

"Yes."

"Were you lying when you testified that Alice Connolly said she thought she'd get away with the murder because she was too smart for everybody?"

"Yes."

"Ms. Harting, is it your testimony today that everything you said on this stand yesterday was false?"

Judge Guthrie leaned toward the witness, his mouth set in a grim line and his forehead wrinkling deeply. For the first time in this trial, his plaid bow tie looked askew.

"Ms. Harting, it is incumbent upon the Court, since you appear without counsel in this matter, to inform you that perjury, which is the making of a false material statement under oath, carries a heavy penalty in Pennsylvania. Do you understand that, Ms. Harting?"

"Yeah," the witness answered, and blinked once. It was the only reaction evident on her face. "Alls I said yesterday was a lie. I lied on Alice and I'm sorry."

For a minute Bennie had no idea how to follow up. So she asked the only question she wanted answered, which had to be on the minds of the jurors. "Ms. Harting, there is one last question. Why did you lie yesterday?"

"Because I wanted Alice to go up for the murder. We was never friends. She did somethin' bad to me, somethin' real terrible, between us. I wanted to get her back, so I called up the D.A." Harting paused. "But las' night in bed I thought about it and I prayed to my Lord Jesus and I knew I couldn't go through with it. I'm sorry. I truly am."

Bennie didn't believe a word of it. Something must have changed Harting's mind about testifying against Connolly. Someone had gotten to her, overnight. Who? Connolly, or someone sent by her. Bennie felt torn, sickened. Harting's testimony today was the truth, but it had come the wrong way. "I have no further questions," she said, and returned to her seat without looking at Connolly.

Hilliard took the podium and swiped his head with an open palm. "Ms. Harting, I must say, I am absolutely astounded at your testimony this morning."

"Objection," Bennie said. "The prosecutor may not comment on the testimony, Your Honor."

Judge Guthrie shifted forward in his chair. "Mr. Hilliard, please."

"Yes, sir," Hilliard said, sighing theatrically. "Ms. Harting, is it your testimony today that everything you said yesterday was a complete and utter fabrication?"

"Objection, asked and answered," Bennie said, and Judge Guthrie groaned.

"Sustained. Mr. Hilliard—"

Hilliard raised a hand. "I'm sorry, Your Honor. This comes as such a shock."

Bennie stifled her motion to strike. Hilliard's histrionics were futile. The prosecutor was in a terrible bind and he knew it. There was no quicker way to lose a trial than to have a star witness recant.

"Ms. Harting," Hilliard said, "you took an oath to tell the truth yesterday, didn't you?"

"Yes."

"Ms. Harting, did you understand you took that oath yesterday?"

"Yes."

"But you didn't tell the truth yesterday?"

"No, I didn't."

"Even though you swore on a Bible, before *your Lord Jesus*, when you took that oath to tell the truth?"

"Yes. I'm sorry. I truly, truly am."

Hilliard nodded. "When you got up on the stand this morning, the judge reminded you that you were still under oath, didn't he?"

"Yes."

"So that means you took an oath to tell the truth today, do you understand that?"

"Yes."

"So you took an oath to tell the truth yesterday and you took an oath to tell the truth today. How do we know you're telling the truth today?"

Bennie rose. "Move to strike this line of questioning, Your Honor. The prosecutor is harassing his own witness."

Hilliard straightened his broad shoulders at the podium. "Your Honor, in view of the morning's events, the Commonwealth requests permission to question Ms. Harting as a hostile witness."

"Granted." Judge Guthrie shifted back in his chair.

"Ms. Harting," Hilliard said, rapid-fire, "were you lying yesterday or are you lying today?"

"I'm tellin' the truth today, I swear it." Harting turned her body toward the jury, though she didn't make eye contact with a single juror. "I am tellin' the truth now, I swear to you. I prayed to Jesus, and he helped me. I done wrong in my life, I know, and I wanted to get Alice back, but it was wrong and I want to do the right thing—"

"Ms. Harting," Hilliard interrupted. "Look at me, not the jury, and please answer my question, and my question only."

At her chair, Bennie could barely listen to the exchange. How had Connolly gotten to Harting, from a holding cell? Had she sent Bullock to the prison last night? He could have represented that he was an attorney and gotten in even after hours. But the prison logs would show a lawyer visit and they could be checked with a phone call. Bennie guessed Hilliard's thinking tracked hers, because he scribbled a note and handed it to an associate, who scooted from the courtroom.

Hilliard resumed his questioning. "Ms. Harting, you say that you prayed to Jesus. Do you attend chapel regularly in prison?"

"Not regular."

"When was the last time you attended chapel in prison?"

Shetrell's eyes fluttered. "I pray in my own way."

"In your own way?"

"Objection, Your Honor," Bennie said. "This is harassment."

Hilliard pursed his lips. "I'll withdraw the question, Your Honor. Ms. Harting, what did you do after you left court yesterday?"

"I went back to the house. To prison."

"What did you do there, Ms. Harting?"

"Same thing as always." Harting shrugged, her shoulders knobby under the thin T-shirt.

"Which is what, Ms. Harting? Do enlighten us."

"Looked at some TV, sat on the unit, then went to sleep."

"Ms. Harting, did you discuss your testimony with any of the other inmates at the prison?"

"No."

"Did you receive any visitors with whom you discussed your testimony?"

"No."

"Did you receive any visitors at all last night?"

"No."

"Did you receive any telephone calls last night?"

"No."

"So, Ms. Harting, it's your testimony that you have not discussed this case or your testimony with anyone since yesterday?"

"No, that's not what I said. I did discuss my testimony with someone."

Judge Guthrie looked over. Bennie tensed. Hilliard looked relieved. "Who did you discuss your testimony with, Ms. Harting?" he asked eagerly.

"My Lord Jesus," Harting answered, with absolute conviction.

Suddenly the D.A.'s associate appeared at the door in the bulletproof shield and was admitted by the deputy. In his hand was a crumpled slip of paper. The associate handed the note to Hilliard, whose face remained impassive. Bennie held her breath. Wanting the truth to come out; not wanting the truth to come out.

"Your Honor," Hilliard said. "I have no further questions."

Bennie sat astounded. The OV logs hadn't shown a visitor? So how had Connolly reached Harting? Had she bribed the guard who kept the logs? *You know how much money is in drugs? You can buy girls, boys, guards, and cops.* The words echoed in Bennie's mind as court recessed for the lunch break, the jury was guided out, and Connolly was escorted from her seat without looking back.

84

Low-rise projects squatted near Philadelphia's business district, ten blocks from City Hall. Their crumbling brick towers stood out in a skyline rejuvenated by the modern geometry of the Mellon Bank Center and the neon spikes of Liberty Place. The mirrored skyscrapers uptown caught the sun like a butterfly in hand, but the projects swallowed it up, superheating the apartments inside. The windows that hadn't been punched out like black eyes were flung open. At each corner of the building were caged balconies, and Lou noticed a line of laundry drying inside one of the cages.

He was sitting in his Honda, parked across the street from the building where Brunell lived. Lou had found the address by looking Brunell up in the phone book. The man had four phones, all listed. It was easier to call the bad guys than the good guys. Lou watched patiently, scoping out the scene before he went upstairs. The foot traffic in and out of the building was steady, and Lou saw all types go in: young black men, white women, businessmen, and pregnant mothers. One kid, no more than twelve, went sailing into the building's entrance on a skateboard, baggy shorts flapping low on his hips. Different as they were, all entered the building and left again fifteen to twenty minutes later. Lou couldn't prove that they were there to buy drugs. He couldn't prove the sun was hot either.

He got out of the Honda, crossed the street, and asked the first person he saw if she knew Brunell. "Up on eight, 803," the older woman said. She seemed resigned to being asked and evidently wasn't worried that Lou was a cop. The drug dealer did business as openly as Woolworth's. How much could that kind of security cost? Half a mil, under the friggin' floor?

Lou found the elevator near the front entrance but it hadn't worked in ages. The call button had been yanked out of its plate and the doors spray-painted with graffiti. He looked around for a stairway. The hall was filthy and reeked of urine. Bags of trash had been set outside apartment doors, contributing to the foul air, though in front of one door sat a tied stack of papers for recycling. Television blared through walls so thin Lou could identify Rosie O'Donnell's laughter. A hip-hop beat pounded from behind a closed door, making him yearn for Stan Getz.

Lou spotted a broken EXIT sign on the wall and followed it around the corner to the stairs. The stairs, concrete with scored metal on the steps, were dark with grime. Cigarette butts and a dead Elmo toy littered the narrow passage. Eight floors. Lou sighed and took the first step.

"I'm here to see Pace Brunell," Lou said, talking through the closed door to the apartment. He was trying to catch his breath from the walk upstairs, staring at the painted-on 803 in cockeyed black letters.

"Come on in," said a man's voice. The door swung open onto a well-built young man with light-blue eyes, densely coiled reddish-brown hair, and a dotting of tiny freckles across his cheeks. His wide nose and broad lips suggested an African-American heritage, but his skin was

white, even pale. He wore a T-shirt and baggy blue basketball shorts that said NOVA.

"Are you Pace Brunell?" Lou asked.

"Sure am."

"Lou Jacobs. Like to come in if I can."

"Step into my office," Brunell said breezily, then closed
the door behind Lou, who glanced quickly around. A saggy
tan couch sat in front of a teak coffee table, but the furniture wasn't what Lou noticed right off. Wrinkled stacks of
fifties, tens, and twenties sat on the table, at least thirty
thou to Lou's eye. Hot damn! Next to the dough was a digital money-counting machine like they have in Vegas, press
a button and it fans out money like cards. Coke packets
wrapped in cellophane and twisted shut at both ends lay
scattered on the table like hard candy.

"See somethin' you like?" Brunell asked, and Lou
shook his head slowly.

"You know, they used to put cigarettes on coffee tables,
in china boxes. Very classy. You could lift off the top and
there were the Camels. Or Pall Malls. Or Old Gold. It
smelled like tobacco when you opened the box."

"Cigarettes will kill ya."

"I know. I miss 'em every minute."

Brunell smiled and flopped on the couch. His gym
shorts rode up, revealing a long scar on his thigh, knotty
with keloids. "It's Friday, you know. I'm busy before the
weekend. You a buyer or what, pop?"

"No," Lou said. "I came to talk about Joe Citrone. You
know him."

"I knew you was a cop." Brunell slapped his leg in self-
admiration. "You from the Eleventh, too?"

"No, I'm retired. I know Citrone protects you, your
operation."

"This ain't a shakedown, is it?"

"At my age? No. I'm trying to find out why a cop named Bill Latorce got dead. I think it has something to do with Citrone."

"Now, why you think that?" Brunell said, his smile vanishing.

"I heard it, over the shuffleboard courts. You remember Latorce, a black cop? He was working with Citrone, keeping you in business."

Brunell stood up quickly. "Time for you to go, buddy."

"But we're having such a nice talk. I think we're, what do they say, bonding?"

"You're crazy, old man." Brunell crossed the room, opened the door, and in one smooth move, yanked a matte-gray Glock from the back of his shorts and aimed it at Lou. "Get out."

Lou eased out of the chair and went to the door. The sight of the gun wasn't good for his heart, but Brunell wasn't stupid enough to kill him. "You remember my name, Brunell?"

"Lou the Jew."

"Get it right when you call Citrone. Tell him I'm the one from the parking lot, at the Eleventh." Lou walked out, and Brunell slammed the door behind him.

85

The press attacked Bennie the moment she pressed through the courtroom doors, shining TV lights in her face and shouting questions in her ear. "Ms. Rosato, what do you have to say to Ms. Harting's testimony?" "Ms. Rosato, were you shocked by this turnaround?" "How's your twin?" Bennie shielded her eyes and fought her way down the marble corridor, with Mike and Ike running interference. "Thanks, guys," she said, as she slammed the door to the courthouse conference room closed, to face two jubilant associates.

"Bennie! We scored, do you realize that?" Judy exulted from her customary seat, and Mary applauded, a standing ovation. Her face was flushed with excitement.

"It's over!" Mary said. "Way to go."

"Cool it, guys," Bennie said, sitting down wearily.

Judy's brow buckled with bewilderment. "Bennie, will you at least smile? Shetrell Harting was the big bang and she just went bust. Hilliard is dead! The prosecution is dead!"

Bennie looked up. "Question number one, why did Harting recant?"

"Who cares? She did!"

"Question number two, what if our client got to her?"

Judy fell abruptly silent, but Mary looked positively stricken. *"Did she?"*

"I think so, I just can't figure out how."

Mary sank into her chair. "I don't think it was anything Connolly did, Bennie. Harting was believable, at least I believed her. She started to do something, then she thought better of it. She bit off more than she could chew. Haven't you ever done that?"

"Yeah, this case." Bennie smiled bitterly.

"Why do you think Connolly got to her? Do you have any facts?"

"What you just saw was too good to be true. You know the expression, DiNunzio."

"Yeah." Mary's father always used to say that. "So what do we do?"

"I'm thinking about that," Bennie said, but Judy, standing above them both, planted her hands on her strong hips and frowned.

"I can't believe I'm hearing this. Bennie, you lectured me at the crime scene on how a defense lawyer isn't supposed to seek justice, he's supposed to get the defendant off. What happened to that?"

"Get the defendant off within the rules, Carrier. Witness tampering is not a trial strategy. I don't like benefiting from obstruction of justice. I play fair."

"But it's not about you, Bennie. You're not the one who's benefiting, Connolly is. It's not you on trial, it's Connolly."

"I know that," Bennie said, though a sinking feeling told her she hadn't been thinking that way. Separating her identity—and fate—from Connolly's was growing impossible.

Judy leaned forward urgently. "Besides, you don't know Connolly had anything to do with Harting's recanting. They were incarcerated in separate places. All we know is,

Harting recanted. We just got a break. We have an obligation to use it."

"An *obligation*?" Bennie laughed, but it sounded like a hiccup. "I see, not only is it okay to exploit it, we're *obligated* to exploit it."

"For sure. We have a duty to represent Connolly to the best of our ability. Zealously. You know what the canons say. You taught me that, remember?" Judy looked like she expected an answer, but Bennie regarded her associate through the haze of a growing headache, so Judy continued. "Look, Hilliard just took a huge blow. If you consider the Harting fiasco, it's really borderline whether he's proved his case. I don't think we should go forward and put on a defense. I think we should rest, right here. Right now."

"Put it to the jury, now?" Bennie asked, struggling for clarity. For the first time in her career, she was at a complete loss during trial. Bennie always knew what to do in court; it was the life part that stumped her. And this was both. "Wait a minute, slow down. You don't make a move like that so fast. I mean, I've never done that."

"Review the case so far, then," Judy said, and summarized the testimony witness by witness, her enthusiasm gathering momentum. When she was finished she sat convinced, waiting for the word from Bennie. "Well, Coach?"

Bennie sighed, tense. "I don't know. Maybe you're right. If we put up a case, the jury will forget about Harting and we'd give Hilliard the time to rehabilitate his case. And Guthrie the chance to torpedo me. Maybe we should take it to the jury."

Mary, sitting between the two lawyers, looked from one to the other in amazement. "Are you two really considering not putting on a defense *in a death penalty case*?"

The question, put so starkly and simply, set the issue in

relief for all of them. They were silent for a moment, each left to her own thoughts, and conscience. "Be right back," Bennie said abruptly, and got up.

"What did you do to Harting?" Bennie demanded.

Connolly scoffed on the other side of the bulletproof glass, in the gray suit she had worn for the second day in a row. "I didn't do anything to Harting."

"You got to her, I know you did. How did you do it?" Bennie leaned forward, bracing her hands on the skinny metal ledge between them. "Did you send Bullock to promise her the world? How did you keep him off the OV logs? Money buys guards, isn't that what you said?"

"You're outta your mind, Rosato." Connolly sat straighter, annoyed. "Harting wouldn't do anything for me. I killed her girlfriend, remember?"

"So why did she recant?"

"Why are you asking me?" Connolly threw her arms into the air. "How do I know? Why'd she make up the story in the first place?"

Bennie stopped short, then eyed the face that looked so much like her own. *Why'd she make up the story in the first place?* Suddenly she realized how Connolly had gotten to Harting. "You didn't get to her last night," Bennie said, thinking aloud. "That's why it didn't show in the OV logs. You went to her after you killed Mendoza and Page. You made the deal before the trial. You had it rigged—the testimony *and* the recanting—*from the beginning.*"

"I don't know what you're talking about," Connolly said evenly. Her expression betrayed nothing, but Bennie didn't need confirmation.

"You told Harting to come forward during the trial. You told her to call the D.A.'s office and offer herself up.

You fed her enough information to make it credible to the jury and to me. You knew Hilliard would see a slam-dunk surprise witness. You knew when Harting recanted it would screw up the prosecution's case."

Connolly smirked. "Don't try to guess how cons act, Rosato. You're an amateur. Shetrell was trying to kill me, why would she make deals with me?"

"Because you made it more profitable to side with you than kill you. What did you offer her? A cheaper supply? You in business on the outside and her in business on the inside?"

Connolly's eyes narrowed. "Why the hell are you here? Shouldn't you be working on my defense?"

"What defense? My associate thinks you don't need one."

"I agree," Connolly said quickly, and her reaction clarified Bennie's thoughts.

"Oh, really? Most defendants in a capital murder case would be shocked if their lawyer was considering not staging a defense. Something about lethal injections makes a defendant hedge his bets."

"I'm not most defendants."

"Yes, you are. You just anticipated that I'd think of it. You knew that when Harting recanted, we'd have a shot at taking it straight to the jury."

Connolly laughed. "More than a shot. I watched the jury when Harting flipped. If you harp on it in your closing argument, I'll get off."

"I gather I have your permission to rest, then. Legally it's your call."

Connolly paused. "If you think it's the right thing to do, sure."

"It certainly suits my needs." Bennie stood up. "I don't want to defend you anymore."

"You're not trying to kill me, are you?" Connolly laughed again, and for the first time it sounded nervous, but Bennie felt too furious to reassure her.

"It's settled, then. We go right to closing arguments. By the way, make sure you listen to my closing. I couldn't control you getting to Harting, but I sure as hell can control what I do about it."

"What's that supposed to mean?" Connolly asked, but Bennie was already out the door.

86

Judge Guthrie was reading the pleadings index as the jury resettled into its numbered seats. "Call your first witness, Ms. Rosato," he said, and Bennie rose to her feet at defense table.

"Your Honor, the defense has chosen not to present any witnesses because the prosecution has not proven its charge of capital murder. The defense moves for a directed verdict of acquittal."

Surprise crossed the judge's refined features, and the lid of his pleadings index dropped closed. "Ms. Rosato, are you saying the defense is resting at this point?"

"Yes, Your Honor." Bennie watched a ripple of excitement run through the jury, and she knew that behind her the gallery would be reacting, too. "My motion is outstanding, Your Honor."

"Denied," the judge ruled. Judge Guthrie looked at Dorsey Hilliard, who was hustling to his feet on his crutches. "Mr. Prosecutor, are you prepared to proceed to your closing argument?"

"Of course, Your Honor," Hilliard said, too quickly to be credible. He collected some papers hastily, either for show or security, since Bennie doubted he'd have written his closing already, and he walked to the podium.

"Ladies and gentlemen," Hilliard began, "this is sooner than I expected to be speaking to you, but just the same,

I'm delighted with the opportunity. You have been attentive and responsive throughout our testimony, and I thank you on behalf of the Commonwealth of Pennsylvania. We thank you also for your common sense and your sound judgment, which is what you will need when you go into the jury room to deliberate today.

"You heard the defense attorney tell you in her opening argument that the prosecution case against the defendant is circumstantial, as if 'circumstantial' is a dirty word. I beg to differ. Murders are rarely committed in broad daylight, in full view of an array of witnesses. In fact, most murders take place without an audience and between people who know each other. People who loved each other, and who fight."

"Objection, Your Honor," Bennie said. "None of those facts are in evidence in this case."

"Sustained," Judge Guthrie ruled, unexpectedly to Bennie, though he knew the bell couldn't be unrung.

"The circumstances of a murder can easily and, quite reliably, point to the killer. Officer Sean McShea and Officer Arthur Reston caught the defendant running from the scene of the crime, and she confessed and attempted to bribe them in order to avoid being brought to justice. Mrs. Lambertsen saw the defendant running from the scene, after she heard the defendant fighting with her lover and after she heard a gunshot. The fact that Mrs. Lambertsen may have been somewhat unsure as to which exact minute she saw the defendant run by is of no legal or factual significance.

"You also learned from Dr. Liam Pettis that the blood spatter on the sweatshirt was consistent with the officers' testimony, and Dr. Mark Merwicke told you, over defense counsel objection, that previous defense counsel had *pre-*

vented the Commonwealth from testing the defendant's hands for residue from firing a gun."

"Objection, Your Honor," Bennie said, rising, and Judge Guthrie shook his head discreetly.

"Overruled."

Hilliard held up a finger. "A word about the murder weapon. The gun. Judge Guthrie will charge you that you're not to speculate in the jury room as to the facts of this case, and so I suggest to you that the fact that the murder weapon was not recovered is not the result of mysterious scheming of a cabal of police officers. The truth is simpler than that: we aren't perfect. We're not TV cops. We don't always find the murder weapon. It happens more than we care to admit and certainly we wish it were not so."

"Objection, Your Honor," Bennie said. "Again, assumes facts not in evidence."

Judge Guthrie shook his head. "Overruled. The Court can take judicial notice of the fact that murder weapons are not always recovered."

Hilliard glanced at the dais, then focused on the jury. "You will hear much, when defense counsel addresses you, of conspiracies and cabals. Of plots and schemes. Of drug deals, of crooked cops. It reminds me of *Alice in Wonderland*. Remember the walrus, scamming the oysters? 'The time has come, the Walrus said, to talk of many things; of shoes and ships and sealing wax, of cabbages and kings.'"

The jury smiled, and the librarian in the front row mouthed the passage with Hilliard.

"The defense has to say *something* to respond to the wealth of state's evidence, so they say what they think you'll respond to, a buzzword. Conspiracy! *Conspiracy?* Are we talking UFOs and little green people? Are we talking

grassy knolls and lone gunmen? Are we talking Washington bigwigs and sleazy payoffs?" Hilliard paused. "The
defense underestimates you, my friends. I have every faith,
and every prayer, that when you retire to the jury room to
deliberate, you will see through the stories of cabbages and
kings and find the defendant guilty as charged, of capital
murder. Thank you."

Hilliard left the podium, and Bennie stood up, feeling
the full onus of the risk she had taken in not presenting a
defense. There was no buffer between her and the verdict;
no testimony to point to, not even physical evidence. It
wasn't between her and Hilliard anymore, or her and
Judge Guthrie, or even her and Connolly.

It was between Bennie and the jurors. It was a relationship, a compact between them. It would happen now
or it wouldn't happen at all. She felt a shiver shoot up her
spine and approached the jury.

87

To Lou, nothing was right about the scene. The sun shone too brightly. The afternoon was too pretty. The cop was too young, and he was killed trying to murder a citizen. The Eleventh was at the cemetery in force, a blue square of dress uniforms, but the inspector hadn't made his typical cameo and neither had the mayor. Lou stood with the press about fifty yards away from the flag-draped casket; even the reporters looked second-string. Lenihan's death wasn't front-page news anymore, and Lou would have missed the obit if he hadn't been looking for it.

It made Lou feel sad, like he'd lived too long. He didn't want to see a world where drug dealers did business in the open and cops murdered their own partners. His eyes hurt suddenly, it was so goddamn bright, and he looked at Lenihan's mother and father, crying behind their son's casket. Then he spotted Citrone standing behind Lenihan's mother and his heart hardened. The cop was in full dress uniform and the badge on his hat caught the sun; he reminded Lou of a toy soldier, tin on the outside and hollow on the inside. Lou wondered if Citrone had gotten the call from Brunell yet.

Standing beside Lou, a young reporter coughed, then lit a cigarette. The acrid cone of smoke disappeared into the fresh air. Lou scanned the rest of the uniforms and found Vega the Younger. He was hoping to see either McShea or

Reston, but they were too smart to show up. Crap. He wanted to get them so bad he could taste it. Not for Rosato, not even for himself, but for reasons that had to do with the way things used to be, with Stan Getz behind "Quiet Nights of Quiet Stars" and bakeries that put cellophane hay on the cookies.

The reporter beside him coughed again, louder this time, and Lou looked over. "You gotta quit smoking, kid," he said. "Now they got the patch, they got gum. I had to do it with one of those plastic cigarettes, like a smacked ass."

"What do you know?" the reporter snapped.

"What do *I* know?" Lou repeated slowly. He considered spanking the kid but then got a better idea. "Let's see, I know that cop over there, his name is Joe Citrone." Lou pointed, and the kid followed his fingers. "He's filthy as the day is long. He's buddy-buddy with two other cops, named Sean McShea and Art Reston—"

Another reporter turned around at the names. "Did you say something about McShea and Reston? Those cops who testified in the Connolly case?"

Lou nodded. "The very same. McShea and Reston aren't from the Eleventh, but they and Citrone, that tall cop behind the family, they're all in business together, running a drug business."

"*Drug business?*" asked another reporter, turning around, joining the group forming around Lou.

"They take and sell the drugs from busts and protect dealers like Pace Brunell, down in the projects. Wait, it gets better. Citrone is responsible for the murder of his partner, named Bill Latorce, who was supposedly killed in the line of duty. One of you smartasses oughta be looking into why a domestic got an experienced cop dead, you ask me."

The reporters started interrupting, but Lou put up his hands. "My advice to you is to get on this story right away. It'll be the story of the decade. Probably win a Pulitzer. Does anybody say 'scoop' anymore?"

Then Lou turned to the kid next to him, whose cigarette hung by its paper from his open mouth. "Put that in your pipe and smoke it," he said, and walked away.

88

Bennie stood in front of the jury and paused before she began her closing, to calm her nerves and gather her thoughts. Again, she decided to go with the truth. It was all she had.

"Ladies and gentlemen, I made the highly unusual decision not to put on a defense case for Alice Connolly, because I do not think the Commonwealth proved its case of murder beyond a reasonable doubt. I do not share the prosecutor's lofty regard for circumstantial evidence, especially in death penalty cases. The prosecutor soft-pedaled that fact in his closing, but I stand here to remind you: the Commonwealth ultimately seeks the death penalty in this case. Keep that in mind at all times. Let it inform your judgment. How sure do you have to be to send a human being to her death? Sure beyond any reasonable doubt."

Bennie paused to let it sink in, and the faces of the jurors were properly grave. "Yet the Commonwealth hasn't provided you with anywhere near that quantum of proof. Nobody saw the crime being committed, and contrary to the prosecutor's assertion in his closing, there are many murders that take place in front of witnesses. You can read in the newspaper every day accounts of drive-by—"

"Objection, Your Honor," Hilliard barked. "There is no record evidence of such shootings."

"Sustained," Judge Guthrie ruled, but Bennie didn't break stride.

"There are no witnesses to this killing, at least the Commonwealth could not produce one, and there are many other facts that the Commonwealth didn't prove, all of which add up to more than reasonable doubt. First, the Commonwealth didn't produce the murder weapon. The prosecutor wants you to forget about the gun, but can you, fairly?" Bennie stepped closer to the jury rail. "Remember their theory of what happened that night. They posit that Alice Connolly shot the deceased, changed her clothes, and threw them in a Dumpster to get rid of the evidence. If that's the truth, why wasn't the gun in the Dumpster with the other evidence? Are you supposed to believe that Alice kept the gun with her? Why would she do that, when she had disposed of far less incriminating evidence? And if she did keep it, why wasn't it found on her?"

Bennie paused, hoping her words had an impact. "It doesn't make sense because it isn't the truth. The truth is that Alice Connolly never had the gun. The real killer had the gun and kept it because it would show his fingerprints, and not Alice Connolly's. As you heard Dr. Liam Pettis testify, the gun could prove that Alice did not kill Anthony Della Porta—"

"Objection, Your Honor," Hilliard said. "Ms. Rosato misstates Dr. Pettis's testimony."

"Sustained," Judge Guthrie ruled, before Bennie could argue, but she had too much momentum to stop now.

"Let's consider the laundry list of other facts the Commonwealth didn't prove. One, the Commonwealth didn't prove motive. A fight? Every couple has rough patches. I myself haven't spoken to my boyfriend in days, but I'm not killing him." The jury smiled, and Bennie forced one, too. "Secondly, the Commonwealth didn't prove how the blood spatter got on the sweatshirt. Third, the Commonwealth didn't prove what time Alice ran by Mrs. Lambertsen's door. Fourth, the Commonwealth didn't prove it was Alice who ran by Mr. Munoz's window. Who can forget Mr. Munoz?"

The videographer laughed, as did the young black man in the back row. It was Mr. Speaker, the talkative one. Bennie smiled in spite of the tightening in her chest.

"Unlike the prosecution, I don't think conspiracy involves little green people. You know that there are many crimes that take more than one person to commit. Think of the Mafia. Think of the Oklahoma bombing. Those are criminal conspiracies, and you don't have to believe in little green people to know that conspiracies are real." Bennie made eye contact with the jurors, and an inquisitive tilt to the librarian's chin encouraged her, so she went for the jugular. "Ladies and gentlemen, the defense believes there is a police conspiracy behind this murder which included Officers McShea and Reston, and that members of this conspiracy murdered Anthony Della Porta—"

"Objection, Your Honor!" Hilliard shouted. "There's no evidence in the record to support these allegations! The only evidence in the record is that Officers Reston and McShea were the arresting officers. Anything else is an unfair inference from the record and pure conjecture on the part of defense counsel!"

Bennie pivoted angrily on her heel. "Your Honor, this is proper argument in a closing. The jury may draw reasonable inferences from the Commonwealth testimony, including what the defense elicited on cross-examination. If I can give the jury an alternative scenario—"

"The objection is sustained." Judge Guthrie's mouth closed firmly, setting his jowls like a French bulldog. "Comment no further on the arresting officers, Ms. Rosato, and resume your argument."

Bennie was dumbfounded. "Your Honor, is it your ruling that I can't present my theory of the way I believe this murder was committed? I'm not bound to the prosecution's theory. That denies the defendant the right to a fair trial."

Judge Guthrie frowned deeply. "You may present an alternative scenario, counsel, but there is no record evidence that any specific police officers were involved in Detective Della Porta's death. You may not confuse or mislead the jury in closing argument. You can present your theory without mention of any purported role of the arresting officers. Please proceed."

Bennie swallowed her anger, thought on her feet, and faced the jury. "Consider this, then. Consider that someone—we don't know who—comes to Detective Della Porta's apartment about fifteen minutes before eight o'clock on the night of May nineteenth, fights with Detective Della Porta, and shoots him point-blank. The killer wants to frame Alice Connolly, so he runs to the closet, which he knows is in the bedroom, grabs one of Alice's sweatshirts, and dips it in Detective Della Porta's blood in a typical spatter pattern he has learned something about. Somewhere. Then he leaves, unseen, and plants the bloody sweatshirt in a nearby Dumpster, knowing it will incriminate Alice."

Bennie spoke urgently to the jury now. She had to make them understand. "Picture that Alice comes in and discovers Detective Della Porta lying dead on the floor. Terrified that the killer is still in the apartment, she panics and runs for her life. Remember, there are ten to twelve minutes between the sound of the gunshot and the time Mrs. Lambertsen sees Alice run by. That's more than enough time, isn't it?"

The videographer inched forward on his seat, but the librarian hung back.

"Think about what I'm saying, ladies and gentlemen. If you can understand how someone else could have killed Detective Della Porta and framed Alice for it, then you cannot, under the law or in good conscience, convict Alice Connolly. And I suggest to you that Alice is being framed—by a police conspiracy."

"Your Honor, objection!" Hilliard said, and Judge Guthrie leaned across the dais with a deep frown.

"Sustained," he ruled. "Ms. Rosato, I warn you."

Bennie bore down. She couldn't win if Guthrie tied her hands, and she had to win. "Ladies and gentlemen of the jury, reflect for a minute on the testimony of Officers McShea and Reston. They said they were in Detective Della Porta's neighborhood, halfway across town, while they were supposed to be on duty. Does it ring true that a cheesesteak was the reason they left their district?"

"Objection!" Hilliard shouted. "Your Honor!"

"Sustained," Judge Guthrie said, reaching for his gavel and holding it poised over the dais. "Ms. Rosato, you may not refer specifically to the arresting officers."

Bennie turned on him, gritting her teeth. "Your Honor, is it your ruling that the defense cannot argue that the arresting officers lied on the stand? The jury is always free to disbelieve the officers, as it is any of the Commonwealth witnesses."

"Ms. Rosato." Judge Guthrie set his gavel down. "You may *not* argue that the police officers were involved in the underlying murder. Any inference the jury would draw in that regard would be unreasonable and speculative. Move on, counsel, before you are cited for contempt."

Bennie ignored the threat. "Ladies and gentlemen, isn't it at least possible that Officers McShea and Reston were on the scene because they were the ones who shot Detective Della Porta—"

"Objection, Your Honor!" Hilliard said, reaching for his crutches and standing now behind counsel table. "Defense counsel is boldly flouting your rulings, Your Honor!"

Judge Guthrie banged the gavel. *Crack!* "Ms. Rosato, this is your final warning. The very next improper reference and you will be held in contempt!"

Bennie told herself to calm down, but she couldn't. Her adrenaline pumped, her heart thumped hard. She was fighting for Connolly's life. The responsibility hit like a freight train. She ignored judge and prosecution, in favor of the jury. "Ladies and gentlemen, think critically about the Commonwealth testimony. Nobody but the arresting officers heard any alleged confession. Nobody but the arresting officers heard any alleged bribe. Nobody but the arresting officers saw a plastic bag. Only the arresting officers testified to these points and that was because they *lied* to you."

Bennie rested her hand on the polished jury rail, its support unexpectedly inadequate. "The Commonwealth's case rests entirely on those lies and it will ultimately collapse of its own weight. I didn't even think it was worth responding to, and this is a *capital murder case* in which the defendant is—"

Bennie caught herself. She was going to say "my twin." She tried to keep a lid on her emotions, then realized she was struggling to suppress the truth. Her own truth. She flashed on the first day she met Connolly, then finding her father's cottage. Reading her mother's note; the drop of blood in the crevice of her arm. And then Bennie knew. She finally let herself acknowledge it.

"Ladies and gentlemen, in my opening argument, I told you I did not know whether Ms. Connolly is my twin. Well, that is no longer true." Bennie's voice grew hushed and she felt suddenly as if she were talking to herself, instead of holding the most intimate of conversations with total strangers, in open court. She was thinking clearly, standing in her own truth. "Though I have no proof, I *know* that Alice Connolly is my twin, as surely as I *know* that she did not commit this murder—"

"Objection, Your Honor!" Hilliard said, rising on his arms. "Move to strike! I demand that Ms. Rosato be cited for contempt."

Crack! Crack! Judge Guthrie pounded the gavel to the desktop, them slammed the gavel down, handle and all. "Ms. Rosato, I've warned you and you've disregarded my warnings. I find you in plain contempt of court! Mr. Deputy, take Ms. Rosato into custody!"

In the jury box, the librarian gasped, the videographer looked stunned, and the other jurors looked equally shocked. Judy and Mary leapt to their feet. Connolly stood up, openmouthed, before an astonished courtroom as a shaken Bennie was taken roughly away.

89

The deputy in the courthouse holding area had seen many a strange sight in his cells, but he'd never seen a sight as strange as this one. He looked through the bullet-proof window of his station at the two cells, each holding a pretty blonde in a gray suit. Each woman sat on the white bench in her cell, rested her chin on her hands, and crossed her legs left over right, at the knees, the same way as the other. But though the women looked and acted like twins, it was obvious they were barely friends.

The guard peeked again. Their heads were turned away from each other, in opposite directions, like newspaper photos of couples in the middle of a divorce. One twin faced the stainless steel sink in the left corner of her cell, and the other faced the stainless steel sink in the right corner of hers. The guard forgot for a minute which broad was the defendant and which the lawyer, then gave up trying. As far as he was concerned, the Lord would be the judge of them both.

"Now what happens?" Connolly asked. She stared straight ahead, not looking at Rosato. Her voice, curiously devoid of emotion, carried through the white-painted bars between their holding cells.

"I'm not sure." Bennie shrugged listlessly.

"Does the case go forward with us sitting here?"

"No. I'm dispensable, but you have a right to be present

at your own trial. The judge will calm down and let me out with a fine, or he'll stay pissed, have Carrier take over the case, and leave me locked up. Either way, it doesn't matter. The case is going to the jury."

Connolly nodded. "What happened to you out there?" she asked after a minute.

Bennie rubbed her face. Her skin felt oddly strange to the touch. "I lost it, I think."

"In *my* case, you *lost* it?"

"Why would I lose it in anybody else's case? I got another twin?" Bennie looked over with a slightly crazy grin, and Connolly rolled her eyes.

"Right."

"There you go." There was nothing else to do but laugh, and Bennie did, briefly.

Connolly raked her hair back. "So, am I screwed?"

"You mean, did I just lose it for us?"

"I mean did you just lose it for *me*." Connolly's voice grew quiet, her features still.

"No, I don't think so. I got my closing out, and the jury didn't like what Guthrie just did. He overplayed his hand. I think the defense is in good shape. In a funny way, what just happened in there could help."

"Why?"

"The jury won't forget it. Also, I was right. I was telling them the truth, and they can feel that. I could feel it." Bennie thought a minute. "It happened."

"What happened?"

"I can't explain it, I just feel it. Sometimes I get the feeling, like a little *click* during a closing, and sometimes I don't. This time I felt the *click*."

"Are you ever wrong, when you think you feel it?"

"Sure."

Connolly blinked. "You've been wrong?"

Bennie leaned her head back against the unforgiving wall of cinderblock. "Sure. I'm human."

Connolly fell momentarily silent. "You didn't mention Shetrell in your closing."

"Harting? No."

"You did it for spite."

"No, not for spite. I might be your twin but I won't be your accomplice."

Connolly slumped slightly and rested her hands between her legs. "You really into this twin thing, huh?"

"That we're twins? Yeah."

"You got all blubbery out there. I thought you were gonna cry like a baby, right in front of the jury."

Bennie smiled sadly. "Are you surprised by that, that I might shed a tear about you being put to death?"

Connolly snorted, then looked away.

"It doesn't mean anything to you, our being twins, does it?" Bennie asked, and watched as Connolly's eyes focused out the door, to the guard's station.

"What if we're not twins, huh? Remember that DNA test we took? What if it comes back and says we're not twins?"

"It can't. It won't. I know that now. I think I always did. Our father—"

"Our father what?" Connolly turned and looked directly through the bars at Bennie. Her eyes were so angrily blue, Bennie drew back. "Our father who art in heaven?"

"Winslow."

"Winslow? Who knows if he's our father?" The sudden sharpness in Connolly's voice echoed throughout the hollow cells.

"I went to his house, in Montchanin. He was away, but I found his clippings. Of me, of my career. There's books of them."

"So maybe he's a freak, ever think of that?" Connolly didn't wait for an answer. "There's a lot of freaks out there. They hear voices, they think the FBI is following them. They think they're married to rich guys. They think they're Mel Gibson. They think they're friends with Steven Spielberg or that he's their real son. You don't know about these people, girl, but I do. You don't live in that world. I do."

Bennie shook her head, no. "There's that picture you gave me, of him holding two babies."

"So maybe one was a friend's baby, or maybe both. Do they look alike to you? You can't tell a friggin' thing from that photo. I don't believe the guy for a minute. I thought he was a crackpot."

"I found a Dear John note, from our mother, leaving him. He even came to her funeral."

"So what? So maybe she left him when she had you. It doesn't mean we're twins. Maybe you're his kid, not me." Connolly grew louder, almost shouting in the cells. "Or maybe it's the other way around, huh? Maybe he's some freak and I'm his real daughter, but I grew up to be a dope dealer. So one day he's watching the TV and he sees you, a big success. We look alike and he gets it into his head that I'm like you. That I'm really your twin. That we're both his kids, his twin girls. So he comes to me and tells me my twin will help me."

Bennie tried to wrap her mind around the situation. When they'd first met, Connolly had tried to convince Bennie they were twins. Now that Bennie had finally come around, Connolly was trying to convince her they weren't.

The reversal made her head spin. "Why are you saying this?"

"What?"

"You're trying to convince me I'm not your twin."

"I'm just saying I don't think we're twins, is all." Connolly's features returned to their familiar lines, and her tone went cold. "I don't need a twin. I don't want a twin. If I get off when this is over, I don't want a twin. Got it?"

There was a loud rap at Bennie's door and the guard's face loomed at the bulletproof window. "Will the real Miss Rosato please stand up?"

"I'm Rosato." Bennie stood up as the guard slid a key into the locked door to her cell.

"Judge wants you in the courtroom. Said you don't need no cuffs."

"What a guy." Bennie walked out into the hallway, which was barely wide enough to fit one person and flooded with harsh fluorescent lighting. The guard moved next door and unlocked Connolly's door with an expert twist of the wrist.

"This could be my big chance, Rosato," Connolly said loudly. "I could tell the guard that I was really you. Then you'd be the one on the hot seat, and I'd go free no matter what the verdict." Connolly stepped into the tight hallway and offered her wrists for cuffing. "How about it? Would you trade places with me now? Would you bet your life on this case?"

"That's enough of that talk," the guard said gently, but Bennie felt too stricken to speak.

Would you bet your life on this case?

Bennie felt like she already had.

As soon as the door to the courtroom opened, Bennie caught sight of Judge Guthrie, who had evidently regained his judicial temperament, for his features seemed composed and his manner calm. The jury was sitting in their paneled box, and a chagrined Dorsey Hilliard was in place at the prosecutor's table. At the bar of court, Carrier and DiNunzio sat on the edge of their chairs, visibly concerned.

Bennie entered the courtroom, and the gallery reacted instantly, fidgeting in the pews for a better look. Reporters wrote furiously in their skinny notebooks, next to sketch artists who drew so deftly they appeared to be scribbling. Mike and Ike sat wedged among them, unhappy as linemen benched in the playoffs.

"Ms. Rosato," Judge Guthrie said, "please approach. Mr. Sheriff, please escort the defendant to her seat at counsel table."

"Yes, Your Honor," Bennie said, her tone professional as she faced the dais and looked Judge Guthrie in the eye. Behind her, Connolly was escorted to counsel table.

"Ms. Rosato," Judge Guthrie began. "The Court found you in contempt for disobeying my order during your closing argument. However, after vigorous argument by one of your associates, the Court finds it would be in the interests of justice for the matter to proceed." The judge nodded grimly in the direction of Carrier and DiNunzio, and Bennie thanked God for Carrier. "You are hereby released from your incarceration and fined a sum of five hundred dollars. Your associate has already paid the sum on your behalf, to the Clerk of Court. Are you finished with your closing argument?"

"I am, Your Honor."

"Then take your seat, counsel, while we continue this final phase of trial. Mr. Hilliard, you may have rebuttal."

Bennie returned to counsel table and checked the jury's reaction. They seemed subdued as a group; the librarian didn't look at her, and even the lively videographer seemed impassive. *Would you trade places with me now? Would you bet your life on this case?* Bennie had felt the *click* during her closing, but she'd been wrong before.

"Ladies and gentlemen of the jury," Hilliard said from the podium, and began his rebuttal, repeating that the jury couldn't infer a police conspiracy from the absence of the murder weapon. He concluded quickly and when he was finished the jury looked somber. Bennie wasn't certain what conclusion to draw from their grave faces; in her experience, jurors usually grew serious when the time of decision was at hand. She wished she could argue again, but the defense didn't get the second shot the Commonwealth did.

Judge Guthrie proceeded immediately to charge the jury, reading them a lengthy recitation of the relevant points of law both sides had submitted, while Bennie sat quietly, only half-listening, slowly realizing that the case was ebbing out of her control. Usually it came as a relief to Bennie when the power, and the ultimate responsibility, shifted from her to the jury. In the past it had meant her job was finished, and after the verdict, she could return to her life. She'd loll around in bed with Grady, then get up and work on the house. She'd visit with her mother, sit with her in the elegant hospital until she'd dozed off.

But when this trial ended there would be none of these things. Nothing but a vacuum, and that was the best-case scenario. What if they lost? Bennie shuddered as the jury filed out to begin deliberations, disappearing through the paneled door. Departing to decide Connolly's fate, leaving Bennie with nothing but emptiness, and fear.

90

The lawyers awaited the verdict back at the office, and Bennie helped the associates gather the trial exhibits and return them to the file. It wasn't the type of clerical task she usually performed, but she knew they'd need her help and part of her wasn't ready to let go of the associates. Trying this case together had brought them closer, like soldiers in the war, and Bennie knew this war wasn't over yet. If Connolly were convicted, there was still the penalty phase of the trial to go, with Bennie putting up the expert and fact witnesses that would be Connolly's last hope. "You got the psych expert lined up, right, Carrier?"

"All taken care of. Ready on phone notice."

"Good. You got the assistant warden?"

"Only the assistant's assistant. She'll say that Connolly was the model inmate, conducted the computer class, and showed rehabilitation potential."

Bennie kept her own counsel. With what she knew, eliciting that testimony would be like suborning perjury. She turned to DiNunzio. "Any luck finding anybody who knew Connolly growing up?"

"No. I made a bunch of calls and got zip."

"No family left at all? Not even cousins or something?"

"None."

Bennie considered the implications. She and Connolly were all each other had left. "You checked on family friends and neighbors?"

"I found an acquaintance who knew her from high school. She said Connolly was always an outsider. Maybe that would help. She said she'd testify. If we need her, I can take her."

"You'll do the direct exam, DiNunzio? No jitters?"

"Not after my contempt argument."

Bennie smiled, surprised. She had assumed that Carrier had handled the argument. "You mean *you* argued that, to Judge Guthrie?"

"Yes," Mary said, and couldn't hide a proud smile. "I got you out of jail. Almost free."

"How'd you handle it? Were you nervous?"

"It didn't kill me, so I must be stronger."

Judy nodded happily. "She was awesome. She had the case law ready as soon as they took you away. It only made sense for her to argue it, not me."

Bennie didn't get it. "You had contempt cases ready? Why? How?"

"I thought you might get into trouble down the line. I would have, in your position. As nuts as my twin makes me, she's still my twin. So I found a few cases this morning."

Bennie laughed, a brief break from the tension. "Well, thanks. You done good." Then her thoughts returned to Connolly. "So we don't have much for the penalty phase, is what I'm hearing. Wonderful." Bennie thought of trying to contact her father. He could tell the story of how he had abandoned Connolly, help her in a way he'd never helped before. She shook it off, then unaccountably, thought of Lou. "You didn't hear anything from Lou, did you?" Bennie asked, and Mary shook her head.

"No, not since this morning."

"He hasn't called in?"

"I checked the messages."

Bennie's mouth made a grim line. "I don't like the sound of that. He should be here. Did he tell you where he was going when he left court?"

"No, he didn't say." Mary frowned, and locked eyes with Bennie.

"Five more minutes, I call his house again."

Mary nodded. "I'll remind you."

"Where do you want these?" Judy asked, holding a file of trial notes.

Bennie looked up from her work. "Stick 'em in the last folder."

Judy wedged the manila folder into the last red accordion file. Fifteen accordians sat in three rows of five on the conference room table, their manila folders straight. Almost all of the exhibits and transcripts cluttering the conference room had found their way into one of the accordians. Bennie wondered if anything else in her life would come back together so easily.

"How long do you think the jury will be out?" Judy asked, stuffing the correspondence file away.

"Not tonight, either way." Bennie checked the small desk clock sitting behind the telephone. 4:32. Only five minutes since the last time she'd looked. "They haven't been sequestered that long, so they're not that antsy, and it's a major case. They'll sleep on it, then decide tomorrow or the next day."

"Sunday? You think they'll go 'til Sunday?" Judy rubbed her neck. "It's not like there's a lot of physical evidence to go over. Either they believe the cops or they don't."

Mary nodded. "People don't like to work on Sundays. I bet they'll come back tomorrow, then go home and rest on Sunday."

Judy squinted outside the large windows of the conference room. The sky was gorgeous and sunny, the humidity mercifully low. "It's supposed to be a nice weekend. They get the weather report, don't they?"

Suddenly the intercom buzzed on the credenza, startling Bennie, who reached for it. The associates froze where they stood. It would be Marshall, the receptionist. "Rosato," Bennie said when she picked up. "Are they back?"

"No, relax," Marshall said. "Turn on the TV. The news is on Channel 10, and we've been getting tons of calls. Something's happening out there."

"Thanks." Bennie hung up and leaned over to switch on the small color Trinitron in the corner of the conference room. "It's not the jury, it's the TV."

"What?" Judy said, as she and Mary gathered around.

"What the hell?" Bennie asked, turning up the sound.

On the screen flashed a series of still photos of police officers hurrying from a cemetery. A voice-over said, "The funeral service of Officer Lenihan was disrupted by reporters today, and Philadelphia's top cop has requested that immediate action be taken against members of the press." The next scene was a head shot of the Police Inspector, his distinguished features marked with undisguised scorn. "I'm shocked by what I heard happened today," he said. "It is an absolute abomination that Officer Lenihan's family was disturbed in their most difficult hour, by a media that seems to know no bounds and have no decency."

A woman TV reporter stuck a bubble microphone in the

Inspector's face. "Do you have any comment about the allegations of corruption against certain members of the Eleventh and Twentieth Districts, Inspector?"

"We have no further comment at this time. An investigation of the districts has been commenced today and will be fairly conducted. Thank you."

"Specifically, are you aware that certain allegations have been made involving members of the police force taking cash payments for protecting drug dealers?"

"I repeat, I have no comment on the particulars," the Inspector said, and walked off-camera as the TV reporter turned and flashed a capped smile.

"That's all from the Roundhouse. Back to you, Steve."

Bennie switched off the television to the sound of the associates laughing and clapping. "Did you hear that?" Judy said, delighted, and Mary's face lit up.

"The word is out! How did that happen?"

Bennie looked grim. "A sailor man we know?"

"*Lou?*" they both said in unison, but Bennie's eyes were pained. Lou wasn't as young as he thought and whatever he was doing would threaten some very dangerous characters, enemies known and unknown. If they were going down, it wouldn't be without a fight.

"Where the hell is he?" Bennie asked, but nobody had the answer.

"Enough with the lecture," Lou said, exasperated, in his chair, but Bennie wasn't finished.

"Lou, the trial may be over, but the conspiracy isn't. They have a business to run, a very lucrative business. You're hitting them where it hurts, threatening not to let up even after the case is over. They'll take you out, Lou. They will."

"Let them try," Lou scoffed, and winked at Mary, who sat off to the side, looking worried nonetheless.

"Bennie's right, and not just because she's the boss," Mary said. "They tried to kill her. They'll try to kill you."

Lou sighed. "Is this what I came back for? To get nagged? At least men lawyers don't nag you."

"Fine." Bennie stood up. "I'm not going to nag you about it. For the next couple of days, you take Ike." She gestured to the opposite conference room, where the bodyguards thumbed through the newspapers. "I'll keep Mike."

Lou looked over his shoulder at the bodyguards. "Split up the kids? Bennie, we can't do that."

But Bennie wasn't laughing.

They worked into the night preparing the death penalty phase of the case, transforming the conference room into a telethon headquarters. Bennie worked the phones and interviewed potential character witnesses, and the associates and Lou called any leads they could reach. No new witnesses could be raised, and the phones outside the conference room's private lines rang until all hours. It was the press, but Bennie wasn't answering. She had to focus on this last part of the trial. It was hard enough, working on the assumption that Connolly had already been convicted of capital murder.

"I'm whipped," Mary said, brushing her hair from her eyes, and Judy looked tired.

Even Lou, previously battery-powered, had come down from his high. He hung up the phone from his last call, beat. "Let's call it a night."

"Agreed," Bennie said. "You all go home. Come back tomorrow morning, around seven."

"What about you?" Judy asked, picking up her bag.

"I'm staying for a while," Bennie said. She was exhausted, but she had paperwork to prepare. "I have a few things to finish up. Lou, you and Ike take the girls home, and you keep Ike."

Lou folded his arms. "No, I'll put the girls in a cab with Ike, who will take the girls home and come back for you. I'll take care of my own ass."

"Lou, we're not discussing this again."

"You're right, we're not. You're nagging, and I'm ignoring you. It's my marriage all over again." Lou stood up and gestured to the bodyguards across the way, who slipped into their sportjackets.

"Lou—"

"Oh, will you shut up? See you tomorrow. Let's go, kids." Lou left the conference room and met Mike and Ike in the hallway.

"Damn," Bennie said, and went after him. She had hired the guards, she could direct them. "Ike," she said, pointing, "you go with Lou. You follow him home whether he wants you to or not, and you sit outside his house if you have to. Keep him alive tonight, so I can kill him tomorrow. Understand?"

"No can do," Ike said. "Lou's not the client, you are."

"What?"

"We can't protect Lou. We have to stay with you. It's in the contract."

"What contract? I didn't sign any contract."

"Our contract with the security company, and the security company's contract with the insurance company. We're only insured to protect you. If something goes wrong, we have to be with you or our company gets sued."

Bennie laughed. "That's ridiculous."

Mike shrugged shoulders like the continental shelf. "That's what they told us. Stay with the designated client."

Lou smiled. "See? It's lawyers, Rosato. They complicate everything. Can't even jump off a diving board anymore because of lawyers. Lady lawyers, probably. They nag you, then they sue you." Lou hit the elevator button in a jaunty way, and the doors opened. He stepped inside and took the associates in with him. "Come, ladies. I left my car at home, I'll escort you home in a cab. See ya, Rosato," he said as the doors shut.

"He's so damn stubborn," Bennie said, staring at the closed aluminum doors, and Mike nodded.

"They all are."

"Who? Old people?"

"Men," Mike answered, and Ike looked over.

91

Judy and Lou dropped Mary off in the cab, then continued down Pine Street in silence. Judy looked out the window, too sleepy to make conversation, which was fine with Lou. He unbuttoned his jacket and relaxed in the torn seat. His car would have been comfier but he'd left it at home in case it had been made at the cemetery or the police station.

Lou watched the cardboard tree swing from the rearview mirror. Funny. All the cabs had those trees, but none of them smelled like pine. The air in the cab stank of cigarettes regardless of the round NO SMOKING sticker, and in the light from the car behind, Lou could see greasy smudges on the plastic separating them from the young driver.

Lou looked idly out the window. Antique shops lined the narrow street, and it was too late for anyone to be on the sidewalks. The cab stopped at a traffic light, and Lou read the sign of one of the shops, MEYER & DAUGHTER. A skinny wood chair sat in the window. "That an antique, Judy?"

Judy nodded. "I bet it's early American. That's all they have in there, real Colonial pieces. The chair probably cost a thousand dollars."

"Get out. Hardly wide enough for a tush."

"Colonial tushes were smaller."

"Ha!" Lou shook his head. "I love it. For old chairs, we pay through the nose. For old people, we can't be bothered."

The cab lurched forward, its interior brighter than before from headlights behind. The car in back of them was tailgating. But why, at this hour of night? With no other traffic? Lou stiffened instinctively and twisted around.

The sight shocked him. There was a patrol car on their bumper. The lights on its roof blazed to life, filling the cab with red, white, and blue. Patrol car number 98.

Fear jolted Lou to alertness. It was Citrone, alone. No siren to attract attention. A cop on a night stop could get away with anything. Lou had seen it happen.

The cab was slowing down, and Lou pounded on the plastic divider. "Keep driving!" he ordered. "Go, go, go!"

"You nuts?" the cabbie asked, recoiling. "It's the cops."

Judy looked back at the lights, the patrol car. "Lou?" she asked, panicky.

"Stay calm," Lou ordered. He would've locked the doors but he wanted Judy out of the picture. The cabbie pulled to the curb and got out. A white spotlight seared through the back window. Beside it stood a tall silhouette whose arm ended in a gun. Citrone was coming at them. Lou's heart fluttered. He was packing, but couldn't chance anything until Judy was free.

"Get out of the car!" Citrone shouted. He pulled open the back door and yanked Lou out of the cab, jamming the revolver into his sternum.

"Relax, Citrone." Lou flattened against the cab, momentarily breathless. The gun bored into his chest. In a second he could be dead. He'd had a good run, it wouldn't be the worst thing. But there was Judy. "I'll go with you. Leave the kid." Lou took a step forward, but Citrone drilled him back with the gun barrel.

"Get out of the car, counselor!" Citrone called to Judy. "Make it fast!"

"I'm coming, I'm coming," Judy said, her heart in her throat. She slid from the backseat and gasped when she saw the gun. She edged away reflexively, her back bumping into the cab, staring openmouthed at Citrone. His face became angles and shadows in the blinding light. His eyes were merciless black slits. He would kill them both. Judy struggled to think through her terror.

The astonished cabbie put up his hands. "I stopped at the light, Officer, I swear. I came to a full stop."

Citrone's gaze darted sideways while he kept the revolver flush against Lou's shirt. "Get lost or you're dead," he told the cabbie. "Come back for the car." The driver's eyes went wide and he ran off, his legs pumping.

"Nice police work," Lou said. "Now let the kid go. She won't say anything."

"Let her go? She attacked a cop on a routine traffic stop. The cab had a broken taillight." With a swift kick Citrone shattered the cab's brake light. Red plastic shards clattered onto the street.

"Come on, Citrone," Lou said. "Everybody knows about the parking lot at the Eleventh. They gonna believe you killed us on a routine stop?"

Citrone laughed quietly. "Me, kill you? I'm not even here. My friend should be along any minute. A state trooper."

Judy forced herself to think. Citrone would shoot them as soon as the trooper got there. What could she do? She didn't have a gun. Then she remembered the boxing she'd watched at the gym. She had surprise on her side, if not expertise. Suddenly she lowered her stance, planted her feet, and threw the first punch of her life, aimed point-blank at Citrone's jaw.

"Ahh!" Citrone cried out. The blow landed badly, but

knocked the cop off-balance. The revolver went off with an ear-splitting *crack!*

"No! Lou!" Judy screamed as Lou's shoulder exploded into bright red blood and tattered fabric.

Lou didn't feel the pain. He threw himself against Citrone's arm and grabbed his wrist, struggling to shake the gun free. It clattered to the street while Lou pinned the stunned cop to the wet asphalt. Judy watched dumbstruck, then realized she had to act. She ran for the gun, snatched it off the street, and raised it with both hands. Her right hand throbbed from the punch, but she looked down the gun's sight to Citrone and braced herself.

"Freeze, Citrone!" Judy shouted, her voice strong with newborn authority, and Lou was already rolling off of the crooked cop, leaving him exposed in the gutter.

"I'll be all right," Lou said, drowsy from the anesthesia. It would hurt if he could feel anything, but he couldn't. He'd never caught one in all his years on the force. His retirement, he had to get shot. Like a schmuck. He eased back on the thin hospital pillow. The bullet had been removed and his shoulder packed and splinted. Nagging him from the foot of the bed, like three harpies, were Judy, Mary, and Rosato.

"You'll be fine." Bennie patted his foot. "Because I'm not letting you out of my sight."

"Me, neither," Mary said. "Not until the entire Eleventh District is behind bars."

"We got 'em, didn't we?" Lou smiled, his words faintly slurred.

Judy grinned. "Oh yeah, we're all over the television." Her right hand was bandaged and sore. She had broken a finger punching Citrone, who didn't have a scratch. Judy needed remedial boxing. "They've stepped up the investigation of the Eleventh."

Bennie nodded. "It's only a matter of time before they call in McShea and Reston, and the cops start diming on each other. The D.A.'s office will make the best deals with whoever comes forward first. The cops know the drill."

Still, Mary couldn't feel happy about it. "Not a great way to do it, though, Lou. Putting yourself in harm's way."

Lou chuckled softly. "Talk to Judy. She threw one of the worst punches I ever saw."

Judy bowed. "Thank you, thank you."

"She saved my life," Lou said, his sentence trailing off. He wanted to thank her, but didn't have the strength to hug her. It was probably for the best. You weren't allowed to hug women anymore. It was against federal law.

"Told you I could box," Judy said. "I'm going twice a week, after this verdict is in."

The verdict, Bennie remembered. She'd been so worried about Lou that she rushed from the office and hadn't thought about it since. Remarkable, considering that the Connolly case had occupied her every thought for days. Lou's surviving the attack had dealt a deathblow to the conspiracy and it would all come tumbling down, starting with Citrone on up, with luck extending even to Guthrie and Hilliard. But the jury would be deliberating under sequestration, isolated. They wouldn't know the police conspiracy had been proved true. They'd return with the verdict, innocent or guilty.

When?

92

B ennie got the call from the Clerk of Court at 10:15 the next morning, and the defense team was at the Criminal Justice Center barely ten minutes later. The lawyers and bodyguards emerged from two cabs, their faces taut as the cab doors opened and the press swarmed, swinging boom mikes overhead. Bennie screened it out. All she could think about was the verdict.

"Get out of my way!" she shouted at the mobbing reporters. She plowed through the crowd and trusted that Mike and Ike had the associates covered. They fought their way into the courthouse, into the elevator, and finally down the hallway to Courtroom 306. The lawyers pushed through the gallery to the bulletproof shield. For the first time Bennie felt relieved to have the goddamn wall of plastic between her and the rest of the world.

On the silent side of the barrier, Judge Guthrie sat atop the dais, apparently reading documents. Courtroom personnel bustled about, getting ready for the verdict. A woman hurried by with what Bennie recognized as an Order Sheet, remanding Connolly to the custody of the prison system until the date of her execution. Bennie looked away and reminded herself the order was just a contingency. Like her, the court had to prepare for either verdict. She put her briefcase down on the counsel table, her mouth dry.

Dorsey Hilliard walked through the glass door, then approached Bennie. He balanced on his crutches as he offered her a hand. "Whatever happens, Bennie, you've been a worthy adversary," he said.

Bennie's throat caught. Her twin's life was on the line, she had almost been killed, and Lou lay wounded in a hospital. "Go straight to hell," she said, and Hilliard withdrew his hand as if bitten. The exchange was gaped at by spectators, captured by sketch artists, and noted by the reporters, to be the subject of a hundred questions later. Bennie put it all from her mind and sat down to wait for Connolly. It wasn't long.

Connolly came through the paneled door of the courtroom, led by the guard, and Bennie felt a painful tug inside. What the tug was, she wasn't sure. Sympathy? Affection? Loathing? She didn't know, but the connection was there, undeniable. They had both chosen the gray suit, for God's sake. But if Connolly felt any connection, it didn't show. Her eyes were slightly sunken, her face drawn, and she walked in a stilted fashion toward her seat at defense table. She sat beside Bennie without looking over, so Bennie stared straight ahead.

"Mr. Deputy," Judge Guthrie said, his lined features tense. "Please call the jury."

The deputy retrieved the jury, and everyone in the courtroom craned their necks to see them as they filed in, searching their faces for clues as to the verdict. But the jury entered the courtroom on the final day as they had on the first, with their heads lowered and their eyes avoiding contact with anyone. The videographer looked grave and the librarian remained businesslike, her lips pressed together.

Bennie took it as a bad sign. Jurors looked solemn when they were about to deliver bad news. A hush fell over the room, even the jaded courtroom personnel grew still, and Hilliard shifted forward in his seat. Bennie didn't miss the gesture. He was eager. He thought he had won a conviction. Bennie felt sick to her stomach.

"Madam Foreperson," Judge Guthrie said, reading from a slip of paper on his desk. "I have received a note indicating the jury has reached a verdict. Is that correct?"

The librarian stood up, resting a hand on the jury rail. "It is true, Your Honor."

"Is this a unanimous verdict, Madam Foreperson?"

"Yes, it is, Your Honor."

"May I have the verdict slip, Mr. Deputy?"

Bennie watched almost breathlessly as the deputy walked to the librarian, took the slip of paper, and handed it up to the judge on the dais. Judge Guthrie opened the paper without betraying its verdict, his actions prescribed by law and tradition. Then, wordlessly, the judge handed the paper back to the deputy, who returned it to the librarian. "Will the defendant please stand?" Judge Guthrie said, his voice echoing in the stillness of the courtroom.

Connolly rose in tandem with Bennie. Bennie couldn't breathe and couldn't see. The courtroom, the judge, and the world seemed to fall away. She imagined she could hear the pounding of her own heart, then of Connolly's, beating in time with hers.

"Madam Foreperson, will you please read the verdict?"

"Yes, Your Honor." The librarian cleared her throat and read from the sheet. "We, the jury in the matter of *The Commonwealth of Pennsylvania vs. Connolly*, find the defendant, Ms. Alice Connolly, not guilty of murder."

Bennie's knees buckled at the words and at first she couldn't believe her ears. What had they said? Had they said not guilty? A shout went up behind her, then a whoop she recognized as Mary's but which sounded far away. Bennie saw Hilliard's face drop into his hands. Only then did it hit her.

They won.

They *won*. Connolly was acquitted. It hit Bennie like a wave, flooding her heart with relief. But not happiness. Happiness was reserved for the truly innocent, and Bennie knew it when she felt it. She couldn't bring herself to face Connolly. She wasn't completely sure why.

Hilliard was rising to his feet. "I request that the jurors be polled, Your Honor."

"Certainly, Mr. Prosecutor." Judge Guthrie faced the jury, as did Hilliard and everyone else in the courtroom, including Bennie, who sat down at counsel table. Polling was more than a formality, she'd seen it disturb jury verdicts before. "Juror Number One, is the verdict the Court just read your verdict?"

"Yes, Your Honor."

"Juror Number Two, is the verdict the Court just read your verdict?"

"Yes, Your Honor."

Judge Guthrie asked each juror in turn, and as each answered in the affirmative, Bennie began to relax into her chair. Her breathing returned to normal and the courtroom came back into focus. She looked at Connolly, who looked pale and shaken as they locked eyes. Bennie imagined the expression mirrored her own, this time not by contrivance. Finally Judge Guthrie polled the last juror. "Juror Number Twelve, is the verdict the Court just read your verdict?"

"Yes, Your Honor."

Judge Guthrie nodded quickly. "The Court accepts the verdict of this jury, it having been duly impaneled, having heard the testimony and the evidence, and having duly deliberated. It is hereby the Order, Judgment, and Decree of this Court that the defendant is found not guilty of the crime of capital murder, as charged. Ms. Connolly, you are released from custody, effective immediately."

Connolly nodded, but said nothing, even after a year in custody for a crime she didn't commit. Bennie could understand it, somehow. She felt her eyes brimming and blinked the wetness away.

Judge Guthrie finished the formalities. "Members of the jury, the Court thanks you very much for your service to the Commonwealth. Please leave your plastic ID holders on the jury rail. You are hereby discharged from your secrecy and you may discuss this matter with anyone, including its particulars. Likewise, you are free not to discuss this matter and may decline any requests for interviews that will undoubtedly come your way." Judge Guthrie picked up his gavel and struck it down lightly. *Crack!* "Court is now adjourned."

Bennie stood up, watching in a daze as Judge Guthrie left the courtroom, then Hilliard. Both of the associates rushed up, hugging her and shaking Connolly's hand stiffly.

"Get me out of here," Connolly said, speaking finally to Bennie, who was already opening the door in the bullet-proof shield, preparing for the media as it surged forward to meet them.

93

Bennie had no comment for the excited press and managed to get through them and into the backseat of a cab with Connolly. She put Mike up front with the driver to intimidate the reporters banging on the cab doors and filming through the windows. The cab could barely inch forward in the crush. "You have my permission to run them over," Bennie said, and the cabbie grinned.

"I read all about you in the papers, Miss Rosato. You, too, Miss Connolly. Congratulations, you all must be real happy." The cabbie hit the gas and the cab took off. "So where you ladies goin' to celebrate?"

"The train station," Connolly answered quickly, and Bennie looked at her in surprise.

"Are you serious?"

"Absolutely."

"You're leaving right now?"

"I told you I wouldn't be hanging around."

"I didn't think you'd leave right away." Bennie felt confused, her emotions bollixed up. She didn't know what to say, she felt too full to say anything, somehow. The cab left the throng at the Criminal Justice Center and stopped at the traffic light. Ahead stretched the wide avenue that was John F. Kennedy Boulevard, which ended in Thirtieth Street Station, a massive edifice in Grecian style. It loomed so close. Only five minutes from the courthouse, with no traffic. Bennie found her voice. "I thought you'd want to . . . come by the office."

"I think I should get outta town. I heard about what happened to your investigator last night."

"But you're safe with me. I've got Mike here, under contract." Bennie gestured at the front seat. "We even have insurance companies on our side."

"No, I have to go." Connolly looked out the open window as the cab traveled smoothly up the boulevard, her blond hair blowing willy-nilly in the humid air.

"But we didn't get time to talk."

"There's nothing to talk about," Connolly said as the cab approached the train station.

"How can you say that? I mean"—Bennie glanced, embarrassed, at the cabbie and Mike, who were pretending not to listen—"we haven't even gotten the blood test back yet. Don't you want to wait until that comes back?"

"Will you give it up?" Connolly turned on Bennie, her brow knotted with contempt. "I told you, I don't want a twin, I don't want a sister. Thanks for getting me off, but don't act like I owe you. I don't. I have to go."

"Where?" Bennie asked, stung.

"None of your business." The cab entered the drop-off area and braked, and Connolly opened the cab door and climbed out. "Bye," she said abruptly, slamming the door closed.

"Should I walk you—"

"No, go!" Connolly waved without missing a beat, she then turned away, jogged across the drop-off island, and disappeared through the entrance to the station.

Bennie sat in the cab, frozen despite the heat, watching the doors of the train station swing closed. It was so strange and sudden; Connolly's departure was as unexpected as her arrival. She didn't have money; she didn't have her effects. How would she get a train? And Bennie didn't know exactly why, but she wasn't ready for Connolly to go just yet. She flung open the cab door. "I'll be back," she called out.

"What?" Mike said, surprised. Then he got out of the car and went after her, but Bennie was already flying into the station.

Bennie spun around in the cavernous concourse, her pumps pivoting on the marble. The walls extended almost a hundred feet high, ending in a ceiling patterned with squares of carefully restored molding. Elongated frosted windows cast muted lighting on the lobby floor. The concourse was almost completely empty. The line at the information desk held only two students with backpacks; there was no business travel on Saturday afternoons and few tourists arrived by rail. Connolly wasn't anywhere in sight.

Where could she be? The ticket counter, of course. Connolly would need to buy a ticket, first thing. Maybe she'd had it planned? Reserved, somehow?

Bennie ran across a floor polished to a high sheen and hurried to the ticket windows. NEXT AGENT AVAILABLE, read the lighted sign over the bank of windows. The white-shirted agents were helping customers. Connolly wasn't among them. Maybe she was using a ticket machine. Bennie scanned the machines in the area, then the telephones. Connolly wasn't in sight. How could she have gone so fast? Then Bennie thought of it. The ladies' room! She took off for the bathroom, behind the ticket counters.

Bennie chugged inside the rank washroom, her pumps clattering over the black tile floor. She looked under each closed stall door but didn't see any familiar gray pumps.

She went back to the mirrors at the bathroom entrance. "Excuse me," she said to a businesswoman applying blusher. "I'm looking for a woman, my twin. She looks exactly like me. Did she come in here?"

"Not that I saw."

"Thanks," Bennie said, and took off. Maybe Connolly was in one of the stores ringing the main concourse. She could be buying coffee, a snack, a magazine, gum even. With what money? Bennie hustled across the lobby, noticing that she'd picked up Mike after the ladies' room.

The large bodyguard jogged to Bennie's side, his jacket open and his tie flapping. "Are we having fun yet?" he asked.

"I'll check McDonald's, you check the bookstore."

"Can't do that. Have to stay with you. The contract."

"Then put on the afterburners." Bennie scooted into McDonald's, but Connolly wasn't there. She checked the bathroom, then hustled through a large bookstore, a video store, a food market area, even a flower shop, all with a barely winded Mike in tow. Connolly wasn't in any of them. Bennie double-checked the gates that went to New York, Washington, and Boston. Even the suburban lines running west and north. No Connolly.

Bennie ended up, exhausted and panting, in the center of the concourse in front of a marble statue. Her suit was damp with sweat and she raked hair from her eyes. She whirled around one final time. The lobby was completely empty. Connolly wasn't up, down, or around. Maybe she had simply run through the station and been picked up by someone. "I can't believe it," Bennie said, as Mike came jogging up on the other side.

"She's gone," he said, finally panting.

"She can't be."

"She is. We looked everywhere."

"We'll wait. She'll show up. She has to."

"No, she doesn't." Mike laid a heavy hand on Bennie's shoulder. "Listen, I've been in security a long time. Before that I did private detective work. I can tell you, if somebody don't want to be found, they won't be."

"We could wait."

"She won't show up."

"Shouldn't we wait?" Bennie's eyes stung. Inside she felt a sort of panic. "Mike?"

"Time for you to go home," the bodyguard said. He looped a strong arm around Bennie's shoulder and guided her out of the train station.

94

Bennie opened her front door and was greeted by an exuberant dog and the aroma of fresh coffee. "No jumping, no jumping," she said to the golden clawing her suit, but her heart wasn't in it. In her hand was the day's mail, which she had retrieved from the slot when she unlocked the front door. There were the usual catalogs, bills, and a *People* magazine, but it was the last business letter that made her breath catch in her throat. The envelope was business white and it had the name of a lab printed in the upper left corner. The lab in Virginia. It was the DNA test results. They'd come in today's mail. *After* Connolly had vanished.

"Bennie?" Grady's voice came from the dining room, over the whine of an orbital sander losing power. He appeared after a minute in a gray T-shirt and jeans, with a coffee mug in hand. He set it down the moment he saw Bennie's face. "Honey, you okay?"

Bennie faced him, uncertain. She hadn't seen Grady in so long she'd almost forgotten what he looked like. Mostly he looked appealing. Curly fair hair, round gold glasses, an intelligent smile. A puzzled expression, but distant. "I think I'm okay," she said, and he cocked his head.

"You won the case. Congratulations." Grady's arms flopped at his sides, but he didn't move to kiss her. "I was thinking maybe we could go out. Celebrate. Get reacquainted."

"Look." Bennie held up the mail. It was hard to speak. The dog danced at her feet, then plopped his butt sloppily on the plywood floor, his tail thumping hard. "The DNA test."

"You're kidding." Grady brushed his hand on his jeans, leaving sawdust handprints on his thighs. "You want me to open it for you?"

"No."

"You sure you want to know?"

"Sure." Bennie looked at the envelope in her hands. "I didn't go through all this not to know. Right?"

Grady nodded. "Sit down, then."

Bennie looked around. The room was a dark shell of lath and plaster. Tile for the new kitchen was stacked in boxes in the center of the plywood floor. "We don't have a chair."

"An excellent point." Grady pulled over a box of tile, and Bennie sat down. "Okay?"

"Okay." Bennie tore open the envelope. A single sheet of paper was inside, reminding her of the verdict sheet earlier in the day. In court she had known what she wanted the verdict to be. This time she was less certain. Bennie extracted it from the envelope and opened it up.

"Well?" Grady asked, standing apart from her, his hands resting on his hips.

"I can't tell." Bennie squinted at the paper, which contained a large table. *Twin Analysis*, said the title. There were five entries of what looked to Bennie like gobbledygook, in columns on the left. CRI-pS194, CRI-pL427-4, CRI-pL159-2, CRI-pR365-1, CRI-pL355-8, p144-D6. The numbers swam before her eyes. At the bottom of the page was a doctor's hasty signature, over a line that read MOLECULAR DIAGNOSTICS LABORATORY. "I can't understand it."

"Let me see." Grady stood behind her and scrutinized the paper over her shoulder. "It isn't very clear, is it?"

"You'd think they could make it easier." Bennie read across the columns of four-digit numbers, under Sample A and Sample B, and noticed something striking. The numbers matched. She read them again, her heart pounding.

Grady looked up from the paper. "You're twins. Lord, you're really twins."

Bennie swallowed hard. She had known it inside, but confirming it boggled the mind. "I couldn't get this yesterday?" she said, her voice almost a cry. "Why didn't I tell them to fax it? She's gone now. Connolly's gone."

"What?" Grady asked, and Bennie told him the whole story, while he settled onto the plywood floor, Indian style, and listened quietly. He fetched coffee for her, and Grady interrupted with only a few questions, managing to learn more than she wanted and even more than she understood. By the end of the conversation, Bennie felt better, but restless. "So, do you think I should try to find her?"

"Connolly? No."

"But she's my twin. I know it now, for sure. She should know that, too."

"It doesn't sound like she cares, hon. She treated you terribly. You almost got killed because of her, and she dumped you at the station. Why would you want to seek her out?"

"Because she's my sister."

"And what of it?" Grady asked softly.

"She's my family, my *blood*, and right now, she's the sum total of it." She gulped her coffee, not wanting to cry.

"You know what I think, Ben? I'm not like you, with this blood thing and all. Maybe it's because I'm not Italian, I don't know." Grady pulled his legs up to his chest, looping long arms around his knees. Bear slept soundly next to him, curled into a cinnamon-colored doughnut on the plywood. "I have a different view of family than you do."

"What do you mean?"

"My brother is a jerk, you know that. A materialistic, mean-spirited jerk. He's not family to me, even though he's my only brother."

"That's not good."

"It's the way it is." Grady shrugged, his fingers still interlaced. "I don't feel tied to him just because he's my blood and shares my genes. Who's your family? Family is who you feel close to, who you love, and who loves you in return. Gives to you. You aren't stuck with the family you're born with. At some point, you grow up and choose your family, Bennie. You make it."

Bennie fell quiet, considering it briefly. The only sound in the room was the dog's snoring. "I don't buy it. I like that bright-line test. Either you're blood or you ain't."

"I know you do, but it doesn't work, does it? It gets you into trouble I needn't detail."

"Is that a fancy way of saying 'I told you so'?" she asked, and Grady laughed, which reminded her of how much fun it was to make him laugh. But you had to talk first to do that, and be around each other. Could they be, again? "So who's my family, under the new improved definition?"

"You tell me. It's your family."

Bennie thought a minute. "I guess Hattie, my mother, and you. Not Connolly? Not my father?"

"Neither, not in my definition."

Bennie swallowed, hard. "At least he kept clippings about me and came to my mother's funeral. And we know he didn't leave her, she left him. We don't know much about him to judge him so harshly."

"Maybe you should find out."

"Maybe I should." Bennie set her coffee mug on the floor and stood up. "Can I borrow your car?"

Grady laughed in disbelief. *"Now?"*

"Can you think of a better time than now?" she asked, and Grady knew any response was futile.

95

It was dusk when Judge Harrison Guthrie set sail in his sixteen-footer, the *Jurist Prudent*. Other sailboats and motorboats were coming in as he set out. To a man, their skippers were burnt from a full day of sun. "Don't stay out too long, buddy," someone shouted to him, boozy, from a motorboat. The judge waved back dismissively. He didn't know the man's name. He hadn't made any friends at the marina, or on the bay, for that matter. He liked his solitude when he sailed and the only friend he needed was his wife, Maudie.

The judge tacked the *Jurist Prudent* into the breeze, a mild gust puffing eastward across the bay. The mainsail luffed as he turned, then snapped as it filled with wind. His wrinkled hand gripped the heavy line with the strength of a much younger man. He'd left the city after the Connolly verdict, stopped home only to change into his clothes and kiss Maudie good-bye. One solid peck on the cheek, like a rubber stamp. He'd been tempted to kiss her on the mouth, but it had been so long since he'd done that she would have found it odd. Then he'd driven down for a quick sail, as was his habit on the weekend. Maudie didn't suspect anything.

The judge looked at the sky, his hand on the tiller and the boat parting the water with ease. The western half of the sky, where the weather came from, was darkening quickly. Nimbus clouds gathered, a deepening gray tinged with soft black at the fringe. The judge could smell the water hanging in the air and feel its dampness on his cheek. A storm was coming, but he anticipated it with a kind of hope.

Maybe there would be lightning. The judge knew a fair amount about lightning, had even studied its history. In early times it was believed to be evil spirits, and villages had rung church bells to ward it off. Later, lightning was assumed to be fire; finally Ben Franklin proved otherwise. Its anatomy was remarkable, too. A ribbon of pure electric energy, three to four miles long, but only an inch in diameter.

The judge's watery eyes searched the sky, growing darker. The storm clouds collected, milling together like old friends. The wind picked up, filling the sails and testing their thick cloth. Judge Guthrie wasn't afraid. He would leave Maudie well provided for, and the children and grandchildren. He had done good work as a lawyer, filed papers to be proud of. Then he had become a judge, the capstone of his legal career. Any of the opinions, concurrences, or dissents that bore his name would stand forever. Making law for all time; making legal history. Judge Guthrie had always written with that in mind, deciding cases under the law, with fairness, decency, and justice. There had been only one exception.

The Connolly case. The judge had been indebted to Henry Burden and it would have been dishonorable to turn him down once the inevitable request had been made. The judge knew that the prosecutor, Dorsey Hilliard, owed a debt to Henry Burden as well, but at least the prosecutor had been acting in faith with his sworn duty as he fulfilled Burden's bidding. The judge had not.

For the first and only time, Harrison Guthrie had opposed the law.

The judge's hand held fast to the tiller and didn't waver, even as his thoughts darkened like the clouds. He had made rulings contrary to law, for the purpose of achieving the wrong result. He had violated his oath and he had disgraced the bench. Even if his misdeeds never came to light, Judge Guthrie knew what he had done. He had acted in combination with murderers, causing death and mayhem. He had profaned the name of justice and transgressed as surely as the robbers, murderers, and miscreants who stood before him day after day. Even Judge Guthrie conceded he should pay for what he had done. No one was above the law, and especially not a judge.

And so Harrison Guthrie judged himself, in the end, and sailed swiftly into the darkness.

96

S tar connected with a right cross that split the skin under
Mojo Harris's eyebrow like a boiled hot dog. *Yeah!* Star
thought. Sweat poured from his face and chest. He danced
backward, light on his feet. It was late in the sixth and he
was a round away from winning. The crowd knew it, too.
The Blue Horizon rocked with shouting and cheering.

Harris staggered back and blood bubbled instantly to
the cut. It gaped open, skin flaps flopping on each side.
Star would have punched Harris again but the ref rushed
between the fighters and steadied Harris's bruised face
while he squinted at the cut. "Can you see, Mojo?" the ref
shouted over the crowd noise. "How many fingers I got?"

"Two!"

"Then box!" the ref said, and Star lunged forward,
swinging. He didn't want the fight stopped, nobody did.
Star knew he'd fought the fight of his life. He'd beaten
Harris on points so far, each round but the third.

Ring! went the bell ending the sixth, and Harris's arms
dropped. He was whipped, dead on his feet. Star glared at
Harris before Harris hustled back to his corner. Star was
tellin' Harris he was licked. Tellin' him that *he*, Star Harald, *owned* this ring now. That the next time Harris came
out, Star would pound his eye 'til it *exploded*.

"Star, come on back!" Star's corner shouted. It was
Browning callin' him in. Star stayed in the ring, lettin'

Harris know. Servin' notice, demandin' respect. The crowd roared at the grandstanding and Star gulped it down like cold beer. His first professional fight, an eight-rounder, and he was about to win it. A TV camera focused on him and reporters took notes. Star felt the best he had ever felt in his life. Except Anthony wasn't here to see it.

"Come on, Star!" Browning yelled. "Come on back! You only got a second, man!"

Star looked at the crowd, standin' up for him. The men clappin', hands over their heads, the women givin' him the eye. Their faces, all excited, so close to the ring he could make them out. Everybody from the gym was there. Mr. Gaines, Danny Morales, and his foxy wife. Everybody but Anthony. It killed Star when he shoulda been the happiest. Where was that squirrel with the hair plugs? Star scanned the crowd and found the dude. He was in the back, his head wrapped in bandages. Makin' sure Star kept up his end of the bargain. *Harris in seven.* Dude better have kept *his* end.

"Star! Come in, get your ass back here! Get your ass back here!"

Star turned and sauntered back to his corner, the crowd on its feet, going crazy for him. They were seeing history and they knew it. Years from now they could say they were at Star Harald's first professional fight. He wouldn't be fighting at the Blue anymore, he'd be at the Convention Center or Bally's. Bruce Willis would sit ringside and the TV cameras would be pay-per-view. Star's purse would go from twenty grand to twenty *million*.

"You got him, man!" Browning shouted as Star sat down in his corner. "You opened him up! When you get back out there, stay upstairs. Circle to the right. Look for a right cross behind your left!"

Star tuned out Browning. His thoughts were on that bitch. She better be dead. He spit his mouthguard into a hand covered in a latex glove while another glove wiped sweat off his face and squirted water into his mouth. A third set of gloves smeared Vaseline on his eyebrows, but Star waved them off. Harris wasn't going to be landing anything in the seventh. Star would knock him out in the seventh.

Ring! It was the round bell. Star got off the stool and jumped to get his blood moving. Loosen up. A gloved hand popped in his mouthguard.

"You know what to do, Star!" Browning started up again. "Finish him off, man! He don't want no more. Can't take no more. Finish him *off!*"

Star charged out of his corner, gloves up, light on his feet. He went straight at Harris, who backed off, his left high, tryin' to protect his eye. Star waited for his moment. Harris didn't throw anything, just danced back like a pussy, gloves in front of his cut eye. Fresh red blood drippin' like tears in a line down his cheek.

The crowd screamed for the knockout punch. They smelled the blood. They knew it was comin'. Star had to throw it. Harris blinked blood out of his eye and backed into the ropes. The cut was so bad the ref would call the fight any second. Star pushed Harris against the ropes, throwing left jabs. Had to get Harris lookin' for the left, so he could throw the right into the cut. Star stayed patient. It drove the crowd crazy. The TV cameras rolled.

Suddenly Star found another way. He caught Harris with a left uppercut to the gut. Harris dropped his right arm, covering up. His left was still high, but he was open. The crowd screamed as Star followed with a left hook to the temple. Harris took one step back, then slumped forward to his knees. The ref waved Star to a neutral corner, but Star didn't move. It was too sweet a sight. Mojo Harris kneeling unconscious in front of him.

The ref shoved Star to the corner and started his count. By the time he got to three, it was over. The ref waved the fight off, a knockout, as Star threw his fists into the air and roared.

After the fight, Star gave interview after interview, talkin' to the newspapers, *Ring* magazine, and even a guy from *Sports Illustrated*. There were so many reporters, Star couldn't even make it into the locker room. He stood outside, jawin' into microphones with white boxes showing the stations. USA, ESPN, KYW. Browning yapped more than Star did, actin' like Don King while other managers sucked up. They was comin' to Star now, but the boxer didn't want to see 'em. Only dude he wanted to see was that squirrel with the hair plugs.

"Star, yo!" said a voice behind him, and Star finished signing another autograph and turned around. It was the squirrel wearin' head bandages that made him look like a dothead. In his hand was a black Adidas gym bag. Make sure it got done.

"Get your ass inside," Star said. He opened the dressing room door, shoved the dude, and shouted at his people to clear out. He locked the door behind them and faced the dude alone. "You do that bitch?" Star demanded.

"Man, you were unreal! I never saw a fight like that! You could take anybody! You could be the champ!"

"I *am* the champ! Answer me. Tell me that bitch is dead."

"She's dead, man. She's history, and you just made me and my boss a boatload." The dude was smilin' like an idiot, but Star wasn't.

"How I know you did her? You bring the proof?"

"Sure. I got it, just like you said." The dude reached into the gym bag and brought out a crumpled paper bag with a greasy stain on the bottom. "Here, look."

Star leaned over and peeked into the bag. The sight turned his stomach. In the bag was a mess of blond hair matted with blood and stuck to a bloody scalp. The skin on the scalp was so white it coulda been a doll's. The smell was disgusting, like fresh road kill. Star pushed it away. "Get that outta my face."

"You said, show me." The dude closed the bag fast and stuck it back in the gym bag. "You wanted proof."

Then Star realized something. "How'm I supposed to know it's Connolly's? Could be somebody else's hair, any bitch's hair."

" 'Course it's Connolly's. Dyed blond and all, just like you said, Star. Look, man, even got the black roots." The dude reached in the bag again, but Star reared back with disgust.

"Get that outta my sight!" Star waved at the bag and watched as the dude put the bag away. It had to be Connolly's, didn't it? Connolly was dead. The bitch was dead. They had held up their side of the bargain, and Star had done more than his part. He'd won by a TKO in the seventh. It made him feel good, where his heart ached.

Finally there was an end to it. Star had gotten justice, for Anthony.

And he was on his way to the top.

Bennie didn't reach the cottage until dark. If she hadn't been there before, she never would have found the place. She pulled Grady's old Saab up to the fork in the road and took the unpaved driveway to the cottage, where she found herself in luck. A light was on inside the house, shining gold through the trees. Winslow was home. Bennie would get to see him. Meet him. Her *father*.

She cut the Saab's headlights, leaving on the low beams as she drove closer. Rocks and gravel crunched under the car's tires. A rusty red pickup stood out in front of the cottage, and Bennie parked next to it. She cut the ignition, got out of the Saab, and walked slowly up to the house. On the way she found herself patting her hair and smoothing down her suit skirt. Might as well look nice.

Bennie stood in front of the screen door, summoning her nerve. From beyond the lighted screen came the unmistakable sound of a man humming. Bennie felt oddly delighted. Her father was humming. What was the tune? She inclined her head toward the screen, and a brown moth fluttered away on dusty wings. She didn't recognize the song, then the humming stopped abruptly.

"Ay? Somebody there?" asked a voice. Elderly, uncertain, even frightened. It touched her unexpectedly.

"It's me. Bennie Rosato."

"Wha?" There was the sound of a dry cough, then foot-steps shuffling softly. In the next minute a long figure filled the dark door and opened it wide.

"Hello," Bennie said, backing the form into the dim room until the lamplight illuminated Winslow's face. His mouth was full, and his face was lean, lightly tanned, with feathery crow's-feet. His eyes were large, round, and as sharply blue as Bennie's. They struck her at once as so familiar, even behind their drugstore eyeglasses, that she impulsively threw open her arms and gave him a hug.

"No!" he shouted, throwing off her arms and recoiling suddenly, knocking an astonished Bennie almost off-balance.

"I'm sorry," she said, flustered. She wasn't even sure what had happened, his response had been so immediate, so violent. Bennie's face flushed with embarrassment and a sort of shame. She didn't even know why she had hugged him in the first place. "I didn't mean . . . I'm sorry."

"It's all right." Winslow patted his chest, over a buttoned-up blue workshirt, as if he'd just received a shock.

"I was only—"

"Quite all right." His wrinkled hand fluttered against his shirt, then moved to right his glasses, though they weren't crooked. "It's all right. It's fine. My. Well." Win-slow coughed again and focused on Bennie. "So, we meet," he said without ceremony, and Bennie nodded.

"Yes. We do." She was trying to recover from her faux pas. "Starting off on the right foot," she said, laughing uncomfortably.

"I thought you might come, when it was over. I didn't know you'd get here before I left. I was hoping you wouldn't." Winslow turned slightly, and Bennie looked down. On the floor stood an ancient tan suitcase, its leather dry and cracked, with a stand-up handle, and next to the suitcase sat a large cardboard box of books. She couldn't help but notice his scrapbooks weren't going with him. She had so many questions, she didn't know where to start.

"Where are you going?" she asked.

"South." Winslow eased his glasses up his long nose with an index finger, its nail dirty.

"Is that all you're taking?" She was thinking of the clippings, and the note from her mother. Had he even noticed it was gone?

"I must keep packing, if you don't mind. My books." He walked to the bookshelf and ran his fingertips over the books' spines. He stopped when he got to one, tapped it thoughtfully, and slid it off the shelf. Then he went to the box and eased the book into it, spine up. "I must take as many of my books with me as possible."

"Is this a vacation or what?"

"No, I just came off one of those, though it wasn't much of a respite, was it?" Winslow smiled tightly, though his voice remained curiously humorless. "You won the case."

"Yes, I did. How did you know that?"

"I was there."

"Where?" Bennie blinked, amazed. "I didn't see you."

Winslow returned to the bookshelf, the second shelf this time, and after a brief examination, selected a volume and walked back to the cardboard box with it. "That's why I put Alice onto you," he said, without looking up from his task. "I knew you'd win."

"How did you know that? I didn't know I'd win."

"Oh, I know all about you. You and Alice. I take care of you both."

"You do?" Bennie would have found it funny, if it weren't her life. "How? I never met you before."

"I take care of my girls. I step in when I'm needed."

His girls? Bennie didn't reply. "Alice and I are twins, right?"

"Yes, quite right." Winslow peered at the shelf and slid out a book, then put it back. "No, not Robert Penn Warren. I can't take the Warren. Oh, well."

"My mother left you."

"A long time ago." Winslow picked a book off the shelf, rubbed nonexistent dust from the cloth cover with his fingertips, then brought the volume back to the box. "Only room for one more."

"Why would she do that?"

"Seemed to think I wouldn't make a good father. Always told me that." He snorted softly, his head bent as he wedged the book into the box. He had a growing bald spot and his hair, once blond, had thinned to gray and was slicked down, curling over his tight collar. "She had lots of ideas like that. Her own ideas."

"Was she right?"

"Ask her."

The statement, coldly delivered, struck bone. "You know I can't do that," Bennie said, dry-mouthed.

"No, and so you'll never know. It's a lot more complicated than you think, not that it matters now." Winslow straightened up, went back to the bookshelf, and removed one more book. He seemed to know which one he wanted, and he placed it in the box with an attention Bennie found infuriating.

"I think it matters. I want to know. How could my mother give up a child? How did she do it, even, and how could you let her? Why didn't you fight for us, or at least take Alice?"

"You've made a success of yourself, and Alice is out of jail. All's well that ends well. Help me with these books, would you? Pick the box up from your side and put it on the couch." As if he hadn't heard her, Winslow bent over and lifted the box, but Bennie snatched it from his hands and stood back in anger.

"Stop and answer me," she said. The heavy box pulled at her shoulders, but she was strengthened by a bitterness she didn't know she harbored. "Why didn't you take Alice? Why didn't you try to see us?"

"Give me my books." Winslow stretched out his arms, callused palms up.

"Answer me first."

"Give me my books." His voice went stern and hard. *"My books!"*

"Here." Bennie shoved the box at him, and he stooped slightly as he absorbed its impact. He struggled to set the box down on the couch, a fact Bennie noted with only a smidgen of guilt. "You have your books, now answer me."

When Winslow straightened, his face was red with effort. "You're angry."

"An understatement."

"You expect me to justify myself," he said, though his tone remained harsh. "You think I don't care for you, or Alice."

"Right. It's a matter of fact, as the lawyers say. You weren't there for us and you didn't try to be."

"You didn't need me. You were doing fine. You never gave anyone any trouble. But Alice I had to watch more closely. She would fall in with the wrong men. I had to step in. When I was needed, I was there."

"What do you mean?"

"When she was sixteen, there was a young man . . .

well, I stepped in. I took care of her. She never knew it was me, I wasn't looking for credit. I saw the situation that arose, and I dealt with it."

"How?" Bennie didn't understand, but she didn't like the sound of it. "What are you talking about?"

"The details aren't your concern. I dealt with the situations that arose. When her most recent situation arose, I dealt with that, too."

"*What* recent situation?" Bennie asked, too edgy to be exasperated.

"With that detective, that Della Porta. He was bad for Alice. A hypocrite, a thief. The worst of a bad lot." Winslow shook his head righteously, but Bennie felt stunned.

"What are you saying?"

"I saw that Alice was falling in with Mr. Della Porta and those others. You were right about them. You figured it out. They were selling cocaine and they involved Alice in their dirty business. They *corrupted* her."

Bennie listened, astounded.

"I went to try to convince Mr. Della Porta to let Alice alone. He wouldn't listen. He refused to let her go. He called me names. He called Alice filthy names, too. *Filthy.* He said she did horrible things, things I knew no daughter of mine could ever do."

Bennie thought back to the trial. The fighting that Mrs. Lambertsen had heard. It hadn't been Della Porta and the cops. It had been Della Porta and her father.

"So I shot him. I didn't plan to. There was no other way. He would have ruined her. He'd choke the life from her if I let him. Like a weed."

Bennie felt a wrenching deep within her chest. She wasn't sure if she could speak. She didn't try.

"Don't let it upset you, child. He was destroying Alice. I had to take care of her. I'm her father."

Bennie shook her head, uncomprehending. "You killed a human being."

"For Alice, I did it for Alice. To save her."

"Save her? You put her on the hook."

Winslow's upper lip twitched slightly. "I didn't know she'd be charged with the murder."

Bennie could barely imagine it. "But you let *your child* be charged with a murder *you* committed."

"That's why I showed myself. Told her to call you. I knew you'd prove her innocent."

"But what if I hadn't?" Bennie exploded, bewildered. "I almost didn't, don't you realize that? It took everything I had—*everything*—and I almost got killed! You killed a man. You almost killed both of your children!"

Winslow looked at her without batting an eye. "If you hadn't won, I would have come forward. They wouldn't have sent Alice to jail then."

"What are you talking about? They wouldn't have believed you. *I* barely believe you!"

"Oh, they would have believed me. I kept the gun. The murder weapon."

The statement shocked Bennie into silence. The only sound in the still cottage was the shallow huff of her own breathing.

Winslow closed the box and looked to the window. "Too bad it's dark outside, I'd show you my garden. The foxglove is in and the rudbeckia just blooming. It took decades to make that garden. It needed to be weeded, tended. Gardens, they need tending."

Bennie's mind reeled. She felt almost dizzy, sick to her stomach. She didn't know what to do, what to say. She had wondered about her father her whole life but couldn't bear to be in his presence a moment longer. He made her skin crawl. He was crazy, insane; he had to be. She swallowed her rising gorge, turned on her heel, and hurried to the door of the cottage. She banged open the screen door, heard it slam behind her, and didn't look back. She ran to the Saab, twisted on the ignition, and drove off in a cold, scared sweat.

It took Bennie all the way to the Pennsylvania border to calm her stomach and begin to understand her reaction. It only became clear because the farther she drove from Winslow's cottage, the easier she breathed. Her heart rate returned to normal. Her viscera stilled. Her tongue tasted vaguely of bile, but she gritted her teeth, stiff-armed the Saab, and steered into the night, racing to lay down as much mileage as possible between her and Winslow.

A lifetime of distance.

Bennie's hair whipped from her face and she hit the gas. The Saab responded as soon as its winded turbos allowed. The car was almost ten years old and Grady had bought it used, but he took care of his car. She thought about Grady then. He took care of things he loved, like his ancient Saab, and her. He made Bennie coffee, held her when she needed it, even backed off when she didn't. Grady was a caretaker of things that caused trouble, talked back, and fell into foul and selfish moods. Of things that could hurt and wound. Of things imperfect.

Of human beings.

Bennie floored the gas pedal when she spotted the orange lights of the airport that marked Philadelphia's southern perimeter. Oil refineries encircled the airport and spewed billows of pollution into the summer night. The air hung a hazy orange and smelled like dry-cleaning chemicals. Still, Bennie felt the urge to go faster, to get to Philly. To a city that smelled like a catalytic converter. To a house that had boxes for furniture and exposed lath for wallpaper. To a man who loved her and took care of her when she needed it. To a dog that would never, *ever* come when he was called.

Bennie wanted to go home. So she drove as far as she could from her father, as fast as she could go, and sped home, there to meet her family.

For the first time.

ACKNOWLEDGMENTS

It wasn't until I was in my thirties that I found out about my sister. Technically she's a half-sister, but when we first met she struck me instantly as a twin—close in age and very much alike in looks, temperament, and manner. I am only now starting to know her and come to admire the journey she took to make her way to me. She is obviously not the twin depicted in *Mistaken Identity*—that much must be crystal clear—but it should come as no surprise that authors often cannibalize their own lives for the truth that makes fiction. My meeting her suggested the gravamen of this novel. For her bravery and heart, as well as her openness and honesty, *Mistaken Identity* is dedicated to her, J.

Special thanks, as always, to my agent Molly Friedrich for her on-the-mark improvements to this manuscript, as well as her expertise, support, and kindness. Thanks to Carolyn Marino, my editor at HarperCollins, who has steered me through six books with this one, yet her support and grace never flags. Thanks also to A. Paul Cirone, for his help, Robin Stamm, for hers, and a bear hug to Laura Leonard at HarperCollins, friend and publicist, who is always cheering for me.

As usual, I got lots of help on the technical aspects of this book, and any mistakes in that regard are my own. Heartfelt thanks to the detectives of the Two Squad of the Philadelphia Police Department, who remain helpful and supportive and serve my hometown in every way. Thanks again to criminal lawyers Susan Burt and especially Glenn Gilman, for superb legal advice in the clutch. Thanks to Nina Segre and Karen Senser, for their insights into women-owned law firms, and their kindness. Thanks to Bob Eskind of the Philadelphia prison system, whose information and access helped me create the fictional prison herein.

Thanks for her time and help to Dr. Jeanne Paulus-Thomas, Ph.D., and her colleagues at the Center for Medical Genetics, Allegheny Health, Education and Research Foundation. Thanks to Doug and Cindy Claffey, who are great friends and who helped with the twin research, firsthand.

There are also great and informative books about twins, reared together and apart, which informed my novel, and for those who want to read more, see Torrey, Bowler, Taylor, and Gottesman, *Schizophrenia and Manic-Depressive Disorder*, HarperCollins (1994); Farber, *Identical Twins Reared Apart*, Basic Books (1981); Loehlin and Nichols, *Heredity, Environment and Personality*, University of Texas Press (1976); and Juel-Nielsen, *Individual and Environment: Monozygotic Twins Reared Apart*, International Universities Press (1965); Schwartz, *The Culture of the Copy*, Zone Books (1996).

Thanks to the folks at a certain gym in Philadelphia, who helped so much with the boxing details and gave me boxing lessons, which I'm sure will come in handy in an alley. Thanks to my anonymous boxer, who gave me insight into the men (and women) who box.

Thanks to the leadership and the librarians of the Free Library of Philadelphia, who let me run wild through the stacks and who have been so supportive of my books over the years. And to Dr. Paul Bookman.

Thanks to my readers, who have been so kind and whom I always remember when I write, and to my many "online editors" who participated in a wonderful experiment to improve the first chapter.

Final thanks and all my love to my family, my parents, and my daughter.

ABOUT THE AUTHOR

Lisa Scottoline is the *New York Times* bestselling and Edgar Award–winning author of thirty-two novels, twelve of which are in the Rosato series. Thirty million copies of her books are in print in the United States, and she has been published in thirty-five countries. She also writes a weekly humor column, Chick Wit, with her daughter, Francesca Serritella, for the *Philadelphia Inquirer*, and those stories have been adapted into a series of bestselling memoirs. Lisa has served as president of Mystery Writers of America and has taught a course she developed, Justice in Fiction, at the University of Pennsylvania Law School, her alma mater. She lives in the Philadelphia area. You can visit Lisa at www.scottoline.com.

MORE FROM THE
ROSATO & ASSOCIATES SERIES BY
LISA SCOTTOLINE

EVERYWHERE THAT MARY WENT
Available in Paperback, eBook, and Digital Audio

LEGAL TENDER
Available in Paperback, eBook, and Digital Audio

ROUGH JUSTICE
Available in eBook and Digital Audio

MISTAKEN IDENTITY
Available in eBook and Digital Audio

MOMENT OF TRUTH
Available in eBook and Digital Audio

VENDETTA DEFENSE
Available in eBook and Digital Audio

COURTING TROUBLE
Available in eBook and Digital Audio

DEAD RINGER
Available in eBook and Digital Audio

KILLER SMILE
Available in eBook and Digital Audio

LADY KILLER
Available in eBook and Digital Audio

HarperCollinsPublishers
DISCOVER GREAT AUTHORS, EXCLUSIVE OFFERS, AND MORE AT HC.COM.

BOOKS BY
LISA SCOTTOLINE

FINAL APPEAL
Available in Paperback, eBook, and and Digital Audio

RUNNING FROM THE LAW
Available in eBook and Digital Audio

DEVIL'S CORNER
Available in eBook and Digital Audio

DIRTY BLONDE
Available in eBook and Digital Audio

DADDY'S GIRL
Available in eBook and Digital Audio

For more details visit:
www.scottoline.com

HarperCollinsPublishers
DISCOVER GREAT AUTHORS, EXCLUSIVE OFFERS, AND MORE AT HC.COM.